A Usable Past

The University of Massachusetts Press   *Amherst, 1984*

A Usable Past

Essays on Modern & Contemporary

Poetry by Paul Mariani

Copyright © 1984

by The University of Massachusetts Press

All rights reserved

Printed in the United States of America

LC 84–2613   ISBN 0–87023–445–5

Library of Congress Cataloging in Publication Data

appear on the last printed page of this book.

Let us now praise famous men: for all the brothers & laymen at Manhattan College, both those who still walk the earth & those who sleep now in His care, first among the dedicated men who taught me how to see, Brother Abdon & Brother Luke, Brother Stephen & Brother Paul, as well as Frank Davies and Harry Blair, Paul Cortissoz & John Fandel, and those whose names I have forgotten, I offer up this book.

Contents

Post–World War II Poets

A Usable Past

Introduction

In retrospect, there is an unforced symmetry to this collection which I would not have expected when I consider the varied conditions under which these essays and essay-reviews were first written. A 100-page section on Williams, then a section half as long on Hopkins, followed by another 100-page section on some of the poets who came into their own after the Second World War, several of them, it will be noticed, influenced either by Williams or by Hopkins.

Simply put, Hopkins was my first love, alpha, a figure I needed very much for my own spiritual and intellectual survival as a young man. I was in my last semester at Manhattan College and it was the spring of '62. Kennedy was president, there was the bimonthly stir of American space shots being covered on the black-and-white television in the lobby outside Plato's Cave at the Student Union Center, and Paul Cortissoz had assigned me—by lottery in essence—to give a class talk on Yeats. But there were enough ardent Irishmen on campus (not a few of them full-fledged supporters of the old Irish Republican Army) and—though it was a Catholic college, there was little enough interest in a dead

Jesuit, and an Englishman at that. In any event I traded my assignment with someone else (it may have been my fraternity brother with the marvelous appellation of Jim Blake) and began scouring the library and the cramped, worried-looking bookstores in the area for anything I could find about the poet who had written "The Wreck of the Deutschland" and those extraordinary sonnets whose contrapuntal effects and Anglo-Saxon percussive rhythms kept ringing in my ears. Thus began a love affair with a poet which has only deepened with the years.

I think now that I decided to stay with English—after desultory beginnings in philosophy and psychology—largely because of these marvelous poems that incorporated a quarter-century-long dialogue with no less an antagonist/lover than God himself. And though I had to leave Hopkins behind in order to prepare myself for a teaching "career," which meant devouring pythonlike the various texts that make up what we used to call—in our prepluralistic innocence—the Great Tradition, I came back to Hopkins when, in early 1967, it was time at last to write a dissertation. Not that Hopkins had been my first choice for a dissertation topic. I would never in all my Jansenistic upbringing have attempted to pursue something I actually loved. Preparing to be a college teacher should be work, hard work, with occasional moments of grace to light the stormy way. Instead, I was set on doing my doctoral work on Carlyle, who had already managed to infect my own naturally asyntactical and crabbed style in ways that would surely have created a hermetically sealed, albeit enthusiastic system of signs even the most charitable of my teachers would have been hard put to understand.

I was saved from that fate by the program director, that extraordinary diva among medievalists, the late Helaine Newstead. And she saved me by the rather simple device of not allowing me to take Carlyle for my topic. A month later, fresh from reading Dwight Culler on Cardinal Newman, I came back to her once more, knees slightly shaking. I would undertake to write on the development of Newman's persuasive classical rhetoric, I proffered now somewhat schizophrenically. But her answer was no to that one as well. And then—belatedly as usual—the obvious solution struck me. Why not do the poet I had always wanted to do anyway? And so I came back with a scheme to do a reading of each of Hopkins's sonnets, from the early undergraduate pieces Hopkins had written as a student at Balliol College, Oxford, to the poem he wrote for Robert Bridges just six weeks before he died at forty-four from typhoid fever. That dissertation—substantially revised and expanded—was published in early 1970 as my first book, with the exact, if somewhat lengthy title, *A Commentary on the Complete Poems of Gerard Manley Hopkins.*

Over the next seven years I continued to publish on Hopkins, all the pieces being commissioned by magazines or as essays in various collections. The "Andromeda" piece, the oldest of the essays in this collection, was originally written for a symposium on Victorian literature in the 1870s held at the University of Massachusetts. What I was interested in showing in this essay was the underlying pressures on Hopkins that prompted him, one day in mid-August 1879, to compose his uncharacteristically allegorical sonnet. What were the psychogenetic pressures that had given rise to this poem? What were the dangers—real or imagined—Hopkins was warning his fictive readers against (fictive because, like nearly everything he wrote, the poem went unpublished in Hopkins's lifetime)? What was the threat? Was it America? Liberalism? Homosexuality? Whitman? Or was it Whitman's English followers, Pater, Swinburne, and the young Oscar Wilde among them? Whatever, mention of Hopkins's apparently nascent homosexual proclivities even as late as 1973 could still raise hackles on some critics. I remember one former nun who confronted me in a barely controlled frenzy before she simply dismissed me as being too young to understand the angelic virtue, whatever that was.

The piece on "The Wreck" was done as part of a collection of essays by acknowledged scholars of Hopkins in honor of the centenary of the writing of that extraordinary pindaric ode reshaped within the context of the late Romantic tradition. What I was particularly interested in examining was the aesthetic tension between Hopkins's quasi-erotic desire to fill the world with worded news of God's presence and his despair that any language—however brilliant, however original—could ever fill the infinite space he saw exploding not only around but—even more frighteningly—within him. Hopkins knew also that every poem carries with it not only its paraphrasable meanings but other meanings conveyed in the music of the poem itself, in the very combinations of syllables on the page, and that this meaning is closer to the heart of the matter for the poet. For this underlying utterance is the poet's primal cry, the sound of the human spirit itself.

This hint, this profound insight into the nature of the poem, I had gathered from Hopkins himself, and I went on to look for evidence of this presence of the poet in the unique music of the poem in another essay I wrote for the *Hopkins Quarterly,* "The Sound of Oneself Breathing," this time following the burdens of Hopkins's own metaphors of breath and air and music, as if just there in the lay of the syllables and the signs Hopkins had used, one might come to touch—however momentarily—what we used to call the soul of the poet. In "A Poetics of Unselfconsciousness," disturbed by what that brilliant critic and high priest of Gnosticism, Harold Bloom, had said about Hopkins's potential greatness as a poet being overshadowed by his prostration before the figures of Milton and Wordsworth, I felt the need to offer a defense that would show that Hopkins, though a Romantic, was struggling to escape the pull toward egoism to create what he called a more "manly" poetry. He was thinking of Dryden and using that poet's somewhat outdated terminology, but he meant by that term what I think we would call a return to a more classical sort of poetry, closer to the *dramatic* lyric and of necessity less ego conscious. In other words, Hopkins, keenly aware of the idiosyncratic music of his own work, consciously began moving (as he believed his beloved Keats had earlier) toward a poetry more in keeping with the spirit of Shakespeare's late dramas and less like his Romantic predecessors (a line that in Hopkins begins with Milton and includes Blake and Keats, followed later in the century by Tennyson, Pater, and Swinburne). By the mid-1970s I was becoming more and more immersed in the figure of Williams, though I would still like some day (some day) to write a critical biography of Father Hopkins, whose presence is now acknowledged everywhere in British and American poetry, Auden, Lowell, Berryman, Ted Hughes, and Robert Penn Warren being just a few of the names of Hopkins's progeny that come readily to mind.

I came to Williams belatedly, some half dozen years after I had found Hopkins. By then Williams had also been dead half a dozen years. But, like Hopkins, Williams answered to a deep need within me. If Hopkins had shown me a religious voice creatively countering the growing agnosticism and nihilism in the literature, philosophy, and politics of the past century, Williams provided for my time what Whitman had provided for the last century: an example of a poet engaged in a lifelong struggle to raise my world—America—to the level of the epic. The Beats, especially Kerouac and Ginsberg, might conceivably have done this for me as well. But my own essentially conservative bent could not easily accept what we used to call such a radically different "lifestyle." I was from working-class stock, bluest of blue collar, obedient to the fathers, bent on entering, not leaving, mainstream America, at least as my family understood the values of upward mobility, none of us at that point having tasted the so-called good life. Now Williams, on the other hand, like Wallace Stevens, was essentially American middle class, professional, in the most immediate sense, and, as Creeley might say, "useful" to society. Here was a practicing doctor and pediatrician, a father and husband, member of the local school board in Rutherford, viewed as a good citizen (except when the McCarthy fever of the early 1950s went after him like a rabid dog and decided this dedicated doctor and outspoken critic was some sort of ill-defined public menace).

But Williams was also a part of the American and international avant garde, a friend of Ezra Pound, Wallace Stevens, E. E. Cummings, H. D., Marianne Moore, Ford Madox Ford, a sometime antagonist or protagonist of Gertrude Stein, T. S. Eliot, Hart Crane, H. L. Mencken, and Wyndham Lewis, an associate of such painters as Marcel Duchamp, Charles Scheeler, Charles Demuth, Pavel Tchelitchev, a father figure for writers as different from each other as were Louis Zukofsky, George Oppen, Charles Reznikoff, John Sanford, Theodore Roethke, Robert Lowell, Allen Ginsberg, Charles Olson, Robert Creeley, Denise Levertov, Gary Snyder, Phillip Whalen, Charles Tomlinson, John Montague, Thomas Kinsella, Amamu Amiri Baraka, Robert Coles, Tom Coles, and —finally—a commanding presence to literally hundreds of other writers, critics, and artists, many of whom Williams never even met.

I began my work on Williams by doing what I call my "homework book," a commentary on the published criticism that had accumulated around Williams's reputation from his inauspicious beginnings in 1909 until 1973, ten years after his death. What I originally thought would be six months' work stretched into two and a half years and was published by the American Library Association in 1975 as part of a series called *The Poet and His Critics*. And then began a series of essays on Williams's late poems, including various aspects of his epic, *Paterson*. Some of these essays were incorporated into what was to become my ten-year effort, my biography of Williams, subtitled *A New World Naked*, published in late 1981. But other essays I'd written on Williams were not incorporated into the biography because my original intention had been to write only a biography of *Paterson* itself. So "The Eighth Day of Creation" (1975) looks at the formation of "Asphodel" and *Paterson* 5 as these poems grew out of the original close of the epic, the first becoming a long lyric apology to his wife, the other a hymn of praise to the feminine principle, both of them—finally—songs of love to the women who had been so important to Williams's growth as a man.

"The Poem as a Field of Action" was originally written in response to a query from the editor of the *Iowa Review* for a piece on Williams and the theory of the poem as a field of action. In the late 1940s Williams gave every indication, as his poems and letters and essays show, that he was onto a new kind of poetry, and he was to point frequently to the changes in the nature of the poems he wrote between the publication of *Paterson* 1 in 1946 and the publication of *Paterson* 2 two years later. Something profound—admittedly difficult to track and to name—had occurred in that period. It was as if Williams had paid his dues to the tradition—to Eliot and Pound and Hart Crane and the Modernist phase of poetry in *Paterson* 1 and had moved into the beginnings of a post-Modernist poetics with the creation of *Paterson* 2.

Apparently, even Williams himself was not sure of what he had discovered in the heat of writing, but he was to return to the second book of his American epic on many occasions in his last years to gesture to the place where the new phase had begun. One senses the change in the way the characters in *Paterson* 2 are fleshed out for us (there are, as Robert Lowell long ago pointed out, almost no human figures in *Paterson* 1) and in the way the characters and the landscapes are made present to us in these pages. We are, in a sense, in the midst of a field, trying to gain our own multiple perspectives along with the poet who walks there, for Williams has taken a great risk to present these figures who speak the imprecise language of the place and who enact in their essential poverty the recognizable gestures of the man and the city which is Paterson and its environs. Even more, one understands— and accepts as fully credible—the despair and tentative hope of the figure who moves through this fallen world, brooding over its debasement, yet aware of a life there that even rampant greed and indifference have not been able finally to kill.

The most recent essay in this collection—"The Hard Core of Beauty" —was originally written for the Bread Loaf School of English. The Robert Frost Lecture for 1983, it is a continuation of my meditation on Williams's post-Modernist phase which I had begun seven years earlier, this time, however, focusing on the lyric poems Williams was writing at the same time he was struggling (composing as a verb here will simply not do) with his epic. I wanted to demonstrate something of the incredible range of Williams's late experiments in the lyric form and to point to some of the directions his poetry was taking before he was hit with the first of a series of strokes which changed forever the very shape of his poetry.

The short essay on Williams and Stevens was presented originally at a symposium co-sponsored by the Poetry Society of America and the CUNY Graduate Center at 42nd Street to honor Stevens's hundreth birthday. Among the others who also spoke that evening were Denis Donoghue, Helen Vendler, Richard Howard, Allen Mandelbaum, and Harold Bloom. My own talk centered on the largely silent dialogue I believe continued between Williams and Stevens for forty years. With the recent publication of Peter Brazeau's oral history of Stevens, we can be even more sure of Stevens's unapproachable and—from a layperson's point of view—almost pathological reticences which included everyone, his old friend, Williams, not excepted. Nevertheless, the dialogue concerning reality and the imagination, including as a subset the problem of the most effective rhetorical strategies for the poem, went on in the midst of the most important forum of all: the poems themselves. In this debate, it seems to me, both men were winners. Contemporary American poetry is richer for both the concretized abstractions of Stevens as well as for Williams's insistent stabbings and questionings. For both poets, we should remember, are grounded in the things of this world.

For me perhaps the most seminal essay in *A Usable Past* is the opening piece, "Reassembling the Dust." Originally delivered as the Abernethy Lecture at Middlebury College in the spring of 1982, this essay is, I see now in retrospect, the suppressed prolegomenon to *A New World Naked*. The introduction one actually finds there is a rather modest affair, and not without reason, the strategy being—simply—one of self-effacement, for I was anxious to get on with the telling of Williams's life story and not with my own. But as the hundreds of reviews, together with letters from well-wishers and irate readers, continued to arrive over the months following the publication of the book, I felt compelled to defend the kind of literary biography I had spent ten years in researching and writing. By literary biography I mean biography that pays attention to literary style, has a strong narrative line, and presents the subject from the perspective of the moment in which that person lived. I wanted as little of the omniscient author and as little of that easy Monday morning quarterbacking—whether invoking the name of

Freud or Marx or whomever—as would suffice to order and make sense of the life. I wanted the men and women who made up Williams's world and I wanted them living and believable and delivered in as much of their human complexity as I could manage. And for the purpose of getting the work written I would as soon rely on the narrative skills of a Joyce or a Flaubert or a Faulkner insofar as those skills are available to the biographer. Finally, I wanted to deliver as little moral judgment on the character as I could get away with. Let the readers judge for themselves and let the readers beware of the implications of their judgments.

Last, I have included a selection of essays written over the past decade that look at several American, British, and Irish poets who have continued to be important to me. There are others, naturally, whom I would like to have included here, both those I have had the chance to write about and those for whom there has not yet been either the opportunity or the time, but who are also important to my own work as critic and as poet. So a number of essays not reprinted here have dealt with poetic sequences by American poets whose practices are as different as Allen Mandelbaum's, Donald Finkel's, Robert Pinsky's, and Daniel Hoffman's. But the essays gathered here all focus on single poets or—as in the cases of Tomlinson, Creeley, and Berryman—on their interraction with Williams or Hopkins.

The piece on Robert Penn Warren, written as the poet was approaching seventy, is in its original form the most problematic of the essays presented here. Written just as Warren was beginning to compose the extraordinary poems of this past decade, it carries with it some of the unease I and others felt with a volume like *Or Else.* Was the book a series of discrete lyrics as well as a single poetic sequence as Warren has claimed for it? And how treat a volume that had what I still feel are some weak poems co-existing with some very strong work? It has therefore been necessary to add an extended coda to this essay in order to take a longer perspective on Warren's brilliant achievement. There are, of course, still a number of poets and critics reviewing Warren's work who feel that these late poems are a falling off from Warren's best work and that he has published entirely too much poetry in the last ten years. But the salutary example here is Thomas Hardy, the poet whom I am most reminded of when I consider Warren's power to evoke a world long gone together with its characteristic attitudes of philosophical uncertainty and unease. Warren seems as intent as Hardy to leave behind a body of work from which the critics will have to make their own selections, and it is now clear to me that the poetry—taken altogether—is a major achievement approaching the scale of his predecessor. Few major American critics—Harold Bloom being a possible exception—seem to be willing to grant this as yet, but I think time is now on Warren's side.

The essay on Charles Tomlinson needs the 1977 addendum which was meant to close the essay as originally written. I see now what I did not see eight years ago: that I was too close to Williams and not close enough to Tomlinson's intent when I wrote the essay and, though what I say there still seems to me true enough, it is also true that it does not say enough. What I would like to add at some point in the next few years is my unstinting praise for Tomlinson's cumulative poetic achievement. He is not an easy poet for an American to read and his pace and philosophical metabolism are slower than either Williams's or mine. A serious student of Wordsworth, his pace is more like Marianne Moore's than any other American poet I can think of. But he is worth our close attention, for few poets writing today can so evoke the signature of air or water or the familiar and unfamiliar landscapes of our century—the English midlands, New Jersey, New Mexico, Provençal, La Spezia—with the moral and aesthetic precision of Tomlinson. Not enough attention has been paid to this poet by American critics (Hugh Kenner being one notable exception), but he is already one of the three or four most important older voices now coming out of England. And if Tomlinson has learned much from his American teachers—Williams, Stevens, Marianne Moore, and Ezra Pound among them—we Americans have much to learn from him about precision of image and word, the values of discretion, and a sense of poetic civility that Yeats for one would have appreciated.

One of the questions that has preoccupied me over the past decade is what to make of the contours of the Williams tradition. The Tomlinson essay itself originally grew out of that impetus, and the Creeley essay, originally commissioned for a special number of *Boundary 2* devoted to Creeley, is a continuation of that interest. Moreover, I have known Bob Creeley personally now for ten years and have come to admire his honesty, his toughness, his hard critical intelligence, his gift for conversation, his humanity, his unswerving dedication to the craft, his unique signature as a poet. As a poet just starting out in the early 1970s, I needed to determine for myself what Creeley had managed to learn from Williams and something of how he had transformed what he'd learned into his own "fire of a very real order." Creeley himself was just starting out as a writer when he began corresponding with Williams in the early 1950s and *For Love,* his first volume of poems, would not be published until three years before Williams's death. But Creeley had the satisfaction of having Williams tell him, after Williams had read the poems in *For Love* in early 1960, that he believed Creeley to have the subtlest feeling for the measure of anyone he had read, Pound alone excepted. High praise indeed. I have not said enough yet about the unique gifts of Creeley, who has been with us, after all, for the past thirty years, but in time I will again add my own voice to the chorus of those who have benefited from the poet's example.

I first met John Montague at the University of Buffalo in the summer of 1974 while I was doing research on Williams at the old state campus. Montague and his wife and his ten-month-old daughter shared a student room across the hall from my own. Thus began a friendship, carried on sporadically by letter and with an occasional visit here in western Massachusetts or in New York City. I read closely everything of Montague's I could get my hands on, some of it in manuscript. And while "Fretwork in Stone Tracery" is a review of two volumes of Montague's poetry published in the mid to late 1970s, I have continued my interest in Montague with a monograph on the poet written for the *Dictionary of Literary Biography* that covers—insofar as an essay can do such a thing—Montague's entire career to date. The man continues to write eloquently and with a rare empathy for his country and its plangent, earthly music. Just now American critics seem preoccupied with another Irish poet, Seamus Heaney, eleven years Montague's junior, and Heaney *is* an extraordinarily gifted poet and the one with whom I feel the closest personal affinity. But it is Montague who now needs the critical attention he has long deserved, and we Americans would benefit by giving him a closer reading.

The Berryman essay was a work of love for several reasons: first, because Berryman has a genius for the unexpected. He can be comic, vulnerable, tragic, coarse, and profound, in electric succession. And, second, in the sequence of poems I chose to treat—the "Eleven Addresses to the Lord" which closes his volume, *Love & Fame*—I read Berryman's long-deferred coming to terms with one of his masters and mine: Hopkins. A poet of gigantic ego and elephantine talent, capable of hurting those he most loved in ways sometimes approaching the diabolic, an alcoholic finally drying out in the late spring of 1970 in a Minneapolis ward, Berryman was reduced in these poems to that bare, forked, essential thing we call unaccommodated man. In this last extremity, then, Berryman found himself calling on his God in a series of poems that have as their model Hopkins's terrible sonnets. What he achieved here are some of the most terrible, terrifying, exhausting, and honest religious poems of our deeply troubled century. For, in spite of Berryman's human failings and his suicide two years after he wrote these poems, few American poets have approached this man on this level of humility. Here is the modern cry *in extremis* of Job to his God, and no poet that I am aware of—not Jarrell or Roethke or Lowell or Plath or Sexton—has surpassed him on this score. Was it not Robert Lowell himself who, just a year before his own death, wrote that he often found himself praying now not *for,* but *to,* this troubled, brilliant poet?

By extension, the short Merton piece began, really, as a Lenten exercise. My oldest son has been immersed in Merton's work for several years now and so, given the opportunity to review Merton's *Literary Essays* for the *American Book Review,* I began reading everything I could get my hands on, in part to satisfy my own Catholic curiosity and in part to continue the dialogue about Merton with my son. What I came to realize was that Merton—Father Louis—was very much on a spiritual journey and that the final chapter of that journey has been eloquently described by Merton himself in what was posthumously published as *The Asian Journal.* It was Jay Laughlin, Merton's (and Williams's) publisher, who spent long months reassembling and transcribing the scrawled notes Merton had left behind at the time of his death in late 1968. In the months leading up to that death (by accidental electrocution), Merton, still searching for a closer union with his God, was in the Far East preparing for the first East-West meeting of Christian, Zen, and Buddhist monks. As wonderful as Merton's essays on Camus, Faulkner, Flannery O'Connor, and the others are, it is in the *Asian Journals* that I believe the full flowering of Merton's spirituality is most evident, and my essay attempts to play the one style—the intellectual signature of the literary essays—against the more deeply human style of the journals.

Finally, a word about the essay on Robert Pack. For ten years now

Bob Pack and I have been reading and commenting on each other's work. I must confess that I did not come easily to Pack's kind of poetry. After all, in some basic ways it would seem to belong to what I call the "opposing" camp. That is, my own proclivities have been with Pound and Williams and Stevens (the last a figure we both share) and not with Frost and Edward Arlington Robinson. But Pack is a consummate teacher and very patient and, slowly, steadily, I have come to reassess my own debt to the narrative tradition in poetry, especially because so many of my own poems are, after all, stories. I had also thought Pack would begin in time to receive more of the attention his poetry surely deserves. But when his *Selected Poems* were met with relative silence, I set out to write an appreciation of his work spanning the last quarter century. This essay is of course only a beginning, but at least there now exists a critical dialogue to which others can add. Perhaps now critics will begin to understand that in Pack we have one of Frost's—and Words-worth's—strong sons, destined to do his best work as he grows older. I for one have not been disappointed. For in the two years since I wrote this essay, Pack has continued to write narrative poems and dramatic monologues that, taken together, have provided a new direction for him and that show him—half way through his sixth decade—to be writing at the top of his form. Moreover, in the recent appearance of Clayfeld, *mensch* and *schlemiel,* who moves against the translucent backdrop of a Freudian sublime, Pack has provided us with one of the handful of fully blooded comic figures in the American poetic tradition.

In the essays themselves I have mentioned some of the figures who have provided me with a usable past. Now I want to close by mentioning the names of several friends whose critical intelligence and commitment to style have meant so much to me, providing me with the example of their own dedication to the craft. I mean the rabbinic intensity and clarity of Allen Mandelbaum, the translator of Virgil and Dante. I mean too the dedication of Stephen Oates, the biographer of Nat Turner, John Brown, Abraham Lincoln, Martin Luther King, and now of William Faulkner. I mean—again—the prose precision and acerbic, saving wit of Frederick Turner, author of *Beyond Geography* and the life and times of the naturalist John Muir. And, finally, I mean Terrence Des Pres, for his book on the survivors of the Nazi death camps and the Soviet gulags, as well as for his essays on politics and poetry. And for something more: his unflinching honesty in the face of our modern terrors that has cost him so much in human terms. It is a commitment not unlike Carolyn Forché's, and for me it verges on the heroic.

There are other debts, too, to the editors of the various quarterlies and reviews in whose pages these essays first appeared. And there are friends, students, colleagues, and mentors on whom I tried out so many of these ideas over the past ten years. For me the writing of poems and the writing of essays, reviews, and biographies are all part of the same activity, as Williams says was true for him as well, all of it flowering out of the gutter of the unconscious. The only difference, perhaps, is one of intensity, due in large part to the nature of revision in poetry, with its responsibility to *present* realities rather than meanings. In retrospect, the writing of my first three books of poems—co-extensive with the writing of these essays—seems now to have been not unlike a mapping of the configurations on the dark side of the moon. Now that I think of it, I have been as surprised as anyone to find the poems blessedly there in the midst of this other activity we call criticism. But one comes to see that the moon's hidden side must have its own complementary if distinctive face. In short, the prose and the poetry have both been necessary phases of that complex fiction we call the self, a self that, as Marisol for one has noted, in all likelihood we will never find.

Paul Mariani
Montague, Massachusetts
25 January 1984

William Carlos Williams

Reassembling the Dust: Notes on the Art of the Biographer

1   "I know of no critics in modern times," Leon Edel, the biographer of Henry James, has reminded us, "who have chosen to deal with biography as one deals with poetry or the novel. The critics fall into the easy trap of writing pieces about the life that was lived, when their business is to discuss how the life was told." From scanning the reviews that greeted (in one form or another) my own biography of William Carlos Williams, I know the truth of Edel's statement. And I mention it because it is a curious phenomenon and, in an age that prides itself on the attention it has given to the critical act, a phenomenon which I find puzzling and hard to explain. It is as though, in the case of biography, the reader somehow believed that the life the biographer has assembled for us existed prior to the writing itself. I am only half playing when I say this, because it is axiomatic that the biographer must always be true to the facts—the literary remains—which he or she keeps finding, trying to make sense of it all in something like a final ordering.

But it is the other half of the problem that I want to look at: the biographer as creator, the dustman reassembling the dust, like the God of Genesis breathing life into a few handfuls of ashes. For the biographer is as much the inventor, the maker, as the poet or the novelist when it comes to creating a life out of the *prima materia* we call words, the very stuff, for example, that I am directing at you this moment. Is it not, after all, the *illusion* of a life which the biographer gives in the process of writing biography, something carried on perhaps over many years, a process of reassembling tapes and letters, discarded drafts and manuscripts, directives and memoes, testaments and check stubs, the feel of names and places revisited, people known perhaps still among the living, words, words transcribed, written, uttered, words, words, and more words, that the biographer must shape and select and reorder, until a figure begins again to live in our imagination? It is extraordinary what the biographer feels when, finally, after writing and rewriting chapter after chapter of a person's life, after having lived for so long with the pale voices of the dead and perhaps with the still-insistent voices of the living who think that they were there, to suddenly feel something like light come streaming into the head, and to feel then the dust of all those words we call "facts" begin to take form, like the shape of the rose (to borrow an image from Ezra Pound) emerging out of the steel-dust particles when a magnet has been placed beneath their surface.

I remember how this moment occurred for me, and I keep learning that something like my own experience has been frequent with other biographers as well. Even after eight years of research, I was still finding Williams's letters in new archives or in private collections (a process, incidentally, that continues and is bound to continue for some time). By then I had already collected thousands of such letters and was beginning to find a certain repetitiveness in the process. I decided at that point to play a game with the new packets of material that crossed my desk and, after looking at the date of a letter, try to guess what the general contents of that letter would be. I soon found that I could guess fairly accurately a good portion of the contents. It was like a tape going over in my mind: this was how Williams would have spoken to Pound at this point, this is how he would have addressed Louis Zukofsky or Allen Ginsberg or Denise Levertov or Robert Lowell. In a sense, then, the biographer had finally managed to become his subject. Other biographers have taken to wearing their subject's clothes or hat or shoes, others find their smoking habits and diets and tastes subtly or not so subtly changing to conform to their subjects', some have even gone so far as to interject themselves on the domestic scenes of their subjects, sometimes with an aggrandizement bordering on the violent, sometimes with something approaching filial piety. You can't live another person's words day in and day out without running up against some such occupational benefits or occupational risks. Those risks will differ of course for each subject, and several good novelists from Henry James on have used the biographer as their protagonist. Most of these novels have been in the tradition of the comedy of manners, though from the biographer's own standpoint I suppose the genre most apt would be the Romantic Quest. And at the heart of the romantic quest, remember, is the moment of the Grail, the visionary moment, the moment of the breakthrough.

Let us call this moment of breakthrough the *illusion* of the saturation point. I stress the word *illusion* because any biographer worthy of the name wants to ingest everything available on his or her subject and the truth is that more dust—new letters, new manuscripts, new memoirs by others who remained silent while you were doing your own work or who were spurred into writing perhaps because of your work—whatever, but more dust—has a way of collecting after your own work, you thought, was done. Such a state of things, this new stirring of the dust, is to be expected and even welcomed, for it shows a continuing or at least renewed interest in a subject that one already had found worthwhile exploring. Call this renewal of interest a kind of second life springing from the first life of the biography.

The only thing which might really trouble the biographer would be, I think, to discover that not only had the dust been stirred again but that something like a new rose pattern radically reshaping the life the biographer had already shaped had been part of the stirring. To watch all the dust reassemble again in a new configuration, and one which seemed to suit the dust more fully. Harold Bloom speaks of the anxiety of the later poet coming into the presence of the father's text. But that is as nothing to Ptolemy's meeting up with a Galileo, the son who would rearrange the sense of the world according to his own discoveries and his own imagination. For is not the biographer's primal desire the desire to father his subject, so that the "world" (i.e., one's interested readers) is satisfied with the illusion the biographer has given it and which can then pass for what one thinks of when one thinks of Subject X? How many of us think of James Joyce without thinking of Richard Ellmann's Joyce, or think of Hart Crane without thinking of Horton of perhaps Unterecker, or of Henry James without thinking of Edel's composite of a life?

How then does the biographer go about accomplishing this rich illusion of a life, this essential fiction? First of all, of course, not all biographers are sufficiently concerned with the shape of their fictions. In this they are like certain novelists in the American realist tradition who want the story without really giving all that much concern to formal considerations. There are those biographers who try to do the impossible by trying to get everything between the covers of two or five or nine volumes, in that attempt (frustrated from the start) emptying the dust bin over the grave of the dead as a memorial so that the dust sifts down and down in the shape of a pyramid, out of which monument the reader is then invited to make his or her own judgment, i.e., one's own private portrait. This gesture of omnipresence and omnipotence on the part of the biographer is perhaps that writer's last infirmity, and many have, finally, wearily, succumbed to that temptation. This is not to make an oblique strike at the long biography, for there is often good reason to publish a book or indeed several books that may exceed even the thousand-page mark. Besides, having perpetrated a long biography myself, I suppose I would like to defend my own actions as well. But Williams died just short of eighty and up to almost the very end he was in the midst of one or another of those American vortices that, like their natural cousin, the hurricane, have a way of forming and splitting up with unseemly haste. I still believe, however, that 800 pages devoted to Keats or to the two Cranes, all figures who died young, will appear excessive to any but the most devoted follower. On the other hand, Edel's five volumes on James, R.W.B. Lewis's biography of Edith Wharton, and Ellman's life of Joyce, each certainly sustained meditations, seem to me appropriate in part because of the creative longevity of each of those figures.

Sometimes a case has to be made for presenting a particular life in detail even as one is in the act of re-creating the life, and that strategy likewise takes time. No one would blink twice if another long life were to appear that dealt with Faulkner or Pound or Eliot or Frost (though it is interesting that Lawrance Thompson's three-volume life should already have contracted to a single volume). But what about Williams? Did he really deserve a long biography? To listen to one camp of critics: no. To listen to another: yes, and it was about time. For part of a biographer's art will have to deal with the question of scope, of size. To do a mural or a cameo or a portrait? You don't just write a long biography by chance, and you will certainly not get it past a trade editor without making a very good case for the length of that life study. I myself was so frustrated by hearing the same myths about Williams—that he was incapable of serious, consecutive thought, that there was no real drama in the life of this New Jersey poet-doctor from a one-horse town, that *Paterson* and Williams's other poems were mostly precompositions, sketches for poems rather than poems, frenetically dashed off between delivering one baby and another—that I was determined to do what I could to set the record straight. With very few exceptions no one who had worked in any way with Williams's life and written of it had given the reader anything like a sufficient sense of just how complex and multileveled that life had been. Nor had anyone yet shown how intimately Williams had touched the imaginative lives of three generations of American writers. Profoundly touched by my own encounter with Williams, I wanted to do what I could as life writer to see at least that Williams was not dismissed now that something like a full picture of the man in his time could be presented. When I was younger it was Richard Ellmann's biographical example in dealing with Joyce that had held me, and I see now that what I wanted to give American audiences in particular was a book about Williams peopled with his friends and enemies that would be a counterpart in every way except in tone to what Ellmann had offered in his homage to Joyce. I make no secrets about it. Call it hubris, but my book would be a way of paying homage to the father, of doing for modern American poetry what Ellman had done for European Modernism. There would be shortcomings of course. There would be little on Frost or Sandburg or Robinson, and less than I would have liked on Stevens or H. D. or even Marianne Moore. But that would be because Williams had touched these lives only peripherally, if at all. In spite of which he would be my candidate for one of the truly major American voices of our century, and here between the covers of this book would be my case.

2   Looking back at what he had achieved in several biographies on late medieval princes and statesmen, Paul Murray Kendall once wrote

that the biographer has the nearly impossible task of grafting stone to rainbow. What he meant by this happy phrase was that the biographer must take the unrecalcitrant facts as they appear to exist—in memoirs, diaries, journals, the rest of it—and so possess this material as to create out of it the rainbow, the living simulation in words of a life from all that we can discover about that person. In the last poem he ever wrote, Hopkins spoke eloquently of this moment of inspiration, the moment of the rainbow, and of that moment's ability to keep *in*-forming its recipient, no matter how long it took the poem to come finally to term:

> The fine delight that fathers thought; the strong
> Spur, live and lancing like a blowpipe flame,
> Breathes once and, quenchèd faster than it came,
> Leaves yet the mind a mother of immortal song.
> Nine months she then, nay years, nine years she long
> Within her wears, bears, cares and combs the same:
> The widow of an insight lost she lives, with aim
> Now known and hand at work now never wrong.

The biographer is both like and unlike the poet. He or she also feels the same strong spur as the poet. But once the biographer has felt that fine delight, that moment of light streaming into the head, the moment of the rainbow, there is still the forbidding pyramid of dust to work with. The biographer may have caught something like the inner life of his or her subject, but how in heaven's name, after all, shall one go about taking all those index card entries and all those interviews done on tape or in shorthand or by telephone and, in the case of the Subject as writer, analyzing or at least accounting for all those marvelous poems and essays, those memoirs and letters and libretti, and transforming all into a readable narrative that shall do justice to the subject? What tone shall he or she take toward the material, what distance assume in relation to the subject, what language employ? What strategies shall the biographer use by which to reassemble the dust and reveal the pattern the biographer believes is somewhere in the midst of all of that?

Biographers seem to have worked, at least until quite recently, pretty much alone. First of all, they still come from widely divergent disciplines. There is, for example, the field sociologist, the journalist, the historian, the psychoanalyst, the feminist, the Marxist, the theologian, the professor of literature, even the professional biographer. Each comes to biography with different attitudes about the field, different presuppositions, different purposes. In spite of which, it seems to me, we must still learn how to tell a good story if we are to tap the peculiar energies of the biography.

And how are we to do that? I think one answer to that question, if I have learned anything from working on Williams, will depend on the specific contours as well as on the underlying myth that spurred someone on, and gave him or her a deep sense of self-definition. I mean anything of course but the public mask, the face most people see when they look at Hemingway or Hart Crane or Emily Dickinson or Thoreau or Emerson or Poe. I mean that it is the biographer's special agony and his or her glory to grasp *that* reality, that radiant gist, that energy and direction, that should inform, *in*-form, a thousand thousand otherwise disparate facts and make them dance together. For without that inner understanding we see as in a glass darkly, as in a winter snowstorm, the figures in the drama blurred, shadowy, halting, moving through a strangely cold and unrealized landscape. I think most successful biographers will tell you (or at least *could* tell you) that there was that moment of light when the inner life of their subject was suddenly revealed. At that point the earlier, partial images fell away and the inner consistency of their subject was impressed upon them. What was many images suddenly coalesced into a unified figure, many-sided but nonetheless possessing a self, and then the dust particles—all those discrete facts— could be arranged into a major pattern. My experience has been that if this moment of light rings "true" to the biographer, then all subsequent finds will accommodate themselves to this pattern. If they do not, if the facts still insist on squiggling all over the surface, then the insight will have turned out to be partly light and partly an *ignis fatuus,* a shadow light beckoning into the swamps. Philip Horton, for example, published his biography of Hart Crane only three years after Crane's suicide, but he was not superseded by John Unterecker, whose life of Crane was published thirty-five years later in a study nearly three times as long. The reason this is so is that Horton managed to catch the truth of his subject and wrote passionately and to the point from that truth. In short, the pattern held.

Writing my own biography of Williams, I think the moment of realization came when I saw how central the myth of success through repeated failures had been for Williams. In teaching *In the American Grain,* for example, it became clear to me that Williams was dividing his protagonists into parts of a cubist mural composed in binary fashion of those who had "apparently" succeeded and those who had "apparently" failed. Among those who succeeded, Williams included Cortez and Jonathan Edwards and Ben Franklin, men whom Williams thought had failed to establish the intimacy necessary for genuine and lasting contact with their world. On the other hand there were such "failures" as Columbus and Montezuma, Père Sebastian Rasles and Daniel Boone, Aaron Burr and Poe. These figures were failures in the eyes of most Americans because they had not achieved the American Dream, ending their lives—all of them—disgraced, lonely, or misunderstood, though what they all had in common was their contact with the ground, a grounding necessarily figured for Williams in the woman, as much the necessary counterpart for him in his art as in his life.

It became clearer and clearer to me as I worked with Williams that he had pursued this theme through twenty years while he wrote his Stecher trilogy and watched his family of immigrants (based as they were on his wife's family) become stranded on the desert shores of that same American Dream. I saw the theme again in Williams's dream of Washington, the father who had persisted in spite of repeated military failures on Long Island and Manhattan and up and down the New Jersey coast until doggedly he had won through and made his dream of America a reality, at least for a short while. I could see the theme at work again more subtly as a way of *in*-forming his epic, *Paterson,* where the poet's desperate search for a language with which to marry himself irrevocably to a place became his all-important work. By then Williams's sense of place had turned into a cry, the cry Williams swore Poe had heard when that poetic predecessor had gone in search of a country. So Williams heard his country crying out against him with all the anger and frustration of a Marcia Nardi, the very real woman whose very real letters he placed into the fabric of his poem by way of a judgment that he was willing by then to bring against himself for his own hubris in attempting to speak for the whole tribe (America) in the first place.

Williams's photographic negative of the American success story, then, became the generative myth, the underlying poetics, if you will, which in turn *in*-formed my own narrative of Williams. Early, Williams somehow became convinced that he was going to live a long and productive life. Somehow—perhaps because his grandmother had lived into her nineties and his mother lived to be a centenarian—Williams believed that the Fates would not cut his own life thread short, as they had cut short the life of Hart Crane. As a corollary to this faith, Williams also came to believe that he would have a very long and recurring creative springtime in which to get done what he knew he had in him to do. In his early thirties he began to envision himself more and more as a revolutionary born into a time of revolutions: the revolution in American art signaled by John Reed and Big Bill Haywood and the Paterson strike of 1913, followed by Pancho Villa in Mexico and—most significantly—the Russian Revolution of 1917. Williams had only begun to come of age at that extraordinary period, and he knew he would need the next half century to work out the complex implications of his own revolution of the word. Incredibly, he nearly got the whole fifty years he'd bargained for, though it cost him more dearly than as a young dreamer he would have thought possible. And it is just there—in the crosscurrents Williams rode, the crest of the dream, the trough of rejection and misunderstanding—that my biography found its own mythic impulse. Here was Williams's version of the American success story experienced day by day in his own life drama.

Many critics and reviewers seem genuinely surprised that Williams could feel almost as if he'd been physically assaulted by the rejections and dismissals of Eliot, Frost, and the New Critics, as though the critics who killed Keats (in Shelley's mythopoetic version of the tale) had resurfaced long enough to bring Bill Williams down. That of course is nonsense, as it was nonsense in Keats's own case, where tuberculosis had a prior claim. But literary infighting, the politics of art, did have its grinding effect on Williams, as it had its effect on Eliot and Pound and Hart Crane and others. And even Gerard Manley Hopkins, who published virtually nothing in his lifetime, could feel a critic's barb by inference and smile sardonically to his friend Robert Bridges that, if such oblique references and dismissal constituted fame, he wanted no part of it. For Williams, however, the case was far more interesting and severe, for it was once easy in American literary circles to laugh Williams off. The *Partisan Review* did it, the Princeton circle did it, including Blackmur and Jarrell and others, *Poetry* did it, and by extension the entire British literary tradition did it. Everybody did it, or so it seemed. And though Williams could forgive, as he forgave the editors of the *Hudson Review* and sent them, in his last years, some of his best work, he could not always forget.

So, when Robert Lowell tried to patch things up between Williams and Eliot in 1948, Williams was willing to go along with the reconciliation (he did after all admire much the Possum had wrought), but he was quick to warn Lowell (and the rest of us) that the younger generations would be hard put to comprehend what Williams's literary skirmishes had cost his battered spirit. Did Williams actually remember Frost's snub at Bread Loaf, offered in the summer of 1941; did he remember it ten years later when he returned again to Bread Loaf? Yes, Williams did remember, as he remembered Eliot's dismissive conduct in 1924, and Duchamps's barb in 1916 and Jarrell's final downward reassessment of Williams when *Paterson* 4 was published in 1951. Williams remembered because literature mattered so much to him. It really did matter how a poet put his or her language on the line. In the long empyrean view, as we turn the pages of our Nortons or other anthologies of American poetry and see Stevens and Williams and Pound and Eliot and Hart Crane enthroned side by side like larger-than-life Byzantine presences, none of this much matters. But in re-creating Williams's life, I learned early that all this of course does matter. It mattered because there was a political and social judgment implicit in telling the world that a poem could be made of anything. I have said it many times, as Williams reiterated toward the end of his life. Anything is grist for the poem. Anything. Make it of this, of this, of this.

"Reading your biography," Williams's younger son, Paul, wrote me, "I can remember Dad's conversations over the dinner table. You brought them back to me. Apparently you were there too." For that is the job of the biographer: to re-create the inner drama of such literary skirmishes for those to whom literature meant life itself. Words, the words of the poem, the words of attack, the words of praise. All these words matter in the re-creation of a life. They matter as much as the victories and defeats of a Caesar, a Vercingetorix, a Nelson, a Pershing, a Patton, even though long after those battle sites have been emptied we may walk there in a tranquility that we throw backwards onto those earlier times ... at our peril. What we want again in the literary biography is the hurl of voices shouting at or past each other, the words actually spoken in mid-passage and not the words remembered after the voyage is over. Discovery by "seaboard," Pound has it, not by Aquinas map.

3   Literary lives, we should keep reminding ourselves, are after all made up of words. And if a biography is composed of words, we should look carefully at the ones we use. Is there, for example, a particular kind of language better suited to the telling of Subject X's life than Y's? Or

at least a particular range of language choices? I think there is, *if* the biographer is able to possess himself or herself of that language. The language used to portray a figure like Henry James should be made to reflect the world of James, just as, in the vast verbal kaleideoscope of things, another language could be made to flesh the world of a Wallace Stevens and another the worlds of a Hemingway or an Emily Dickinson. Some will, I know, object to such an organic view of biographical language. Some may, for example, claim that such a suggestion smacks of what, in the days of neo-orthodoxy, was once called the mimetic fallacy: the attempt to imitate reality with language, or (in this case), the attempt to imitate the world of Subject X by seeing that world through the lens of Subject X's own language. Imagine doing Faulkner in the style of *As I Lay Dying*; or Joyce in the style of *Finnegans Wake*; or Emily Dickinson in the style of her own poems . . . or even of her letters. Other biographers will reject my suggestion because they do not have the ability to reconstruct either their subject's language or even the illusion of that language.

Of course such a direct imitation is not exactly what I have in mind either. What I mean is rather a simulation of the language of the subject whose life we are retelling. This is not to say the language that we hear in Williams's or Stevens's poems, or in the novels of Faulkner or Hemingway, but rather a simulation of a person's characteristic diction and syntax as we can discover those in letters, tapes, and memories of their speech: in short the language staple, the language as they themselves used it everyday. To tell the story, that is, from the eye and mouth of Subject X, rather than from the outside, or at least to do this (more likely) as a strategy part of the time.

Let me give you an example of the kind of thing I mean. One critic took me to task for quoting some of the salty language and four-letter words that Williams finally managed to get into his written and spoken language. It apparently took Williams until he was in his thirties before he felt comfortable about doing this, having for so long been under his mother's injunction never to do or think a wrong thing. In allowing myself to reveal this "darker" side of Williams, this particular critic argued, I had revealed myself to be, like Williams, rather coarse minded; by which he meant, presumably, using language unfit to be uttered in the presence of the truly great, such as Henry James and Proust and Dostoievsky, Mallarmé and Kafka. But it seems to me an easy enough trick for the critic to summon at least by name such an impressive pantheon, such a philosopher's circle, and yet never once rise above the humdrum quotidian of what passes for literary salon talk. There are very few of us indeed who have not at one point or another in our lives employed stereotypes in our language or found ourselves resorting to Chaucerian substandard English. Maybe it is because I am of a later generation, but if I had written the life of "Vinegar Joe" Stilwell I would not have agonized over Stilwell's characterization of polio-stricken FDR as "rubberlegs," as that fine biographer Barbara Tuchman says she did in writing *Stilwell and the American Experience in China* a dozen years ago.

It seems apparent—to me at least—that biographers cannot afford *not* to reveal the darker shadows of their subjects. For, like the novelist, they must remain absolutely true to their subject. Biographers may well regret that their subjects used such language, just as they will probably regret the banal or vicious stereotyping of which their heroes were guilty (by which I mean comments about race, about religion, about sexual differences or preferences), but if it is part of the record, then certainly a representative portion of that material will have to be recorded or we falsify the story. Biographers must know not only what their subjects said in the prepared speech before the podium in the glare of the public light, or reveal not only the moments of lyrical perception and the splendid repartee; they must also show what the subject felt in the privacy of a letter or what was remembered off the record in conversation with a friend, an enemy, an outsider. Such glimpses will be rare enough anyway once the eulogizing and sculpting into marble begin. As a rule of thumb, therefore, biographers would do well to learn from the linguist that all language—however highly charged—is acceptable if it helps to reveal the full dimensions of the subject, the chiaroscuro of light and dark that renders the portrait plausible.

Let me add, so that I am not misunderstood on this point, that I have little patience with those biographers who seem to be out to reveal the little or big secrets of their subjects for the pleasure of the scandal itself, without taking the necessary responsibility of placing those shortcomings in their correct perspective. There are biographers, regrettably, who show no real understanding of their subjects, who do not have the ability to show us the underlying strengths of a figure, and so set out to debunk (in a way Lytton Strachey himself never did) by holding up the shabby truths they have discovered like so much unwashed underwear. I find something disturbing, for example, about the treatment accorded Elvis Presley by his most recent biographer, Albert Goldman, not because he bares Presley's dark side, but because he seems to have gone to such disproportionate length to reveal what he learned from those figures, some of them mere hangers-on and some outrightly hostile to Presley, who surrounded the singer in his last depressed years. What this biographer fails to show us, meanwhile, is the very real hold Presley's music had on millions of Americans and others. We have the sordid facts of Presley's last years, the quantities of uppers and downers consumed, the casual sexual interludes, but where is the dream of the young singer before it soured, where is the truth of the legend that touched so many who make up the democratic ground of America? And why did that legend have the effect it did? It is not to be found, this other Presley, in Goldman's telling.

Norman Mailer, on the other hand, taking much less promising material in the life and death of convicted killer Gary Gilmore, did manage to explore the reality of the American West and to place the tragicomic inversion of this world against the troubling and stark vision of early Mormons coming by wagon train to Utah. Mailer's is not, perhaps, a "true" biography because he is enough of an iconoclast to break generic bindings when he can, but for biographical texture his book by and large succeeds where Goldman's fails. This is because Mailer had the imagination to find a vehicle for Gilmore's felt sense of reality in the relentless, quotidian, and ultimately stark quality of the language he himself used, a language that employs the techniques of journalism in much the same spirit of Andy Warhol painting his meticulous reproductions of Campbell Soups: a medium of flat, unadorned, and even tacky sentences, precise as plastic rulers, the thin tissue of syntactical connectives simulating the thin tissue of unconnectedness that turns out to have been Gilmore's life. What strikes us too is that it is a life shared, except perhaps for its explicit violence, by millions of Americans. Goldman's language, on the other hand, strikes me as made up of a Madison Avenue confectionery of tinsel and plastic, half glitter and half function, much of it having the texture of that imitation marble where Presley's body lies, and serving much the same purpose of preserving a corpse.

What then of the cool, detached stance of the narrator as the model for the biographer, the speaker keeping an objective distance? Again, it is a matter of literary strategy, and I can see where an aloof, objective tone would do well for a life, say, of the historian Gibbon, or for a life of Baudelaire or Flaubert. But for the most part this sort of scientific detachment belongs rather in the case history or in those situations where the biographer needs to employ an ironic detachment to best engage the reader. This mode comes close to the finest reportorial prose, and might serve well in presenting a life of Nixon, say, or Kissinger. In most cases, however, where one is giving a life story, it should be the unfolding inner drama that asserts itself, whether that life is revealed in the poems and novels of a writer, or in the realized places of an explorer, a soldier, a statesman—in the operating room, over a Sunday dinner, on an assembly line, or on a lonely road lost somewhere at night. Let objectivity and distance be relegated to the preface of the biography or to the notes or the afterword or the index.

What we want after all in a biography is the subject alive and moving, and if this means evoking the Muse of the novelist as well as the more familiar Clio, that is all to the good. Let us see Hemingway driving his ambulance on the Italian front lines, or fishing for trout on Lake Michigan or beginning to go to pieces in his mountain home in Ketchum, Idaho. Let us see Faulkner stopping to chat with friends on the town green in Jefferson or drinking some of the local whiskey with the other hunters by a campfire at night, creating the Snopes clan half out of thin air, half out of the reality of the hill people. Let us see Dickinson stoop to stare quizzically at a bumblebee bumping about its work in the June sun there in the south garden of her home in Amherst. Whitman tracking through the dirty snow of a cobblestoned alley in the Brooklyn of the late 1840s, his head filled with an aria he'd heard at the opera house across the river the night before. T.S. Eliot, tall and stoop-shouldered, in morning coat and frayed slacks, hair slicked and parted down the middle, a dog-eared copy of the Temple Classics translation of Dante's *Inferno* in his coat pocket, on a lunch break now from his wearying duties as clerk at Lloyd's, and staring down at the waters of the Thames, to recall that other great river with its brown gods, the Mississippi at St. Louis, along whose shores he had grown up. Let us see the mistakes and slights and economic worries, the estrangements and erotic engagements and the imaginative breakthroughs of these figures as and where they occurred, at eye level, and not through the clairvoyant eye of the omniscient and omnipresent narrator who, with deistic hindsight, looks out over it all and passes final judgment. We want the life, the life and not the marble tribute.

And yet we do want to see what these figures managed to achieve in their lives as well, for we have not chosen this man or that woman to blood with ten or a dozen years of our own life without hoping to have something in return. Writing a biography is, after all, rather like falling in love. At some point we must have seen something like a greatness in our subject, or if not that at least a uniqueness, demonic or otherwise, an achievement, or—if the life is minor—a special peculiarity in the life, a hunger at least for something, an ideal, however flawed, that draws the biographer on day after day. It was Geoffrey Wolff in his biography of Harry Crosby, that minor luminary of the American 1920s, who said that it was his subject's determination to transform himself through his own suicide into the Great Poet that held him riveted. Harry Crosby determined, Wolff tells us, "to translate himself from a Boston banker into a Great Poet by the agency of Genius," a genius "he calculated to attain by the agency of Madness." What is more, the final weird apotheosis of that madness would take the bizarre shape of Crosby's self-immolation. By keeping his word, Wolff argues, Crosby authenticated his life. "It is awful," Wolff tells us, "to watch someone with good eyesight and all his senses on full alert walk with gravity and determination toward the edge of a precipice, and keep going." Wolff disclaims any design on his readers; he is clearly not after a type or a lesson in the figure of this twenties American expatriate. Nor, he argues, is it the biographer's task to shape a subject's life to fit to a standard of morality or conduct, since the life, if sufficiently grasped, is always greater and more complex than any code or system superimposed upon it. And yet, we read lives because they do teach us something about human and moral conditions that none of us, I suspect, can ever escape or ever afford to dismiss. And they teach us even as they hold and fascinate us endlessly. A life unfolds, gathers to a greatness of momentum and complexity, and then inevitably begins to unwind, like those presences of Yeats's in the heavenly city of Byzantium, spinning in counterclockwise fashion, divesting themselves of the very lives into which they had spent the better part of their time on earth winding themselves in the first place. This process of self-realization unfolds about us and within us every day, occurring to a billion and a billion people. And yet. And yet what infinite variety within that basic arithmetical pattern we call life, we call death. Alpha and omega.

4   Which leads me then to a word about the aesthetic strategy of endings and beginnings. Jay Martin began his life of Nathaniel West with the moment of West's death. In a skillful narrative passage, Martin

re-creates the scene: a California highway, summer, 1941. West and his wife, Eileen, slumped over in their new station wagon, West's body resting on the horn, still sounding, the car demolished, the two of them dead. Having killed off his subject, Martin explained a few years ago at an English Institute session on biography, he could get on with the business of recounting West's life as it would lead up to this irrevocable terminus. Like a butterfly collector, Jay Martin had his specimen pinned, with all its gorgeous colors on display. Justin Kaplan, in his biography of Whitman, appears to have employed a variant of this killing off of the subject by beginning his life of the poet in old age, waiting for the very thing he had all his life yearned after: sweet death and surcease. Only in the fourth chapter, then, do we see Whitman's own beginnings. By adopting this narrative strategy, it seems to me, Kaplan allowed us to see Whitman at the end of his biography not in death, but as an old man at Camden, walking through the tall meadow grasses and summer flowers along the peaceful river, himself at peace at last, like that other bearded patriarch, Monet in his gardens at Giverny. But such a death-in-life scene as a strategy for Williams seemed particularly inappropriate, since death was the very thing Williams had struggled all his life against. Even Williams's still lifes, Jarrell has reminded us, swarm with a vigor that most poets never get into their presentations even of men and women. How much more so, then, in the life of the man himself.

I can tell you now that I had more trouble with the opening passages than I had with anything else in the writing of my biography. I wrote and rewrote those pages, trying to discover the most effective way to begin that book and introduce the reader to my version of Williams. I did not want to begin right off at the beginning. Rather, I wanted to present an image, a scene, that would catch something of the man's gestures and vitality but that would also signal something of the under-lying drama of that life. For a long time my opening put young man Williams in an open boxcar with a group of other teen-aged boys as the freight train ground slowly over the Hackensack River. In that scene Williams, sitting on the wooden floor, watches as one of the boys, a local kid from Rutherford with the marvelous real-life name of Dago Schenck, dives from the boxcar and down into the muddy river below. Such a scene, I had imagined, would have suggested Williams's own early passivity, his own delayed springtime—sexual, emotional, creative—as he bided for his own moment to make the great leap. It was a leap that came, finally, in spite of his feelings of inadequacy and cowardice, only with the decision to begin *Paterson,* a decision that was not made until Williams approached his sixtieth year. This opening scene would have been the only partially fictive scene in the entire biography (at least to my knowledge), and by its placement as entrance song would have stood as an implicit statement to the effect that the biographer, if he is to make an artful biography, must use fictive devices so that the underlying truth of a person's life may be revealed. It would have said, essentially, that in writing biography what the biographer must finally deliver, in spite of all the research one can do, is not the life itself but a reconstruction, a simulation, a dramatization, an illusion. In short, the biographer's reality is ultimately one more version of what Wallace Stevens meant by the Supreme Fiction.

Finally, however, I did not go with that opening, because my own thinking had shifted as I moved toward the completion of the biography. The original opening had stood as a metaphor, which is what I thought I had wanted in the first place: a scene that might reveal in microcosm the essential direction of a life. But that scene had been partially manufactured, as if to say: look, in spite of the years I've lived with Williams's spirit, I cannot give you the whole truth about him. And then it struck me. What hubris to suppose I or anyone ever could have done that. For to do that would have been to deny the central mystery of the human condition, which no one—not Darwin or Jung or Freud or the biographer—can ever fully reveal.

Once I understood this truth along my pulse, I could try another entrance into my biography. It would be a much humbler moment this time, and yet one filled with significance, if only its metaphorical significance could be made to resonate. Such oblique metonymical strategies, a method of appearing to address a subject directly while revealing something other by implication, had been one of the lessons Williams as poet and as man had taught me. Approaching seventy and with most of *Paterson* behind him by then, Williams had finally gotten around to doing his public *Autobiography.* It is an effort filled with many good and true stories; indeed, it served as a primary source for my own biography, especially of Williams's earliest years. But it is a text filled too with significant omissions and distortions, and it was shaped according to its own *in*-forming myth, for Williams had meant to show the world how a small-town boy and provincial doctor had stayed at home while the others—like Pound and Eliot and McAlmon and H.D.—had gone running off to Europe. Williams's reward for staying at home had been to catch the prize, for by age seventy he knew he'd won through to being at least in some sense a representative American poet, a son in the venerable tradition of Emerson, Thoreau, and Whitman.

In the final scene of the *Autobiography*, Williams leads the reader back to the river, to the Great Falls at Paterson, this time in company with a friend and Williams's own grandson Paul. It is early winter and there are ice formations everywhere about the park that sits above the falls. Young Paul asks his grandfather to hurl one of those "ice cabbages," as he calls them, into the river below, and that act of hurling the object into the Passaic evokes in Williams's mind the image of Sam Patch, the local daredevil who had leapt from this very spot several times in the 1820s until he died, the clotted river finally killing him. Young Paul is of course both terrified and fascinated by the sheer magnitude of the spectacle, and yet he wonders out loud just how deep the river is at that point. So Williams ends his own life story here, at this place and at this moment, the present, with the son of his son calculating when and how he might ever duplicate Sam Patch's leap, the very leap Williams himself had finally willed himself into taking when he chose to begin writing *Paterson*.

It was with this scene, then, that I decided to begin my biography. In studying the original drafts for the *Autobiography* now at the Beinecke, I learned by chance that this visit to the Falls had taken place on New Year's Eve, 1950. The moment of Janus: the exact fulcrum on which the century itself rests. A looking forward and a looking back. By beginning just here, then, I would take Williams's own narrative closure and begin all over again for myself, telling Williams's story partially as Williams himself had seen it, but taking my own leap, as we all must, by restructuring Williams's rendering with my own. It would mean supplanting Williams's later version of the American success story as he'd presented it in the *Autobiography* with the deeper version that had guided him all those years while he had had to fight like a bantam to achieve a voice and have that voice heard. And of course, on the darker side, I would have to fill in the silences that Williams, with his wife, Flossie, looking over his shoulder, had chosen not to look at again in telling this official version of the story. And so I would begin by asking the same question that Williams had had his grandson—my own contemporary (and luckily my namesake) ask: Just how deep did the river (of Williams's life) really flow? What, in other words, had it really cost this American (one like me, of mixed ancestry) to dream of a language rising out of a particular ground, and to pursue that language and that dream daily for nearly eighty years?

The answers, such as they were, took over 800 pages of print, answers recapitulated for the reader once more in the biography's final pages. For the strategy of juxtapositions in that closure was meant to suggest that Williams's life, like the lives of his own heroes—Washington and Boone and Poe and even his own father-in-law—was both a vindication and a personal tragedy of a very real order. The single-minded pursuit of Williams's dream had cost him dearly in terms of his own life and the lives of those dear to him, especially his wife, whom he had loved in spite of self-preoccupations, infidelities, and the rest of it. I meant to suggest as much when I showed Floss discovering her husband's small and wasted body turned toward the wall after the man had suffered one cerebral hemorrhage too many, and then juxtaposed that death with Floss's own death one May morning thirteen years later. Floss remains in part a silent presence throughout the biography because, after all, it is her husband who is taking center stage here. But this death was hers. And when we learn that at the end Floss made the decision to be cremated and her ashes scattered rather than rest beside her husband in death, it comes as something of a shock. I myself chose not to speculate on the reasons for that final decision, thus reminding the reader again that in *any* life, no matter how long, much must remain, finally, a mystery. That having been understated, I could then get on with the business of the literary and imaginative significance of Williams's life, the legacy this flawed giant had left us, his sons and daughters.

5   Last, a word about the overall strategy of the biography. What I attempted there was something like a calculus of indeterminacy, a strategy of wresting success out of defeat. In my version of the metapoetics of the biography, I would inundate the reader with the river of facts surrounding Williams even as the reader should become aware that, if Williams's was a representative life, a life shared on many counts by many Americans in his roles of father, husband, lover, physician, citizen, and artist, it had somehow managed to move along another and unduplicated axis as well. In spite of failure after failure in that life, therefore, a crosscurrent paradoxically makes itself felt in the biography that, especially with the decision to finally do *Paterson*, resulted in Williams's

breaking through and giving us a poetry commensurate with our particular sense of reality; that is, we, a people at cross-purposes with ourselves yet jostling in our pluralistic society in a kind of antagonistic cooperation.

On this level, the biography was an attempt to duplicate the central paradox of *Paterson*, which after all contains Williams's true autobiography, that poem which tells us finally that it is not any system of values that holds us together, whether we see those values as political, economic, or societal. Instead, what we get in *Paterson*—and what I tried to echo—is the sense of a life caught in the flux of reality itself, a life that, while in danger of being pulled under by the overwhelming flood of events, dares to question at every turn, responding to the flood of experience as well as it can at every moment. If it is *Paterson* then that contains the central Williams, it was my special task as biographer to respond as fully as I could to what that poem had to teach me as a life replica, my biographical form answering to Williams's more complex autobiographical one. "Weakness dogs him," Williams confesses toward the close of his epic,

> fulfillment only
> a dream or in a dream.
> No one mind
> can do it all, runs smooth
> in the effort, *tout dans l'effort*. . . .

It is the artist-father consoling the artist-son even in death. If I have told the life failingly, that too may be forgiven and may even be a virtue in the way we say that sweeping the dust together can be a virtue, apart from the elusive rainbow I earlier evoked. Williams for one knew that, being human, there could be no other way but to go haltingly when it is a man and not a god who is left to tell the story, to collect the dust and try to breathe life into it all again. *It is all in the effort*. . . . Let that be the biographer's as well as the poet's final defense. That and the intercession of the text itself, and the man or woman caught shimmering (perhaps) in all that dust.

1983

The Poem as Field of Action:
Paterson

A plan for action to supplant a plan for action:
In those dark days of December 1940, with the German Stukas dive-bombing over London, ringing the city with fire, T. S. Eliot, from his fire station post on the roof of Faber & Faber's offices on Russell Square, caught in that apocalyptic moment, that scene from Dante's hell, the Pentecostal moment as well. And so,

> After the dark dove with the flickering tongue
> Had passed below the horizon of his homing,

Eliot could begin to compose, in what would have seemed a most inauspicious time, the last of his *Four Quartets*, could sum up a lifetime's concentration on his craft, words fluttering about the ineffable Logos. "We shall not cease from exploration," he concluded, in sprung four-stressed lines, alike and yet so unlike those quatrains he'd done twenty-five years before,

> And the end of all our exploring
> Will be to arrive where we started
> And know the place for the first time.

Looking at the bombed city blazing in the predawn dark, he might feel he had earned the right to invoke the idea of mystical union, could now call on the presences of that anonymous English mystic who had penned *The Cloud of Unknowing* back in Chaucer's time and of Dante, whose paradisal rose, aflame now on the horizon, could evoke the whole company of the blessèd, purged, now, in those refining fires. Let the fire bombs do their worst, consigning whole streets to fiery destruction. Here, still, was a heart that could sing in that pyre that

> all shall be well and
> All manner of thing shall be well
> When the tongues of flame are in-folded
> Into the crowned knot of fire
> And the fire and the rose are one.

Little Gidding would be Eliot's final important poem. And though he still had another twenty-five years and a number of verse plays to write and the Nobel Prize to accept, and though he would continue to be lionized, to be the darling of the universities even after his death, he would stop with this poem, believing that he had extended the poetic line as far as he felt it ougl.. reasonably be extended in his time. The period of experimentation was over; it had ended with the poetic apotheosis of *Little Gidding*, though he was too modest to name the event outright. "So here I am," the loose Alexandrines of *East Coker* lament,

> in the middle way, having had twenty years—
> Twenty years largely wasted, the years of *l'entre deux guerres*—
> Trying to learn to use words, and every attempt
> Is a wholly new start, and a different kind of failure
> Because one has only learnt to get the better of words
> For the thing one no longer has to say, or the way in which
> One is no longer disposed to say it.

So, addressing the British Academy in 1947 on the subject of his revisionist stance on Milton's influence, Eliot, standing there in the direct line of succession, closed his speech with a series of somewhat churchly sonorities.[1] "We cannot," he intoned, "in literature, any more than in

the rest of life, live in a perpetual state of revolution." Poetry, he reminded his listeners, had not one but *two* functions. It should not only
help to purify the dialect of the tribe, as Mallarmé had enjoined, but
it should also prevent the language "from changing too rapidly," for
"a development of language at too great a speeed would be a development in the sense of a progressive deterioration." And that sort of
breakdown and deterioration of English posed a very real threat to the
tradition in A.D. 1947. Had not the Modernists, himself among the
leaders, already established a new poetic diction for the young to explore and utilize? Let the young, therefore, turn to Milton to see how
a long poem might be written, let them turn to Milton that they might
"avoid the danger of a *servitude* to colloquial speech and to current
jargon." Beware the breakdown of forms, "the pointless irregularity."
Milton's greatness, this wayward son had come to see, lay just there, in
his adherence to the great tradition of English verse, in his "departure
from, and return to, the regular measure." In his adherence to the
established norms, paradoxically, Milton had achieved his greatest freedom. "In short," Eliot summed up, "it now seems to me that poets are
sufficiently liberated from Milton's reputation, to approach the study of
his work without danger, and with profit to their poetry and to the
English language." And there Eliot felt he could let the issue rest. The
period of poetic experimentation was now at an end. It had, as it turned
out, coincided exactly with Eliot's own years of development. Now let
the young, in this postwar time, consolidate and employ what their
ghostly masters had indeed achieved for them.

When the *Enola Gay* lumbered off its Pacific runway on the morning
of August 6, 1945, it carried in its womb a single bomb. Over the city
of Hiroshima (population 245,000) the bomb-bay doors of this other
dark dove opened to release that single, comic-lumpish bomb. What
happened then was radically unlike anything that had ever before happened in the long history of war. Within moments enough energy had
been released to kill 80,000 people and seriously burn, break, and poison
another 80,000. It was the first act of a new kind of war; a new kind
of energy had been unleashed, which stunned not only those on whom
it had been dropped, but also the very ones who had dropped it as
well. Wars do release energy, William Carlos Williams knew, and
though they release it wastefully, destructively, they do release it. For

the very *fact* of the atom bomb, staggering in its implications, once grasped, came to inform the very core of Williams's poetics, to stand as metonym for the vast open fields of poetry that had not yet been tapped.

No wonder, then, that Williams, who was still searching for a new measure even as Eliot spoke for a new stability, should lash out against him. In an essay published in *Four Pages* in February 1948—one of those ephemeral "little magazines" that constituted for Williams the cutting edge of the avant garde and that together made up the incredibly tough flower that might (in time) break the very rock on which the academies stood—Williams swung out against Eliot and the pernicious influence Milton's poetry could still have on the young.[2] Milton's capital offense (and Eliot's as well) was to have perverted "the language in order to adhere to certain orthodoxies of classic form." Like Milton, Eliot already belonged to the "old" and both were mountains fallen "across the way modern poetry must take to get on with its work." What was Eliot *really* up to, after all, Williams wondered, in "throwing the young against [such] an earthworks as Milton"? Wasn't it that he feared *they* just might "DISCOVER a means, a means for expression, an enlargement of mood and style in our day which Mr. Eliot has never sighted"? Milton could still effect a destructive influence, had, in fact "converted" Eliot himself "over a lifetime." In time Eliot himself had become the Milton of the mid-twentieth century, the singer of his own "enlightened and distant world." Some of Milton's early poetry—the experimental work (and here Williams placed *Samson Agonistes*)—the young could use to good effect. But the later Milton had better be avoided, because there was new work to be done, "enormously difficult work unlike anything Milton [or Eliot, he might have added] ever conceived, a negative which his best scarcely envisions."

From the late thirties on and throughout the forties, as he moved by halts, blurts, and many false starts toward the realization of the major form he'd spent thirty years preparing the way for—the form of his long poem *Paterson*—Williams's letters, notes, essays, and lectures are likewise preoccupied with one overriding question: the question of clearing the field in order to find a new form, the need felt marrow-deep to move, as he told Horace Gregory in mid-1944, "into the field of action and go into combat there on the new ground."[3] The poem as field of action, as battlefield, where the new, still-green open formations might successfully rout the older, entrenched forces of orthodoxy: the sonnet, the blank verse line, the octosyllabic couplet, the iambic pentameter, all drawn up in their imposing columns, their flanks supported by systems and ideologies of all sorts, protecting those shell-like forms, those stale linear configurations. "The artist," Williams had written in March 1938, "is to be understood not as occupying some outlying section of the field of action but the whole field, at a different level howbeit from that possessed by grosser modes." [4] And what were those grosser modes? Again and again, Williams insists, they are any of those special interest groups—usurious in the truest sense—that would use poetry for their own special interests: parties and ideologies and churches of all sorts. Fields of knowledge of whatever kind were, by their very nature, parties, divisions, factions, offering partial solutions, containing in their very incompleteness—as against an expanding universe—the seeds of their own destruction, their own shell-like (Shelley) deaths. Only in the well-made poem, the poem that adequately incorporated in its expanded base the fact of a living, sensuous, present-day reality (as opposed to an ideological or intellectualized reality) might the poet manage to beat time, that all-consuming fire, at its own game. "Formal patterns," Williams insisted in what is a key into his own poetics, "formal patterns of all sorts represent arrests of the truth in some particular phase of its mutations, and immediately thereafter, unless they change, become mutilations." [5]

Therefore, just as General Braddock had learned the hard way when his closed formations, his well-ordered columns, had run smack into an ambush deep inside the New World wilderness, you either adapted to the new conditions by dispersing your forces in an *apparently* random formation, or your lines went under. Enter, then, the all-important dissonance, the unstable element recharting the settled periodic maps, enter Pan, that disturbance buzzing gleefully in the harmonious choir, so that the phoenix might once more rise out of the destruction, the de-creation, of the old nest, plastered together from all those old bits of form.

Williams came to harp on the need for a new line, a new measure, until he was sure his audiences thought him obsessed. At least from the twenties on, the insistence on the need for new forms, for what later became the emphasis on the variable foot, is everywhere in Williams's poetry and criticism. It threatened to become polyvalent, omnipresent, a stridency, so much so that Williams came in time very near to apologizing for bringing the issue up just one more time, and then, having said that, proceeding to expound on the need again. Looking back now with the hindsight of thirty years, it should become more readily noticeable what it was that Williams was rejecting, and why (though the battle is even now far from won). In his notes for the series of lectures he delivered at the University of Washington in July 1948, subsequently published in part and included in his *Selected Essays* under the title, "The Poem as a Field of Action," Williams struggled to articulate his own sense of how the poem might develop in the next twenty to thirty years.

At the very time he began taking notes for that series of talks—on odd scraps of prescription paper and random pages in that notebook he kept by his bedside while recuperating from an operation in February 1948 and later while at Atlantic City with Floss for a few days—Williams was also smack in the middle of organizing *Paterson* 3 and still had *Paterson* 2 fresh in his memory.[6] The actual working out of the new measure in the only place it mattered, finally—the poem itself—was nearly concomitant with the attempt to articulate the very need for that new measure. No sooner had Williams come in from exploring the field than he would try to say what it was, exactly, he had found out there. And he had found, in the little magazines, the young and the near-young out there in those same fields, listening carefully, and even then demonstrating in their own poems the truth of what Williams was saying in the summer of '48. The news, he felt, could be read in the new work of poets like Louis Zukofsky[7] and Theodore Roethke and Charles Olson, and even younger poets like Robert Creeley and Denise Levertov and Allen Ginsberg and others.

There were, Williams told his audience, two traditions, one representing stability, the other—the viable tradition—representing change. Change in the forms of the poem, Williams said, was absolutely necessary to avoid stasis, stagnation, a marmoreal fixity.[8] And, in fact, the best poems in the poetic tradition proved that it was only when the form had sufficiently changed from its predecessors that it could truly be said to have entered that tradition. By change, however, as he had been at some pains to point out in his "Letter to an Australian Editor" in late 1946, he meant a structural change in the poem arising out of a deep understanding of one's society—that fructifying female, the language as really used—and not the androgynetic habit of the son feeding off the forms of the father without recourse to the changes in the matrix of the living, pulsing language itself. What Pound and Eliot had done—and they were simply the most important examples—was to go running off to Europe, to a ready-made culture, where they could, in tapeworm fashion, feed off the figures of the great tradition, in effect "translating" the dead masters into their own idiom. The effect, however, was to use those masters as "the fixed basis of their divagations," altering their sources without ever breaking clear of them. What resulted was a stasis, a blockage, which prevented the idiom from coming over unhampered, unfettered, without literary construction or falseness. That blockage created an artificiality, turned the language into a sort of wax container housing a language smothered in honey.

Recall just how beset by the forces of the "great tradition" Williams felt in the mid-forties, by what he termed the "party-line" boys. (For a start, he would have tossed the *Partisan Review,* Conrad Aiken's recent *Anthology of American Poetry*—which had failed to include him—and those two Anglo-Catholics, first Eliot and now the young upstart Auden into that stew.) And recall, too, to shift the force of the field metaphor ever so slightly, that a field must first be cleared and new furrows, new lines made, before there can be new growth, new flowers. (Hence the central importance of Poe's example in clearing the field in Williams's essay on Poe in *In the American Grain,* the essay with which Williams had originally wanted to close his book.) In the mid-forties, it was the example of Auden in particular that Williams held up for examination and for rejection.[9] Why, really, had Auden come to the United States, Williams asked. Because, he felt, Auden had come to realize that he was rapidly becoming "breathless" in England, had already come to the end of his poetic resources, and so had been drawn to America hoping he could find a new, more flexible measure.

Let Auden write as much as he liked about the impoverished industrial landscape or write all the occasional pieces he wanted. But, unless they contained an expanded and flexible structure, they remained lifeless. And yet (at least in Williams's reading), Auden was perceptive enough to see that the poetic staple in England had become too rigidified, too stable to admit of real experimentation, so that it was no longer able to contain a significant part of his own world and his own reality. And, in spite of their expatriation, both Eliot and Pound had unavoidably carried with them the seeds of the American language. That language might be constricted, rejected, spurned as an embarrassment. But it was this very unstable element, this dialect phase of the English language, that had entered into their poetry to save it in a way that Auden's best work could not match.

But there were other contemporaries of Williams's who had also failed to develop adequate formal means. If the poem was "a construction embodying the reality of the moment," then Hart Crane—that other American contender—had also failed. For Crane's lines did "not disturb the bed of the form": only his surfaces were new. He had cultivated the blank verse line, this poet, who, cruising the bars in the Red Hook district of Brooklyn looking for companionship, used to give his name out as Kit Marlowe, and that line had become his poetic signature. He had chosen, rather, to cultivate a stable field, those elaborate Elizabethan sonorities with their "heady metaphors," had chosen instead to plaster new lexical configurations on the older English forms. There was, Williams insisted, "no new structure" in the man, "no new bones," only an outmoded Symboliste pastiche.

And Stevens. The trouble with Stevens, Williams had remarked back in 1937, was that, when he used the blank verse line, he felt compelled to say something important.[10] Early in his talk, "An Approach to the Poem," delivered at the Kenyon Conference in mid-July 1947 and given again at the English Institute meetings held at Columbia that September, Williams spoke of his having read Stevens's lecture which had been presented before a Harvard gathering the previous February and subsequently published in the *Partisan Review* (where Williams saw it): the piece entitled "Three Academic Pieces." Without stressing the fact that his own poetics was in sharp contradistinction to his old friend's, Williams in effect rejected Stevens's contention that the modern structure of reality resided in the accuracy of the resemblances between things, ideas, facts, and their lexical and metaphoric referents: that metaphor was at the core of the poetic act. For Stevens, the singularity of poetry rested in the fact that in "satisfying the desire for resemblance it touches the sense of reality, it enhances the sense of reality, heightens it, intensifies it." [11] The essay is not one of Stevens's better efforts, and a comment he had made a few months earlier, when he was preparing his talk, reinforces the sense of just how great the distance between Stevens and Williams had become on the question of form in poetry. In December 1946 Stevens had written a friend that he had not read *Paterson* 1 because there was "the constant difficulty" in reading Williams that the man was "more interested in the way of saying things than in what he has to say." But, Stevens insisted, people were "fundamentally interested in *what* a writer has to say. When we are sure of that, we pay attention to the way in which he says it, not often before" (italics added).[12] So, first there was the paraphrasable content, and *then* there was the form. But, Williams argued in his talk, the poem was "made up of nothing else" than a new reality superseding the particular occasion out of which it had arisen, and only as that was made manifest by the *form* of the poem. The reality lay just there, then, in the particular *form* of the utterance, in the precise shape in which the words jostled along the line.

If these figures—and a host of other poets besides—had failed to sufficiently engage the structure of the poem, still there was a tradition of innovation in modern American poetry. It was a tradition that had tried, however haltingly, to achieve a radically new measure, a new structure that could respond adequately to the complex reality of the living language itself. For the Americans there was, to begin with, the example of Walt Whitman's "formal excursions," the "cry of a man breaking through the barriers of constraint IN ORDER TO BE ABLE TO SAY *exactly* what was in his mind." [13] His greatest contribution to the development of American poetry had proven to be a negative but nevertheless all-important one: "the break he instituted with traditional forms." What Whitman had done in effect was to break down the complex associations of the old forms to their "nascent elements" for future poets to recombine into new forms "as the opportunities of a new language offer." [14] Was something like *Song of Myself* a free verse poem? Yes and no. Yes, because the poem lay there on the page in its "free" verse form. But, in a deeper sense, no, because if one could only look deep enough into the elements of the line, one would see that there really was no such thing as free verse without a governing principle of some sort. Free verse poems were, in fact, "poems to which the ordinary standards of measure have not been found applicable or to which they have not been applied. They are, or represent . . . a new association of the prosodic elements in the making (or might be so) or of unrecognized elements waiting for final assessment." [15]

The history of American poetry since Whitman had shown two distinctive trends: a regression back to the older, safer rules of English prosody—poetry via Saintsbury—or an irregular advance, often "bizarre and puzzling," a venture out into the unchartered reality all about us, after a new measure, those new forms made by recombining the most basic element of the poem: the foot itself.

There already existed a tradition of innovation in the search to expand the resources of the poetic foot. There were, for example, Hopkins's poems in sprung rhythm, with their all-important emphasis on the stress quality of the language.[16] And there was Robert Bridges, both in such early pieces as "The Dead Child" and "London Snow," with their modified sprung-syllabic base, and in the later sprung music of *The Testament of Beauty*.[17] These were the important early English innovators, though, of course, there was the special—and complex—case of Ezra Pound, Williams's early master and amiable antagonist. Pound's greatest importance as a poet for Williams rested in the work he had done with the line. "Time," he wrote of Pound in January 1950, "is the pure element of Pound's success." It was a quality in his lines—this "joining phrases to time"—that "makes most other contemporary verse sound juvenile by comparison."[18] It was not with the ideogram nor with his ideas on the cancer of usury that Pound had made his greatest contributions. In fact, Williams was afraid that Pound's ideas had blocked the poetry (at least until the Pisan *Cantos* were published), so that his "present line" (the poetry of the thirties and early forties) had become "repetitious, tiresomely the same or positively decayed."[19] All Pound had done was to put the same kinds of content into a form he had created between 1915 and 1925. He was the androgyne par excellence and in that sense, as Williams had said a quarter of a century earlier, the "best enemy" American poetry had. And he was still the one man from whom Williams could continue to learn how to refine his craft.[20] But in the mid-forties, Williams was primarily troubled by Pound's apparent rejection of the technical means and his continued reliance on the content, which was after all, relatively unimportant in the poem *as* a poem.[21]

So Williams had again looked over the fields of his contemporaries, evaluating their relative strengths and deficiencies, the strategic entrenchments, and that unguarded break in their defenses: the critical weakness in the line itself. That weakness was acting as a cancer, undetected, ignored, so that, unawares, many of the structures of his contemporaries had become grids or cages, entrapping rather than freeing that elusive beauty: Kore, the radiant gist, the goddess herself. What field tactics could Williams point to, how expand the field of action to include an expanding reality? One thing the atom bomb had done: it had shown what could be done, what might be done, if the irritant disturbing the structural valence of the line itself could be charted and then utilized.

Most contemporary poetry was being brought stillborn into the world because the line itself, which had once contained life, had become increasingly rigid, had moved with the passage of time toward the stability of inert lead.

The problem lay, then, in the elements that made up the line itself and finally in the concept of the foot itself. That was where the stasis lay, in something as elementary as that. To continue to write on in the old iambic pentameter, with its accentual-syllabic guidelines, was to write in a leaded form. Smash the foot, determine what it was that was disturbing the periodic table, find a new measurement consonant with our own sense of time, and the effect in terms of a released energy could be as revolutionary for good as the bomb had been for destruction.[22] Eliot and Crane and Stevens and a multitude of others had for too long played at conventional warfare. New, revised tactics, as disciplined and as regulated as the old, but more in line with the modern world: that was what was needed! That alone would raise our own moment into reality. Otherwise we merely dreamt on, our world, our people, our time slumbering on into oblivion.

All well and good. But there were difficulties. "Maybe I am dreaming." Williams had confessed to himself, "maybe what I conceive is impossible. I may be excusing myself, for I do not seem to have succeeded so far in making studies of what I *think* can be done. I write about it in all my so-called criticism, but I have not, in my own work, made some practical tests. I just go on writing, which isn't what I want to do." [23] And yet, when he wrote this, in January 1947, he was on the brink of writing the "Descent" passage and of tapping into the energy flow disturbing the metrical valence (though it would still be several years before he realized what he had achieved). In the meantime, there were possibilities that he could articulate: things to avoid as well as things to look for.

He saw, for example, that the trouble with English poetry from Chaucer's time on (he did not know Anglo-Saxon poetry well enough to feel free to comment on it) was that it was a rhyme-poor language, and that poets had continually distorted their syntax to make it conform to the endurable limits of the old metrical patterns. Rhyme patterns had never much troubled Williams after he reached thirty; he had simply dropped the device, except for occasional effects, soon after his first, privately printed volume, *Poems* (1909). Early he had learned that a

good modern poet could not invert the phrase and still write good modern poetry. And yet, how many poets, in order "to gain wit [and] fluid-
ity," had "perverted the prose construction"? The meter could only be
twisted, forced, strained so much, and then the poet was forced to
"invert the phrase *or* go dead." [24]

But so-called free verse was not the answer, for without discipline the
line simply went slack, sputtered off not into prose but a bad poem.
Who did the contemporary practitioners of the craft think they were,
Williams warned, to assume that they could "do what the greatest ge-
niuses of the language can do, with freshness, originality, and WITHOUT
new devices or structures." [25] A new measure, a new government of the
works, a new open formation: that was what was needed if the poem
were once again to become a sensual reality, become again a fit abode
for the muse.[26]

Well, then, what could he point to? What examples of this new
measure could he offer young poets in 1948? As for actual evidence of
the new work, people would have to search for it as he had: in all those
little magazines and in the anthologies. For good work, tentative as it
was, *was* being accomplished. He could urge them to study their own
idiom, the American language, the dialect phase, the green shoot stem-
ming from the solid English trunk, study it as *he* had, by listening to
the rhythms of the language as it got itself spoken daily in the streets of
whatever polis or place one found oneself. He could urge them especially to listen hard for the pace of the language, its phrasing, its "acceptable pauses and interludes," its breaks, its heaves, its breath, its very
life.[27] He could urge them further to attend carefully to speed values in
their lines, to try to trace across the page "the mere brushing of a meaning" rather than to plod on with metrically "correct" lines, which could
not hold the elusive life necessary to any good poem. He could urge
them too to utilize those loose, colloquial phrases that were in the very
grain of the spoken language and that gave the line a certain freedom
of manner, a sense, as he put it, "of emotional drive and reality." An
idiomatic freshness coupled with an intense care for a syntactic structure that, on the other hand, should be packed tight with meaning, even
if that were expressed elliptically, with all the leaps and disjunctures of
the mind itself, as Joyce for one had done. *There* was a poetics Williams
could subscribe to. For it was words and only words that could unlock
the mind, new combinations of words, as free as possible of their old
associational weights, words new to the consciousness, new in their mea-

sure, radiant tracings of the ever-fleeting moment. That was how one began to create a field of action.

And that is something of what Williams was saying about the poem in the years immediately following World War II. But that was only half of it, for was not the real proof *only* in the poem itself, the well-made poem? "The most I can say concerning the poem is inevitably only second best beside the poem itself," Williams had warned his Washington audience at the outset of his talks. "This is a permanent and irreversible qualification. It is the poem, the new poem, the invention it implies that takes the cake. Never forget that. The achieved poem needs no bush of argument any more than did good wine in the old days" (PFA). Which suggests that it would be profitable to look at *Paterson* as well as at some of the shorter pieces Williams was writing at about the same time he was formulating his "so-called criticism." When Williams was writing criticism, especially for his college audiences, he felt the revolutionary's need to make himself not only widely understood but also widely accepted. But in the act of enunciating what exactly it was that he was charting in this unexplored new world, what often came across were two things: a sense of enthusiasm often bordering on the urgent, and a Cassandra-like frustration about being unable to say clearly what it was he was actually seeing.

But in his poems, Williams is a different kind of person. There the hesitancies and the false steps and the frequent descents in *Paterson*, for example, are in fact all part of a brilliant guerilla tactic as Williams brings the city into alignment with himself. He is the patient strategist, mapping out his lines, shifting his metrical emphases, retreating, like Washington across Long Island and over New York (Williams's own metaphor) until he can take the field by storm in New Jersey. Consider, for example, how Williams says "Raindrops on a Briar," a poem first published in early 1947:

> I, a writer, at one time hipped on
> painting, did not consider
> the effects, painting,
> for that reason, static, on
>
> the contrary the stillness of
> the objects—the flowers, the gloves—

freed them precisely by that
from a necessity merely to move

in space as if they had been—
not children! but the thinking male
or the charged and delivering female frantic with ecstasies;

served rather to present, for me,
a more pregnant motion; a
series of varying leaves
clinging still, let us say, to

the cat-briar after last night's
storm, its waterdrops
ranged upon the arching stems
irregularly as an accompaniment.

(*Collected Later Poems,* p. 99)

What Williams has given us is both an action poem and, effectively, the poetics behind such a poem. Consider the effects of the phrasing, the double caesure in the first and last lines of the initial stanza, the varied pace, the effect of the syntax as it pushes forward and the counterpressure of the voice slowing the line down with its various asides and qualifiers as it attempts to make sure that the reader understands that it is painting he is talking about (though it is writing he is actually performing). Consider such idiomatic interpolations as "for that reason," "on the contrary," "precisely," "merely," "for me," and "let us say." Consider the compression of the lexical package he gives us, of how to paint in words an un-still life, first negatively ("not children" and not simply the male or the female aspects of the reality under consideration and certainly not the stillness of the situation), and then positively giving us a dynamic, unquiet "still" life where the unsteady and irregular waterdrops "clinging still" to the "arching" stems (how active are those present participles, how shimmering that stillness) give us the illusion of freshness, of the life still clinging to the ephemeral moment, as though we were still witnessing the effects of "last night's / storm." That moment, that image and the voice speaking the words together create a field of action, a dynamic stillness over which a violent activity has passed, where the effects of that energy are still present.

But what of the larger field, of *Paterson,* embodying as it does in its very pages Williams's long, often frustrating search for a viable form. Think back to the early attempts, to poems stretching as far back as "The Wanderer" (1914), the various sketches, the aborted plans throughout the twenties and thirties, Williams's telling Pound in 1936 about that projected "magnum opus I've always wanted to do," the long sounding out, "working toward a form of some sort." [28] In the spring of '42 he plunges into the writing of what he thinks of as a relatively short long poem, and begins amassing page after page of an introduction, as he tries out one approach after another. And even with the presence of David Lyle on the one hand and of Marcia Nardi on the other—his Noah Faitoute Paterson, his Cress—Williams cannot break through an overwhelming sense of construction into a satisfying form.

In January 1943, he is telling his publisher, James Laughlin, that the poem is "crying to be written" as an answer to "the kind of thought that destroyed Pound and made what it has made of Eliot," an answer that will allow the local culture to infiltrate the city. In August of that year he is telling McAlmon that he is writing "an account, a psychologic-social panorama of a city treated as if it were a man, the man Paterson," but that though he has already "done a hundred pages or so," he is still finding it extremely difficult to work at his poem.[29] Again, in early 1944, he tells Charles Abbott, curator of the Poetry Collection at the Lockwood, that he has been trying to push himself forward, that he is blocked because he cannot find the right way into the poem, though now he thinks he can see his way clear. The long "Introduction" already amassed, he is hoping Laughlin will publish separately (though it is not to be).[30] And in July, he writes Horace Gregory from his vacation cottage in West Haven, Connecticut, that he is "aligning" a whole sheaf of papers into something like the final draft of his "Introduction," a fact he repeats to Wallace Stevens two weeks later. Speaking of his poems in *The Wedge* (1944) to Marianne Moore that November he admits that there "is too often no convincing form or no form convincing or promising enough to hold me over or take me over to some more satisfying invention." [31]

And then, on New Year's 1945, he confesses his profound sense of failure to Horace Gregory:

All this fall I have wanted to get to the "Paterson" poem again and as before I always find a dozen reasons for doing nothing about

it. I see the mass of material I have collected and that is enough.
I shy away and write something else. . . . I am timid about beginning what I know will surely exhaust me if I permit myself to become involved. Just yesterday I learned one of the causes of my
inability to proceed: I MUST BEGIN COMPOSING again. . . . The old
approach is outdated, and I shall have to work like a fiend to make
myself new again. But there is no escape. Either I remake myself or
I am done.

By early February, however, the blockage has been dynamited, and Williams can write Gregory that his friend Kitty Hoagland has already typed
out "the first finished draft of the 1st quarter of the 'Paterson' thing." At
the same time he is already asking Laughlin where to send his "contribution to the meal of the gods," though it may prove to be little more
than "perhaps a radish," once the draft has been finished ("sometime
before St. Patrick's Day").[32] By early 1945, then, Williams has achieved
a major form that, with a plenitude of variations, will be repeated
throughout the rest of the poem. It is the first book of Paterson.

And yet, if one compares the typographical layout of Paterson 1 with
that of Paterson 2, compares them without recourse to the content of
each, as Fabre might examine a fish, one will note that there are distinctive and even radical line differences between the two. Most of the verse
sections of Paterson 1 are in columns, in lines varying from the epiclike
opening,

> Paterson lies in the valley under the Passaic Falls
> its spent waters forming the outline of his back . . .

to the shorter lines of a passage like

> We sit and talk and the
> silence speaks of the giants
> who have died in the past and have
> returned to those scenes unsatisfied . . .

to the terse quatrains of

> Who is younger than I?
>   The contemptible twig?
> that I was? stale in mind
>   whom the dirt. . . .

But with *Paterson* 2, which Williams apparently began in earnest in January 1947, lines and parts of lines are spread out across the page, as Williams begins to literally split up his poem into its constituent elements, in search of the radiant gist he believes he can discover if he can only name the element disturbing the metrical tables. Here in the second book of his long poem, Paterson, that sleeping giant of a man/city, begins to stir now from the whole dream of the poem,[33] and it is in the very lines of the poem itself that we come into at least a momentary contact with reality, since, most profoundly, it is only in learning how to measure correctly that we have empirical knowledge of a place.

So it is that in *Paterson* 2 the characteristic gesture of the man/city is of a man walking, as Paterson begins now to walk concretely across the charged female, Garrett Mountain, stroking her into a concomitant response. It is in this measuring of foot moving out from foot as Paterson begins the ascent, first up the same traveled footpaths as the others, but then, soon, cutting off across the open field on his own, that the poet's thoughts begin to flame into action. Garrett Mountain, we realize, becomes a metaphor for the woman awakening to desire, becoming a charged field, as the male principle begins to instruct his thoughts concretely over her. Leaving the beaten path, the old line (tradition), Paterson recalls how those old singers on the mountain had nearly killed someone for trying to expel them by force from a garden (the Dalzell episode), and then enters the old field with its "old furrows, to say labor sweated or / had sweated here. / a flame / spent." These, then, are the old furrows, old lines, old measures Paterson has come upon, breaking down once more to their original formlessness. But just there, arising out of this scene of apparent formlessness, here at this de-creative juncture, as the poet half stumbles in his halting measure, there, "before his feet, half tripping, / picking a way," suddenly there is "a flight of empurpled wings": grasshoppers in flight, the imagination itself aflame. From the imagination, from the very "core [Kore] of his mind," out of the de-created, "disintegrating" mound, emerges a red basalt grasshopper, the stone (the female) shaped, "instructed / to bear away some rumor / of the living presence that has preceded / it."

Out of the breakdown of the old forms, then, the emergence of the new, the still living. There, literally, in that unpromising field, Paterson has discovered a field of incessant activity, where stones—heavy words, things themselves—find their "counter buoyancy / by the mind's wings." As the poet "walks" across the page/field half stumbling in his halting measures, he is paradoxically creating a new measure. Watching the grasshoppers transforming themselves into act as they whiz and blur forward in irregular patterns, Paterson recalls that stone grasshopper, that stone stroked by the phallic chisel (as inert words are stroked into life by the phallic imagination) and comes to realize that the poem, and in fact his own sense of identity, must be created foot by foot, step by step, in halting measure:

> Before his feet, at each step, the flight
> is renewed. A burst of wings, a quick
> churring sound. . . .

Truly, then, here in this most unpromising of places, this abandoned field, Paterson has witnessed an annunciation, as these grasshopper/ seraphim, these "couriers to the ceremonial of love," announce by the very presence of their activity, a new poetic life, a new inspiration for Paterson.

There are, of course, the forces of authority that would strike out at this elusive beauty, this new field of energy, as it tries to push itself up through the old imprisoning lines, the metrical grid over the "cellar window" (and remember, it is in the cellar that Paterson will discover Kore / Persephone, the beautiful thing, misused, raped repeatedly, but lying there on those stained sheets, her beauty *still* essentially intact). Like Kore, the elusive mink of *Paterson* 2 is another of those female images creating a dissonance, a disturbance in the (water) table, the atomic periodic grid, and the forces of stasis (the status quo: the academy, the churchmen) though they try to kill that beauty, cannot.[34]

Throughout Book 2, Paterson will continue to walk, stroking the rock beneath him. And there, whether ascending the mountain, or, later, descending, he will encounter the various forces of repression: the Eliot-like figure combing out the "new-washed Collie bitch," until the lines lie "like ripples in white sand," a tame design stroked into the British pedigree. This figure of the English establishment will reappear later to look down on the haranguing minister Klaus Ehrens, who is, like Williams himself, the figure of the Protestant protesting. There is also Lambert's Castle, its phallic tower dominating the mountain, a reminder of another (economic) form of repression, recalling the English immigrant who, like Alexander Hamilton before him, saw the masses of people as some "great beast" to be exploited, maimed, crippled, crying out in their great crippled language. And there is the woman herself, Cress, one with the very field over which Paterson walks, crying out for the poet who will marry her and thus create the antagonistic harmony of the poem itself, but who instead all but pulls the poet under as her neuroses dominate the field at the close of the second book.

And yet Williams knows and knows deeply that the poet "will continue to produce only if his attachments to society continue adequate. If a man in his fatuous dream cuts himself off from that supplying female, he dries up his sources." [35] So here, on this Sunday in May, among these working-class families and couples from the mills and factories of that city from which the poet draws his sustenance, indeed, his very identity, Paterson/Williams has come to be fed, to translate the roar of the river everywhere about him into the measured poem: "I bought a new bathing suit, just / pants and a brassier," and "Come on! Wassa ma'? You got / broken leg? . . . What a bunch of bums! Afraid somebody see / you? / Blah! / *Excrementi!*" But also, the "featureless" harangue of the minister preaching outdoors on Garrett Mountain near some stone benches, his words "arrested in space":

> Don't think
> about me. Call me a stupid old man, that's
> right. Yes, call me an old bore who talks until
> he is hoarse when nobody wants to listen. That's
> the truth. I'm an old fool and I know it.

And of course there is the poet's own voice, arising out of the same place, arising into newly measured cadences, triple-plied, falling and yet buoyant, a descent becoming at last a new ascent:

> The descent beckons
>   as the ascent beckoned
>   Memory is a kind
> of accomplishment
>   a sort of renewal
>   even
> an initiation, since the spaces it opens are new
> places. . . .

It is a line so new for Williams that he will not at once realize its full potential as a new measure, will not see for several years yet that he has created a slower, more meditative measure that he will call upon in his sickness, when his characteristically nervous, sharp body rhythms will pace more slowly.[36]

But Paterson's voice here in Book 2 is more usually a falter, as the lines break up to make their own frequent descents. How often that voice must confront the petrifying stasis of an unchartered language, as when it laments:

> The language   •   words
> without style! whose scholars (there are none)
> •   or dangling, about whom
> the water weaves its strands encasing them
> in a sort of thick lacquer, lodged
> under its flow   •

And then the field itself threatens to become lead-bound, blocked, divorced from the supplying female, to become an "unmoving roar!" Only by breaking "down the pinnacles of his moods / fearlessly— / to the bases; base! to the screaming dregs," only in that terrifying descent leading, as Williams well knew, to wisdom but also to despair, can the poet hope to win through, finding in the structure of the language, in the inner structure of the elemental foot itself, "something of interest."

Name it, name that elusive something that Paterson finds of interest in the three quatrains that conclude *Paterson* 2—except for the fragmentary refrain and then the long complaint of Cress whiplashing into the poem and drowning out Paterson himself. Name the measure of lines like these, where anapests give way to spondees:

> On this most voluptuous night of the year
> the term of the moon is yellow with no light
> the air's soft, the night bird has
> only one note, the cherry tree in bloom
>
> makes a blur on the woods, its perfume
> no more than half guessed moves in the mind,

where a loose, triple measure seems to hover over the lines:

> On this
>   most voluptuous night
>   of the year

```
the term of the moon
              is yellow
                        with no light
the air's
        soft
              the night bird has
only
          one note
              the cherry tree in bloom. . . .
```

Is it the variations in the caesura that Paterson hears, breaking the lines into irregular triads, or is it something else? Hard put to it, Williams himself does not seem to have had a readily articulated answer. His own critical comments on the poem as a field of action, its energy released and realized by a new, more flexible measure, are maddeningly scattered all over the earth. And yet, when brought together, their dismembered corpse will yield up a unified sensibility if not an answer. And what we are finally given is the sense of a man coming down hard again and again on the work he has already achieved with that deeper mind that never sleeps and that cannot wait for the critical clarification, not even if that clarification should eventually come from the poet himself.

In the very weeks that Williams was typing out his first drafts of *Paterson* 2, including the "Descent" passage, his old friend Kenneth Burke, in one of those characteristically Aristotelian gestures of his, sent Williams a long summary of Virgil's "plan" in writing the *Aeneid*. *Paterson* 1 was, of course, already published, but perhaps Williams might consider planning out the remaining books of his long poem, and thus reinforce its sense of a major form. But Williams knew, as of course Burke too in his heart of hearts knew, that Virgil had never "formulated any such preliminary plan as this before beginning composition on the *Aeneid*." No, the critic, he insisted, must come after. "For if the poet allows himself to fall into that trap (of listening too early to the philosopher) he will inevitably be of little use to the very philosopher himself as a field of investigation after he, as a poet, has completed his maneuvers." And maneuvers, of course, took place on fields of intense action across which the poet/tactician must move, stumblingly, haltingly, while his "nascent instincts" probed "into new territory." Even Einstein himself, working with other fields of action, had acknowledged the primary importance of this a priori mode of strategy called instinct. Better to keep poet and critic separate, "to penetrate separately into the jungle, each by his own modes, calling back and forth as we can to keep in touch for better uniting our forces." [37]

There was, then, talk about the poem as a field of action and the poetic field of action itself. Williams at different points did act as critic, but it was usually after the fact itself, after he had already made those heated forays of his into the unchartered territory of the spoken language. And when he emerged, try as he might—and his own attempts are better than any critic's in his own lifetime were—he could only stumble by fits and starts to say where it was he'd been and what he'd seen, pointing over and over again in the general direction of those fields radiant with activity.

1976

The Eighth Day of Creation: *Rethinking* Paterson

Even before he finished the last part of *Paterson* as he had originally conceived it—with its four-part structure—Williams was already thinking of moving his poem into a fifth book. The evidence for such a rethinking of the quadernity of *Paterson* exists in the manuscripts for Book 4,[1] for there Williams, writing for himself, considered extending the field of the poem to write about the river in a new dimension: the Passaic as archetype, as the River of Heaven. That view of his river, however, was in 1950 premature, for Williams still had to follow the Passaic out into the North Atlantic, where, dying, it would lose its temporal identity in the sea of eternity, what Williams called the sea of blood. The processive mode of *Paterson* 1-4 achieved, however, Williams returned to the untouched key: the dimension of timelessness, the world of the imagination, the quiet, apocalyptic moment, what he referred to as the eighth day of creation.

The need for imaginatively apprehending such a dimension had impressed itself on Williams in several ways: two operations in 1946, a heart attack in early 1948, and the first of a series of crippling strokes which began in 1951 and continued thereafter with increasing violence until his death in 1963. The impulse for summing up the life of the man/city Paterson in the mode of the eighth day of creation—a gesture that finds its analogue in the image of a Troilus viewing his Cress and his embattled city from the seventh sphere[2]—is no doubt anterior to these repeated intimations of immortality, but such accidents did reinforce the necessity for a new mode of saying, and, with it, a new way of seeing. But perhaps "new" verges on an unnecessary immensity, since it does not place the emphasis precisely where it belongs. "Life's processes are very simple," Williams wrote in his late thirties. "One or two moves are made and that is the end. The rest is repetitious." [3] So the apocalyptic mode is not really *new* for Williams in the sense that basically new strategies were developed for the late poems. Williams had tried on the approach to the apocalyptic moment any number of times; so, for example, he destroyed the entire world, imaginatively, at the beginning of *Spring and All* to begin all over again, in order that his few readers might see the world as new. And in *Paterson* 3, the city is once again destroyed in the imagination by the successive inroads of wind, fire, and flood, necessary purgings before Dr. Paterson can discover the scarred beauty, the beautiful black Kora, in the living hell of the modern city. These repeated de-creations are necessary, in terms of Williams's psychopoetics, in order to come at that beauty locked in the imagination. "To refine, to clarify, to intensify that eternal moment in which we alone live there is but a single force," Williams had insisted in *Spring and All*.[4] That single force was the imagination and this was its book. But *Spring and All* was only *one* of its books or, better, perhaps, *all* of Williams's books are one book, and all are celebrations of the erotic/creative power of the imagination.

What *is* new about the late poems is Williams's more relaxed way of saying and with it a more explicit way of seeing the all-pervasive radiating pattern at the core of so much that Williams wrote. In fact, all of *Paterson* and *Asphodel* and much else that Williams wrote, from *The Great American Novel* (which finds its organizing principle in the final image of the machine manufacturing shoddy products from cast-off materials, the whole crazy quilt held together with a stitched-in design) to "Old Doc Rivers" (which constructs a cubist portrait of an old-time doctor from Paterson by juggling patches of secondhand conversations, often unreliable, with old hospital records), to "The Clouds" (which tries to come at Williams's sense of loss for his father by juxtaposing images of clouds with fragmentary scenes culled from his memory), in all of these works and in others Williams presents discrete objects moving "from frame to frame without perspective/touching each other on the canvas" to "make up the picture." In this quotation Williams is describing the technique of the master of the Unicorn Tapestries, but it serves to describe perfectly his own characteristic method of presentation. It was a method he learned not only by listening attentively to Rimbaud, Stein, and Pound, but by having watched such cubist masters as Picasso and Juan Gris and Braque in the years following the Armory Show. "The truth is," Wallace Stevens remarked in an essay called "The Relations between Poetry and Painting" which he read at the Museum of Modern Art in January 1951, "The truth is that there seems to exist a corpus of remarks in respect to paintings, most often the remarks of painters themselves, which are as significant to poets as to painters . . . because they are, after all, sayings about art." [5] Williams would have agreed wholeheartedly.

It is, specifically, this cubist mode, eschewing the fictions of perspective for a strategy of multiple centers mirroring one another, that suggests Williams's radical departure from a logocentric poetics, such as we find in the poems of Hart Crane or T. S. Eliot. So, for example, in the late winter of 1938, Williams uses Dante's *Divina Commedia* and "the fat archpriest" of Hita's[6] *El Libro de Buen Amor* as analogues, modes for two antithetical traditions: the tradition exemplified by T. S. Eliot (Williams's archenemy) and Williams's own tradition. Dante, Williams felt, had laced himself too tightly within the constrictions of two formal "necessities": the philosophical and theological underpinnings that everywhere ground the *Comedy*, and the triadic mode of the *terza rima*. But the Spanish priest, with his looser, episodic structure and his "flat-footed quadruple rhyme scheme," placed no barriers between himself and his imagination. What Williams sensed in the priest's open form was a texture that at least manured "the entire poetic field." There was in his poem a tolerance for the imperfect, "a glowing at the center which extends in all directions equally, resembling in that the grace of Paradise." [7] Whether that phrase describes *The Book of Love* or not, it neatly encapsulates two of Williams's long poems: *Asphodel* and *Paterson* 5. (It also describes the *Pictures from Brueghel* sequence read as parts of a single poem, but since Williams was returning in the very late work to the sharper, more nervous mode of *Spring and All*, was in a sense leaving Paradise by the back door, they belong to another meditation.)

The formal emphasis we are searching for might be phrased this way: what marks poems like *Asphodel* and *Paterson* 5 as different from his earlier poetry is that Williams has come out on the other side of the apocalyptic moment. He stands, now, at a remove from the processive nature of the earlier poetry, in a world where linear time—the flow of the river—has given way to the figure of the poet standing above the river or on the shore: in either case, he is removed from the violent flux, from the frustrations of seeing the river only by fits and starts. Now the whole falls into a pattern: in Book 5 Paterson is seen by Troilus/Williams from the Cloisters at Fort Tryon Park, the line of the river flowing quietly toward the sea, the city itself visible as a pattern of shades, a world chiming with that of the Unicorn Tapestries, the world of art that has survived. From this heavenly world, the old poet can allow himself more space for rumination, for quiet meditation. It is a world that still contains many of the jagged patterns of Williams's own world of the early fifties: the Rosenberg trial, the cold war, Mexican prostitutes and G.I.s stationed in Texas, letters from old friends and young poets. But all of these are viewed with a detached philosophical air, as parts of a pattern that are irradiated by the energy of the imagination. For it is Kora who, revealed in the late work, glows at the center of the poetry, extending her light generously and tolerantly "in all directions equally." It is Kora again who, like the Beautiful Thing of *Paterson* 3, illuminates the poem, but it is a Kora apprehended now quite openly as icon, the source of permanent radiance: the fructifying image of the woman, the anima so many artists have celebrated in a gesture that Williams characterizes as a figure dancing satyrically, goat-footed, in measure before the female of the imagination. Now, in old age, Williams too kneels before the woman who remains herself frozen, a force as powerful and as liberating as Curie's radium, supplying light and warmth to all the surrounding details, tolerantly, democratically.

The icon presupposes a kind of paradise, or, conversely, most paradises are peopled at least at strategic points with figures approaching iconography. Dante for one felt this. It is no accident, then, that, as Williams moves into that geographical region of the imagination where the river of heaven flows, he will find other artists who have also celebrated the light. And there, in the place of the imagination expressly revealed, will be the sensuous virgin pursued by the one-horned beast, the unicorn/ artist, himself become an icon in this garden of delights. Three points demand our attention, then: (1) the movement toward the garden of the imagination, where it is always spring; (2) the encounter with the beautiful thing, Kora, the sensuous virgin to whom the artist pays homage; (3) the figure of the artist, both the all-pervasive creator who contains within himself the garden and the virgin and also the willing victim, a figure moving through the tapestry, seeking his own murder and rebirth in the imagination.

First, then, the fitful but insistent movement in the late poetry toward paradise, toward what Williams called the river of heaven, the Passaic seen in its eternal phase. While Williams was at Yaddo in July and August of 1950, writing furiously to complete the last book of *Paterson* as he had until then conceived of it—as a four-part structure—Nicolas Calas (another poet and artist-in-residence at the colony and an old acquaintance of Williams) showed him the work he had been doing on Hieronymus Bosch's fifteenth-century triptych, the *Garden of Delights*. Calas had pored over every inch of Bosch's work with microscopic care, using hundreds of photographic close-ups to examine the plenitude of detail that makes up the painting. As Williams read through Calas's commentary—his working papers—which attempted to decipher the painting's total complex of meanings, Williams was "appalled," as he said in the *Autobiography*,[8] at the sheer amount of scholarship that had been brought to bear on this medieval artifact. Calas's study of Bosch's apocalyptic icons stuck with Williams. A year later, in August 1951, while he was still recovering from the stroke he had suffered in March, Williams wrote an appreciation of Calas's achievement in giving the modern world a contemporary Bosch.[9] "It makes the 15th century come alive to us in a way which is vivid with contemporary preoccupations," Williams wrote (Calas). It was *not* the revelation of the *medieval* imagination that Calas had stressed, but the *timeless* imagination. Here was one of the old masters whose way of seeing his fifteenth-century world differed only in accidentals from twentieth-century man's way of looking at his own world. Calas had made Bosch's mind work "as if it were a contemporary mind," and—Williams threw out in an important parenthetical aside—"we know the mind has always worked the same" (Calas). In this view, then, Bosch was brother to the surrealists, whose chief importance, Williams had said elsewhere, was that they too had managed, through the use of free association, to liberate the imagination.

And Bosch was also brother to the cubists. In presenting his subjects without worrying about the illusion of perspective, a later preoccupation inherited from the Renaissance, he, like other old masters, had refused, like Williams, to see time as predominantly linear, or, even worse, progressive. What Williams discovered was that the old masters had had their own way of transcending the idiocy of the single, fixed perspective. Like the cubists with their multiple perspectives, their discrete planes apprehended simultaneously, the old masters had also moved their subjects outside the fixed moment. They were able, therefore, to free themselves to present their figures in all of their particularity both within a specific moment and at the same time as universal types or patterns, moving frequently to the level of icon. This shift in perspective helps to explain the similarity (*and* difference) between the achievement, say, of a volume like *Spring and All* and the later poems: the analogue, except in terms of scope, is between the cubist perspectives of a still life by Juan Gris and the multiple perspectives of the unicorn tapestries centered around the central icons of the virgin and the unicorn.

But what apparently struck the most responsive chord in Williams was that Bosch, in Calas's judgment, had managed to achieve the eighth day of creation, the apocalyptic vision itself, had in fact managed to annihilate time, to be in at the end, to see the pattern of his whole life as something accomplished, the artist looking in upon his own world and finding himself there. "Men do not die if their meaning is kept alive by their work," Williams wrote in the same essay, with an eye turned on himself, "hence the masters secreted their meaning in their paintings to live" (Calas). Williams was willing to acknowledge the need for the hermetic nature of Bosch's painting, which, elucidated by the teachings of St. Augustine and St. Gregory, pointed toward "the disastrous effects of the teachings of heresy generally over against the solid foundation in virtues of the true church" (Calas). But the *particular* force of the triptych came from the face looming out of the right corner, much larger than any other and the only face in the painting showing any particular character. This nearly disembodied face was, according to Calas (and Williams agreed) the face of the artist himself, looking back "with a half suspected smile . . . directly at the beholder" (Calas). This face, peering out from the mass of hundreds of fantastic and monstrous details, amounted to a "confession" of sorts, the artist revealing his subconscious world with all of its attendant erotic fantasies. Together, the hundreds of human and animal and abstract figures, many of them frankly sexual, provided an explanation or, better, an "evocation" into the inner reality of Bosch himself. In revealing or confessing himself so fully, Bosch had transcended the limitations of the self, giving those who could read him an intimate glimpse into themselves as well. Here was a "picture of how a contemporary mind, with all its shiftings as in the subconscious, in dreams, in the throes of composition, works" (Calas).

In a sense, then, Bosch, like Williams, had read Freud's *Interpretation of Dreams* to good advantage. The left triptych represents the earthly paradise, the only kind, finally, Williams was concerned with. And there Christ, the figure of the Creator, is about to present the virgin, Kora, as Eve, to the bridegroom. In that primal gesture, Bosch seems to suggest, nature has begun to manifest its tensions. Already death has entered the garden; the monstrous, as in the two-legged dog, has infiltrated Bosch's world. Williams's garden of delights in *Asphodel* contains the same kinds of potential tensions, but all are presented tolerantly, all, even the damned, sharing the light of the imagination. Bosch's triptych, I suggest, then, chimes with Williams's *Asphodel*, a poem in three parts and a coda. Both are, basically, confessions; both present a series of discrete images held on the same plane by the artist. Linearity is eschewed for a mode of cubist simultaneity, and both poem and painting contain versions of the garden. Moreover, if one "reads" Bosch not from left to right but as one might read one's image in a mirror, in reverse, then one begins with the artist in hell and moves to a new beginning, with the bridegroom beholding the luminous bride, the sensuous virgin, apprehended on the eighth day as in the primal garden.

In originally conceiving of *Paterson* in four parts, Williams had, as he pointed out, added Pan to the embrace of the Trinity, much as he felt Dante had unwittingly done in supplying a "fourth unrhymed factor, unobserved" to the very structure of the *Commedia*. (This factor appears if we note the creative dissonance developed by the unrhymed ending reappearing in any four lines after the initial four.) The world of *Paterson* 1–4 is very much a world in flux, a world in violent, haphazard process, where objects washing in or crashing against the surfaces of the man/city Paterson are caught up into the pattern of the poem even as they create in turn the pattern itself. So such things as the chance appearance of a nurse who was discovered to have a case of *Salmonella montevideo,* written up into a case history in the *Journal of the American Medical Association* for July 29, 1948, or a letter from a young unknown poet from Paterson named Allen Ginsberg, or a hasty note scribbled by Ezra Pound from St. Elizabeth's Hospital in Washington, letters from Marcia Nardi or Fred Miller or Josephine Herbst or Edward Dahlberg or Alva Turner find their way into the action painting of the poem. The lines too are jagged, hesitant, coiling back on themselves, for the most part purposely flat, only in "isolate flecks" rising to the level of a lyricism that seems without artificiality or undue self-consciousness, a language shaped from the mouths of Polish mothers, but heightened.

The first four books of *Paterson* are, really, in a sense, the creation of the first six days, a world caught up very much in the rapid confusion of its own linear, processive time, where the orphic poet like the carnival figure of Sam Patch must keep his difficult balance or be pulled under by the roar of the language at the brink of the descent into chaos every artist encounters in the genesis of creation. What Williams was looking for instead in a fifth book, after resting from his unfolding creation, was to see the river at the heart of his poem as the ourobouros, the serpent with its tail in its mouth, the eternal river, the river of heaven. This meant, of course, that time itself would have to change, and a new time meant a relatively new way of measuring, meant a more secure, a more relaxed way of saying. That was a question, primarily, of form, and the emphasis on the variable foot, which the critics went after all through the fifties and sixties like hounds after an elusive hare, was in large part a strategy of Williams's own devising. But it was an absolutely necessary strategy for him, because just here the real revolution in poetry would have to occur: here with the river, metaphor for the poetic line itself.

The river of heaven became almost an obsession for Williams in the early fifties. First he had considered viewing *Paterson* 4 under that rubric; then he had begun a long poem called *The River of Heaven*, which became instead *Asphodel*. In June 1950, Allen Ginsberg had written Williams (in a letter that finds itself caught in the grid of *Paterson* 4) that he'd been "walking the streets of Paterson and discovering the bars." "I wonder," he asked, "if you have seen River Street most of all, because that is really at the heart of what is to be known." [10] There were a number of bars along River Street, especially in the black section, which he recommended to Williams in the summer of 1952. "What I want of your son," Williams wrote Louis Ginsberg, "is for him to take me to a bar on River Street. . . . I don't know what the joint is like or whether we'd be welcome there but if it's something to experience and to see I'd like to see it for I want to make it the central locale for a poem which I have in mind—a sort of extension of *Paterson*." [11] From River Street, one of the oldest streets in Paterson, which follows the course of the Passaic, Williams could view through the painted glass of an old tavern turned bar the Passaic River surrounded by a cosmic harmony of sorts: the dance of the satyrs, swinging to jazz, on the eighth day of creation. Things have a way of changing, however, and the river of heaven finds its enactment not in the back room of the Bobaloo, but as it flows through the unicorn tapestries, the unicorn emerging from its waters, having escaped the silent hounds, threaded teeth bared, baying his imminent murder.

"Maybe there'll be a 5th book of Paterson embodying everything I've learned of 'the line' to date," Williams told Robert Lowell in March 1952.[12] And, indeed, much of the new book does incorporate Williams's late development with the line, including the three-ply line of *Asphodel*. But the manuscripts reveal an interesting change in Williams's collage for Book 5, which refocuses the emphasis of the entire book and brings us from the river to the icon. Williams had intended to include a long letter to him from Cid Corman dealing with the whole question of modern prosody and, in fact, even in the galleys, he had included that letter. But in its place Williams inserted at the last minute a letter from Edward Dahlberg that he had received in late September 1957 when he was putting the finishing touches on Book 5.

What Williams saw in Dahlberg's letter was a modern, living, breathing analogue for Brueghel's *The Adoration of the Kings* in the Danish woman surrounded by the police, and the placement of Dahlberg's letter focuses the attention away from the question of the line (which had in any event been attended to by Sappho and Bessie Smith) and onto the modern representation of the central icon of Book 5, the beautiful thing, Kora. It is the icon that includes, really, all of her sisters, from the "young woman / with rounded brow" who listens to the "hunter's horn" and who alone can lure the unicorn-poet, to Williams's own English grandmother (whose presence had marked his initiation into the filthy Passaic forty years before and who rounds off the conclusion of *Paterson*). And it includes as well the virgin in Lorca's *The Love of Don Perlimplin*, Osamu Dazai's saintly sister, "tagged" by her lover in *The Setting Sun*, those Mexican whores turning up their dresses in a short sketch by a young writer named Gilbert Sorrentino who had sent Williams his manuscript for the poet's comments, a young girl Williams remembered who'd gone swimming naked with him and all the boys at Sandy Bottom some sixty years before, and, finally, Sappho singing and Bessie Smith singing and the 3,000 years between them now as nothing.

In his 1928 novel, *A Voyage to Pagany,* Williams removed what is in fact the central chapter because the editors found the book too long to print in its original form. That chapter, "The Venus," describes a scene between a young fräulein and Dev (for Evans Dionysius) Evans. There the American doctor and the German girl sit in a quiet spot south of Rome which still bears evidences of having been in some remote past a pagan grotto, while Evans tries to explain the elusive beauty he is searching for in America. It is clear from Williams's description that Evans is in fact speaking to a modern-day incarnation of Venus herself, specifically Botticelli's sensuous virgin. But this Venus is about to enter a convent because she has not found the figure of the artist who can fully liberate her, although Evans's new-world paganism attracts her. The steady glance of this German Venus continued to haunt Williams, and he found that glance again in the figure of another Venus in a garb very like a nun's: Brueghel's Virgin. A buxom German peasant girl, she holds her baby boy upon her knee, as later, in the *Pictures from Brueghel,* she will pose in icon fashion, detached from the quotidian bustle everywhere apparent, as she does too in Giotto's "Adoration of the Magi," which Williams celebrated in "The Gift," a poem also from the mid-fifties.

It is she, Kora, around whom all of *Paterson* 5 radiates, and, in the tapestries, she appears again with the tamed unicorn amidst a world of flowers where Williams had always felt at home. In a sense, Marianne Moore's real toad in an imaginary garden finds its correlative here in Williams's icons of the virgin/whore situated among "the sweetsmelling primrose / growing close to the ground," "the slippered flowers / crimson and white, / balanced to hang on slender bracts," forget-me-nots, dandelions, love-in-a-mist, daffodils and gentians and daisies.[13] We have seen this woman before: she is the woman in *Asphodel* caring for her flowers in winter, in hell's despite, another German Venus, Floss Williams. Which, then, is the real, Williams's wife seen or his icon of the wife? And his wife seen now, at this moment, or his wife remembered, an icon released by the imagination from time, ageless, this woman containing all women? Rather, it is the anima, the idea of woman, with its tenuous balance between the woman glimpsed and the woman realized, the hag language whored and whored again but transformed by the poet-lover's desire into something virginal and new, the woman and the language translated to the eighth day of creation, assuming a new condition of dynamic permanence. In this garden, the broken, jagged random things of William's world are caught up in a pattern, a dance where the poem, like the tapestries themselves, can be possessed a thousand thousand times and yet remain as fresh and as virginal as on the day they were conceived, like Venus, from the head of their creator.

The woman is of course all-pervasive in Williams's poems. What is different now is the more explicit use of Kora as the symbol, in fact, the central icon in the late poems. Two examples from the earlier sections of *Paterson* will serve to illustrate differences in the handling of his women. In *Paterson* 1, Williams sketches the delineaments of the giants, the female of the place, Garrett Mountain, resting against the male of it, the city of Paterson. "Paterson," the genesis of Book 1 begins, "lies in the valley under the Passaic Falls / its spent waters forming the outline of his back," Over "against him, stretches the low mountain. / The Park's her head, carved, above the Falls, by the quiet river...." [14] Williams, as Michael Weaver has noted, may even have had Pavel Tchelitchew's *Fata Morgana,* his painting of two reclining earth figures, a man, a woman, in mind. [15] This pattern of the unroused lovers is evoked obliquely later in Book 2 when Paterson/Williams, walking on Garrett Mountain, notices a young couple lying partly concealed by some bushes, intent on each other while Sunday strollers float past them on all sides: [16]

> But the white girl, her head
> upon an arm, a butt between her fingers
> lies under the bush
>
> Semi-naked, facing her, a sunshade
> over his eyes,
> he talks with her
>
> the jalopy half hid
> behind them in the trees—
> I bought a new bathing suit, just

>   pants and a brassier:
>   the breasts and
>   the pudenda covered—beneath
>
>   the sun in frank vulgarity.
>   Minds beaten thin
>   by waste—among
>
>   the working classes SOME sort
>   of breakdown
>   has occurred. . . .

Mural has become cameo, but the image of reclining lovers remains, substantially unchanged. In terms of strategy, however, Williams has purposely not pressed his parallel home. For the attention must be riveted first on the actuality of the encounter: it is midmorning in late May, probably 1942 or '43. Or for that matter '33 or '73. These are probably young second-generation Polish- or Italian-Americans, surprised by eros on this, their day off, intent on seizing the day before returning to the silk mills or locomotive works in the industrial town sprawled out below them. But for this moment, the pattern of young lovers persists as archetype, fleshed out in these particular working-class people who impinge upon Williams's consciousness.

There is another interesting image that Williams found *too* explicit to finally place in Book 4, but the various manuscripts for that book mention it several times. In the modern Idyll that begins *Paterson* 4, Williams gives us a strange love triangle that spells frustration from whatever angle of incidence we follow: the love triangle between Corydon, an aging, lame lesbian and would-be poetess, well educated in the classics and in French literature, whose penthouse apartment in the East 50s overlooks the river; her maseusse, a young (twenty-one-year-old) nurse from Ramapo (perhaps a Jackson White) trained at Passaic General Hospital in Paterson (where Williams served for some forty years), and Dr. Paterson himself, that married man and aging lover. Paterson is driven wild by the young virgin's beauty; indeed he cannot even think unless she first removes her clothes. For Williams she is, explicitly, the very incarnation of Goya's famous Maja Desnuda. And if for Dr. Paterson she remains the elusive new-world beauty who cannot give herself to the new-world poet but follows instead the old-world hag (Europe) into a world cold and alien, she is first and foremost a real woman, someone from Williams's own past, an incarnation of the unattainable reclining nude, the odalisque, Olympia, more fleshly cousin of Stevens's Mrs. Pappadoppoulos. Goya's nude seems to have informed Williams's realization of Phyllis in the unpublished sheets of the Idyll, but Williams carefully removed the scaffolding in the published version.

Paterson 5 eschews such oblique stratagems, however. Williams has made that consummate metapoem far more explicit for several reasons, one comes to realize: first, because no critic, not even the most friendly and the most astute, had even begun to adequately sound the real complexities of the poem by 1956, ten years after *Paterson* 1 appeared. (Indeed an adequate critical vocabulary for the kind of thing Williams was doing does not seem to have been available then to the critics and reviewers.) Second, Williams felt the need to praise his own tradition, his own pantheon of artists, to pay tribute to those others who had also helped to celebrate the light. Williams would show that, on the eighth day of creation, all of the disparate, jagged edges of *Paterson* could, as he had said in his introduction, multiply themselves and so reduce themselves to unity, to a dance around the core of the imagination.

In the dreamlike worlds of *Asphodel* and *Paterson* 5, filled as they are with the radiant light of the imagination, all disparate images revolve around the virgin/whore, including the "male of it," the phallic artist who is both earthly Pan and unicorn, that divine lover, who dances contrapuntally against his beloved. Williams, perhaps sensing that the old, crude fight against the clerks of the great tradition had been sufficiently won by that point to let him relax, chooses now to celebrate a whole pantheon of old masters in *Asphodel* and again in *Paterson* 5.

And if the presences of Bosch, Brueghel, and the master of the unicorn tapestries are the central presences in the three late long poems, still, there is room to celebrate a host of other artists who dance in attendance on the woman as well. We can do little more at this point than enumerate some of them: Toulouse-Lautrec, who painted the very human turn-of-the-century Parisian prostitutes among whom he lived; Gauguin, celebrating his sorrowful reclining nude in *The Loss of Virginity*; the anonymous Inca sculptor who created the statuette of a woman at her bath some 3,000 years ago; the 6,000-year-old cave paintings of bison; Cézanne for his patches of blue and blue; Daumier, Picasso, Juan

Gris, Gertrude Stein, Kung; Albrecht Dürer for his *Melancholy*; Audubon, Ben Shahn, and Marsden Hartley.

We come, then, finally, to our third point: the figure of the artist himself, the male principle incessantly attracted to and moving toward the female of it: the anima. And here we are confronted with the comic and the grotesque: the figure of Sam Patch or the hydrocephalic dwarf or the Mexican peasant in Eisenstein's film, and, in the late poems, the portrait of the old man, all of these finding their resolution and comic apotheosis in the captive, one-horned unicorn, a figure, like the figure of the satyr erectus, of the artist's phallic imagination. There is, too, Brueghel's self-portrait, as Williams thought, re-created in the first of Williams's own pictures taken from Brueghel, and imitated in a cubist mode. That old man, with his "Bulbous nose" (one thinks of Williams's own early poem celebrating his own nose) and his "eyes red-rimmed / from over-use" with "no time for any / thing but his painting." [17] And, again, there is the head of the old smiling Dane, the Tollund Man, seen in a photograph; it is a portrait of a man, a sacrificial victim, strangled as part of some forgotten spring rite, the features marvelously preserved intact by the tanning effects of the bogs from which he had been exhumed after twenty centuries of strong silence, that 2,000-year-old face frozen into something like a half-smile. That face chimes with Brueghel's face as both chime with the strange, half-smiling face of Bosch peering out from his strange world where order has given way to an apocalyptic nightmare.

But the male remains the lesser figure of the two in Williams. As he told Theodore Roethke in early 1950, "All my life I have hated my face and wanted to smash it." [18] (It was one reason, he told Roethke in the same letter, that he could not even bear to speak of Vivienne Koch's critical study of him which had just appeared. What mattered was not the man himself, but the man's work.) He was willing, however, to let the icon of the unicorn, the one-horned beast, stand. And he let it stand because it represented the necessary male complement to the female of it, the object desired, the beautiful thing: the language in its impossible edenic state. No one but the virgin can tame the unicorn, the legend goes, and Williams had, like other artists before and after him, given himself up to that elusive beauty. Like Hart Crane in another mode, he had given himself up to be murdered, to offer himself not, as Pound had, to the pale presences of the past, virtually all of them male voices, but for the virgin, Kora. And yet, there was a way out, a hole at the bottom of the pit for the artist, in the timeless world of the imagination, the enchanted circle, the jeweled collar encircling the unicorn's neck. In the final tapestry of the series, the unicorn kneels within the fence paling, (pomegranates bespeak fertility and the presence of Kora), at ease among a panoply of flowers forever on the eighth day of creation, a world evoked for Williams out of the imagination, the source from which even the author of Revelation must have created his own eighth day in his time.

What was of central importance to Williams was not the artist, then, whose force is primarily directional and whose presence is in any event everywhere, but the icon that motivates the artist and urges him on: the icon of Kora, the image of the beloved. And this figure appears, of course, everywhere in Williams's writing, assuming many faces, yet always, finally one. Asked in his mid-seventies what it was that kept him writing, Williams answered that it was all for the young woman whose eyes he had caught watching him out there in some audience as he read his poems. It was all for lovely Sappho, then, and all for Venus. Consider for a moment the example of other modern poets: Yeats's Helen of Troy, Stevens's fat, voluptuous mundo, or Pound, finding a shadow of his ideal beauty in the *yeux glauques,* the lacquered eyes of Jenny in those Burne-Jones cartoons, or the eyes of the goddess momentarily penetrating through the very walls of Pound's tent at the U. S. Army Detention Center at Pisa in that summer of '45. With them Williams places his own icon of the woman rising out of the hell of his own repressions. In the world of art, in that garden where spring is a condition of permanence, where the earthly garden chimes perfectly with the garden of paradise, the eye of the unicorn is still and still intent upon the woman.

1975

The Hard Core of Beauty

Williams's *Paterson* is so large and so complex an achievement that we have tended to overlook the body of shorter poems the man wrote during the years he was in the midst of that hurricane of activity. When we think of the highlights of Williams's career as a poet, we think naturally of groupings, of certain mountain configurations rising out of the surrounding foothills and plains. We will probably think first of terrain like *Spring and All* and *In the American Grain* written in the 1920s, then of *Paterson,* whose most virulent phase of activity occurred in the 1940s, and then—at the last—of those experiments from the 1950s gathered into Williams's last book of poems: *Pictures from Brueghel.*

But such an overview leaves out of the varied terrain whole river valleys, moraines, islands, and peninsulas which make up the continent that is Williams's achievement. During the years when he was working through the formal implications of the modern epic, Williams was also rethinking the transformative possibilities of the lyric poem itself.

Perhaps this was inevitable, since Paterson itself could not go forward until Williams could find a new kind of lyric poem upon which to build his epic. One sees these moments of lyrical crisis in Williams's theory and practice in 1938, when he approached the problem with his "Parody for the Poem Paterson," the title itself revealing the anxiety Williams was feeling as he seriously approached the borders of his epic for the first time. And one sees the same thing happening again in 1942 and in 1944: the need to find a new lyric form supple enough, fluid enough, to carry the weight of the territory he was exploring for the first time. It is the major reason, I suspect, that he watched Wallace Stevens so carefully during these years. What he was looking for was authority, authority and its concomitant sense of ease with the things of this world, and for that who better than the Stevens of *Parts of a World?*

Williams has so many different kinds of faces that he continues to appeal to a wide range of poets, many of whom we think of as belonging to different traditions, different bands of the poetic spectrum. Louis Zukofsky, Charles Olson, Allen Ginsberg, Robert Creeley, Denise Levertov, Gary Snyder, Robert Lowell, Theodore Roethke, A. R. Ammons, Diane Wakoski, Marvin Bell, Charles Tomlinson, and John Montague, for example, have all acknowledged their various debts to Williams. And yet each of these poets has a voice distinctively his or her own. How then can we rightly speak of Williams as progenitor? Part of the answer, of course, lies in Williams's enormous versatility and in his ability to always be beginning again, something Wallace Stevens had warned Williams against doing as early as 1916. But this continual revolution of the word is one of Williams's great strengths, a revolution that continued until the night itself intervened.

So it is with the period that saw the publication of the first four books of *Paterson*: the five years between 1946 and 1951. From the time he published *Paterson* 1 until the time he suffered his first stroke in the spring of '51, Williams seems to have composed sui generis a new poem —a new kind of poem—each time he wrote. And yet, this extraordinary, extra-*Paterson* activity has yet to be adequately mapped by anyone to my knowledge. In fact, we do not have an accurate enough chronology of the order in which or the order by which Williams composed these poems. Ironically, it is these same poems, gathered along with *The Wedge* into Williams's *Collected Later Poems,* that have been used and reused by poets too impatient to wait for the critical cartographers to tell them what they have known was there all along. Years ago they learned the way to the secret source and have been drinking from its waters for a long time now.

My instinct, for example, would be to point to the poems of Frank O'Hara, Robert Creeley, and Marvin Bell which use a recognizably colloquial voice moving easily and even randomly from idea to idea, while the poems themselves actually establish a surprisingly complex grid of oblique analogues and equations, all pulling eventually in the same direction. These are poems in which we the reader must make constant adjustments to see how the vivid, talky fragments do cohere. Such a poem seems to look at you and say, well, I'm not after the big philosophical formulations, I'm not going to talk with that deep crescendo voice that seems to incorporate and implicate the great tradition and the past. No, I'm just going to talk about a few things on my mind right now.

If we believe that is all the poet is doing, however, we are in danger of being taken in by the mask of easy intimacy, for the poet's designs on us are every bit as serious as the voice of a Milton, a Shelley, a Stevens. When we think of a poetry of ideas written by a twentieth-century American, is it not Stevens who first comes to mind? But in Williams one senses an engagement with the specifics of things, the flux of names informing the surface of the text, so that the intersections of loci established by this naming grid act as so many points of energy to be accounted for in understanding the text. To read a poem by Williams demands a new measure of the inclusive capabilities of the poem. With Williams we really are on new ground and, unless we realize this, we are in danger of being like those early explorers in the new world who did not understand where they were and so passed on incommunicado.

In constructing my biography of Williams, I had necessarily to sift through thousands of documents—letters, essays, poems and drafts of poems, notes, lecture notes, notes written or typed to himself so that he could see what it was he was thinking about a problem. What I was in search of was evidence of what Williams himself was after as he traced the elusive core of beauty as that core revealed itself in his life. It is true, as Hugh Kenner has said, that one often gets the sense in Williams of a man gesticulating with his hands to something out there that keeps eluding him: the mystery of a poetry so good, so exacting, that it had yet to be written. But that is only part of the story, for most serious poets must understand that feeling: not satisfaction for what has been achieved, but a desire for what remains absent and elusive and teasingly just beyond one's reach. If Williams desired the Perfect Woman, if he desired to realize in the common, overused, misused language of one's time and place the dream of the perfect poem, he still managed to make a body of poetry, and it is that body— the habeas corpus of that achievement as Williams might have said —that must finally be judged.

The work goes on. The early period has received a great deal of attention in the past decade. And so have the poems of the late period —from "The Desert Music" up through the poems in *Pictures from Brueghel*. But this is not so of the poems that Williams wrote just prior to his late flowering, poems every bit as good as those that followed. They are, in fact—in spite of much critical opinion to the contrary—more intelligent and ultimately more satisfying poems as well. And this, I think, is the secret the poets have known.

Shortly after World War II ended, Williams began composing again with the speed and voluminosity of a man for whom time is running out. He was approaching seventy and still believed his best work lay before him. We can feel something of the urgency and despair he was feeling in the second, third, and fourth books of *Paterson*. The same is true of the tenor of his essays, lectures, and letters written during this period as Williams tried to determine what the poem in its post-Modernist phase would look and feel like. He talked about it— some would argue he talked too much about it—but, more important, he wrote new poems as well, not only for the vast mural of *Paterson* in lyrics like "I remember / a *Geographic* picture," or the extraordinary interweaving of voices that begins the second part of *Paterson* 1 and goes on, uninterrupted by prose, for several pages, or the "Without invention" section of *Paterson* 2, but in dozens of sketches and cartoons, some of them meant most likely for *Paterson* itself, but which Williams decided to detach and to publish separately as poems, where the themes that were preoccupying him in his own version of "The Prelude" might assume their own resonances.

And many of these "exercises"—if you will—rivulets from the activity of the Great Falls washing over Williams—are extraordinary poems, written in a number of styles that show some of the directions in which post-Modern American poetry has moved. And this they have done so skillfully and so transparently that many critics are still not aware of the new directions Williams's poetry took as he continued to experiment in poetry like Picasso with his painting, breaking new ground and beginning again with the building materials of the poem in his sixties.

Consider, for example, three poems from this period, each dealing with the erotics of the imagination worked against a profoundly felt absence. Each of these poems has at its core the figure of the Perfect Woman (whether evoked sympathetically or with fear and loathing) which is itself a symbol of that desire that moves the speaker to the use of words. And yet the tone, the rhetorical strategies, the formal components of the poems themselves, are different in each poem and branch off into different directions in the history of post-Modernist American poetics. All three poems were written between 1946 and 1948. They are: "The Birth of Venus," "The Hard Core of Beauty," and "All That Is Perfect in Woman." And all of them can be found in *The Collected Later Poems.*

During the late 1940s Williams continued his experimentation with a wide variety of line lengths and stanza forms, ransacking the anthologies and the current little magazines to discover from his predecessors and his contemporaries forms—syntactical forms, stanzaic forms, metrical forms—he could use in the creation of a new poetry. A quick survey of *The Collected Later Poems* itself reveals at least the following: the three-line, four-line, five-line, and variable-line stanza, all cutting across the poem's syntactical patterns and thus creating a musical counterpoint. There are verse paragraphs shaped according to the arc of the thought expressed, sonnets or antisonnets of eleven, twelve, and fourteen short lines, lines of seven and even more accentual stresses, very short lines, alternating long and short lines, lines that are as four-square and compact as if they were in pressurized containers, and lines that seem to drift free of any formal anchoring. There are lines with medial and even initial caesurae (the latter introduced by a colon), and there are refrain lines. In short, there is a sense of the new here everywhere, the sense of a beginning over and over again. Only the iambic pentameter, it would seem, has been avoided.

In looking through these poems, then, one comes away with the sense of a great energy expended, as if Picasso were to pick up and discard a dozen styles as the imagination moved him. And, as with Picasso, we will not discover in these texts any immediate or easy order. Let us examine the three poems earlier mentioned in the order of their complexity—their metonymical indirection—and then make some observations on that order as discovered in the poems themselves.

1   The first poem is "The Birth of Venus," published in the Rome-based magazine *Botteghe Oscure* in 1948. On the surface of it, this is another of Williams's spring poems celebrating once more the return of the goddess into the poet's world. The goddess—or the Godhead, as he calls her in another poem—is nothing less than the feminine principle of regenerativity (to phrase it more abstractly than Williams himself might have liked) figured doubly as Persephone and Venus. Does not the title itself point to Botticelli's painting of that name in the Uffizi, before which Williams had twice stood: first in March 1910 when he toured Italy with his brother Ed in his twenty-seventh year, and then with his wife fourteen years later during another March, this one in 1924. It is a world of springtime Williams evokes in this poem, a world stirred into realization by the memory itself. The rhythms of the poem underscore this meditation. What Williams uses here is a five-line stanza with an uncharacteristically long line that can expand or contract to anywhere between four and seven stress units of what appears to be quantitative measure. And if it were not for the forward momentum of the poem's meaning, the need to get said what must be said, one would read the rhythm as slow, stately, meditative, the phrasal units creating at least two medial caesurae within each line. The effect of this is that the poem's tensions work against themselves, so that in one sense the poem reads like a hurried and pained reflection on a world quickly going to hell and in another sense reads as a rehearsal for the long poem Williams would begin composing in the step-down triadic foot (that long, maxi-Alexandrine line with its own two pronounced caesurae) four years later in "Of Asphodel, that Greeny Flower." In both poems it is the Keats of the odes who informs if not the pace then certainly the strategy of the meditation on absence and desire.

Consider how Williams begins "The Birth of Venus" by making vivid to the mind's eye what the second stanza will take away. It is an evocation, this opening, of that February springtime Williams and Floss had experienced together a quarter of a century before, the play of waves on the Mediterranean at Villefranche in southern France, whether in sunny, calm weather or in storm. We know from the diary Williams kept at the time how intensely he watched the waves for

some sign. And the speaker of this poem knows that today, even as he
thinks about them, the waves again

> are rippling, crystal clear, upon the pebbles
> at Villefranche whence from the wall, at the Parade Grounds
> of the Chasseurs Alpins, we stood and watched them; or
>   passing along
> the cliff on the ledge between the sea and the old fortress, heard
> the long swell stir without cost among the rock's teeth. But we
>
> are not there!

Here the seaswell phrasing and the connective tissue of the syntax
itself draw us forward from line to line in growing expectation until,
in near despair, the speaker (and we) are pulled up short. Now, at
sixty-five, Williams has seen the world redefined by the cataclysm of
World War II. In a letter written a few years earlier, he had confessed
that he had no desire to return to France since the France he had known
in the mid-twenties had been altered by the war beyond what he was
ready to accept. But at least the changing and unchanging waves would
have remained the same. How beautiful to stand before those waves
and to listen.

But we are not there, he cries, not there this April to see the waves
lapping the shore and not there—even more important—in our imaginations, even though, he has reminded us, it would be money in our
pockets to value such things. But this is the world of the new cold war
that has swept over our world so soon after the end of the war itself.
And yet, Williams risks, is not the Black Sea this April also "blue with
waves / under a smiling sky"? As (again) with the North American
coast—the Labrador North Shore, for example, up which he and Floss
had sailed in the summer of '31, when Williams, drawn to those icy
waters, had been—he tells us—the only one on their cruise ship to dive
into them, slicing his stomach in the process on the Venusian shells
lining the water's shallow bottom.

Spring is here, Williams cries, here in Russia and France and in
America, a spring indifferent to national boundaries and doing all it
can to thaw the cold war, just as, when the world has turned to bask
its other side half a year hence, spring will begin again to "enliven the
African coast southward." And again, Williams repeats with growing
alarm, "we not there, not there!" And we understand now with that

refrainlike lament that that is the plight exactly of the dead: not to be there.

"Why not believe that we shall be young again?" Williams asks with a rhetorical directness and urgency characteristic of this new, late strain in his work. It is a rhetoric that goes beyond, simply, the earlier phrasing of "so much depends upon" or of the mandarin wryness of "rather notice, *mon cher.*" We will see this newer strain of address in "Asphodel" and in "For Daphne and Virginia," something brought on by the sense of time running out and the need to say what has to be said, as directly as he can. Is it not what we desire, Williams asks, this persistence of springtime in our lives, the possibility of holding onto our youth, the Sapphic bracelet spotted under the waves in the mind's eye, as new now as when it was first made those thousands of years ago? It is an artifact as replete with nostalgias as any Grecian urn.

And yet it is death we keep hearing about, the deaths of soldiers on beaches like Villefranche with its once-sleepy French garrison, only now those beaches have names more familiar to Williams's first audience: Omaha Beach and Juno, Iwo Jima, Okinawa. For is it not death that colors the "small waves crimson"? It is an image that seems to have obsessed Williams's imagination in these late years: the bodies of young men lying face down or half buried in the sands or bobbing face up at sea, and it may owe something—this preoccupation—to Williams's daily worry about his two Navy sons: Bill serving with the Navy Seabees in the far Pacific, Paul on destroyer duty in the North Atlantic. We will see this drift out into the crimson sea again and again in the last pages of *Paterson 4,* even as another war was beginning in Asia, this one in a place called Korea. Do we not believe that war is inevitable, Williams suggests, and so consume our daily drafts of poison from the news Mithradates-like, preparing for the final catastrophe?

But about life and eros and springtime, about the gentleness of eternal spring we are less certain. The shells that ripped Sebastopol, for example, a fortress-city "fired by the Germans first, then by the Russians," remain indifferent to our agony. Not, of course, Williams is quick to add, that sunlight playing on the waves is any less indifferent to our cries. The difference, therefore, is in us. But at least we need not choose to fix our imaginations on death. It is a crucial observation for the poet approaching his own end. We do not have to dwell on the human torment that informs so much of the *Iliad,* for example, or on the various battlefields of Amiens, or on the reported atrocities during the Japanese invasion of Manchuria in the 1930s, even now with China, like Russia, becoming the new enemy to be feared.

Nor do we need to sacrifice our lives in skirmishes with death (our own or—vicariously—the deaths of others) to appease the gods within us in order to *feel,* Williams insists. Life is gentler than that, ready to share its pleasures, if only we would let it. Thus Williams, in his own version of the Paterian aesthetic. Let us rather experience the exquisite pain of "almond blossoms" or "an agony of mimosa trees in bloom," he offers instead, even the "sense of viands," as his friend, dear Fordie—Ford Madox Ford—dead now and buried in Provence, had time and again reminded him. The poem is constructed on this double-edged principle of the deathlike things Williams would reject and the absence of the beautiful thing he would make present to the imagination. "I see a schoolboy when I think of him," Ille says to Hic in Yeats's *Ego Dominus Tuus,* "With face and nose pressed to a sweet-shop window. . . . Shut out from all the luxury of the world [to make] luxuriant song." Keats. There is much of Keats in this most American of poets and surely loss is a large part of their likeness to each other.

The argument goes that art and beauty must have their blood sacrifice, that the flowering of a culture is based on the bonemeal of thousands of victims who served to make that flower bloom. Williams knew the arguments and he even knew their validity. And yet . . . would there be no Pinturicchio, no Picasso, no Botticelli, he asks, "no frescos on the jungle temples of Burma," no cathedrals even, no Columbus starting out from Huelva to discover the beautiful thing over the wide waters, but for the exorbitant costs of death and war? Perhaps, Williams realizes, perhaps he is a fool. Perhaps the world of flowers is itself filled with its own internecine strife, as one flower crowds out or succumbs finally to another, so that the quietude such a pastoral world evokes is merely a lie. Perhaps. But must we, Williams asks again, imitating the very polarities of the poem itself, must we fill our imaginations with images of death before we can feel we have earned the right to enjoy the world? Must we constantly undergo a physical or imaginative death in order "to be born again"? That last phrase resonates, of course, with traditional religious significance. For what the poem asks during this particular April is if indeed we need Good Friday before we can again experience a new eastering.

The tension bonding this poem together suggests that Williams's answer to this question is yes, even though the answer Williams provides in terms of the poem's rhetoric is otherwise. For what the poem's structure tells us is that spring is made sweeter because we know that soon enough death will take it and eventually the perceiving I itself with it. What is there to do, then? Forget restrictions, forget taboos, sanctions, punishments, and let Eros—even in its culturally forbidden manifestations—flourish where and as they will. "Let the homosexuals seduce whom they will," Williams nearly shouts in his poem. Let them seduce whomever they will "under what bushes along the coast of the Middle Sea / / rather than have us insist on murder." For are not all governments, he adds, by the fact that they *are* governments, an acknowledgment that the human dream of eternal spring has been defeated? Why do we check our impulses with something far worse, Williams aks in his own version of Pater's aesthetic? Why do we allow a pornography of violence and death to flourish, shells exploding everywhere, while we shun the lovely shell of the body?

What then is there to do? One can *wish,* which is, the poem's logic tells us, already to fail, because by wishing we admit that we do not yet possess what we so desire. In other words, it is truly an absence only that we possess. And yet and yet, Williams ends his poem, in a sentence whose characteristic ambiguities of syntax keep cutting back and forth:

> I wish we might
> learn of an April of small waves—deadly as all slaughter, that we
> shall die soon enough, to dream of April, not knowing why we
>   have been
> struck down, heedless of what greater violence.

That is, if I read these lines correctly, with an eye on that dash, that infinitive, and those particles, what Williams asks here is why we cannot learn that death is there for all of us regardless of what we would wish otherwise. Moreover, the very idea of resolution in death, the way we comfort ourselves, is by way of an image of an unending dream of springtime itself. And here the infinitive is crucial—*to dream of April*—for the very thing we wish for in death is what death itself may deprive us of forever. Nor is death the answer, for we shall never understand why the greater violence of our own deaths (more final than any imagining of it) had to be at all. In short, instead of rehearsing our own deaths in the rumors of war and violence we are daily fed, Williams suggests, why not read in the sea the eternal return of spring? For if death is as real as eros, it follows that, conversely, eros must be as real as death, and sweeter to dwell on.

If "The Birth of Venus" looks half forward to the later, meditative cadences of a poem like "Asphodel," the Williams so many like because he seems at least accessible, as if—after a lifetime of fighting—the old revolutionary had stopped long enough to sip a glass of orangeade and to dwell on his world, the other half of the equation is to remember just how urgent-sounding this poem really is. Ironically, the long lines themselves do not slow the poem down, for there is a forward momentum to them that works against the meditative form. It would take two strokes to slow Williams's poetic metabolism down.

2   There is about the second poem, "The Hard Core of Beauty," an even greater insistency created by the sexual tension swarming just beneath the poem's surface. This is a poem of intense desire where the poet searches for something in the world around him that he believes can sustain him. In this the concerns here are the same as those Williams was preoccupied with in *Paterson* 2 and 3, poems contemporary with "The Hard Core of Beauty." The characteristic pattern of search and discovery and the intensity of the search in personal costs have not radically altered for Williams. How could they? Williams's own face is still straight ahead, searching for something even as he moves through his world, having repeatedly paid the price in his daily ministrations as a physician and as a poet to have it. The speaker is like that white rabbit Alice saw, busy looking for something as he moves through the space of this poem, and we will have to walk very fast (or very slow) in this world of appearances if we are to keep up with him.

Williams does not tell us where, exactly, he is in this poem, but the place should be familiar to anyone who knows his world. It is the world many of us have come to call, simply, Paterson, thus identifying the man and the city. But it is, more specifically, the old meadows to the east of Rutherford, near the place where the sports complex sits today. In letters he wrote his son Bill during the latter's tour of duty in the Pacific, Williams spoke about many things, one of them being the new construction going up over the meadowlands where he and a younger Bill had gone fishing and crabbing years before. Now a new bridge has gone up and the old highway has become a dead-end, something to be abandoned.

"Abandoned." The word will gather to it a force similar to that of Keats's "forlorn" by the time it is repeated near the end of the poem. First, we see, it is only the dead-end highway that has been abandoned to give way to the new. But by poem's end it is nothing short of "the whole great world" that we have abandoned . . . and for what? What is Williams really doing in this poem among these houses. What he frequently did in his ministrations: looking about him to stare in wonder at the life around him. But in this poem there is a further clue in the strange simile Williams throws out mid-way through the poem, where one of the jerrybuilt houses is described as possessing "a second floor / miniscule / portico" glimpsed in the distance as looking like the "peaked . . . palate / of a child." Williams is probably out again making house-calls this spring morning, probably looking in on some child, with a sore throat perhaps. These are working-class dwellings, the kind one sees (for example) in the poorer Italian neighborhoods like Greenpoint in Brooklyn or East Rutherford and Lyndhurst and Garfield nearer Williams's own home. We hardly look at such dwellings twice, even from the air as we circle Newark or Kennedy airports. Beauty, we say, if it exists, must surely have found a more fitting habitat than this.

But Williams believed—because he needed to believe—otherwise. Kenneth Rexroth once told Williams that he—Williams—was the most Franciscan poet he knew, in his pastoral concerns, his generosity towards the poor, whatever. But I now think that Williams's need was too great, too unsettled, ever to be Franciscan. The green glass of the broken bottle shines so brightly in Williams's poem just because it is set on a pile of waste cinders in the back of that contagious hospital in Passaic. In short, it is the context of absence that makes the beauty we do find so much more valuable. After all, Williams argues here, it is not the presence of beauty that is the "most marvellous," but rather the "classic attempt / at beauty."

Having witnessed at first hand the truly marvelous Greek ruins at Paestum, the Roman ruins of Herculaneum and Pompeii in the shadow of Vesuvius, and the ghostly shadows of that early center of the world, the Foro Romano, and having stood before the treasures of Florence and Venice, London, Amsterdam, Paris, and Vienna as well as of New York itself, the white city shimmering like a flower to the east, Williams knows as well as Pound and Eliot that those working-class homes with their asbestos shingle siding and peeling paint, their potted geraniums and plum trees "(one dead) surrounded / at the base by worn-out auto-tire casings," are surely no equal to the classic splendor of Europe. Pound might dismiss Hoboken as seen from the lower west side of New York City as the entrance to hell, as Williams himself once did in *Paterson* 4, citing no less an authority than Dante when he warned those crossing under the tunnel at 34th Street to abandon all hope. And even fastidious, correct Henry James had shuddered at the chuffing industrial troglodyte that was New York as he sailed safely to the south of it in 1906. But Williams is after something deeper here, something truer and more profound than satire will allow. Not what is there, then, but what has been attempted in spite of the odds against it. Praise then for "the classic attempt at beauty," even here in Bergen and Passaic counties, praise for the instinct in the poorest of us for grace and beauty and symmetry, signs of praise that will give glory to the Godhead.

The Godhead. Hardly is the word out. . . . An ambiguous term at best in the poet who had written, fifteen years earlier, of "The Cod Head," with its piscean, evolutionary, downward-spiraling, and sexual overtones. Who is this "Godhead," then, that we wittingly or unwittingly pay homage to? It is the feminine principle itself, the she who "poked" —that *onoma kurion,* that precise American epithet—who *poked* "her twin shoulders, supporting / the draggled blondness / of her tresses, from beneath / the patient waves." It is Venus rising from the mottled waves again like the Botticellian woman in the Uffizi at Florence. It is, in short—to return to the title of the poem—a mind's eye vision of the beautiful thing herself, the hard core of beauty: Venus, Persephone too, returned from the underworld on this Sunday afternoon in spring in the late forties . . . as always.

What is it, then, this desire of the imagination to possess the core of absence and make it present, the thing itself made more desirable by its very absence and flowering now in the imagination? What, indeed, does it mean to possess the woman in the sexual act, the self filling the hollow core (as though any man could posess the core, Kore herself!) In our very frenzy to possess the world, have we not instead abandoned her, finally, for "nothing at all," for a dream deferred again and again instead of snatching at and possessing what we can? And yet that "lost world" (lost because there is so little left of Greece and Rome, but lost too in the sense of some mythic Eden lost, the place that never was, except, perhaps, in the amniotic waters of our first world), that "lost world of symmetry / and grace" is *still* there, still that ideal we desire to possess. The evidence is there, Williams tells us, if only we will look. It is there in the way, for example, the occupant of this house has "piled" the bags of charcoal "deftly" under the "shed at the rear." It is a sign of order, of that need in all of us for "symmetry / and grace" and— beyond that—there is the ditch behind the shed itself that turns out to be a dead-end (which juxtapositioning of ditch and dead-end might suggest to most of us a meditation on thanatos), but rather "a passageway through the mud" leading to eros, "to pleasure, / pleasure; pleasure by boat / a byway of a Sunday / to the smooth river." In spite of the obstacles that we or others put up against pleasure, something there is in us that *will* find a way to the river and, of course, to the woman waiting there.

Two poems, one by Robert Frost, one by Ezra Pound, come to mind here and will prove instructive as comparisons. We don't usually think of Frost and Williams in the same breath, but in fact the two men were very much aware of each other's work even if, as it seems to have been with Frost, by way of dismissal, when he lumped Williams in with the New York crowd back in 1932 during a talk at—of all places—Williams College. Williams was in the audience to hear that remark, though Frost wrung his hands by way of apology next morning at the Williams Inn. At Frost's sixty-fourth birthday party (really his sixty-fifth) held in Montclair, New Jersey, in March 1939, Williams and Frost agreed to exchange books, a bargain Williams kept but Frost did not. And in 1948, the year Williams wrote "The Hard Core of Beauty," he reviewed Frost's "A Masque of Mercy" for *Poetry*—unfavorably.

The poem of Frost's Williams seems to be echoing in his own poem is the often-anthologized "The Wood Pile." Out walking in a frozen swamp, Frost's speaker discovers a cord of split wood left there, apparently, to rot. "I thought," the speaker says, "that only / Someone who lived in turning to fresh tasks / Could so forget his handiwork on which / He spent himself" and so "leave it there far from a useful fireplace / To warm the frozen swamp as best it could / With the slow smokeless burning of decay." In other words, Frost's speaker surmises, here is a sign of pleasure—a readymade, as it were—discovered in this New England swamp, a sign that someone has been doing good work for the sake of the work itself. Of course Frost is up to his old tricks, having fun here at his speaker's expense. For if the speaker had earlier in the poem laughed at the small bird that (he imagines) acts as if the poet were following it, we can smile now at the mirror image of the speaker for constructing the motivation for a "someone" completely absent from the poem itself. How do we know, after all, why someone left that wood in the middle of this swamp, like some jar in Tennessee? We don't. The wood has been left there—a sign of order—and that is all we know. Whoever chopped that wood may have in the meantime moved away, may have met with an accident, may have ceased to live, or may still come back for that cord. That is, if that someone has a life distinct from the fiction of the poem, which is doubtful. So the poem moves back self-reflexively on itself, becomes consciously a poem about a poem. For the only wood pile we have, finally, is the wood pile of the poem itself, and Frost is left reflecting on the mirror act of leaving one's own signs behind one, one of those—like Williams—who turns "to fresh tasks" and leaves us who come after wondering what the old signs of order were meant to signify . . . if anything.

And so with Williams, at his own "swamp's center," finding even in a house on a dead-end road viable signs of the "classic attempt / at beauty," an instinct still "intact" and discovered *there,* an instinct for a "lost world of symmetry / and grace." That is what is "most marvellous" for Williams in his daily rounds as a doctor and as a pediatrician, the Rutherford leech-gatherer moving in a world that most would ignore if they could but to which Williams responds with profound tact and desire.

There is the story Frank Gill of the *New Yorker* tells, of going the rounds with Williams in the winter of 1950, a few years after he wrote "The Hard Core of Beauty." Gill was interviewing Williams for the magazine and Williams, busy with his appointed daily house calls, asked Gill to accompany him. At one modest working-class home, Gill remembers, Williams stood at the door talking with a mother, her hair still up in pink curlers and dressed in a plain robe holding a baby who had just decided to wet its diaper. After a few moments, Williams walked back to his car, got in, jotted down a phrase the woman had made (probably without realizing the linguistic gist of her own remarks) on one of those ubiquitous prescription pads of his, and then began driving to his next patient. As he did so, he quipped something about that being the most beautiful woman he'd ever seen. We may forgive Gill perhaps for reserving judgment, but Williams was not being ironic. This woman too was one more example of the hard core of beauty Williams found everywhere, partially out of despair at its absence, or— more positively—by its always radiant potential as much as by its always tarnished real presence, the light shining through the smear, the necessary stain.

And so in the poem itself. If we look at what the speaker sees, the scene is plain enough; a decayed entranceway where the paint has been blistered by the sun, and inside "a painted plaque showing / ripe pomegranates." And what ancient memory of the myth of Kore, of Persephone, is present there? Persephone, kept in hell half the year because she had eaten seven seeds of the fruit of the pomegranate. And do the people in whose home Williams finds this picture know their Ovid and the story of Ceres' search for her daughter in Pluto's underworld kingdom? Do they know of Kore's mother who was

>   determined
> To have her daughter back, but the Fates forbade it.
> She had been hungry, wandering in the gardens,
> Poor simple child, and plucked from the leaving bough
> A pomegranate, the crimson fruit, and peeled it,
> With the inside coating of the pale rind showing,
> And eaten seven of the seeds. . . .

"I love pictures," Williams wrote in his essay, "Effie Deans":

> Nine times out of ten when I go into a house and have to wait a moment or two for whoever it is to appear, I begin looking around for pictures. And it's surprising how often I find interesting ones to look at, in the plainest households sometimes. . . . A physician often comes upon delightful *objets d'art* inauspiciously lighting the days and years of some obscure household in almost any suburban town—anywhere, everywhere on his rounds. . . . My own small town Rutherford is like any other in that. . . . All are not prize pieces but what I see always has interest, sometimes charm and associational qualities of note and occasionally great beauty.[1]

Rarely great beauty, then, but surely the associational quality that—in the imagination—makes present what is after all absent, and makes it *more* present to us because of the despair underlying our great desire to possess it. Prisoners understand this, the monk who wept at the beauty of the color red after denying himself color for half a year seems to have understood it, and Williams, too, out of his own great hungers, understood it.

The second poetic passage I would like to consider is Pound's own version of the goddess who appeared in his makeshift U.S. Army tent in the Detention Center at Pisa in the summer of 1945, when Pound was in near despair over the real possibility that—as Williams himself knew—he might be hanged on charges of treason against the United States government. Suddenly, "listening to the light murmuring," Pound begins with a wonderful synaesthetic phrase early Yeats would have applauded, suddenly

> Ed ascoltando il leggier mormorio
> > there came new subtlety of eyes into my tent,
> whether of spirit or hypostasis
> > but what the blindfold hides
> or at carnival
> > > nor any pair showed anger
> > Saw but the eyes and stance between the eyes,
> color, diastasis,
> > careless or unaware it had not the
> whole tent's room
> nor was place for the full *Eidos*
> interpass, penetrate. . . .

In 1947 Williams had read the Pisan *Cantos* with close attention, looking for evidence there of the new in the first work of Pound's that Williams had seen since communications between the two had been interrupted by the war. We have Williams's own word for it that he was absorbed more by the proselike verse passages in the Pisan *Cantos* than he was by the high lyrical epiphanies themselves, because the important work was being done just there. But Pound's vision is a wonderfully lyric moment, and more so if the reader knows the writings of the medieval philosophers of light, is aware of the assonantal and linguistic intricacies of Guido Cavalcanti's poems, and understands the fine gradations of terms like *hypostasis* and *diastasis* in their philosophical, theological, and medical colorations.

Freud might say that Pound, out of his intense isolation, had projected the goddess's eyes into his tent. And so has Williams, not in Pisa but there amidst the drabness of northern New Jersey, seeing *his* goddess "poking" her shoulders from beneath the "patient waves." Unlike Pound, Williams does not worry about the nature of his vision, does not attempt to understand the philosophical underpinnings of what he has been privileged to see. It is enough that, out of absence, out of the need for beauty, beauty has responded. It is there, has always been there, will, like the Godhead it is, always *be* there, waiting, patiently, beneath the surface of things. It is a vision of all gentleness, the feminine rising out of this place like the baby girl in *White Mule* who enters, "as Venus from the sea, dripping," "screwing up her tiny smeared face," this Venus, however, letting out "three convulsive yells" before she lies quietly. She is also like the young girl whom Williams admits he had waited for in the poem, "Eternity," who had suddenly appeared out of the dark

> bare headed, in pearl earrings
> and a cloak. Where shall
> we go?

> The boy friend was expecting me
> it was hard to
> get away.

Williams knows that the king of the underworld is also a jealous god and that the presence of the woman must necessarily be short-lived. Hell wants its beauty back. In the meantime, we wait for the goodess with her bedraggled golden tresses to announce herself by poking her bare head for a moment into view from the waters of the polluted Passaic or the Hackensack or Berry's Creek. Praise her.

3   The third poem I want to look at—briefly—is the most difficult and the most problematic of the three: "All That Is Perfect in Woman." It is a poem that refuses at its core to reveal itself because its obscure allusions and its thought units keep shifting from stanza to irregular stanza, killing (as Williams phrased it in *Paterson* 4) the explicit sentence. We know at once that we are in the presence of a compelling mind, but we are denied easy entrance—as Williams earlier complained of Pound—into the rooms of the poem by the very swiftness of the poem's forward movement from stanza to stanza as well as by the privacy of allusions. In a very real sense, this poem wishes to hide as much as it wishes to communicate.

It is only by degrees that we come to understand that Williams is once again preoccupied with the conflict between eros—sexual desire—and its absence in death. But there is a new twist here, for it is death itself that lures the poet on in spite of himself, as though death wore the mask of eros, now, as though the realization of our desires were to lead inevitably to our deaths. This poem, then, is a darker vision of the woman than Williams has allowed himself in either of the other poems. But it is as if Williams had finally to admit in the poem that his preoccupation

with eros could and did lead—in spite of protestations to the contrary—
to the sea and to death. Again, it is the primal image in Williams of the
woman's beauty caught in the sea itself: Kore/Venus breaking from
the waves of the unconsciousness, this time, however, with the face of the
Medusa entwined in the dangling hairlike tentacles of the Portuguese
Man o'War, which image closes the poem.

Appearance and reality. That preoccupation of the poets and philosophers which was old in Plato's time. There is the image of Joppolo
Schmidt playing himself—the original G.I. Joe—in a film about the
war, a bad film, really, "a pathetic scene laid // upon thin slices of
sympathy," the sands of some Pacific island played out instead on the
beaches of Miami a few years after the war. Against that, Williams
juxtaposes what he as a doctor knows is the reality of war: the corpse
mangled beyond recognition, the foot with three amputated toes, the
"head partly scorched, / hairless and with / no nose!"—images of a
world where surrealism has become reality, where the face of war is
seen as a woman by whom we seem perversely attracted, willing our
own annihilation, and lured on by the symbol

> whose blue eyes
> and laughing mouth affirm
> the habeas corpus
> of our resignation.

Resignation. Resignation as we re-sign values to the image of the woman.
Perverse desire become indistinguishable from the wish for death itself.
We have only to leaf through any one of several hundred issues of *Life*
magazine for the period from 1945 to 1950—the period we are discussing, though we could extend that survey right into our own moment
—to understand what Williams despaired of. There on the front cover:
the face of a starlet or a bathing beauty leaning invitingly toward us.
And inside, between the covers: the death of a sulky driver caught on
film, or the suicide of a Japanese officer, or news of some new "treach-
ery" by Russia or China, or—over it all—news of the bomb and its
effects, all made acceptable as coffee-table entertainment by the glitter-
ing prose of *Life*'s and *Look*'s writers.

"God but when I look at the LIFEs, the LOOKs—a grinning blond
with her ass over the edge of an iron pipe in gay sunshine, against bluest
of blue water," Williams wrote his young friend, Bonnie Golightly, in
January 1948, "virginal hips and a magnificent FUTURE of selling it

HIGH—I want to puke: not at her but at my own bitter indifference—bred of too much knowledge, too great an insight into cause and effect." [2] And what is that knowledge? Is it not in part the masculine "blow-torch flame," so effective in burning soldiers out of caves and foxholes "at exorbitant cost" to the spirit no less than to the usurious national debt? Is it not the same destructive energy that will finally burn away even this symbol of virginity, which in its puritanical frigidity and terrifying innocence longs only "for snow and // a quiet life" (a dream also to be purchased "at exorbitant cost" to the highest bidder) and which sick union must continue to blossom—as it already has—into the terrible new birth of the mangled corpse?

Toward the close of his poem, Williams evokes the figure of Garcia Lorca, the poet he had read carefully and written of in 1939, even as the Spanish Civil War was ending in defeat for Williams. If you could only have been alive for this, Williams says with evident bitterness, for this, which—we can believe—Lorca would have understood: how it all ends in the sea of destruction, in the sea which knows fecundity and gaiety and, of course, death.

There is, then, in Williams in these years when he was writing *Paterson*—and in these poems—a complex preoccupation with the dynamics of his own erotic desire which had dogged him since youth. In practice, what this suggests is that even at sixty-five he had not yet come to terms with the woman in himself. Part of the problem, he was willing to contend, was in the false and even destructive images of the woman that culture in his own country had offered him. As a doctor and as a poet he knew that the peak-a-boo soft porn of the popular magazines—from *Vanity Fair* in the twenties to *Life* in the forties—as well as the "girlie" previews available in New York City and on the movie screen—were at the heart of it insidious and grotesque distortions of the woman, reducing her, as he once wrote, to the feverish image of the "All-American fuckable girl." It is something of that image, in large part re-created and "sold to the highest bidder" by the power brokers in this country (most of them men), to which Williams knew he had fallen victim himself more than once. The destructiveness of that erotic illusion is what he seems to have wanted to evoke in the ironically titled "All That Is Perfect in Woman." Hart Crane too had evoked an image of the advertising agencies' perfect woman back in the twenties in the "Virginia" section of *The Bridge*. And he too had taken the type of the virginal woman made to sell everything from cereal to cars to the war itself with the promise of what Williams had called a certain bliss between thighs, thighs concealing grotesquely there "a delicious / lung with entrails / and a tongue or gorget."

But there was something else, too, in the feminine principle—call it a counterforce—that continually drew Williams back to women, to his patients, to his friends, to his wife, to the world of generativity itself. This principle of the feminine was a good and, despite his personal failures, failures for example that he had diagnosed as part of the American sickness in *In the American Grain* back in the early twenties, it was a good that sustained him in all seasons of his life. It was, as he himself tells us, the indestructible, merciful hard core of beauty at the heart of the mystery we call life.

1983

Williams and Stevens: Storming the Edifice

Though it was always a stately saraband between the two of them, at most a little jocularity, a touch of banter that turned more circumspect with the years, Williams and Stevens watched each other through gun-slit turrets for forty years. The two had known each other from the old days in New York, talking over cocktails at Walter Arensberg's place on the upper East Side or Alfred Kreymborg's rooms in downtown New York, before Stevens moved to Hartford, the old insurance capital of America, in 1916. It was Stevens who early established the rules of poetic license and etiquette for the two of them. For Williams saw from almost the beginning that Stevens, approaching forty, was becoming, for complex reasons of self-preservation, something of a grand edifice. Thus, when Williams, on his way north in August 1922 to stay with his wife's family in southern Vermont, decided to "drop by" with his eight-year-old son, Bill, and his dog to see Stevens, the visit became—as Stevens confessed to Harriet Monroe a few days later—something of an ordeal, both men as nervous as two belles in new dresses. Perhaps the new dresses Stevens referred to were his *Harmonium* and Williams's *Spring and All,* both major books of poems, and both published a short time later. Whatever, Stevens did his best to make Williams feel right at home by putting him and his son and the dog up at a nice hotel in Hartford. That gesture was indicative of the separation Stevens demanded from others, including his own family, and which he made sure he received. His Hartford edifice, like the edifice of himself, was off limits to nearly everyone, and Williams was no exception.

For his part, Williams invited Stevens to stay with him at 9 Ridge Road—as Pound, Zukofsky, Burke, Cummings, Maxwell Bodenheim, Wally Gould, Robert Lowell, Allen Ginsberg, Tom Cole, and others would do—and he repeated the offer on many occasions. Take the bus out from the 43rd Street terminal, get off at the Rutherford railroad station, take a five minute's walk, and you were there. But always Stevens would demur; there were errands to run when he was in the city, a pair of shoes, a gallery exhibit to take in, before returning on the train to his home and office. Thus, though they were less than three hours away from each other and often much closer—as when Williams stayed at the beach at West Haven each summer—Stevens never availed himself of Williams's hospitality, and Williams—after that visit in '22 —never again stopped off at Stevens's, though he did several times nod in the direction of Stevens's home as he traveled north to Cummington or Wilmington or Middlebury. So much for the social groundrules.

There were other gestures, of course, other measures by which these two giants, as they grew toward their majority, eyed each other through slits in those gun turrets: these two contenders with differing ideas as to what a poem should be. They had profound respect for each other, and they knew that every shot they fired toward each other's walls should count. The game was to do this with every intention of scoring very palpable hits and yet do it without ever losing good form. With other contenders, even with Pound, Williams made the ground rules by which he would play, so that he must have taken Stevens very seriously, as Stevens took Williams. So, for example, Williams went after Eliot with an anger and vengeance that frustrated Williams all the more because Eliot assumed an air of disdain and aloofness as against an unworthy Pindaric adversary, refusing to engage in the contest with him, at least openly. Williams began attacking Eliot in print in 1918, and he was still at it as late as the closing of *Paterson* 5, published in 1958. Eliot was the expatriate, the traitor, the hypocrite, possum playing dead, a poet manqué, cribber of other people's lines. As for Eliot, the only words he uttered directly against Williams were delivered during his tenure at Harvard in the early thirties, when he remarked that Williams might be a poet "of some local interest, perhaps."

With Pound, Williams had a lifelong love/hate relationship. Pound was the great verse experimenter, the subtle translator snatching lost music out of the living air, the man with an exasperatingly "correct" understanding of the importance of greed and conglomerate interests as the destroyers of culture and so the great sin of our times. Yet Pound, too, was the best enemy American poetry had: Lord Ga-Ga, Mussolini's dupe, out of step with the country he had scorned.

These relationships, one should note, were out in the open, as were Williams's feelings about Marianne Moore, H.D., Cummings, Frost, Hart Crane, Auden, Dylan Thomas, Robert Lowell, Conrad Aiken, Denise Levertov, Olson, Creeley, and others. It was his singular relationship with Stevens, however, that was so much more oblique that most critics have failed to notice just how central that relationship and its attendant dialogue was for both men.

In the beginning—the period from 1915 until 1923—it was a matter of two poets writing, appearing together in the same little magazines, like *Poetry*, *Others*, the *Dial*, the *Little Review*, and *Broom*, or the exchange of an occasional note. When Williams served as editor for the July 1916 issue of *Others*, for example, he asked Stevens to contribute a poem and then took—with corrections or emendations furnished by himself—Stevens's "The Worms at Heaven's Gate." Williams had liked that poem, especially, he said, because it was more direct and less "as iffy" than most of Stevens's efforts. It was not so much a tenuous, impressionistic "seem," this poem about the reality of death, but "be," and Williams told him to take his suggestions. "For Christ's sake," he told him, "yield to me and become great and famous." And Stevens did.

When, at the beginning of 1918, Williams sent Stevens a copy of his *Al Que Quiere!*, Stevens responded that the book struck him not as a unified structure with a developed point of view, but more as a miscellany. "My idea," Stevens told him, "is that in order to carry a thing to the extreme necessity, to convey it one has to stick to it. . . . To fidget with points of view leads always to new beginnings and incessant new beginnings lead to sterility." Williams made two observations in his "Prologue" to *Kora in Hell*, where he printed Stevens's letter. First: now that he had figured out what Circe's tricks were, and he had learned to double-cross the old bitch muse, what was he supposed to do? Marry her? The second observation was one he'd heard from Skip Cannell, who knew both Williams and Stevens in the old days: that Wally was a "Pennsylvania Dutchman"—a roi and a roi and a roiroi—who had suddenly become aware of his earthy habits and taken to "society" in self-defense.

The thing with Williams was this: he had known Stevens in the old days in New York, the place where both of them had first become poets and where both had served their long apprenticeships, and Williams had watched Stevens with the trained eye of the physician, waiting for signs of a repressed Dionysian streak in Stevens to proclaim themselves, to suddenly "wink" even as he held forth in mock-serious declamatory mode, as in his "To a High-Toned Old Christian Woman" or, again, in the exacerbated voices of *The Comedian as the Letter C*. Wasn't this the same Stevens who liked to dance at gatherings of the New York artists, the same Stevens who had taken part in all-night ragtime sessions as a cub reporter and law student living in a hall bedroom on the lower East Side back in 1901 and 1902? Hadn't Stevens, depressed by his living alone and his failure as a reporter working for the *Tribune*, once thought of suicide? "There is . . . the story of the down and out Stevens sitting on a park bench at the Battery," Williams had written William Van O'Connor in '48,

> watching the out tide and thinking to join it, as a corpse, on its way to the sea (he had been a failure as a reporter). As he sat there watching the debris floating past him he began to write—noting the various articles as they passed. He became excited as he wrote and ended by taking back to the *Tribune* office an editorial or a "story" that has become famous—in a small way among the newspaper offices.
>
> But that finished him as a newspaper man. It may very well be that that moment was his beginning as a poet.

And had not the Baroness Elsa von Freytag-Loringhoven—head shaved, her left profile purple, her right saffron, wearing tartan and sardine cans suspended from her breasts, the woman whom Hart Crane once called the embodiment of Dadaism and who had struck mortal terror in him, this woman who had pursued Williams himself out to Rutherford and waited in his car to grapple with him so that Williams had had to take boxing lessons to defend himself from her—had not this same woman once pursued Stevens as well, when, seeing her in the Village attired in such fashion, Stevens had dared to applaud her? For years after, Williams wryly noted in his memorial piece on Stevens in *Poetry*, Stevens had refused to venture below 14th Street for fear of running into her again.

Williams never tired of these stories or legends about an all-too-human Stevens. He needed them to remind him of the man, before he had begun turning slowly into golden bird or sacred text for seminars. He needed to remember *that* Stevens in order to keep himself from being drawn into those ethereal spaces in Stevens's imagination where he himself, Antaeus-like, would have begun to shrivel.

What these two unlikely sons of Emerson and Whitman were really engaged in, of course, was a struggle to determine the nature of reality and the imagination and the direction American poetry was to take in the twentieth century. In reality, this almost invisible war was one of the most significant dialogues into the nature and practice of American poetics—two giants contending, watching each other's moves. Hugh Kenner almost had it right when he spoke of Stevens's radical mistake in refusing to read Williams's *Paterson* when the first book appeared. "I have not read Paterson," Stevens wrote José Rodriguez-Feo just before Christmas 1946. "I have the greatest respect for him, although there is the constant difficulty that he is more interested in the way of saying things than in what he has to say." But beneath that stance of apparent nonchalance and indifference was a giant who was, in reality, watching. Stevens, like others, had been aware of Williams's epic for a number of years, and it is quite probable that Stevens's own "Description Without Place," written at the very moment that Williams had finally finished the first book of *Paterson* and sent it off to the printer's, was the deeper catalyst that persuaded Stevens to do his own poem about the "idea that we live in the description of a place and not in the place itself," as he explained to his old friend, Henry Church.

Certainly, when Williams read Stevens's poem in the *Sewanee Review* in September, he felt compelled to answer it with his own, significantly titled, "A Place (Any Place) to Transcend All Places." Williams told Byron Vazakas—an old friend of Stevens's, incidentally, who also hailed from Reading—that Stevens's poem had had to be "answered." But what he didn't say was that Stevens's talk about the "seeming of the

Spaniard," the "hard hidalgo," was Stevens up to his old tricks again.
To Stevens, Williams was Carlos, the wild man, the Spaniard of the
Rose as in his "Esthétique du Mal" (1944). Now, a year later, Stevens
wrote:

> Thus the theory of description matters most.
> It is the theory of the word for those
>
> For whom the word is the making of the world,
> The buzzing world and lisping firmament.
>
> It is a world of words to the end of it,
> In which nothing solid is its solid self. . . .

When Stevens wrote this and then added that it was men who made
themselves their speech and invented "a nation in a phrase," that all
places were, essentially, casts "Of the imagination, made in sound,"
Williams saw redder than those "rubies" Stevens spoke of "reddened
by rubies reddening."

Well, damn it, Williams insinuated in his own poem, what about
New York, Wally old boy. Let that be the common meeting ground of
these two old New Yorkers, the place where they had met previously
as poets, before both had begun—by 1945—to become elder presences:

> In New York, it is said,
> they do meet (if that is
> what is wanted) talk but
> nothing is exchanged
> unless that guff
> can be translated: as
> to say, that is not
> the end, there are channels
> above that, draining
> places from which New York
> is dignified, created. . . .

Consider New York, consider it as a flower out of which the poem
might be created, but consider too the incredible complexity of the city's
root system, all that waste and excrement, and all those millions of
words spent each day on the air in order to make possible the fertile
poem. It was not ideas that made the city, but rather the city that fed
the mind and flowered into the poem.

Imagine it! Pears
philosophically hard. Nor
thought that is from
branches on a root, from
an acid soil, with scant
grass about the bole
where it breaks through.

No ideas but in things, Wally, no ideas but in things. And then, more
directly, Williams bantering his old friend with the memory of the
Baroness who had once chased him in that *civitas dei,* that same city of
the mind, below 14th Street:

—and we have
: the memory of Elsa
von Freytag Loringhofen,
a fixation from the street
door of a Berlin
playhouse; all who "wear
their manner too obviously,"
the adopted English (white)
and many others.

Like Wally, who had learned to "wear his manner too obviously," who
—as Williams had noted in 1937 reviewing Stevens's *The Man With
the Blue Guitar*—thought he always had to say something important
when he used the blank verse line. "Obscene and abstract as excrement,"
Williams ended his own poem, suggesting again that it was the sharp-
edged gritty things of this world that nourished the imagination.

One could go on discussing the nature of this most important of dialogues. One might ask, for example, why Williams became so touchy
about Stevens's formulation of Williams's poetry as the juxtaposition of
the romantic and sentimental with the deliberately tough guy "antipoetic," a term Stevens devised for Williams in his Preface to Williams's
Collected Poems, 1921-31. Twenty-five years later Williams was still
vehemently denying that there was any such thing as the antipoetic in
his poems, even though that term had been picked up and used in a
hundred subsequent reviews of Williams's work. One might talk about
the radical anxiety created in Williams in 1944, stuck after several years
in the making of *Paterson* 1, because in order to make it his own "Parts

of a Greater World" (the phrase is Williams's own) he would have to incorporate what he called Chaucer's cosmopolitan, sophisticated, assured tone as he'd heard it in *Troilus and Cresseida* and somehow include that voice into the fabric of *Paterson*. And when Williams told Vazakas and Marianne Moore that he'd heard that voice in only a few American poets, including one now dead poet who had taught it to Stevens, the implications were clear: that the wild Spaniard, master of the breathless, enthusiast of wheelbarrows and spring weeds and muddy rivers, would now have to show that he could do Stevens's best cosmopolitan voice as well when he needed to. It was one thing to be called the Buffalo Bill of poetry at forty; it was another to suffer oneself the indignity of that appellation at sixty. Williams had to feel he could assume the urbane, aloof manner when it mattered, though that too was only a mask, a mask of indirection, which Williams also distrusted.

It is sobering to remember Stevens at Bard College in March 1951. Williams was to have been there to celebrate with Stevens when Stevens received an honorary degree from the college, but he had just suffered his first stroke three days before and was struggling to keep from going under. Stevens therefore gave his introductory remarks (they are in the *Opus Posthumous* collection), and then—amidst the peal of thunder and a standing ovation—he turned to Ted Weiss as he left the room and remarked that it looked as though they hadn't needed Williams— the old man—after all. That was Stevens winking for a minute, opening one of the windows of his massive edifice, skipping a little hoorah that —though he was four years older than Williams—he'd managed somehow to outlast him. Coming from one of the Pindaric contenders for the wreath, such joyous hullabalo is understandable. And Stevens did, after all, write Williams a few days later to say how sorry he was for what had happened to his friend, and happy too to learn that Williams was rapidly recovering.

The last word, however, was Williams's, merely because, as he himself noted in his farewell to Stevens written in the fall of 1955 a few months after Stevens's death, he had managed to outlive him. What he wanted to do in remembering his friend, he wrote, was to break down the edifice Stevens had spent years acquiring, to remember instead the poet of the "hibiscus," the poet of the "Jar in Tennessee" and "Bantams in Pine Woods," Stevens and the baroness. Had he known the story of that shark Hemingway (age thirty-six) circling Stevens (at fifty-six) in a makeshift boxing ring in Key West in February 1936, Williams would have understood the need of Stevens's repressed Dionysian mode to surface ever so grotesquely to taste blood, even if it were his own. Eyes philosophically blackened.

And what of those last poems of Stevens's, with titles like "On the Way to the Bus," and "Not Ideas About the Thing But the Thing Itself"? Stevens, at the end of his poetic career arriving at lines like these:

> At the earliest ending of winter,
> In March, a scrawny cry from outside
> Seemed like a sound in his mind.
>
> He knew that he heard it,
> A bird's cry, at daylight or before,
> In the early March wind.

And Williams, beginning *Paterson* 5 in March 1956, the first spring after Stevens's death, watching the three fox sparrows out his rear window, and beginning again, in what was both an answer to and tribute for his dead friend:

> It is early . . .
>   the song of the fox sparrow
> reawakening the world
>   of Paterson
>   —its rocks and streams
>   frail tho it is
> from their long winter sleep
>   In March—
>   the rocks
>   the bare rocks
>   speak!
> —It is a cloudy morning
>   He looks out the window
>   sees the birds still there—

In one of the very last pieces of prose criticism Williams ever wrote— his introduction to a new translation of Villon's poetry into English, written in late 1959—Williams pressed the argument against Stevens's poetry of indirection for the last time. Villon, Williams said, thinking of his own practice undoubtedly, had been "a wholly responsible man," wholly responsible for his statements: when he used "a figure of speech it was not 'as if' but coming from *himself* in one of the disguises that the world forces us to wear." No escaping the persona, Williams knew, but under that the refusal to use "the indirect approach, even at the excuse of art." "As if." That signature of Stevens's, and to a lesser extent Williams's own device years before, the conditional masquerading as certitude, giving rise to ghostly presences in the poem hovering over the void. The magician's trick.

When Stevens had died, Williams had been for so long out of touch, out of direct contact, with him, that he had had to write directly to Norman Holmes Pearson for whatever biographical information Pearson might be able to give him. Who, after all, knew Stevens by then? At the funeral there had been almost no one, no neighbors, no poets, only a handful of presences from Yale, including Pearson. Williams had wanted to know Stevens more intimately, to know him as a man, but Stevens had demurred, had insisted on keeping his distance as he turned slowly into his own sacred text. And now the man was gone. Try frantically as Williams might to flesh again that presence, Stevens was gone. What Williams must have known was that the real contender—not Eliot and not even Pound, but Stevens—had made the total leap onto the bright page. Yet Williams kept his silence as well, continuing the hidden skirmish in the poetry itself. It would remain for others to mark the evidence there—in the poems—that two giants had wrestled, hurling poems like bouquets at one another, each gathering strength from contact with the earth or the air as was needed.

1980

Gerard Manley Hopkins

The New Aestheticism: A Reading
of "Andromeda"

For all its surface transparency, Hopkins's allegorical "Andromeda" has been subjected to a number of widely varying interpretations. But its underlying thrust seems to be a conservative reaction to the spread of a new moral anarchy in the poetry of the 1870s, an anarchy "more lawless, and more lewd" than anything the Victorian British public had as yet encountered. Hopkins's poem, written in August 1879, points to the spectre of Swinburne's "man-god," Walt Whitman, the "wilder beast from West," the phallic dragon, the prophet of a new freedom from established order and sexual restraint, and hence an apocalyptic beast. This is not the Whitman familiar to twentieth-century Americans, but rather the embodiment of a humanistic mysticism, the incarnation of a new paganism walking over the prostrated form of an apparently dead Christianity, for which Swinburne had acted as prophet in his "To Walt Whitman in America" (1871). It is a Victorian view of the poet of democratic America, and even Swinburne, as his later letters and criticism testify, did not quite know what to make of Whitman's message.

More personally, "Andromeda" bears witness to Hopkins's own attraction and repulsion—for the most part unconscious—for a sensuousness and freedom manifested in the predominant art movement of his time—the New Aestheticism. Hopkins's ambivalence, which shows up in his nostalgia for a moral order oddly combined with a manneristic style (an unmistakable sign of aesthetic decadence), is a touchstone of most of the Victorian writers. Such a reading of "Andromeda" as I am attempting here implies that the complex of the poem—its rhythms, images, syntax, diction, resonance—says more than any prose paraphrase of the poem can. And, what is more, the poem may very well lean toward the very thing it seems to be rejecting. To give three other examples of such a tension: Keats's ambivalence toward harvest and completion in "To Autumn," Yeats's attraction for "the young / In one another's arms" in "Sailing to Byzantium," and Sylvia Plath's emotional attraction for her dead father even as she tries to exorcise him in "Daddy."

Hopkins himself mentioned the poem directly only twice, both times in letters to Bridges: once in August 1879, to say he had written "Andromeda," and again in early May 1881,[1] to say that Hall Caine would not publish the poem in his conservative sonnet anthology, despite the poem's alleged metrical regularity. Both times Hopkins commented only on the poem's style. In the earlier reference he calls attention to his attempt "at a more Miltonic plainness and severity than I have anywhere else. I cannot say it has turned out severe, still less plain, but it seems almost free from quaintness and in aiming at one excellence I may have hit another" (*Letters to Bridges,* p. 87). That is all we ever hear of "Andromeda" from Hopkins.

But that is not all we have heard from the commentators. A number of critics have given us the significance of the Andromeda legend for Hopkins, their readings becoming more complex as they have attempted to become more specific. They have agreed only with this irreducible minimum: the poem is about a future but certain rescue of Andromeda by her bridegroom Perseus from the threatening beast. For that, in its barest outline, is what the legend is about. But who is Andromeda, who Perseus, who the beast? W. H. Gardner early made "Time's Andromeda" the Church of Christ; the "rock rude" St. Peter; and the "wilder beast from West" a catch-all for "the new powers of Anti-

christ, which for [Hopkins] would include rationalism, Darwinism, in-
dustrialism, the new paganism of Swinburne and Whitman, possibly
Nietzsche." [2] This works well, but only if Andromeda is disassociated
from England or the Catholic Church in England and is seen as the
Roman Catholic Church, pursued by new forces rising in the Western
world. Jean-Georges Ritz, on the other hand, sees the "rock rude" not
as Peter but as England itself, and Alan Heuser, taking his hint from
Hopkins's commentary on a passage from Revelations 12, sees Perseus
as Gabriel or Christ "steaded" in Gabriel, or, perhaps, as St. George
of England (*Poems*, p. 277). In my *Hopkins Commentary*, I have given
alternate readings, based on the assimilation of the legend of Perseus
slaying the beast with the legend of St. George, patron saint of England,
slaying the dragon, a legend writ large in the stars themselves, but I
have emphasized the Englishness of Hopkins's references. Elisabeth
Schneider, taking a new tack, has given us a radically new reading
which sees Andromeda as England or the Church in England looking
off westward by "both horns of shore" at the increasing roar in Ireland,
and quotes from Hopkins's letters to show that he was acutely aware
of the Fenian threat not only when he was in Ireland, but at the time
the sonnet was composed. John Wain, in his 1959 essay, "An Idiom of
Desperation," separates himself from what he calls the "orthodox"
commentators, and refuses to read "Andromeda" in any definite allegorical relationship: "When Hopkins feels the story of Perseus and
Andromeda strongly enough in his blood to write a poem about it, he
is not constructing an allegory in which this 'stands for' that." [3] But
while Wain's reading of the poem's syntactical ambiguities is interesting, his overall thesis that you don't ask a poet like Hopkins what
his poetry means is open to question.

"Andromeda" is, to begin with, atypical of Hopkins. It is his only
sonnet ("Peace" poses a special case) to use a sustained allegorical
frame. So, while the outline of the poem is clear—the theme of rescue
is a recurrent one in Hopkins's poetry—my essay is an attempt to approach the poem in the light of the particular moment in which it was
written, to show that Hopkins's use of the Andromeda theme was not
peculiar to him, and to suggest not only some of the probable influences
on the poem, but also the *most* probable significance of the allegory.
For it is of course reasonable to read the poem as the concern of a
Victorian Catholic with the larger threats of materialism, unbelief, and
political anarchy. But when Hopkins came to actually write the poem

those forces were translated into images and rhythms and pressures that reveal the particular spectres inhabiting the landscape of his imagination. Still, I am awkwardly aware that Hopkins assumed his best Gioconda smile while I was writing this piece.

But I have attempted this study because I believe the largest pressing requirement in Hopkins scholarship which has yet to be done is to place the poet within his own Victorian context. This means not only chronicling the day-to-day events of the man's life, or a portion of it, as in the precise and scholarly study that Alfred Thomas, S.J., has given us in his recent *Hopkins: The Jesuit Years*. It means also attempting to demonstrate judiciously the nature of the external pressures, the particular intellectual pollen that Hopkins, with his special psychic and physiological strains, drew into himself and that flowered in his poems. Even the influence of the literary magazines, such as the *Academy* and the *Saturday Review,* and of the newspapers, particularly the *London Times,* on Hopkins needs to be shown.[4]

So the influences at work on Hopkins when he composed "Andromeda" on Tuesday, August 12, 1879, may be considered under three headings. First, looking backward and broadly, there are the Victorian (and Romantic) treatments of the Andromeda legend which Hopkins probably knew. Second, there is a dispatch in the *Times* that appeared the morning the poem was written and that may well have been the immediate catalyst for the poem. Third, there is the whole question of Hopkins's being attracted to and repelled by the Dionysian freedom implicit in the New Aestheticism, particularly as manifested in Swinburne and in Swinburne's paeans to the "god-man" Whitman.[5]

Among the other Victorians who were fascinated by the Andromeda story, as William C. DeVane has pointed out, was Browning, who used the legend both early and late. He employed it in *Pauline* (1832–33), in *The Ring and the Book* (1869), and in the late "Parleying with Francis Furini" (1887).[6] And in 1868 William Morris published his first volume of *The Earthly Paradise,* which contains the Andromeda story under April: "The Doom of Acrisius." Hopkins not only read in but seriously considered reviewing this volume of poetry. There even seems to be a direct echo of Morris's lines describing the rock on which Andromeda was chained—the line "From horn to horn a belt of sand there lay" and, again, "The bay from horn to horn"—in Hopkins's Andromeda looking "off by both horns of shore." [7] An earlier literary influence on "Andromeda" may have been Kingsley and also Shelly's

"Adonais." Shelley uses the Andromeda motif in his elegy to represent the draconic critical attack on the poetic force (Urania), with Keats in this instance serving as Perseus-savior. Andromeda-Urania laments that she is "chained to Time, and cannot thence depart" (1.234), a line that finds its echo in Hopkins's "Time's Andromeda."

In 1875 and in the years following, Edward Burne-Jones, whose work Hopkins admired and whom he mentioned in his journals and letters to Dixon, did a series of ten small watercolor studies of the legend of Perseus in preparation for a larger group of oils. And when we recall that Dixon was a friend and Oxford schoolmate of both Morris and Burne-Jones, it is quite possible that Hopkins either saw Burne-Jones's studies or at least knew of their existence. Moreover, Swinburne, whose importance I will deal with shortly, dedicated his seminal 1866 *Poems and Ballads* to Burne-Jones.[8] In these studies of the Perseus legend, as in "The Doom of Acrisius," Perseus seems often to suggest a Christ figure. He certainly represents St. George, a favorite subject of the pre-Raphaelites.

The Perseus-Andromeda myth was even used as an allegory in the popular magazines. In the short-lived *The Mask: A Humorous and Fantastic Preview of the Month*, edited by Alfred Thompson and Leopold (Monk) Lewis, there is at the beginning of the December 1868 issue (its last) a two-page fold-out illustration of Andromeda chained to a rock with a sea-beast rampant and Perseus hovering above, ready to strike. This is accompanied by a one-page essay, "The Modern Andromeda: A Political Fable," in which readers are asked to "apply" the myth "politically to the events of the day, in any way they may prefer." [9]

On the same day that Hopkins wrote "Andromeda" at Oxford, the *Times* ran the following dispatch from the Vatican:

> The Latin text of the Encyclical expected from Leo XIII on the teaching of philosophy (*Aeterni Patris* [On Christian Philosophy]) is published in this evening's *Osservatore Romano*. His Holiness commences by remarking that the greater part of the evils which afflict society in the present day are due to the inculcation of false philosophy, and adds that while sound philosophy is a help to the understanding of supernatural truth false philosophy dissuades from its acceptance. Philosophy, in order that it may attain its end, must be subject to the faith.... He deplores that scholastic philosophy

has been abandoned and that various and opposed systems have prevailed instead, which have given rise to great inconstancy of doctrine.

Among the "many blows and banes" under which Andromeda had had to suffer patiently—and the *Times* for August was rife with them: two colonial wars, in Afghanistan and Zululand, the ominous news of the new Krupp armaments, the indifferent destruction of Italian art treasures, the American threat to British industry reported on by Gladstone—the worst for Hopkins, reinforced by Leo's encyclical, seems to have been the wrongheadedness of much modern philosophy, particularly the spread of a new anarchy, "more lawless, and more lewd." That anarchy seems to have been linked, perhaps unconsciously, to the brazen spectre of Swinburne's republican man-god, Walt Whitman. And given the tenor of the times, with good reason.

Although Whitman's *Leaves of Grass* had first been published in 1855, it went through a number of revisions before it gained widespread notice in England in the early seventies. And then Whitman was vigorously saluted and attacked throughout the decade not just as poet, but as spokesman for the new social and individual freedom. "He disturbs our classifications," Edward Dowden wrote in "The Poetry of Democracy: Walt Whitman" for the *Westminster Review* (July 1871). "He attracts us; he repels us; he excites our curiosity, wonder, admiration, love; or, our extreme repugnance." [10] But Dowden's is in all a very favorable review, perceptive and surprisingly clear-headed, which can accept the abstractions of Whitman's democratic morality. In the same year, however, Swinburne had ushered Whitman in as a god, as the incarnation of Freedom. And it is Swinburne's portrait and, to a lesser degree, George Saintsbury's 1874 review of Whitman, that are most relevant here, for Hopkins received much of his own slant on Whitman from Saintsbury, and much of his own poetic rhetoric from Swinburne.

Because Hopkins did not achieve anything like fame until the 1930s, we forget that Swinburne and Pater were only seven and five years older than Hopkins, and that Whitman himself, while twenty-five years older than Hopkins, outlived him. In 1882, three years after the writing of "Andromeda," Bridges accused Hopkins of imitating Whitman's manner in composing "The Leaden Echo and the Golden Echo." In a rather well-known reply, Hopkins admitted that, though he had read very little of Whitman, perhaps "half a dozen pieces at most," he knew that Whitman's influence went deep. In fact, he said, "I always knew in my heart Walt Whitman's mind to be more like my own than any other man's living. As he is a very great scoundrel this is not a pleasant confession. And this also makes me the more desirous to read him and the more determined that I will not." [11] The bulk of Hopkins's argument revolves around Whitman's rhythm, which Hopkins insists is closer to prose and only superficially like his own sprung rhythm. Both prefer an Alexandrine line. But, Hopkins insists, "I came to it by degrees, I did not take it from him." And this is true. If a source for the Alexandrine had to be cited, Swinburne is the more correct choice. On the other hand, Swinburne himself seems to have been influenced by Whitman's rhythms, which he had discovered as early as 1862, when he himself was twenty-five.

But what did Hopkins mean by calling Whitman a scoundrel in confidence to Bridges? It is clear that he understood Whitman to be homosexual, promiscuous, perhaps even an anarchist. It is what nearly every conservative British critic noted in discussing Whitman's impact in England in the late sixties and seventies. It is what George Saintsbury implied in his review of *Leaves of Grass* in the *Academy* for October 10, 1874, a review Hopkins read carefully, in saying that Whitman's "ideal republic" could be promoted by a "robust American love." "In the ears of the world," Saintsbury either naively or hypocritically insinuated, "(at least on this side of the Atlantic) incredulous of such things, he reiterates the expressions of Plato to Aster, of Socrates respecting Charmides, and in this respect fully justifies (making allowance for altered manners) Mr. Symonds' assertion of his essentially Greek character, an assertion which most students of Whitman will heartily endorse." [12] So we know what Hopkins insinuates when, speaking of the corporal works of mercy to Bridges in January 1879, he remarks that "even Walt Whitman nurses the sick" (*Letters to Bridges,* p. 63).

By his own admission, Hopkins had not read very much Whitman. His view of the poet, therefore, seems to have followed that of the conservative Augustan English critics, critics like Buchanan and Saintsbury (whose style, however, he did find somewhat vulgar), who, while they admired Whitman, were somewhat uncomfortable with his barbaric yawp and message. Saintsbury's review had begun by saying that, while

Whitman had "been praised, with discrimination as well as with emphasis, by Mr. Swinburne," Swinburne's plaudits were "mainly a passport to the favour of those who would be likely to appreciate Whitman without any passport at all." And although Swinburne's more balanced and less exultant criticism of Whitman appeared in *Under the Microscope* (1872) only a year after his ecstatic ode to the American, Whitman remained linked with Swinburne and the new pagan aesthetic throughout the seventies. Given Hopkins's own tendencies and self-imposed checks, the nature of Swinburne's praise for Whitman would have been enough to make Whitman suspect.

That Hopkins followed Swinburne's career with interest from the mid-sixties on is clear from the numerous references to Swinburne in his letters. Except for Bridges, Patmore, and Dixon (with all of whom he corresponded) Hopkins seems to have followed *no* contemporary poet as closely as he did Swinburne. Writing to his friend Baillie in September 1867, the twenty-three-year-old Hopkins used Swinburne as an example of the impossibility of separating the moral from the aesthetic impact in a work of art, especially where the subjects are extreme cases of immorality (*Further Letters*, pp. 228–29). Hopkins had undoubtedly been reading from Swinburne's *Atalanta in Calydon* (1865) as well as from *Poems and Ballads, First Series* (1866), although his own prosody does not show marked signs of Swinburne's influence until about 1870 in "Ad Mariam."

Hopkins's view of Swinburne remained ambivalent throughout his life. Swinburne's genius, Hopkins felt, was astounding, even if limited. But Swinburne himself was one of "those plagues of mankind." [13] His poetry was unique among the Victorians in its "effort at establishing a new standard of poetical diction, of the rhetoric of poetry," but it was blighted in being "essentially archaic" (*Correspondence*, p. 99), biblical, and Elizabethan in diction. Still, Hopkins's own poetry, even to its phrasing, as Schneider has shown, was powerfully influenced by Swinburne's new rhetoric. Take, for example, these lines from Hopkins's "Spelt from Sibyl's Leaves" which date from late 1884:

> her wild hollow hoarlight hung to the height
> Waste; her earliest stars, earlstars, ' stárs principal, overbend us

and compare them with Swinburne's "Hesperia," which appeared in *Poems and Ballads, First Series* eighteen years before:

when the moon overhead
Wanes in the wan waste heights of the heaven, and stars without
    number
Die without sound.

Hopkins, of course, improved tremendously on Swinburne's anapestic series, (and on his Alexandrines as well), by purposely breaking the drugging monotony of that series with his own sprung rhythm, consciously restructuring the foot to emphasize the stress rather than the syllabic count. But the rhythmic and imagistic influence is clearly there.

There are two Swinburne poems that, I would suggest, provide close parallels in terms of their imagery, syntax, and dramatic movement to "Andromeda." A large number of Swinburne's poems are deliberately republican, sensual, and blasphemous. Such qualities were obviously aimed at the heart of the Victorian bourgeoisie, even though many more enlightened critics also took offense, or attempted to dismiss the poems as the ravings of a frantic, naughty boy. But two poems in particular would have been offensive to Hopkins, and these seem to be echoed in "Andromeda": Swinburne's "Hymn to Prosperine" and "To Walt Whitman in America." In the first, the speaker is a Roman pagan of the fourth century, who laments the Edict of Constantine proclaiming Christianity the state religion. The persona is clearly Swinburne marking the still central but weakening hold of Christendom on Europe in his own days. Both lament the loss of the good old colorful, fleshly paganism and the presence of a pale, restricting Christianity. The lines that seem most to have influenced Hopkins, by the way, are precisely those that John Morley quoted in his now-famous attack, "Mr. Swinburne's New Poems: *Poems and Ballads*," which appeared in the August 4, 1866, number of the *Saturday Review*, a magazine that Hopkins's family regularly read and that Hopkins quotes from or alludes to more than a dozen times in his letters.[14] The relevant passage begins:

Sleep, shall we sleep after all? for the world is not sweet in the end;
For the old faiths loosen and fall, the new years ruin and rend.
Fate is a sea without shore, and the soul is a rock that abides;
But her ears are vexed with the roar and her face with the foam of
    the tides.

The old paganism is cast "Far out with the foam of the present that sweeps to the surf of the past." The sea, thus identified with time and with fate, rolls "white-eyed and poisonous-finned, shark-toothed and serpentine-curled," its "crests . . . as fangs that devour." Christ and Mary are usurpers, pale and virginal, but Proserpine's "deep hair" by contrast is laden with those omnipresent Swinburnian flowers. The speaker admits defeat, but knows that time itself shall at last bring rescue in the shape of death and annihilation.

Swinburne begins "To Walt Whitman in America" by asking the vatic bard to sing across the ocean for the English "in the tempest at error, / With no light but the twilight of terror," a phrase that suggests the restless stirrings on the continent of the regime of Louis Napoleon, the Italian struggle for unification, the rise of Germany. Whitman's voice is a "song" with "thoughts as thunders in throng," a "blast of the breath of the west, / Till east way as west way is clear," which for Hopkins would certainly have been no song, but "roar" of "A wilder beast from West than all were." Whitman's new man, synonymous with democratic freedom, is asked to come, with "Eyes trembling, with tremulous hands," to the aid of the enchained spirit of England:

> Here as a weakling in irons,
>   Here as a weanling in bands,
> As a prey that the stake-net environs.

When, when will this new redeemer, this Whitmanian spirit, "this earth-god Freedom," come? For "God is buried and dead to us, / Even the spirit of earth, / Freedom," and men, divine men, are crucified anew. Finally, Swinburne sings the inevitability of Freedom's advent. However long it labors to arrive, it labors steadily on. He also stresses the equivocal temporal sense of "till," repeated five times in syntactically parallel order, with its sense of "until" as well as of "while," of movement toward as well as of end already present in vision. Whitman's song of freedom, bound now in time, gives way to the larger vision of a platonically ideal freedom, a disembodied presence, discovered in an astral eternity, apocalyptic, synonymous with God. While eschewing such Wagnerian immensities, Hopkins manages to achieve the same effect in "Andromeda" with the ambiguity in line thirteen of "then" followed by the infinitive, "to alight," and a present participle, "disarming," so that Perseus's descent, coming as a thief in the night, when "no one dreams," is a direct response to Andromeda's frayed patience. But it is also a response that, while *seeming* to occur in the present time of the poem, is in fact a future action. But because "to alight" is a verb of such swift action, the neutral infinitive resonates, shimmers with action, giving a sense of present happening to what is grammatically atemporal.[15]

Still, if Hopkins's "Andromeda" is so directly concerned with the influence of Swinburne and Whitman, why did Hopkins choose to employ for the first time such a severe Miltonic style? First of all, there was Bridges's insistence that Hopkins write more plainly, more closely in Milton's own style. But there are two other likely reasons as well. This was to be a more public poem, like "The Loss of the Eurydice" of the year before, and therefore needed chastening. And Hopkins wanted to divert his more individual and Romantic style in the direction of a more classical and "manly" style, a quality he sought increasingly as he grew older.[16] A "manly style" was not only his concern, but the concern of a number of critics writing for the established literary magazines in the seventies, such as the *London Quarterly*, the *Saturday Review*, the *Athenaeum*, and the *Academy*, as a reaction against the new aestheticism of Rossetti and Swinburne, what Buchanan called the "Fleshly School of Poetry." Among the "manly" poets, as one critic listed them in "The State of English Poetry" (*Quarterly Review*, July 1873), were Shakespeare, Milton, and Dryden, all of whom Hopkins emulated. So the style of "Andromeda" seems to be Hopkins's reaction to his natural inclination for the sensuous music of Swinburne and for Whitman's longer line: a tightly controlled form as against Whitman's lawless line, and, more particularly, a "chastened" style as against Swinburne's sensuous rhythms.

Hopkins probably saw Swinburne only once, when he took his degree at Oxford on May 29, 1868. And when Hopkins did see him, Swinburne was in the company of Simeon Solomon. His journal entry for May 29, 1868, merely says, "Saw Swinburne. Met Mr. Solomon."[17] Solomon, three years younger than Swinburne, was a member of the Royal Academy and then at the height of his brief fame. Solomon and Swinburne had been carrying on an affair of some years standing, until Solomon, having picked up a casual lover in early 1873, was arrested and imprisoned on charges of homosexuality, after which he was shunned by everyone, including Swinburne (who could not forgive Solomon for his infidelity and did not need the notoriety of his company). Solomon's family were good friends of Walter Pater and his family, and three weeks after taking his degree Hopkins lunched with Pater, visited Solomon's studio, and then the Royal Academy exhibit, perhaps in company with Pater and Solomon.

Solomon is not mentioned by Hopkins again, but he is mentioned here because when Hopkins returned to Oxford in December 1878 and saw Pater, one of the few Oxford people he did see much of at Oxford, he may well have inquired after this bright young man whose star had so ignobly set. Hopkins himself had once seriously considered becoming a painter, but thought that the strain it would have been on his passions would be too "dangerous." Certainly Solomon would have been for Hopkins a particularly sad case of the moral debility to which the unchecked artistic life could lead. Buchanan himself had used Solomon as a kind of ready-made insult, as an extreme type of the fleshly poet, in attacking D. G. Rossetti in his "The Fleshly School of Poetry" (October 1871). A comment such as "Like Mr. Simeon Solomon, however, with whom he [Rossetti] seems to have many points in common...," was certainly intended to mean more than that both Solomon and Rossetti were painters.

Perhaps Swinburne's name also came up between Hopkins and Pater, for back in early June 1873, shortly after Solomon was arrested, Swinburne had written to a friend that "I have been spending a fortnight in Oxford where I saw and spoke with a great friend of poor Simeon's, Pater of Brasenose, who has seen Miss Solomon, and appeared to have more hope of his ultimate recovery and rehabilitation." [18] If Hopkins owed Swinburne a literary debt, so did his tutor, for Pater had told Swinburne, perhaps at the time Hopkins saw Swinburne himself, that he had been inspired by Swinburne's style. Swinburne modestly wrote Lord Morley in April 1873 that

> I admire and enjoy Pater's work [*Studies in the History of the Renaissance*] so heartily that I am somewhat shy of saying how much, ever since my telling him once at Oxford how highly Rossetti (D. G.) as well as myself estimated his first papers in the *Fortnightly,* he replied to the effect that he considered them as owing their inspiration entirely to the example of my own work in the same line; and though of course no one else would dream of attributing the merit to a study of my style of writing on such matters, I suppose, as Rossetti said, that something of the same influence was perceptible in them to him. (*The Swinburne Letters,* pp. 240–41)

It is difficult to believe that Hopkins and Pater did not discuss, at least indirectly, Swinburne's moral impact on the New Aesthetics during their Oxford talks in 1879. In fact, Hopkins, writing from Oxford in late February of that year, seems to couple William Hurrell Mallock's satirical portrait of Pater in *The New Republic*, where he is called Mr. Rose, with Swinburne, when he says that Bridges's poems are "marked with character throughout and human nature and not 'arrangements in vowel sounds,' as Mallock says, very thinly costuming a strain of conventional passion, kept up by stimulants, and crying always in a high head voice about flesh and flowers and democracy and damnation" (*Letters to Bridges*, pp. 72–73). Now those alliterative couplings neatly suggest four of Swinburne's perennial concerns, more so than Pater's. For, as Hopkins knew, Pater was more of a moralist than Mallock gave him credit for. Had he not removed his famous "Conclusion" from the second edition of the *Renaissance* because it might be misused by the "wild" young? It is the kind of sacrifice of art for a higher good, as David Downes notes, that would not be lost on Hopkins.[19] Hopkins mentions Mallock twice in two letters written in February 1879, and he seems to have read Mallock's *The New Republic*, a popular satire in its day. The idea of a new republic, it will be remembered, had been used by Saintsbury in his review of Whitman, and republicanism was very much in the air in England in the seventies with the increasing importance in the British newspapers of America, Italy, France, and Germany.

The New Republic is interesting because it brings together under a transparent fiction so many of the important voices of the mid-seventies: Ruskin, Arnold, Tyndall, Jowett, Pater, and refers repeatedly to Mallock's giants: Tennyson, Browning, and Newman, against whom the newer voices are implicitly measured. Structured in the form of a symposium (after Plato's *Republic*), the figures gather at a country house one weekend to discuss the nature of the ideal republic of late Victorian England. Pater comes in for some rough treatment as the ivory tower aesthete living in the gorgeous world of the private imagination. There is a great deal of talk, but little resolution, although Mallock seems particularly concerned about the disappearance of God. But for all the civilized conversation, the last word is given to Mr. Herbert (Ruskin) and crashes in on us like a breaker. In an otherwise rather tame book, this scene still has an earnestness and intensity which move us. Standing on a private stage with a backdrop painting of a "gorge in the Indian Caucasus," a discarded scene from a rendition of *Prometheus Bound*,

where another mythological figure was chained to a rock, Herbert cries
out to an audience composed almost completely of the doubters, the
atheists, and the indifferent, to, in fact, the informed reading public of
the seventies:

> But suppose we accept denial, you will say, what then? Many de-
> niers have lived noble lives, though they have looked neither for
> a God nor for a heaven. Think of Greece, you will say to me, and
> that will answer you. No—but that is not so. . . . The Greeks never,
> in your sense, denied God. . . . Do not think you can ever again be
> as the Greeks. . . . History, . . . though it seems to repeat itself, . . .
> never can repeat itself. . . . The modern philosopher . . . thus know-
> ing the source of light [to be God] can at once quench it.
>
> What will be left you then if this light be quenched? Will art,
> will painting, will poetry be any comfort to you? . . . [Will these
> magic mirrors] be any better than the glass mirrors in your drawing
> rooms, if they have nothing but the same listless orgy to reflect?
> For that is all that will be at last in store for you; nay, that is the
> best thing that possibly can be in store for you; *the only alternative
> being not a listed orgy for the few, but an undreamed-of anarchy
> for all*. . . . Am I a believer? No, I am a doubter too. Once I could
> pray every morning, and go forth to my day's labour stayed and
> comforted. But now I can pray no longer. You have taken my God
> away from me, and I know not where you have laid Him. My only
> consolation in my misery is that at least I am inconsolable for His
> loss.[20]

Orgy or anarchy for Mallock's new republic, Greek companionship
and the exclusion of culture, philosophy, and manners in Whitman's
ideal, universal republic. "One is inclined," Saintsbury says in his review of Whitman, "for very many sound reasons, and after discarding
all prejudices, to opine that whatever salvation may await the world may
possibly come from other quarters than from America." And this is what
Hopkins's poem also means: salvation will not come from this new
charlatan, this Anti-Christ, this "wilder beast from West than all were."
And Christ *will* rescue his rare-dear Britain, synonymous for Hopkins
with a Britain restored to Catholicism. It is a theme reiterated a number
of times in the poems Hopkins wrote in the middle and late seventies,
as in "The Wreck of the Deutschland" and "The Loss of the Eurydice,"

a hope that refused to die,[21] even in the face of the seemingly inevitable sea tide of influence of Whitman, Swinburne, Rossetti, Pater, and, shortly, Oscar Wilde, the "utterly utter," as Hopkins called him.[22]

There are, undoubtedly, other psychogenetic pressures at work in this poem. So, for example, Hopkins's eye may or may not have caught the announcement in the *Times* for August 9, 1879, of a painting, the *Head of Gorgon*, by Madame la Duchesse Colonna de Castiglione. It would have reminded him, perhaps, of Pater's discussion of the Medusa of the Uffizi, which Pater attributed to Leonardo da Vinci in the chapter on that artist in *The Renaissance* (1873). Of the Medusa Pater had already written that it reflected "the fascination of corruption [which] penetrates in every touch its exquisitely finished beauty." [23] This fascination with corruption Hopkins would have seen in the new self-conscious decadence of style and thought, the new amorality, of Swinburne and Whitman, perhaps in his friend Pater, and felt, as his poems indicate, in himself. It was a decadence in art, tied in the popular mind with a decadence in morality, which many critics were to decry with increasing alarm for the rest of the century while the younger aesthetes enjoyed shocking their bourgeois readers.

Hopkins's "lewd" beast is not, I think, Ireland, but the complex demon of sexual anarchy roaring out of the west. Had "Andromeda" been published in the early eighties, as Hopkins had hoped, I do not think many of its Victorian readers would have understood the beast to be much more than a new ugly threat to Britannia from America, more dangerous than, but akin to, the republican shocks from the east—from France and, more recently, from Germany, like some prophetic "rough beast" slouching "towards Bethlehem to be born." But a close study of the poem's texture, placed against the historical moment in which it was created, reveals other, more revelatory forces and counterforces active in the poem. "Andromeda," then, contains within itself the tension between Hopkins's aesthetic mannerism and his moral conservatism, for beneath the allegorical surface of the poem lies a central Victorian dilemma: the demands of morality and the lure of art for its own sake.

I have attempted to demonstrate here the validity of my hypothesis as Schneider did hers, by an accretion of circumstantial evidence, by a bombardment or, it may be, a mudslide, of possible cultural-historical connections. But the deeper burden of this essay has been to point to a viable method of criticism which has as yet been used only sparingly with Hopkins. It is a method that is necessary if we are ever to have a likeness of Hopkins that will include the man's own backdrop and particular self, and not merely indoors studio work or the Byzantine gold foil of much new criticism, where the poem becomes a timeless and universal artifact. We want the particular man and the particular time and place reflecting each other, an interpenetration both ways.

1973

The Cry at the Heart of
"The Wreck"

When the tug *Liverpool* churned through slogging seas that Tuesday
morning in early December 1875, chuffing out from the Harwich rescue
station into the slate gray North Atlantic, twenty and more miles south-
east toward the Kentish Knock, what was it that its rescue crew and
reporters for papers like the London *Times* and the *Illustrated London
News* saw? They would have seen, of course, the bow of the large
(328 feet) North German steamer, the *Deutschland,* wedged into
treacherous shallows, the stern still lifting and falling like some giant
toy, its screw propellers useless, sheared off in the desperate last-minute
attempt to clear the shoals. They would have seen fishing smacks
hovering near the crippled ship's sides, their crews out early for the
day's take, stripping the ship's dead, those bobbing bodies, of their
purses, wallets, wedding rings, whatever. And they would have seen
some of the sixty and more corpses themselves, either on the ship or
floating on the rough icy waters, dancing with the waves, and one, the

corpse of a sailor, his head gone, swinging with the lilt of the ship's pitch, still attached by his waist to a rope tied taut to the rigging, a bell tolling the just-past storm and his efforts to rescue some now-dead woman or child who had cried out from the deck for help. Once aboard, they would have seen those corpses afloat or sunk in the flooded compartments, and—a rare sight—the bodies of four nuns, one six feet if she were an inch, their blue hands clenched, swaying in the swamped saloon. (A fifth had been pulled loose from that closed circle and sucked out into the water sometime before dawn.) Later, after all the bodies that had been recovered had been brought into the deadhouse at Harwich and photographed for identification purposes, some of the survivors would remember that, at the height of the storm, as the black tides rose over twenty feet, the tall nun, the one who was evidently the superior, had cried out over and over again in German, "O Christ, Christ, come quickly!" until the sea had stopped her mouth. What had she meant? Was it terror? hallucination? a cry to have the ordeal over and done with, as with that body they'd found behind the wheelhouse, its wrists roughly slit?

Sometime the following morning—December 8, the solemn feast of the Immaculate Conception—a young (thirty-one) second-year theology student at St. Beuno's College in North Wales heard and, it being a holiday, probably read the first news dispatches in the *Times* of the wreck of the *Deutschland*. Mr. Gerard Hopkins, S.J., had seen and felt the snowstorm that had covered Wales and caused the *Deutschland* to sail thirty miles off course and into that smother of sand, had in fact slept soundly at the very time people were dropping exhausted from the freezing rigging down onto the deck or into the raging seas. Shipwrecks had always interested him (he liked reading of violent action, he once told his brother Everard); and all this week and the next and the next after that he would scan the published reports of the disaster, would read the demands for official inquiries into the conduct of the Harwich rescue station which had failed all through that Monday storm to respond to the *Deutschland's* distress signals, and he would shake his head at the reprehensible conduct of his countrymen who had been more intent on plundering than on rescuing the survivors. On Christmas Eve he thanked his mother for sending along the news clippings of the wreck. (In her thoroughness she had even sent along some duplicates.) And sometime, probably during the week of the disaster itself, Hopkins had even been told by his rector, Father James Jones, S.J., an

Irishman in his mid-forties, that perhaps someone could, even should, write something about the special circumstances of this disaster, which had seen these five German nuns, a cloistered community of Franciscans from Westphalia, exiled by the virulently anti-Catholic Falck Laws and forced to emigrate to a sister house in Canada, all drowned off the English coast. There had been a solemn funeral Mass for the dead sisters at Stratford-le-Bow, at which Cardinal Manning himself had delivered the address, and the four nuns whose bodies had been recovered had been put to rest at Leytonstone, very near Hopkins's own home in Hampstead. The whole incident had, as Hopkins wrote his mother that Christmas Eve, "made a deep impression on me, more than any other wreck or accident I ever read of." [1]

Father Jones, who appears to have understood the special needs of his sensitive theology student, seems also to have realized that indeed it might be good to have someone write something about the disaster, and even to have suggested—or at least given permission—to Hopkins to go ahead and do some verses. After all, Hopkins had in the past done a few occasional pieces, including, very recently, an Englishing of a hymn (wrongly) attributed to St. Francis Xavier for the Jesuit saint's feast day on December 3. And Hopkins—in the flush of his learning Welsh—had even tried his hand at a version in that difficult tongue of the same hymn and for the same august occasion, though few if any of his fellow Jesuits could have said if that attempt had succeeded or failed.

So here was a man who for seven years now had kept his muse silent, considering his priestly vocation to be at odds with his poetic one, who had done only such occasional verse as his superiors had requested, and who now in the winter of 1875 had received what he interpreted as permission to do something on a much-publicized disaster. Consider that for those seven years of silence his closest and most constant companions had been his fellow Jesuits: novices, philosophy students, theology students, figures like Father Henry Coleridge, S.J., and Mr. Francis Bacon, S.J.; that his daily studies and readings at meals consisted of, among others, Suarez and Molina, Rodriguez, Augustine's *Confessions*, Francis Xavier, Ignatius Loyola, Newman and Patrignani, Segneri and Salazar. Consider the fact that when Robert Bridges wrote, asking him what he had read of Hegel, Hopkins had written back that he had little time for any reading other than his theological studies and that, in any event, he would have preferred Duns Scotus to a—

pace tua—dozen Hegels. Suarez and Scotus have never constituted the average literary staple of British readers and seldom have they served as muses for British poets. They might, some of these figures, rightly belong to the vast, forbidding shelves of required reading for all those generation of English divines, themselves no longer read, but relatively little of all that has found its way into our English texts and anthologies.

And *what* was Hopkins to write, and what form to use? We have little hard information to reconstruct a psychogenetic reading of *The Wreck* poem, but we do know that Hopkins began, by his own telling, with the present twelfth stanza, began, that is, in a narrative mode, to describe the actual events of the disaster as he had learned them from the papers—"On Saturday sailed from Bremen, / American-outward-bound, / Take settler and seamen, tell men with women, / Two hundred souls in the round"—and that he soon enveloped the narrative in the larger modality of the Pindaric ode, as the disaster became a cause for celebration, a victory over death itself. Hopkins knew well that English was not rich in ode literature, but he clearly wanted that form for its formal freedoms and its celebratory tradition. For what had happened out in those deep waters was tragic only if viewed from its dark underside and in the short view. What he wanted, rather, was to correct that partial vision, to stress upon his readers that what had happened might well be cause for rejoicing.

There is in "The Wreck" ode a religious intensity, an emotional force comparatively rare in the English language. Hopkins's poetry, as he himself admitted, must be prepared for, takes some getting used to. Otherwise it will seem forced, strange, indeed even repellent. "The Wreck of the Deutschland" in particular generates the reaction one associates with the kind of intense, subjective religious response one might make in the midst of a long and serious spiritual retreat. Its priorities and sense of reality belong, finally, to that order of experience that to anyone with even a taste for Plato may well be the "truer" order, its news truer even than the truth of the *Times*. Hopkins himself offered the poem only to the *Month,* the literary paper of the Jesuits of the English Province, offered it in fact to Father Coleridge, his "oldest friend in the Society." And when, after holding on to the poem for several months, the editor finally rejected it in September 1875, Hopkins considered the matter of publication closed. If the Jesuits found it too idiosyncratic, then what would others think? If Hopkins thought of an audience beyond his own Lord, it was those British Catholic readers who might, one would have thought, have given the poem at least a sympathetic reading.

Midway through the ode, literally at the heart or "midriff" of the poem, Hopkins, "here all alone" in his room at St. Beuno's, in the very process of discovering his own response to the wreck, finds himself weeping at those events as they stress themselves in upon him. But these, he sees, are tears of joy, joy at the realization of the wondrous ways in which God works even in times of great storm and stress. By a long and intense meditation in the Ignatian mode on the words the tall nun had uttered, her counterstress to the "unshapeable shock night" of the storm, words that had in fact been spread all over England, Hopkins comes to see by degrees their inner significance, their unerring aim, their true inscape. From personal experience and personal witness, he is able to tell not only what that cry meant but, indeed, what the probable effect of the nun's response has been on the others, including the "comfortless unconfessed" of them. What she had felt so intensely there in her last extremity had been the foredrawing of her whole being toward her Lord and Master, as her whole self, now on the brink of dissolution, like some "lush-kept plush-capped sloe," had answered with a *yes* to Christ's stress straining against her midriff. That, then, was the meaning of her cry, the real presence of her Lord comforting her and her sisters, with the storm and its attendant figure, death, transfigured for them in recognizing and accepting God's will for them. In a flash, the storm king has become the solicitous bridegroom.

Hopkins could, of course, respond to the sister's cry because he had already said *yes* to the stress of Christ's terrifying and terrible presence. At some point, somewhere, before some altar in the depths of some nameless night, most intimately, he too had felt God's inescapable presence and had confessed him "truer" than even his tongue could have confessed. So now Hopkins, again pressed to it, can utter in the lexical plenitude of his magnificent ode something of that primal cry. Now, as God's finger touches him anew, Hopkins realizes that it is the same source of inspiration that had touched the nun that night. And that stress sets lexical flecks flashing off from that arch, original cry, that *yes,* that first, best word. As with the original act of preaeonian creation, it is in the selving, the stress of proclaiming one's self, in which the Utterer begets the Uttered, the Word, Christ, *Ipse,* the Sacrificed, that the dapple, stipple, dazzling multifoliate plenitude of · the entire creation is likewise struck off. "It is," as Hopkins wrote in his notebook during the Long Retreat of his tertianship in the fall of

1881, "as if the blissful agony or stress of selving in God had forced out drops of sweat or blood, which drops were the world . . . [creating] one 'cleave' out of the world of possible creatures." [2]

So too with the act of creating the utterance which is the poem, moving by necessity beyond the original instress, the unnameable name of Christ, the Sacrificed, the *Yes*. So too the direction that Hopkins's poetic response will take must also, of necessity, come to "one 'cleave' out of the world of possible creatures." There is, of course, at the heart of this ode, and the reeving or roping in its two parts, the original *yes* of the sacrificed Christ on the cross to which Hopkins had responded with his own *yes* and to which the nun had likewise responded with hers in that storm. In turn, her response had triggered a fresh response in Hopkins, and may well have triggered all those possible other *yeses* of the other shipwrecked souls, and, finally, by an extension outward, the possible *yes* of every reader of Hopkins's publication of her good news. So there is the explicit petition at the conclusion to Part 1:

> Make mercy in all of us, out of us all
> Mastery, but be adored, but be adored King

and the doubling of that petition at the end of Part 2:

> Let him easter in us, be a dayspring to the dimness of us, be a
> crimson-cresseted east,
> More brightening her, rare-dear Britain, as his reign rolls,
> Pride, rose, prince, hero of us, high-priest,
> Our hearts' charity's hearth's fire, our thoughts' chivalry's throng's
> Lord.

One notices other mathematical proportions between the parts of the poem, as one would expect from the poet who fretted over the inner nature of the parts of the sonnet and could see in a tree its sonnetlike inscape. So there is the play between threes and fives, numbers echoing the eternal trinity and the aeonian lovescape of the crucified Christ, doubled in the stigmata of St. Francis of Assisi as well as in the sealing in death of these five Franciscan nuns, as sign begets sign. So, if one considers the stress patterns of each stanza in Part 1 (Part 2 contains an extra stress in the first line of each of its stanzas), we get the following count: 2-3-4-3-5-5-4-6, which splits down the middle into another 3:5 ratio. Again, the middle of each stanza divides around that same stress count. This can hardly be accidental, especially when one considers such lines as "Be adored among men, / God, three-numbered form," or, in the corresponding penultimate stanza of Part 2, the line, "Mid-numbered He in three of the thunder-throne!" And there are these lines as well:

> Five! the finding and sake
> And cipher of suffering Christ,
> Mark, the mark is of man's make
> And the word of it Sacrificed.

We ought not be surprised, though, to find such structural chimings of these sacred numbers repeating themselves in the very placement of stresses in the poem. As with Providence itself, Hopkins's poem leaves little to randomness, to the chance happening. And so, if we continue to look along the line of this 3:5 ratio, we see that one of the structural turning points of the ode occurs in the very center of the twenty-first stanza, three-fifths of the way into the poem itself. There, the plight of the nun reaches its uttermost pitch, as the elements conspire to destroy these "loathed" and "banned" exiles. But, even as it reaches that crescendo, the temporal gives way to the eternal, and the "storm flakes" become "scroll-leaved flowers, lily showers" in Christ's eyes (and now ours), as once again the Word calms the endragoned seas.

So the number five, read aright for (and as) Christ's sake, rings out its inner significance for Hopkins. And the day too that he came to those sisters? Had that been random, without meaning? They had been sealed into their *martyrdom*—for those Falck Laws had killed these cloistered nuns as much as anything—sometime before December 7 had dawned. December 7: the eve of the Immaculate Conception, the "Feast of the one woman without stain." And that fact likewise rings with significance for Hopkins alone in his room in that dark Advent season. For Mary, herself conceived without sin, without the blight man had been born to and that had twisted the heart to lean "unteachably after evil," had been able to likewise conceive Christ without stain.

But there is that other conception, Hopkins sees, when heart and mind, feeling the keen instress of God's grace, utter as one that Word/ word "outright," that is, right out, but also correctly. And so too the nun's utterance, her own conceiving of the ordeal she is undergoing, her reading aright "the unshapeable shock night," brings the bride-groom to this virginal maid and chimes with Mary's own *yes,* her *fiat.* And that primal cry and first stress, echoing the stress of the crucified

Christ, once proclaimed, ripples outward across the foundering wreck in the dark, as word begets word, chiming likewise perhaps—for it is a question Hopkins poses and poises here in stanza 31, and not a certitude —in those other poor souls. Did they too, some of them at least, as their numbed hands clawed against the cold rigging before they dropped heavily into the black waters, did they confess that name somewhere deep within themselves? For Christ, that enormous lover, that compassionate giant, harrowing hell with his man-marked wounds, sweeps down even after the drowned for "The-last-breath-penitent," after any sign of a counterresponse in his beloved, to take him or her home with him.[3]

"You understand of course," Hopkins wrote his agnostic friend Bridges in mid-January 1879—and when Bridges bridled, Hopkins explained his intentions and then dropped the subject for good—

> You understand . . . that I desire to see you a Catholic or, if not that, a Christian or, if not that, at least a believer in the true God (for you told me something of your views about the deity, which were not as they should be). Now you no doubt take for granted that your already being or your ever coming to be any of these things turns on the working of your own mind, influenced or uninfluenced by the minds and reasonings of others as the case may be, and on that only.[4]

But the kind of assent Hopkins was speaking of did not rest alone or even primarily on intellectual arguments (as Hopkins well knew, even if he did not say so to Bridges). It depended, rather, on responding—at whatever the personal cost—to the stress of Christ's own love for the human race in spending himself on the cross. If Bridges could, then, bring himself to put himself out for others, as, for example, by giving alms to those in need at one of the hospitals where he served as a staff physician, then Hopkins was convinced that Christ would not be behindhand in his own counterresponse. Bridges, one gathers, answered something testily about not being interested in donning hairshirts or that sort of thing. Pushed to it, he had retreated from Hopkins's suggestion, as many naturally would, to give until there was some "sensible inconvenience," as Hopkins had put it, to give, that is, till the giving hurt.

It was no idle advice Hopkins offered, for that had been precisely what he himself had done again and again, responding to his Lord's emptying of himself (which was what the *kenosis* Paul had spoken of in his letters came to) with his own emptying of himself. Where was it Hopkins had first confessed the Lord's terrifying yet consoling presence? Had it been his conversion experience at the small country church at Horsham that summer of 1866, while he was studying for his examinations with Alfred Garrett and taking those long, quiet country walks? "It was this night I believe but possibly the next," Hopkins wrote in his journal for July 17 of that year, "that I saw clearly the impossibility of staying in the Church of England, but resolved to say nothing to anyone till three months are over" [5] Was it sometime during the first week of that long retreat two years later at the Jesuit novitiate at Roehampton? Or was it another time? We do not know and Hopkins's ode does not say, though it celebrates from its first word to its last, and in all the extraordinary verbal pyrotechnics in between, the mastery of Christ over his creation.

And what a dapple of language it is, with its rich *cynganhedd*, words chiming against words, all foregrounding the inner radical significations of those lexical echoes. In stanza 8, for example consider the incrementation of *lash, last, lush, plush, flesh, gush, flush, flash, last, first, feet,* as those words move (one would think) inevitably foredrawn toward the feet of Christ, toward the Sacrificed Word, as tongue utters now "the best or worst / Word last!" Consider too how these chimings foredraw toward their inevitable lexical complementation, *lash* and *last* and *lush* and *plush* and *flesh* all brought hovering about that guessed-at *yes,* the *fiat* of Hopkins, the surrender of the nun. And yet, in another of those Christian paradoxes, for all the poem's incredibly rich language, its images of a "dappled-with-damson west," its sea "flint-flake, black-backed in the regular blow," its "rash smart sloggering brine," its May season with "Blue-beating and hoary-glow height," for all this incredibly varied wording and compounding of words, Christ remains "Beyond saying sweet, past telling of tongue."

Until very near the end of his relatively short life, Hopkins would continue to oscillate between lexical plenitude and lexical spareness, counterpointing the starkness of some of his dark sonnets against the verbal richness of such pieces as "The Leaden Echo and the Golden Echo" or his unfinished "Epithalamion." That oscillation, one comes to see, reflects Hopkins's consciously failing attempts to utter what can, finally, only be imperfectly uttered no matter how rich the verbal lode one has at one's command. The opposite tack *in extremis,* one sees, would be to elect silence, and we know that Hopkins tried that way as well, and more than once. One of the things that "The Wreck" ode says, and says so well, is that the poems' inscape, its central significance and "uttermost mark," is the simple *yes* paid out to Christ, to the first word, the alpha of the creation and of this other poetic creation echoing that, to the *Thou* which sits at the head of the ode, as well as to the poem's and creation's last, best word, that signature of apocalyptic closure, the omega word, *Lord*. And so the extraordinary baroque uncoiling of those 280 lines in between this first and last word loops out in its own unreeving to fold back, in an imitation of the great procession of all creation out and back to God, to the primal utterance, that sign, that cipher, that Word.[6]

1976

A Poetics of Unselfconsciousness

In *The Anxiety of Influence* (1973), Harold Bloom, acting as one of Blake's initiates, notes that, if this late in the curve of what is called the Great Tradition no poet can *be* a Covering Cherub, "Coleridge and Hopkins both allowed themselves, at last, to be dominated by him, as perhaps Eliot did also." By the Covering Cherub, that angel forbidding access or return to a state of paradise, Bloom signifies "that portion of creativity in us that has gone over to constriction and hardness," a condition of anxiety where the poet is finally overwhelmed by the pressure of the tradition from realizing his own creative potential. Bloom's view of Hopkins—both here and elsewhere—has about it something perversely appealing in its challenge. It is a fresh reassesment of Hopkins which, in my own critical swerve, might be paraphrased in this way: Hopkins is, finally, one of Romanticism's weaker figures, for fifty years overestimated, lugged out by a series of apologists rather than by critics as the idiosyncratic diamond, the proto-Modern, whose stylistic strategies seemed for a while to outshine these other poets in the Victorian pantheon: Tennyson, Browning, Arnold, Rossetti.

134 GERARD MANLEY HOPKINS

One could, in fact, look at Hopkins's place in the Great Swerve in the following light: Hopkins's poetic father, Tennyson, swerves in his fall to escape the musical language of his father, Keats. In the next generation —Hopkins's own—young Swinburne takes the Keats/Tennyson line, stretching it almost beyond meaning as the iambic is pulled out like taffy into the anapestic mode until it risks the giddy delights of a musical parody of its forbears. Hopkins watches and secretly welcomes this music of his eccentric older brother, realizing that the music of their father, Tennyson, has in fact been altered, realizing too that Swinburne's defection (to the camp of that vulgar, vital Walt Whitman) and his consequent new voice can, with the proper discipline and training under stress, be altered into a brave new style. We have with Hopkins, then, a case not only of oedipal but of sibling rivalry, giving rise to a double swerving which begins to have the complexity of a molecular helix schematized, resulting in a style that, while Hopkins might at times view it as a mirror image of what his grandfather Keats might have done had he lived long enough, is still clotted, constipated, idiosyncratic enough to make itself susceptible to successful parody. Such, indeed, might run the schemata of the *advocatus diaboli* playing his compounded chess game in the mirror that hangs in the critic's closet.

Actually the truth of the matter is both less and more spectacular. Having lived daily half my life with Hopkins, having entered my own commentary on the text, and even, palimpsest-wise, having commented on the commentaries and been commented upon in turn, I have kept a kind of silence now on Hopkins for several years, in part chastened by those gray apparitions warning that one who would dare to speak on Hopkins must listen to the poet for a long time. So I have kept busy weaving on other looms while I waited for Hopkins as one waits to come to term or to terms, watching as the light gathered in the gloom. I suppose Hopkins has come to mean for me what G. K. Chesterton is for Wilfred Sheed or what Virgil seems to have been for his best modern translator, Allen Mandelbaum: a beckoning presence replete with landscape, a way of seeing, a consolation, a check against shrillness.

Having grown older (if not wiser), the commentator looks at Hopkins in the light of the whole Romantic tradition, by which immensity is meant poetry in English since Blake, including such labels and divisions as Victorianism, Modernism, even post-Modernism, and sees in Hopkins not the Covering Cherub—the ghosts of Keats and Tennyson —but a poet attempting to get out from under the Romantic revolution in sensibility altogether; to check the romantic ego, the flaunting Self, and to find a way to sing the divine praises in a time when the singer has accepted it as a "given" that his audience (which includes the artist's Idea of his audience) wanted him to expose his heart, his mind, himself as much as his song. Hopkins found himself in an age of more or less wild romantics—Rossetti, Morris, Swinburne, young Wilde, younger Yeats—where the figure of the Self rings in its shrillnesses and melancholies (and there are genteel varieties of both), sings not only of arms and the man, of love and war, but foremost of itself. By comparison, we find our own fathers almost deferential. And if British poets writing today look at American poets (defensively) as demolition workers smashing the architectural wonders of the past, their sensibilities offended or amused at the sight of Ginsberg dancing nakedly before them, howling out his neuroses defiantly, comically, with great verve, they, more circumspect and reserved, though they sing with the show of a great discipline of the minimal in a minimal key are, finally, in the same camp with their American cousins.

For a long time there have been attempts—by poets and critics—to check and perhaps even reverse the Romantic floodtide with its overriding sense of ego, of the Self as center in our poetry. But it is always an inside job, always the Romantic protesting the seemingly inescapable condition of his own Romanticism. And what Jarrell says of T. S. Eliot —that he was a Romantic desperately opting for a new classicism—is as true of a Zen poet like Gary Snyder or a Trappist like Thomas Merton. And so too with Hopkins, for he was a rather extreme Romantic who, for the sake of his own growth, tried desperately to come out from under that condition, tried to radically alter or "soften" his own ego, to sing the divine praises without dwelling so self-consciously on his own voice. That view, I believe, goes a long way to explaining his silences and his attempts to reshape his very way of singing. It even helps to explain why the poet became a generally despised Jesuit, hoping by that gesture to move as far from the underlying assumptions of his age as the Jesuits themselves were from the center of the vortex of Victorian England.

Perhaps Hopkins's dilemma was, by its very nature, insoluble: if he sang, the song he sang would be distinctive, an unmistakable signature. And there would be, as his particular examination of motives would make clear to him, the danger of dwelling too long on the distinctive contours of his own praise rather than on the One being praised. In effect, Hopkins would be participating in the sin of Lucifer, in love with the sound of his own voice, a preoccupation that had led directly to his own downfall, the Self—in the figure here of Milton's Satan—aware of its fall from grace, yet perversely insisting that at least what was left to it, its own cacophonous scrapings, were its own.

Hopkins makes some extraordinary and revealing comments on Lucifer which can refer just as well to the figure of the artist as Romantic, as Prometheus; we have, in fact, the artist-figure of Milton's own Satan. Sometime during his Long Retreat (the date can be narrowed to November or December 1881), Hopkins commented on Lucifer's fall, a result of an exclusive "instressing of his own inscape," a preoccupation with the self rather than with giving praise to God, the very reason for his having been called into being. Here is Hopkins:

> For being required to adore God and enter into a covenant of justice with him he did so indeed, but, as a chorister who learns by use in the church itself the strength and beauty of his voice, he became aware in his very note of adoration of the riches of his nature; then when from that first note he should have gone on with the sacrificial service, prolonging the first note instead and ravished by his own sweetness and dazzled, the prophet says, by his beauty, he was involved in spiritual sloth . . . and spiritual luxury and vainglory; to heighten this, he summoned a train of spirits to be his choir and, contemptuously breaking with the service of the eucharistic sacrifice, which was to have a victim of earthly nature and of flesh, raise a hymn in honour of their own nature, spiritual purely and ascending, he must have persuaded them, to the divine; and with this sin of pride aspiring to godhead their crime was consummated.[1]

And again, in terms that might apply equally to Carlyle, Whitman, Swinburne, Wilde, and Hopkins himself:

> This song of Lucifer's was a dwelling on his own beauty, an instressing of his own inscape, and like a performance on the organ and instrument of his own being; it was a sounding, as they say, of his own trumpet and a hymn in his own praise. Moreover, it became an incantation: others were drawn in; it became a concert of voices, a concerting of selfpraise, an enchantment, a magic, by which they were dizzied, dazzled, and bewitched. They would not

listen to the note which summoned each to his own place ... and distributed them here and there in the liturgy of the sacrifice; they gathered rather closer and closer home under Lucifer's lead and drowned it, raising a countermusic and countertemple and altar, a counterpoint of dissonance and not of harmony.[2]

Here, then, is Satan's sin. And the Romantics'. Bloom, following Milton (and Blake) sees that poetry, by which he means the English tradition following Shakespeare,

> begins with our awareness, not of a Fall, but that *we are falling.*
> The poet is our chosen man, and his consciousness of election comes
> as a curse ... [that] "I *was* God, I *was* Man (for to a poet they
> were the same), and I *am* falling, from myself." When this con-
> sciousness of self is raised to an absolute pitch, *then* the poet hits
> the floor of Hell. .... There and then, in this bad, he finds his good;
> he chooses the heroic, to know damnation and to explore the limits
> of the possible within it.[3]

The alternative to the strong Romantic poet, Bloom says, is "to repent, to accept a God altogether other than the self, wholly external to the possible. This God is cultural history, the dead poets, the embarrassments of a tradition grown too wealthy to need anything more."

Hopkins's dilemma is just there and may be phrased this way: I reject "the damned subjective rot" (it is his own phrase) that underlies so much Romantic poetry, that crippled Keats, made Blake "crazy," makes Browning sputter, makes Whitman an abomination, drives Swinburne senseless, and makes my own poetry suspect. What, then, is the alternative? How do I escape an excessive indwelling on my own inscapings (here read "poems"), so that I can escape the charge of self-consciousness, watching my own quaint moonmarks, even as I do my part to sing the divine praises?"

Part of the answer is offered in Hopkins's sonnet on Henry Purcell: the singer must keep his attention riveted on the realization of the object. If he does this and does it well, something of his own distinctive individuality will flash or ripple off the song in the act of its being sung. If the singer begins to dwell on his own singing, however, his song falters, becomes cacophonous, fails. Then it is one's sweating self and not the *other* that occupies the central space of the poem/song, and both singer and song fall.

By long attention to its contours, something of the underthought of "Henry Purcell" will flash off, at least in a jagged pattern. Bridges had his own troubles with the sonnet, which Hopkins sent him shortly after he wrote it in April 1879, while he was stationed at Oxford. In a letter written at the end of May of that year Hopkins has to explain not only the argument of the sestet, but the words, *sakes, wuthering, moonmarks*. In January 1883, he finds himself writing out a long prose argument of the entire sonnet for Bridges. And again, that February, he is at pains to gloss the sonnet's opening phrase for him, with its "singular imperative (or optative if you like) of the past." On top of this, Hopkins had appended his prose argument to the poem when he first sent it off to Bridges. The essential argument would seem to go something like this, and Hopkins is of course speaking about Purcell in terms that apply equally to himself: over and above his (Purcell's/Hopkins's) ability to give utterance to the manifold "moods of man's mind," which he shares in any event with many artists, he has been able to express in his art his own individuality, his own "forgèd feature," his very "abrúpt sélf." Intent only on the divine cry of his occasion, intent only on his praise, his "air of angels," something of his very self flashes off him. Hopkins calls these a person's *sakes,* that which marks his works as unmistakably his, "something distinctive, marked, specifically or individually speaking." The simile Hopkins uses to drive home his point is, ironically, Romantic in its idiosyncracy, but, I think, telling to the underthought of the poem. For Purcell is like "some great stormfowl"—an apt description in itself for the strong artist—whose quaint moonmarks on the undersides of its wings are transformed in flight into a colossal smile scattered, flashed, off it. Hopkins's stress on Purcell's great wings raising the artist into his divine "air of angels" is the exact counterpointing to Purcell's antiself, the arch-figure of the subjective Romantic artist, turned in on his own voice like Lucifer himself.

(I think, incidentally, it is the figure of Purcell as counterstress to Satan that explains the importance of the opening quatrain of the poem. Purcell, enlisted to a formal heresy for Hopkins, might seem to have been pulled down with Satan in his aeonion fall from grace. But there is so "arch-especial a spirit" in the man's "divine genius," a whole bent working exactly counter to Satan's song of self-praise, that Hopkins cannot believe that Spirit damned. For Hopkins's own purity of intention in his uttering forth is as much at stake here as Purcell's.)

Hopkins's attempt to escape his own self-consciousness by stressing the act of singing rather than the singer is, of course, still a Romantic answer. For *someone,* even if it is not the poet himself, is still there to notice the individualizing marks of the singer, the special moonmarks on the wings of those two stormfowls: Purcell *and* Lucifer. I am risking understatement when I state the obvious: that Hopkins's style is one of the most Romantically idiosyncratic in the language. And even a touch of Hopkins is immediately noticeable. (There are radioactive traces of Hopkins in poets as dissimilar as Berryman, Lowell, Stevens, Tomlinson, Hughes.) And Hopkins's failure and refusal to publish his poetry had the (perhaps) unintended and ironic effect of throwing the poet's voice back on itself, of heightening its idiosyncrasies.

Hopkins knew his own bitter self-taste, knew it as well as Milton's Satan knew his, and even experienced the perverse joy of being thrown back upon his sweating self. In his verse-play fragment, *St. Winefred's Well,* Hopkins's Carodoc, having just killed innocence and beauty with the slaughter of Winefred, having turned in on himself, rejecting God and that mob, mankind, exults:

> one part,
> Reason, selfdisposal, ' choice of better or worse way,
> Is corpse now, cannot change; ' my other self, this soul,
> Life's quick, this kínd, this kéen self-feeling,
> With dreadful distillation ' of thoughts sour as blood,
> Must all day long taste murder. ' What do nów then? Do? Nay,
> Déed-bound I am; óne deed tréads all dówn here ' cramps all doing.
>   What do? Not yield,
> Not hope, not pray; despair; ' ay, that: brazen despair out,
> Brave all, and take what comes. . . .

Milton's Satan never damned himself with greater force, nor Macbeth, nor Byron, nor Baudelaire themselves. Hopkins, scratching out these lines in Dublin at about the same time he was writing his terrible sonnets, knows what despair tastes like, and even that perverse pleasure that knows the self is damned and knows at least that what remains is one's own.

Hopkins knows this, but does not opt for it. Instead, he opts for the counterposition, for the great sacrifice of Christ, a *kenosis,* an emptying out of the Godhead in the incredible act of condescension that is the Incarnation. The way out of the dilemma of the self then, is to sing in harmony with the chorus. And for Hopkins this means a return to the fountainhead of the tradition, a movement toward the Shakespearean mode (and toward Dryden in his prose), which is the determining and central condition of the English language for Hopkins, a condition anterior to the swervings of Milton, Wordsworth, Keats, Tennyson, Swinburne. Hopkins finds himself returning to a pre-Romantic mode in the very choice of language he attempts: a swerving away from the Spenserian/Keatsian/Tennysonian music toward the austerities of Dryden and the late Shakespeare. And since in fact Hopkins's own bent is for the line and luxuriousness of Keats, he will insist, as a counterweight, on metrical stress, a muscularity grating against his very self. By moving back to the fountainhead of the tradition, Hopkins hoped to escape the more flamboyant idiosyncrasies of his style and to move toward the anonymity of the chorister who lends his voice to the swelling litany of praise before God. To escape his own powerful voice, he endured long stretches of silence, an apparently cavalier indifference to the state and condition, even to the continued existence, of his parcel of songs, at the same time that one detects a nostalgia for that very same exceptional corpus of poems. He knew better than anyone what the self-sacrifice of his poetic gift would cost him, and it helps to explain his impatience with someone like Bridges, who, having opted for his own songs and their attendant fame, did not then push harder to spread that fame abroad. But by the strict, unmerciful logic of his own position, Hopkins could not bring himself to spend time trying to get his own work published. He had chosen instead to keep his attention riveted on his own perfect model: the Christ who had emptied himself at almost every turn, had continually held himself back, had made it no snatching matter to make a grab for what was rightfully his: the Godhead itself. So someone else (perhaps Bridges) would have to notice Hopkins's distinctive markings, his own "pelted plumage under / Wings" and, as editor, sing his friend's praises. For Hopkins there could be no (conscious) song of himself.

Given his very strong ego, Hopkins's emptying out of himself naturally came very hard for him; it takes an incredibly heroic strength to follow to their logical conclusion the dictates of a position as ascetic and unwestern as the one Hopkins found himself in and to alter, in the process of altering one's consciousness, one's very muse for something like the "greater glory of God." Moreover, that position was not made easier for the man by finding himself in a country as unfriendly as Ireland was to Englishmen in the late eighties, when the Star of Balliol, as Jowett had called him twenty years before, found himself teaching classics to a host of mostly mediocre Irish undergraduates and grading hundreds upon hundreds of Latin and Greek state examinations, especially when he knew he was slowly dying and suffering intense migraines daily and yet felt it a weakness to complain about his sickness. Let angels fall from heaven, Hopkins says in a sonnet written just two months before his death. At the least *they* are towers; at least theirs is a "story / Of just, majestical, and giant groans." But what in or out of hell are the rest of us, finally? The greatest of us—and the language is woven inextricably into the lexical fabric of Shakespeare's great tragedies—"blazoned in however bold the name"—is still only "Man Jack the man." Paradoxically—as of course Hopkins knew—the greatness of a man flashes off him clearly in his weakness rather than in his strength, as in the close of the last poem he ever wrote. It is not *his* explanation for his long silences and sparse creativity he offers Bridges. It is, rather, an explanation offered by him *and* his divine lover in a language devoid of the baroque, the idiosyncratic:

> O then if in my lagging lines you miss
> The roll, the rise, the carol the creation,
> My winter world, that scarcely breathes that bliss
> Now, yields you, with some sighs, our explanation.

Those sighs, one comes to see, are working in two ways: they are sighs for what one has lost. But even more, they are the sounds lovers make when they have finally moved beyond the click of syllables.

1976

The Sound of Oneself Breathing

The critical act of attention in this century tends to be eye-centered, with the reader, like the poet, zeroing in on the image, the metaphor, the symbol, the icon. Beyond that is an attention to the sound of the poem: to chimings picked up by the ear—assonance, consonance, rhyme, aural parallelisms. But there is something more, which the reader can sometimes pick up or at least feel is present somewhere just off the screen of consciousness. This ghostly presence suggests the sort of dynamic metaphor felt somewhere along the reader's marrow. It is an image or icon that suggests an activity with its own independence and life. It is a kind of metaphor, really, that goes deeper, goes beyond the radiant stasis of even the most pervasive theologically centered icon to partake of the very act of the poet's utterance. And more, it does in fact transform the poet's utterance, giving that utterance an unmistakable authenticity. Admittedly this is a difficult topic about which to write convincingly, but it is a subject that has shimmered on the fringes of much avant-garde criticism I have seen in the past few years, and it is something to which I should like to address my attention now.

Consider the difficult example of Gerard Manley Hopkins. A good critic of Hopkins (like Robert Boyle, James Cotter, J. Hillis Miller, Elisabeth Schneider, or half a dozen others) could demonstrate convincingly the nearly constant presence in Hopkins's poetry of a dimension of theological iconography acting as a kind of underthought or second voice grounding and underpinning the paraphraseable content of the poem. Two examples of the kind of thing I am talking about may suffice here. Addressing his attention to the sestet of "As kingfishers catch fire," Boyle draws our attention to the homophonic pun on "I/eye," a chiming with very serious theological overtones, instressing as the lines do the activity of the Trinity in the acts of the just man.[1] Here are the lines:

> I say more: the just man justices;
> Keeps gráce: thát keeps all his goings graces;
> Acts in God's eye what in God's eye he is—
> Chríst. For Christ plays in ten thousand places,
> Lovely in limbs, and lovely in eyes not his
> To the Father through the features of men's faces.

What Boyle does with these lines is to point not only to the "I/eye" identity, where the just man "acts in God's eye and in God's I what there he *is*—the 'I' of Christ as well as his own," but to Hopkins's seriously playful recapitulation of the three persons in the Trinity, where the just man, acting as Christ's eye/I, plays before the Father in God's eye/I, lovely in all those eyes/I's not his, ten thousand specific personalities reflecting through the Spirit the faces of the Son in his attention to the Father. That metaphoric yield is significant.

And so is this, an example taken from Cotter.[2] At the close of Hopkins's great caudated sonnet, "That Nature is a Heraclitean Fire," there is the extraordinary incremental chiming catalogue which suggests in its own protean lexical shifts the profound theological idea of death, sacrifice, and transformation, but a transformation that raises the self of self to a radically new cleave of being. Much has been done with this line, and quite ably; but what Cotter adds is the deeper significance of the term "matchwood" in the marvelous close of the poem, where the *I am* embedded in "diamond" is carried to the forefront of the poem:

> This Jack, joke poor potsherd, ' patch, matchwood, immortal diamond,
>> Is immortal diamond.

That matchwood, Cotter sees, is more than merely the kindling that will be transformed phoenixlike into diamond: it is a lexical signature for the Great Sacrifice itself, as this Jack's wood (cross) is made to match his Master's in death. Dying in Christ, he comes to live in Christ. Cotter, especially, has made it abundantly clear to many of us that Christ's in-scaped love—in Hopkins's reading of the world—underlies many of Hopkins's poems, which would seem to have their energies focused on some natural image, some land, water, or treescape. A more careful meditation on the poems, however, reveals a level of linguistic reso-nance, hinting at a traditional corpus of images associated by long use with the Great Sacrifice. Christ's last words, the lance, the gall, wood, nails, the outstretched arms and buckling body: all point toward the right reading of all that Hopkins sees in the fact of creation about him. And nearly all this imagery works by way of visual or linguistic chiming: *these* scenes in nature or these packed phrasal units, as with the poetics of the Ignatian meditation, suggesting the primal theological drama of sacrifice.

What I should like to examine more specifically here, though, is the authenticity of the aural/visual metaphoric complex of breath and inspiration, especially as this informs—literally—the texture, the saying, of the last two sonnets Hopkins wrote: "The Shepherd's Brow" and "To R. B." There is in these last-breath utterances the encoding of a kind of psychological and religious resolution which comes to one only slowly and by degrees. Read aright, they signify not failure but victory. But the critics know, of course, that they are speaking to readers of widely divergent backgrounds, and so must try their best to ground their "findings" in a critical vocabulary that can be understood and perhaps shared.

For me, Hopkins's last two poems form the two halves of a diptych concerned, apparently, with the problematics of human weakness, the loss of inspiration, and the laughable yet titanic struggle to accept or at least acknowledge failure. What hinges these two poems together (poems composed less than three weeks apart) is the complex natural metaphor of human breath. Human breath, that is, as the poet's aware-ness at some level of the presence of divine inspiration or inbreathing—the Spirit's indwelling—and human breath as the sine qua non for all poetic utterance. For Hopkins, as for Milton, the utterance should be the child of *both* indwelling activities: the human, the divine. That is, even beyond the pictorial or iconographic traces of metaphor in the poem is an authenticity of utterance which marks and validates the distinctive presence of the very inspiration that Hopkins has made the subject of these last poems.

But first, by way of contrast, consider the sounds of oneself breathing in an earlier poem that also uses the breath/air/spirit/inspiration lexical complex: the opening and closing sections of "The Wreck of the Deutschland." "Thou mastering me / God! giver of breath and bread." Hopkins initiates that ode, announcing thus dramatically the alpha and groundswell of his inspiration. And, having followed the procession of the word out, the ode rounds on itself, calling at its dramatic climax on the Spirit and on the Sacrificed Word to reveal to the poet what it was the nun meant by her last, frantically repeated utterance before the sea stilled that breath forever. "Breathe, arch and original Breath," Hopkins cries, summoning like Milton before him the Creating Spirit. And then again: "Breathe, body of lovely Death," the repetition driving home the urgency of Hopkins's beseeching. So the nun breathes in Christ's "all-fire glances" and utters the word "outright," signaling with her last breath a sign to "The-last-breath penitent spirits." There has been an intense inspiration, flamelike, devouring, and there has been a complementary expiration with the woman's last breath. It is the kind of parallel that the imagination finds at some level aesthetically satisfying.

Margaret Clitheroe, too, pressed to death, catches, in Hopkins's telling, the crying out of God, "The Utterer, Uttered, Uttering," a superb metaphor for the three distinctive activities of the Trinity: for the Self who utters eternally, for the Self who is eternally uttered, and for the eternal act of that *in*-spiration that coevally partakes of that divine selving, the Self that proceeds from the wellspring of that aeonion Verb. Intent only on that divine cry, intent only on imitating Christ's final yes, Margaret's response is reduced by the extremity of her situation to a counter cry ending like the nun's, in a primal "choke of woe." No matter what glottal, dental, or sibilant, that final expiration is for Hopkins the all-important signature. Still, in both these examples, the metaphor of breath remains largely a linguistic strategy of the logocentric poet, whose distinctive register here is an enthusiasm (in its radical sense of divine indwelling) born of deep meditation, employing the Ignatian exercises as prelude to uttering the word.

As a reading of the corpus will tell us, Hopkins is a distinctively air-centered poet whose tactile imagination is self-reflectively aware of the

very air he breathes in, breathes out. Take, for example, the fine metaphysical conceit of "The Blessed Virgin compared to the Air we Breathe,"
which Hopkins composed in May 1883, while at Stonyhurst. "Wild air,"
he exclaims:

> Wild air, world-mothering air,
> Nestling me everywhere,
> That each eyelash or hair
> Girdles. . . .

It is this very air, as pervasive as grace itself,

> which, by life's law,
> My lung must draw and draw
> Now but to breathe its praise.

The Incarnation itself, Hopkins suggests, was initiated by the fiat of
Mary; by this she was impregnated with the Word; by *this* inspiration,
this indwelling, she could in time deliver *that* Word, distinctive, a
fleshing-forth of that *yes*. In the forward riding of time, moreover,
Hopkins suggests that that indwelling, that inspiration, becomes available to others, since the facticity of the Incarnation continues to touch
people even more closely than the very air we consciously or unconsciously keep breathing in. So we take in air that we may breathe out
airs, as breath is transformed into air, melody, song, word.

Hopkins's use of the air/breath metaphor appears both early and late
in his sermons, letters, journals, retreat notes, as well as in his poems.
But it undergoes a subtle and important alteration in those last two
sonnets. In the first of these, "The Shepherd's Brow," Hopkins stresses,
instresses, the nature of the aeonian fall from grace—Satan's narcissistic
insistence on indwelling on his own beauty—comparing those "just,
majestical, and giant groans" to Man Jack's (and his own) poor gasps.
Hopkins, sick, diarrhetic, suffering from migraine headaches, in fact
dying in the spring of 1889, hears now the sputter and sucking sounds
of his own raspings, each breath a painful recollection of his absolute
dependence on air, that sound serving as signature of his own poor
mortality, and sees that his feverish body is feeding carrionlike off its
own bone-fire. Over and over again, those sick lungs must suck in the

very air that will be expelled as complaint, until, at poem's close, the poet prays that his comic, overly dramatic "tempests" may be tamed. He prays too that his fever, the only fire he is capable of self-generating, may be quieted. The last lines, following the pause, the hiatus, of the Miltonic rhotomontade, capture quite marvelously the quintessence of utterance diminished to gasp, the poet reduced to little more than a sputtering blowpipe hissing out its barely directed flame:

> . . . in smooth spoons spy life's masque mirrored: tame
> My tempests there, my fire and fever fussy.

The emphasis, then, is on the repetitive nature of the rhythm of breathing, and the linguistic counters register that emphasis, moving through an arc that begins with the *groans* of the mighty fallen, proceeding out in a kind of inversion of the aeonian De Processu, the Word returning to its own Source, drawing to its own lexical swerve the terms *breathe, gasp, breath, tones, voids,* and terminating at last mockingly, to the poet's own self-inflated *tempests.*

"To R. B.," however, considers the whole question of inspiration (and, in its encoding, fame) not from the human perspective this time, but rather from the divine side. And the marvelous control, the absence of that anxiety so characteristic of Hopkins's extraordinarily powerful dark sonnets of 1885, testify to this other dimension. True poetic inspiration is for Hopkins, as for Milton (whose lines Hopkins seems to have been mulling over frequently in the winter and spring of 1889), from the Holy Spirit. Rather than a constant inbreathing, however, such an inspiration strikes the mind with the force of achieved sexual ecstasy, impregnating the womb of the very self with the force of an actual, sensible impress. Such tremors, we know from experience, of course will not stay. That "fine delight" breathes when and as it will, often, as Hopkins once told Bridges, coming "unbidden," unsummoned, even unasked for. But the mind *will* harbor that insight, *will* continue to direct it, though in fact the inspiration already contains the dynamics and potential for its own inner development. And though it may take years before the word is finally realized, the Word was already there, waiting.

If by the late 1880s Hopkins scarcely breathes his raptures now, it is because the Spirit seldom moves him sensibly. But in fact his winter world can and does—paradoxically—yield, give up, produce—an explanation that is, finally, not only his but the Spirit's as well. For this sonnet is *their* explanation, and it has produced this final child, this last utterance, this last magnificent poem. Like "The Shepherd's Brow," this poem also ends on a string of strong sibilants. But these *s* sounds have quite another effect upon the reader, the effect here of a quiet and profound surrendering, as of a woman remembering her lover's embraces now she has come to term.

In discussing "The Wreck of the Deutschland" through the lens of "The Shepherd's Brow," Fr. Boyle astutely sees Hopkins as giving over, finally, any illusions of being a Catholic Milton for his time, as mocking himself for having tried in his great ode to "justify the ways of God to men." That seems to me a satisfying way of speaking about the problem of anxiety over the colossus of the tradition. If, as I pointed out some years ago, *Paradise Lost* and George Eliot's remarks about Milton in *Middlemarch* provide several of the key images for "The Shepherd's Brow," *Lycidas* seems in its own way to have informed "To R. B." That echoes of *Lycidas* should float just beneath the surface of this poem reveals in fact part of the poem's underlying tension and resolution. Milton, of course, is a subject that occurs frequently in Hopkins's letters to Bridges and, we may assume, in Bridges's lost letters to Hopkins. Bridges's essay on Milton's prosody, which grew eventually into his important monograph on that subject, was of course well known to Hopkins from its manuscript inception in 1886. Hopkins referred to it frequently, spoke highly of it, showed it to potential readers in and around Dublin, even offered Bridges suggestions on it. In fact, the only extant letter we have from Bridges to Hopkins, dated May 18, 1889—when Hopkins lay dying in the Jesuit infirmary at St. Stephen's Green—is a little note meant to cheer Hopkins up, and mentions having sent Hopkins "a budget of notes on Milton's prosody." [3]

In fact, Milton and Bridges and the whole subject of fame and inspiration seem locked into the linguistic grid of "To R. B." And *spur*, a word that appears only once in all Hopkins's poetry, seems to provide a key. "When I spoke of fame," Hopkins had written to Canon Dixon ten years before, "I was not thinking of the harm it does to men as artists: it may do them harm, as you say, but so, I think, may the want of it, if 'Fame is the spur that the clear spirit doth raise To shun delights and live laborious days'—a spur very hard to find a substitute for or to do without." [4] Of course Hopkins had given over trying to publish his own poems, though it must have rankled deeply, not for the sake of fame, but for what he there called "the loss of recognition belonging to the work itself." [5] Had he not in fact upset Bridges in the very same letter in which he enclosed the sonnet to Bridges by laughing at his friend for desiring fame even as he was publishing his poems in a limited edition of twenty-four copies? [6]

> But the fair guerdon when we hope to find,
> And think to burst out into sudden blaze,
> Comes the blind Fury with abhorrèd shears,
> And slits the thin-spun life.

The blowpipe flame, in Hopkins's laboratory image of the Bunson burner, needs breathe only once to impregnate the imagination. And then what is needed is the leisure, the period of slow ripening. But now, cutting off the chance for any further development: those abhorrèd shears, the fact of death. The corrective to all of that, of course, is the "perfect witness of all-judging Jove," who pronounces lastly on each deed. "The only just judge," so Hopkins's apparent gloss on these lines would go, "the only just literary critic is Christ, who prizes, is proud of, and admires, more than any man, more than the receiver himself can, the gifts of his own making."

What the last poem tells us, then, is that Hopkins has come to accept his very human condition. We might corroborate this from his last letters to Bridges and to his parents; for the first time he no longer seems anxious about unfinished work, about the stacks of examination papers to be graded, about the political tensions in Ireland which had made his five years there such a difficult experience. Instead, he seems to have accepted in the very lay of the syllables of his last poem the historic condition—Jowett's Star of Balliol teaching classics in provincial Dublin—to which his call to duty had brought him. Now, he says (and the word is uttered three times here), *now* his winter world can yield up not *his* explanation only, but the Spirit's as well. Ironically, for the first (and last) time in the poetry, the density of anxious fretting in the introspective sonnets has lifted. One senses that Hopkins has come to accept himself, the apparent failure signaled by his long poetic silences, but the movement of the Spirit operating as well within the poet. Affective and elective wills have for once meshed. The voice in this song is aware of the cost of silence to one's poetic reputation, aware, but willing without anxiousness for once to pay the price. For once, then: something. For once, the poet's breath, haggard and diminished though it is, has responded fully to that "arch and original Breath," as authentic expiration answers, now, as best it can, to authentic inspiration.

1977

Post-World War II Poets

Robert Penn Warren

Since his *Selected Poems: New and Old, 1923–1966,* for which he was awarded the Bollingen, Warren has published three books of poetry: *Incarnations* (1968), the 380-line *Audubon: A Vision* (1969), and now, nearly seventy, he has published a new volume, a long sequence made up of discrete entries, ambiguously titled *Or Else: Poem/Poems 1968–1974.* That is three volumes in six years, years when Warren has also been busy writing fiction, a monograph on Theodore Dreiser, another on *Democracy and Poetry,* a time too when he was also editing an excellent two-volume college textbook-anthology of American litera-ture for St. Martin's Press. Warren is a dean of American letters, dis-tinguished not only as the anthologizer, but as one of those anthologized. He is also one of the very few who has managed to capture a Pulitzer for both fiction—*All the King's Men* (1946)—*and* poetry—*Promises* (1957). And there are other signs of recognition as well: the National Book Award, the National Medal for Literature.

And yet it is hard to gauge precisely the man's reputation in 1975, to say just where the poetry stands today. Over a glass of beer I ask one poet, a dozen years Warren's junior, what he thinks of Warren's latest volume; he is noncommittal, barely shrugging his shoulders, asking me what *I* think of it. Another colleague, a specialist in Southern fiction who regularly teaches *All the King's Men,* confesses that he has not kept up with Warren's poetry. And a young poet—in his late twenties—scratches his head, says, "Is he still around?" One thing is certain: Warren *is* still very much around; he is, in fact, something of a presence. But that is also one of the reasons it is so difficult to get one's metaphorical hands around him, to accurately take the man's measure. There are nine novels, now, a play, a book of short stories, the seminal critical essays, two studies on race relations, ten volumes of poetry, and more. The stiff, magisterial reality of a dictum like *ars longa, vita brevis* weighs heavily on one's shoulders (meaning I cannot read it all), and since the published criticism on Warren's poetry (what there is of it) seems with few exceptions inattentive to the man's real and underestimated importance, the critic is forced back on the poetry itself, a form of collapse this master of the old-style New Criticism would very much enjoy.

A brief look at Warren's *Democracy and Poetry* can help to focus on his primary concerns in *Or Else,* for at bottom the concerns of the essays inform the poems themselves. This is a relatively modest but delightful book, a fleshing out, really, of the two Jefferson lectures Warren gave in 1974 as part of the National Endowment for the Humanities Program. The subject of these lectures, Warren tells us in his preface, is really the grid of interrelations formed by the trinity of democracy, poetry, and the self. For most of his life, Warren has been centrally concerned with the act of discovering himself as a man springing out of a specific place and a specific time. The kind of reflective overview such a man can offer us is invaluable, and I'd like to see this little book done in an inexpensive format for students of American literature; it provides one way into the central importance of the literary "documents" that are our heritage.

It is particularly important to remember the moment out of which these two essays were born. When Warren gave the Jefferson Lectures in early 1974, Nixon was still beseiged in the White House, still denying any central complicity in the whole Watergate mess. At one point in his essays, Warren quotes from the White House tapes; in this excerpt Nixon is discussing with Haldeman how his daughters should spend their time before the opening of the '72 Republican Convention:

President: For example—now the worst thing (unintelligible) is to go to anything that has to do with the arts.

Haldemann: Ya, see that—it was (unintelligible) Julie giving [given?] that time in the Museum in Jacksonville.

President: The arts you know—they're Jews, they're left wing—in other words, stay away.

How are the arts to fare, then, in an America that has moved this far from the leadership afforded by a figure like Jefferson himself? The first essay serves as a review of our literature which Warren sees as a criticism —"often a corrosive criticism—of our actual achievements over the years in democracy." What Warren does with the brilliance and grace that over forty years of teaching has given him is to point to "the decay of the concept of self" which has occurred in the actual unfolding of our democratic experiment over the past two centuries.

In the second essay, Warren documents—at some length—what most of us already feel along our pulse: that the decay of the concept of a real self is related "to our present society and its ideals." This is the reading of a moralist, a conservative in the best tradition of Edmund Burke, and it leads to a discussion of poetry not as a diagnosis of our ills, but as a form of therapy, as a way of allowing all of us to realize our most central selves. Poetry, for Warren, has all along been his "central and obsessive concern." Far from being a superfluous avocation, it has provided him with what it can provide others: a way "to grasp reality and to grasp one's own life." It is the "Archimedean point from which we can . . . consider the world of technology, and indeed, of de-mocracy. And . . . the world of the self." *Or Else* is the latest chapter in Warren's exploration of that self which he has inhabited now for seventy years, a self caught up in time, place, memory, and that other condition we call love.

Or Else, Warren tells us in a prefatory note, "is conceived as a single long poem composed of a number of shorter poems as sections or chap-ters. It is dated 1968–1974, but a few short pieces come from a period some ten years before, when I was working toward a similar long poem." Those few short pieces—seven of them—were first published as part of a ten-piece sequence at the beginning of the *Selected Poems* in the section called "Notes on a Life to be Lived." From *Incarnations*, as he reminds us, he has transposed the two-part "The True Nature of Time." But he has also borrowed his three-part "Homage to Theodore Dreiser" from his 1971 monograph of the same title. Together, these poems make up a quarter of the book's hundred pages. And most of the other pieces have appeared separately in a large number of wide-circulation magazines. I remember, for example, being stunned by the power and timeliness of "News Photo" when I first read it in a copy of the *Atlantic Monthly* in some doctor's office (although as I reread it now, it seems to have yellowed somewhat in a surprisingly short time).

What is new here, though, is the arrangement of the volume as sequence, forming a kind of trajectory like a comet seen at evening, the old poet singing vespers in a time of general drought. Warren suggests both the image of evensong and of parched wilderness in his epigraph to the entire collection, a passage taken from Psalms: "He clave the rocks in the wilderness, and gave them drink as out of the great depths." There are wasteland images everywhere in this book: landscapes (almost all of them American places) the poet remembers or through which he is now passing. Consider, for example, New York in the late sixties:

> Times Square, the season
> Late summer and the hour sunset, with fumes
> In throat and smog-glitter at sky-height, where
> A jet, silver and ectoplasmic, spooks through
> The sustaining light, which
> Is yellow as acid.

Times Square, where old men, coming out of "the hard-core movies" at that hour, stare at the sky, trying not to call attention to their drawers "drying stiff at the crotch." Another American image is Warren's recollection of the last lynching in Gupton (Guthrie?), Kentucky, circa 1915, when some "fool nigger" made the mistake of shooting a member of a posse out looking for him and was hanged by Warren's neighbors quickly if not cleanly:

> When the big
> bread truck they had him standing on
> drew out, he hung on with both feet
> as long as possible, then just
> keeled over, slow and head-down, in-
> to the rope, spilling his yell out. . . .

Vermont in a time of drouth shrinks to a handful of images; it is a time when

> The heel of the sun's foot smites horridly the hill,
> And the stalk of the beech leaf goes limp,
> And the bright brook goes gray among boulders.

And Warren's own childhood in Guthrie in blazing summer is remembered as a small white house, the pasture "brown-bright as brass," singing "like brass . . . with heat," a heat so bright it is "leprous." Or another remembered image—this time from "Rattlesnake Country," of an artificial oasis in mesquite country, where "wicker chairs, all day, / Follow the shimmering shade of the lone cottonwood," and where

> all day,
> The sky shivers white with heat, the lake,
> For its fifteen miles of distance, stretches
> Tight under the white sky. It is stretched
> Tight as a mystic drumhead. It glitters like neurosis.
> You think it may scream, but nothing
> Happens.

One of the most powerfully realized of these landscapes is the image of a black sharecropper's hovel remembered from the Depression. Here Warren slows down the image, freezing it, rendering it immovable, implacable, one of those secret images we carry with us into death, an image stripped of sociological significance, even of philosophical "meaning," and presented instead as the hard thing itself. The force of the image as it unfolds in "Forever O'Clock" demands that the entire poem be read slowly, meditatively, with attention to Warren's techniques for retarding the syntax, slowing the long falling lines until you too think you are in the world of no-time, where the minute hand on the old clock trembles, suspended between one stroke and the next:

> A little two-year old Negro girl-baby, with hair tied up in spindly
>   little tits with strings of red rag,
> Sits in the red dust. Except for some kind of rag around her middle,
>   she is naked, and black as a ripe plum in the sunshine.
>
> Behind the child is a gray board shack, and from the mud-chimney
>   a twist of blue smoke is motionless
>   against the blue sky.

> The fields go on forever, and whatever had been planted there is
> not there now. The drouth does not see
> > fit to stop even now.

This reads like a Zen study in composition, and in fact many such visual meditations are scattered throughout the volume, as though the poet were composing (in both senses of that word) his world as parts of an extended indwelling on the mystery of being, moving logically and inexorably to the final poem, a composition without human figures, the ghost-poet looking out from his livingroom over the Connecticut countryside. He stares out onto a place of trees and blue hills where depth, as in Cézanne's landscapes, is both suggested and denied, where verbs of force suggest incessant motion, activity, the presence of a primitive, insistent life force, where, finally, a hawk, "Entering the composition at the upper left frame" perches and then, "in an eyeblink, is gone." That "is," suggesting being, presence, is the final verb in the entire sequence, but it is immediately negated by the last word, *gone*: "is gone"—presence moving inexorably into nonpresence.

It is this paradox, of a reality so much in flux that what is is always becoming was, that constitutes one of Penn Warren's most characteristic concerns, and that, for me at any rate, is both a strength and a weakness in the poetry, at least when I measure it against the sense of immediacy, of present-ation, that I find in long sections of Pound's *Cantos* or something like Williams's *Desert Music* or some of the younger poets working in that tradition (and even in some of the old Objectivists). You do not have to read very much of Warren's work in whatever genre to see that he has been preoccupied for most of his life with the nature of time and with one of its principle corollaries: history. Consider for a moment the gradual education of Jack Burden in *All the King's Men*, digging into the epic loam for so many Southern writers—the glory and human tragedy of the Civil War—to reconstruct the shadowy figure of Cass Mastern, adulterer, penitent, Christlike noble soldier, romantic icon, dead in an Army field hospital outside Atlanta, defending a society from which he is morally alienated. Or consider the posthumous education of Thomas Jefferson in the commanding *Brother to Dragons* (1953), the paragon of Enlightenment principles coming at last to accept his blood affinity with his own sister's son, Lilburn, who one night in December 1811 systematically meat-cleavered a sixteen-year-old black slave named George, throwing the bloody pieces into a fire.

Warren's ability to reconstruct our past, to flesh it out into a meaning, is for him, as he says at the end of "Rattlesnake Country," "The compulsion to try to convert what now is *was* / Back into what was *is*." And one of the most compelling attempts comes in the central image of his recent *Audubon: A Vision*, in the long second section called "The Dream He Never Knew the End Of," which takes up fully half the poem. That whole section derives from a single incident in Audubon's *Ornithological Biography* (1839), which Warren has included in Volume 1 of his *American Literature: The Makers and the Making*. In this episode, Audubon quite matter of factly describes a night of terror spent in a wilderness cabin watched by a one-eyed Indian, while a prairie woman and her two drunken sons prepare to kill him (and the Indian) for his watch, but who are stopped by the chance appearance of some frontiersmen. I quote at length from Audubon and Warren because we can see here Warren's characteristic concern for translating dead history into living drama. Audubon, watching his "hosts" carefully as he pretends to sleep in a corner of the cabin with his dog, speaks:

> I turned, cocked my gun-locks silently, touched my faithful companion, and lay ready to start up and shoot the first who might attempt my life. The moment was fast approaching, and that night might have been my last in this world, had not Providence made preparations for my rescue. All was ready. The infernal hag was advancing slowly, probably contemplating the best way of despatching me, whilst her sons should be engaged with the Indian. I was several times on the eve of rising and shooting her on the spot:— but she was not to be punished thus. The door was suddenly opened, and there entered two [RPW has three] stout travelers, each with a long rifle on his shoulder. . . . The tale was told in a minute. The drunken sons were secured, and the woman, in spite of her defence and vociferations, shared the same fate. . . . Day came, fair and rosy, and with it the punishment of our captives.
>
> They were now quite sobered. Their feet were unbound, but their arms were still securely tied. We marched them into the woods off the road, and having used them as Regulators were wont to use such delinquents [a euphemism for lynching], we set fire to the cabin, gave all the skins and implements to the young Indian warrior, and proceeded, well pleased, towards the settlements.
>
> During upwards of twenty-five years, when my wanderings ex-

tended to all parts of our country, this was the only time at which my life was in danger from my fellow creatures.

How to recapture that moment, to dig under the prose stratum covering that event, and, like an alchemist, transmute dusty *was* into electric *now,* another of Warren's lexical and ontological signatures? For at the moment the woman moves toward him, Audubon suddenly ceases to be the observer-narrator and becomes a character in the unfolding of the narration, the event itself partaking of fairy tale and nightmare:

With no sound, she rises. She holds it in her hand.
Behind her the sons rise like shadow. The Indian
Snores.
        He thinks: "Now."
            And knows
He has entered the tale, knows
He has entered the dark hovel

In the forest where trees have eyes, knows it is the tale

They told him when he was a child, knows it
Is the dream he had in childhood but never
Knew the end of, only
The Scream.

But no scream now, and under his hand
The dog lies taut, waiting. And he, too, knows
What he must do, do soon, and therefore

Does not understand why now a lassitude
Sweetens his limbs, or why, even in this moment
Of fear—or is it fear?—the saliva
In his mouth tastes sweet.

"Now, now!" the voice in his head cries out, but
Everything seems far away, and small.

But the "event" is interrupted, the mother and sons "trussed up" to await the morning. Where Audubon is devoid of any but the most summary kind of reflection, however, Warren is preoccupied with the artist and sometime portrait-painter instinct in his protagonist. What, really, was the *meaning* of that event for Audubon? The woman, Warren's Audubon comes to realize, will complete the dream which he has all his life been dreaming: the dream of learning how to die. Warren as well as Audubon is spellbound, in fact sexually aroused, by the woman's cold acceptance of her fate:

> Under
> the tumbled darkness of hair, the face
> Is white. Out of that whiteness
> The dark eyes stare at nothing, or at
> The nothingness that the gray sky, like Time, is, for
> There is no Time, and the face
> Is, he suddenly sees, beautiful as stone, and
> So becomes aware that he is in the manly state.

The execution scene itself, hurried past by Audubon, is told with characteristic precision by Warren, who knows how to enact the violent event which is so much a part of our history. "The affair was not tidy," Warren offers with typical understatement:

> bough low, no drop, with the clients
> Simply hung up, feet not much clear of the ground, but not
> Quite close enough to permit any dancing.
> The affair was not quick: both sons long jerking and
> farting, but she,
> From the first, without motion, frozen
> In rage of will, an ecstacy of iron, as though
> This was the dream that, lifelong, she had dreamed
> toward. The face
> Eyes a-glare, jaws clenched, now glowing black with congestion
> Like a plum, had achieved,
> It seemed to him, a new dimension of beauty.

That kind of clarity and moral insight into the human condition in my reading places Warren in some very good company: Hawthorne, Melville, Mark Twain, Faulkner, Flannery O'Connor. But also with Theodore Dreiser, whose gift, in Warren's phrasing, was

> to enact
> All that his deepest self abhors,
> And learn, in his self-contemptive distress,
> The secret worth
> Of all our human worthlessness.

It ties him too with young Flaubert in Egypt, capable of screwing the local dancing girls with a vengeance ("That night three *coups,* and once / performs cunnilingus"), and even of buggering a bathboy, "in a clinical spirit and as / a tribute to the host country," carrying home with him the "trophy" of syphilis. And yet here too is someone capable of praising God that he can observe with precision "the motion of three wave-crests that, / in unison, bowed beneath the wind. . . ."

Time is an obsession with Warren, here as in his other work: the sense of time running out, with its attempts, usually fumbled, to order one's priorities, to somehow grasp the mystery of its passing. Approaching his own end, though in no hurry to do so, Warren keeps swinging back to his own beginnings. Many of these poems are about his own youth, half a century and more gone. In "Time as Hypnosis," he harks back to a snow storm in Kentucky during his twelfth winter, when he walked all day in the strange whiteness: "I looked back, saw / my own tracks march at me. / Mercilessly, / They came at me and did not stop." A childhood Christmas is reenacted in bold surrealistic strokes in a scene where Warren tries to reenter the irrecoverable past to discover his dead, rotting parents waiting for him in "I am Dreaming of a White Christmas." It is a haunting argument that, indeed, we cannot go home again. Several poems, notably "Ballad of Mister Dutcher," "Small White House," and "Forever O'Clock," evoke his lost Southern youth. There is, too, the "mesquite, wolf-waiting," "Rattlesnake Country," remembered images of France, and other landscapes transfigured by lust, anger, love, terror, small deaths. Warren recalls a drunken romp in New Orleans as a young man with two nameless friends when they looked up into the raw face of God in all of their splendid drunkenness and, unlike Housman's Terence, "mouthed out our Milton for magnificence." Now one of those men is dead while the other spends his retirement deep-sea fishing, sometimes coming "back in with no line wet." In these pages Warren remembers the pain he felt at his mother's death, when he stood by her hospital bedside and wondered if he too would, like her, someday have to wear false teeth:

> She is lying on her back, and God, is she ugly, and
> With gum-flabby lips and each word a special problem,
>   she is asking if it is a new suit that you are
>   wearing.

> You say yes and hate her uremic guts, for she has no
> > right to make you hurt the way that question
> > > hurts.
>
> You do not know why that question makes your heart hurt
> > like a kick in the scrotum,
>
> For you do not yet know that the question, in its
> > murderous triviality, is the last thing she
> > > will ever say to you. . . .

There is too the recollection of his father's terrible virtue, an old man with "blanket / Over knees, woolly gray bathrobe over shoulders, handkerchief / On great bald skull spread, glasses / Low on big nose" reading Hume's *History of England,* or Roosevelt's *Winning of the West,* or Freud on dreams, or Coke or Blackstone. How to explain his father's going, his disappearance into the past, that "unnameable and de-timed beast" which lifts its brachycephalic head with its dumb, "magisterial gaze" looking into the distance?

And how to redeem the time, to understand the fact of being, to learn to live well so that one can at least die well? These are very old questions, shared by all, or at least most, of us. One thing the poet can try to do is to keep the past—which annihilates but also preserves—from slipping away. And this Warren does by blooding that past with his words. The other thing, tied to this evocation, is to celebrate the redemptive presence of love. There are few explicit love poems in this volume, although of course many of these poems are poems of concern, for one's parents, one's children, one's place. But two poems in particular are centrally concerned with the man's love for his wife: the exquisitely lyrical "Vision Under the October Mountain," with its vision of a floating mountain, gold in the golden autumn air, and its mode of address, all the more powerful for its slight self-consciousness and indirection:

> I want to understand the miracle
> of your presence here by my side, your
> gaze on the mountain. I want
> to hear the whole story of how
> you came here, with
> particular emphasis on the development of
> the human scheme of values.

But the poem that I find particularly attractive is "Birth of Love," with Warren watching his wife, her body "marked by his use, and Time's," rise at the lake's edge one summer evening after sunset to dry herself. The title refers, of course, to the image of Venus Anadyomene, and this husband and lover, still, out in the darkening lake, sees his wife frozen for a moment in an attitude resembling the goddess's. That moment, he knows,

> is non-sequential and absolute, and admits
> Of no definition, for it
> Subsumes all other, and sequential, moments, by which
> Definition might be possible.

That is the hard-won moment, when meaning falls away and the woman simply *is,* is before she climbs up through the path and is gone. All he can do, the poet realizes, in that gathering gloom, is to cry out from the heart in silence that some star may protect her. In a sense, his own tenuous presence in the poem becomes a problem in spatial composition, for time alone is enough to radically alter one's location: the poet sings and then, in an eyeblink, like the hawk, is gone.

I could quarrel with certain things in Warren I find alien to my own sense of poetics: a sometimes loose, rambling line, a nostalgia verging on obsession, a veering toward philosophical attitudinizing, the mask of the redneck that out-rednecks the redneck. But I would rather leave such critical caveats for others. There is enough here to praise, and I have been given to drink from a spring clear and deep.

1975

CODA: January 1984   When I first wrote this review of Warren, exactly ten years ago this month, Warren was approaching seventy and I was thirty-three. I now feel compelled—it is Warren's achievement over the past decade which itself compels me—to make far greater claims for him than I was able to make then. Like Harold Bloom, I am a late convert to Warren; like him, I believe that Warren's late poetry—by which I mean the poetry he has written since he reached seventy—makes him the foremost poet writing today in the American Romantic tradition. Warren's vision is troubled, cantankerous, the vision of a man who has eaten bitter fruit all his life and who knows that everything he utters will be uttered through clenched teeth. The image, from Jeremiah, is his own for himself. By extension, we his readers cannot have escaped tasting that same grittiness of the fallen self that has so shaped Warren's poetic voice. "I am gall, I am heartburn. God's most deep decree / Bitter would have me taste: my taste was me." So Hopkins, and so, with a vengeance, Robert Penn Warren.

A friend who knows Warren personally tells me that Warren keeps Hardy's *Collected Poems* by his bedside. Whether or not that is the case, it should be. For Warren is clearly paralleling Hardy's poetic example in its most rigorous outlines. Warren's poetry radically changed somewhere around 1960, that is, when he was in his fifties. For his part Hardy turned his attention almost exclusively to poetry at the same age, that is, after reeling from the critical reception of *Jude the Obscure*. True, Warren has been publishing poetry since the beginning of a career that is now sixty years old, and for a long time it looked as if he would be remembered as a novelist (*All the King's Men*) who also wrote some very good poetry. Now it is clear that, like Hardy, Warren is foremost a poet. And it is precisely the work of the past ten years that has convinced me of his greatness.

Since my review was published, Warren has proceeded to publish, along with several other books, five more volumes of poetry. *Selected Poems: 1923–1975* (his *third* selected poems!) appeared in 1976, and contained a new sequence as well as a reordering of priorities to favor his later work. Two years later *Now and Then: Poems 1976–1978* was published. Two more years and another volume, *Being Here: Poetry 1977–1980*, followed the next year by yet another volume, *Rumor Verified: Poems 1979–1980*. And then, in 1983 came his book-length poem in the *Audubon* mode, *Chief Joseph of the Nez Perce*. Together, these volumes—along with the very good work appearing recently in such places as the *New Yorker* ("New Dawn," one of the best anti-nuclear poems so far written, which appeared there in mid-November 1983, is but one example)—demonstrate that Warren is one of those poets whose late poems are not a falling off or even a stasis, but rather an extraordinary late flowering. In this Warren joins that select group of poets who continued to write and write well right up to the last: Stevens, Williams, Yeats, and Hardy. That is heady company for any poet to be classed with, but I believe that in the final assessment Warren must be numbered among these voices.

I say this, as aware of Warren's shortcomings as I am of Hardy's with whom I would compare him in stature. I know what the anti-Warren critics say: that he has published far too much in these last years, that he is garrulous, that his diction is old-fashioned, harking back to an earlier high-Romantic mode, or—conversely—too crabbed, too mannered in the style of Hopkins, that he keeps replaying the same tunes of self, history, and time on the old gramophone, that he is often vulgar, that his portrayal of Joseph, the great chief of the Nimipu, is an embarrassment in which Joseph is made to speak Indian Ugh-talk, that Warren is given attention today primarily because of his venerable stature as encroaching octogenarian and elder statesman of American letters. But if we make the best case for all of these negative assessments, Warren, no less than Hardy, rises above them to take his solitary position of eminence above any other American poet who would attempt the high style of the Romantic sublime today.

Like Bloom, I too do not often feel comfortable with Warren. Not because I am a Gnostic—I do not think I am, though I have been so charged in print—but because I feel uncomfortable with the radical and perhaps not even secular Calvinism underlying Warren's vision. Warren reminds me sometimes of that old Confederate Stonewall Jackson sitting on a pine-rail fence sucking on a lemon, waiting, planning out his strategies. And though he has seen more of the world than most of us will ever see, and has lived and taught in Yankee Connecticut for many years, he was shaped by the old South and, when the chips are down, when he is exasperated by his search for the consolations of philosophy, he will suddenly shift back into the world and language of the poor Southern white. He is looking for correspondences, for some sort of sign of God's presence, asking with the insistence of a redneck shit-kicker (I say this with grudging admiration, a New York City boy recognizing in the Guthrie boy an even greater toughness) if the final sign he has spent his life looking for won't be something like the image memory has dredged up from his childhood:

> Tinfoil wrappers of chocolate, popcorn, nut shells, and poorly
> Cleared up, the last elephant turd on the lot where the circus
> had been.

One aspect of Warren's Southern heritage is the strong, rhetorical and narrative tradition of Southern writing which has informed his poetry for the past quarter century. It has taken me a long time—and much reading of Faulkner, Dickey, and Smith—to appreciate this literary tradition which after all flies in the face of all I was taught to admire in my Modernist masters: brevity, lack of connectives, eschewal of narrative line, the ability to let the image talk (Eliot's objective correlative, so to speak) rather than rely on a poetry of statement. And I still think that some of Warren's poems—like Hardy's—suffer at times from too many philosophical and theological abstractions. But what I have come to see is that Warren has set up a strategy (not unlike late Stevens and Eliot in *Four Quartets*) between meaning and being. That is, Warren allows himself to ask the large philosophical questions so that we may see, finally, after having knocked our heads against the wall for sixty or seventy years, just how unanswerable those large questions are. And then he gives us something else: the consolation of what it *means* to *be* here. So the repetitiveness of the philosophical questioning is most likely part of Warren's final strategy. I have tried and tried, he seems to say. I have listened and I have watched for any sign, no less than Edward Taylor did three hundred years ago, no less than Emerson himself did, but I cannot read the signs, if they *are* after all signs. Coming late in the Romantic tradition, Warren sees himself as a poet singing at evening, like some thrush, perhaps, who

> knows the hour past song
> Has come, [when] the westward height yet
> Stays sallow, and bats scribble
> The sky in miniscule murder, which,
> From one perspective, is beauty, too.
> Time will slip in silence past, like God's breath.

If the bats in their search for prey can be said to "scribble," they write their message on the twilight in a language for which the poet has no key (other than the primitive one of survival). Try as he may, he cannot interpret nature's signs in any finally optimistic sense, and he will not manufacture his answers to console us or himself. At least with Hardy there was a residual nostalgia, the vestiges of a liberal humanitarianism, an old man projecting himself onto his readers as in "Afterwards," seeing himself as one who thought of such natural sights and was at home there. Warren's stance in these late poems is more like

Larkin's in "Aubade," an old man staring at the ceiling of his bedroom in the dark, waiting for the light of predawn to enter the room
so that he can witness at least one more precious day. He is afraid,
though he does his best to cover that fear over for his family's sake.
But the darkness is so very deep and no past glory, no past memory of
love or anger or even of violence can sustain him for long. He wants
the feel of reality, not of dream, and that reality takes the same shape
that it took for Dr. Johnson: the plash of cold water, stroke on stroke,
the sharp zing of a tooth cracking, the incessant drip drip of a Vermont
thaw signaling the coming of another season. In his own poem, "After-
ward," clearly modeled on Hardy's, Warren, having looked at the cold
options of glacier and night desert open to him, chooses instead the
warmth of company where, after a time at least, some sort of trust
and mutual comfort is possible. Even the great poet is, after all, a
human being like the rest of us. At the close, then, not more light, but
more warmth.

And yet Warren has come to understand that the past need not be
only a burden, for it too—as Eliot saw—can sometimes redeem the
present emptiness. Increasingly as Warren has grown older, images of
his childhood and his youth crowd on him, becoming more vivid than
most of the present. So, in "October Picnic Long Ago," the poem that
opens *Being Here,* Warren remembers a picnic with his family which
took place seventy years ago. He himself was six, then, and he recalls
his father talking about the future, as men will, when his ship would
finally come in. But his mother knows better. She knows that if she
is to have happiness, it will have to be in the present, in what she now
possesses. Even then, of course, this time-obsessed poet knows, the
future was lying in wait, for the moment only chained up like some
mad dog, while the mother—happy in the October day and in her family—sang. Now of course his mother and father and most of his friends
are dead, as Warren's other poems tell us, and the poet is—willy-nilly
—the late solitary singer singing of what is as night comes on.

It is instructive to consider the poem that closes this volume, for
Warren has deliberately and subtly juxtaposed that past image of childhood innocence and lyrical blessedness with the image of the poet now,
alone, walking in the New England woods at night. He has been walking a long time, thinking of a warm hearth and of someone to receive
him, though he has been out so long now that he is not sure that there
even is such a thing as a destination any more. He passes someone in

the dark and wishes him well, though that other is probably—and eerily—none other than himself. The final sounds in this poem belong not to the poet or to his mother but to nature itself, and if we do not know what they mean, it is probably just as well. For what, if anything, are we to make of the "crack of bough burdened with snow" and the dubious benediction of the owl, one of Warren's predators—like the hunter God he often invokes. The world has grown more and more present to Warren with time, so much so that not only have the animals and birds become more prominent, but the weather itself, and the trees and the very rocks, which soon he knows he must join forever. Warren has an image of his father, reading philosophy as he sits wrapped up against the cold. And he is his father's son, one of those in search of meaning and scanning the text of the world for signs. But even more so, in these late poems, he has come to appreciate what it was his mother taught him early, to sing while there was still time to sing.

It would take a monograph to say what needs to be said about Warren's achievement, his honesty of diction, his uncanny ability to flesh out in precise imagery such concepts as time and history and self, his range of language, from a language very much in the demotic American grain (in Williams's sense) and moving up to the sublime, and finally, his ease and surety in employing a panoply of poetic forms. And this note is only intended as the coda to an earlier essay review. But I want to end by looking at one of the great poems of our time and one that embodies, incarnates, the native sublime for us. It is a poem that Bloom has already singled out for praise: the poem that concludes the volume, *Now and Then:* "Heart of Autumn." It is fall and the great geese are heading for warmer waters, though some of them—thanks to the hunters—will never reach that destination. Death comes unexpectedly; the wounded geese do not even know what has happened to them. Unbeknown to them, the poet suddenly realizes with a shutter, they are enacting his own story. For they have risen into the autumn skies to cry out with their "imperial utterance," calling out the joy of their nameless tragic destiny. In this, the poet has come to understand, they seem to know more perhaps than the poet knows about himself. And if it is the path of some inner logic, this pull to the south, or merely the path of folly, where the hunter lies in wait, what matter finally? What does matter is the great wing beat across the heavens. Wing beat, high beat, the poet hears and for a moment imagines himself transformed and following in their wake. And now his heart

is impacted with a fierce impulse
To unwordable utterance—
Toward sunset, at a great height.

Only a great poet could have uttered these lines, a cry beyond the human while yet partaking of our humanity. Approaching eighty and his own sunset, Warren has mastered a great height.

1984

Charles Tomlinson

In an issue of the *Review* a few years back, there was a cartoon of
the English poet Charles Tomlinson sporting a Mexican sombrero and
poncho, looking somewhat stiff and uncomfortable in such foreign
garb.[1] He has been made to look there very much like the English
tourist on holiday in New Mexico. It is, of course, of the very nature
of cartoons to flatten out and exaggerate in order to make their point,
and the point here is that Tomlinson reversed what had been, until
his generation (with a few notable exceptions), the acceptable manner
of things: New World neophytes settling, like James, Pound, H. D., Eliot,
in London as the most natural place to learn their craft. Instead, Tomlinson has come to the New World in search of becoming, at least in
terms of his craft, more "Americanized." This exchange has proved
to be, however, a somewhat risky affair. We have, for measure, the
earlier examples—and only partial successes—of Lawrence and Auden,
who also attempted to export American homemade goods, and Tomlinson, with a great deal of good will, seems to have grafted the new onto
the old stock with mixed results.

Nonetheless, Tomlinson may yet prove to be—for he is just fifty—what Calvin Bedient has described him as: "the most considerable British poet to have made his way since the Second World War." [2] If a term like "considerable" tends to wobble, however, Tomlinson is, truly, a prodigious observer—of nature, of artifact—possessed of the painter's acute eye for design that we particularly associate with the Ruskin of *Modern Painters* and with Hopkins in his journals. For twenty years Tomlinson has set himself squarely against the English voices we evoke most readily when we consider poetry written in Great Britain since Dylan Thomas's untimely departure from the scene. This difference was most marked in the fifties, when Tomlinson spoke out repeatedly against the rhetorical resonances of New Apocalyptics like Thomas and Barker as well as against the prevalent *Kulturbolschevismus,* the "common style" of poets like Larkin and Amis. These latter two Movement writers, made very much aware of an England greatly diminished in grandeur, of an island nation besieged by the cries of nationalism at its own doors and reminded daily of its drab industrial sprawl and its blighted pastoral landscapes, had become by the late fifties the recognized spokesmen of Tomlinson's generation. To further isolate and make himself even more "unseasonable" (the term is Bedient's), Tomlinson turned his back on what he considered other excesses: those associated with the Liverpool scene and the Beatles, as well as those being championed by the British critic A. Alvarez in the sixties, the American confessionals.[3]

Constitutionally, Tomlinson is quiet, reflective, meditative, a poet in some ways like Larkin, who also distrusts excesses of any kind: apocalyptic moments, trombone finales. He is a poet of true intellectual powers, a classicist, really, whose natural affinities seem closer to the late Augustans, and to Donald Davie and Yvor Winters in our own time. This essential reserve, however, this kind of latter-day poetic Toryism, has—at least in my reading of the poetry—acted as a weakness as well as a strength. When Tomlinson was still in his mid-twenties and looking hard for suitable models, he began to read seriously and to champion several of the American modernists, including, most notably, Stevens, Pound, Marianne Moore, and Williams—figures, as he has called them, of energetic contemplation. Some of these influences are readily apparent in any reading of Tomlinson's poetry, and anyone who has even thumbed through *The Necklace* (1955) will feel that he or she has entered into a strange, still, imagistic world that looks very much like the world of Stevens's

"Thirteen Ways of Looking at a Blackbird." For lines like the following are consciously playing with the contours and rhythms of Stevens's "The Snow Man":

> when the truth is not good enough
> We exaggerate. Proportions
>
> Matter. It is difficult to get them right.
> There must be nothing
> Superfluous, nothing which is not elegant
> And nothing which is if it is merely that.[4]

Thus, about a dozen years ago, Tomlinson exported a product as recognizably "American" as the variously called staggered tercet, three-ply step-down line, or triple-decker, which we associate with Williams's late phase. Williams first used the staggered tercet in the "Descent" passage in *Paterson* 2 and perfected it in such classic pieces as "Asphodel, That Greeny Flower," "The Ivy Crown," and "To Daphne and Virginia." We know by now, of course, that Williams himself had the examples of Mayakovsky and of Pound's translations of Guido Cavalcanti's *Donna mi priegha* as models for the staggered tercet, but it was Williams who, for us, made the form his own.[5] Making it his "own" should not, of course, be construed to mean that no other poet can use it, but that it has its own internal structures, its own poetic logic, which cannot be indefinitely reworked and still be expected to function as a form.[6]

Tomlinson, in a gesture of homage, attempted in *A Peopled Landscape* (published in 1963, the year Williams died) to adapt Williams's tercets and make them his own. Hayden Carruth, however, reviewing Tomlinson's volume for *Poetry,* was particularly upset that anyone, much less an Englishman, should have tried to use this form.[7] But Carruth missed the point, I think, for Williams's aim was to extend the limits of the poetic line and to pass it on as part of a heritage springing out of his own experience with the American language, formalized into a variable pattern. The fact that Tomlinson experimented with the pattern only in this one volume and in his contemporaneous book of translations from Machado suggests that he had achieved the modest success he may have been looking for.[8]

It is not really surprising that Tomlinson should have tried this form, for it is Williams's poems written in staggered tercets, with their meditative pace, their sense of ceremony, and even, in Tomlinson's sense, their civility, that have most appealed to the British. In fact, if one were pressed to point to the one poem that most Englishmen might "safely" enjoy—in a country where Williams's works have met with only mild success, and then only since the poet's death—that poem would be "Asphodel." Certainly, the few reviewers who even deigned to notice Williams in the sixties when his work finally found a British publisher, pointed to the grace, to the "traditional" qualities of this late poem. Finally, they said, this American had come round to their way of thinking. He had ceased his long, weary search for an American language and American forms and had entered at last into the venerable English meditative tradition. In short, they were still not hearing Williams's distinctive voice, nor had they managed to chart his particular homegrown strategies.

Admittedly, Williams's staggered tercets look easy to imitate. What makes the form distinctive, however, is the masterful sense of open-ended meditation, of mellow rambling counterpointed sharply against a grid of hesitancies, so that we get the sense of a mind quietly but desperately seeking the fiction of an inner peace. This, decidedly, is not Tomlinson's own cast of mind: his intellectual powers are sharper, colder, more disciplined, more self-evidently in control of the utterance. There is in much of Tomlinson's work the sense of a finely controlled desire for the formal means necessary to modify his own poetic line, a means he does not seem to have been able to find among his own British contemporaries, so that he has turned to the older generation of American poets. When, however, he used a form as distinctive as the staggered tercet, what he wanted was a "propriety of cadence," a measure he could adapt to reinforce, shore up, what with hindsight looks like a conservative pastoral vision. The result is that these step-down lines feel peculiarly artificial when measured against Williams's best poems in the mode.

Compare, for example, Williams's "Address" from *Journey to Love* (1955) with Tomlinson's "The Picture of J. T. in a Prospect of Stone," from *A Peopled Landscape*. Both poems use the staggered tercet, and both are addresses of sorts: Williams's to his younger son, Paul, then in his late thirties, and Tomlinson's to his young daughter. Consider, too, that Williams was in his early seventies, near the end of his career when he wrote his poem, and that Tomlinson was only in his mid-thirties and at the beginning of his when he sketched his "Picture."

Moreover, a man gives advice to another man, even a son thirty years his junior, with more deference and tentativeness than he uses when he is addressing, even indirectly, a child. Still, a close comparison of how each poet uses the step-down line should be instructive.

The voice we hear in Williams's "Address" is tentative, uncertain, the syntax itself reflecting the sense of a man who feels he must say something, but is uncertain of exactly what it is he must say. Williams begins the poem with an address seemingly directed not so much toward his son as—at a step removed—to a look "approaching" despair he has caught in his son's eyes. It is a look he knows well, he admits, for he has seen it reflected "in the mirror," has seen it, too, in other men and women. Apologetic, hesitant at this intrusion on his son's privacy, he still knows he must say something, however haltingly, as hesitancy shifts to hesitancy, verbal qualifiers extending out from the main trunk:

> To a look in my son's eyes—
>   I hope he did not see
>   that I was looking—
> that I have seen
>   often enough
>   in the mirror,
> a male look
>   approaching despair—
>   there is a female look
> to match it
>   no need to speak of that. . . .[9]

How much is confessed here, and yet how much is left unstated. What, for example, does Williams mean by that "female look" of despair? That he has seen it in the eyes of his own wife? In the eyes of his son's wife? The "meaning" here reduces to this: "To a look in my son's eyes . . . [a look] that I have seen . . . in the mirror." The rest is an attempt, a purposely failing attempt, to say what he cannot adequately say, or will not say. That inadequacy, that pressure felt along the line itself of a man forcing an unwilling self to get said what must be said as he approaches death, that pressure of words pushing fitfully forward in starts, qualifiers, asides, is the exact opposite of the kind of rhetorical assurance and formal control we will find in Tomlinson's poetry.

The look he sees there in his son's eyes, Williams says, is like the look that Bobby Burns must often have had in *his* youth, a look which "threw

him / into the arms / of women" (JL, 30). It is an oblique confession
of the poet-father to the son, a confession of unhappiness in which father and son, and presumably men of all ages, have shared. Men act like
this—with abandon—to forget their despair, Williams explains to his
son,

> not defiantly,
> but with full acceptance
>   of his lot
> as a man. . . . (JL, 30–31)

For all his excesses, whatever they were, Burn's wife forgave him—as,
presumably, Floss has forgiven Williams, or as his son's wife will forgive his son—when he was

> too drunk
>   with Scotch
> or the love of other women
>   to notice
> what he was doing. (JL, 31)

Yet there is nothing that can erase that look. Not war, not even money.
What does remain, however, is a kind of difficult integrity such as that
which Williams insists Burns (and Williams himself) maintained. For
while Burns wrote some of his most beautiful songs for other women,
they were "never for sale."

Williams begins by addressing his son, opens the field of the poem
to include himself—and by extension other men, other women—and finally focuses on the figure of Burns, another singer and married lover
like Williams. So the poem ends with a kind of oblique confession in
which one senses that, despite the feeling of openness and frankness,
more has been left unsaid than said. It is the integrity to one's sense of
oneself, finally, that Williams stops on—"stops on" rather than "stands
on" because the sense of an ending here is tentative, with the tentativeness and momentary resolution of a person in the act of addressing another in what must be an ongoing process. Williams's conclusion is un-
sure of its own conclusiveness. In short, the strength of Williams's
staggered tercets seems to lie, paradoxically, in their tentativeness, in
their apparently artless vulnerability.

Once we understand the inner tension of the staggered tercets—the
way the syntax gropes across the line breaks with a stumbling prosaic

grace—then the line can indeed be used by other poets. Tomlinson's whole sensibility, however, his entire intellectual constitution, is foreign to this kind of utterance. I can think of no major British poet—except for Hopkins and Larkin in certain moments of intense private stress—who would not feel embarrassed and uneasy with the kind of voice I have described in "Address."

Tomlinson himself has told us what he was looking for in the staggered tercets in his "Letter to Dr. Williams," published in *Spectrum* in 1957, where he praises Williams for his

> propriety of cadence
> that will pass
> into the common idiom
> like the space
> of Juan Gris
> and Picasso. . . .[10]

It is a form with its analogue in the spatial angularity and fragmentation of cubism, a form "invented to be of use" for the "rearticulation / of inarticulate facts." [11] Here, in fact, the young Englishman himself makes it clear that his own intentions are no doubt different from Williams's—since propriety of cadence does not alone adequately describe the staggered tercet—but that the form itself is flexible enough to allow other voices to fit into it. And yet, one may ask, how far can one stretch or contract even a variable measure before it loses its elasticity and becomes brittle?

At Hugh Kenner's suggestion, Tomlinson began a correspondence with Williams in December 1957, shortly after he wrote his poetic "Letter" to Williams in staggered tercets.[12] He was out, he said, to be the second Englishman—the first being D. H. Lawrence—to read Williams correctly. Since part of that reading focused on the ability to use Williams's step-down lines, it is interesting to watch Tomlinson's changing attitude toward them. At first, Tomlinson is aware only of what he calls his own "technical incompetence" in trying to use what is, he admits, Williams's own form. He recognizes, too, that part of the difficulty resides in his being an Englishman, raised on a different tradition, a different kind of cadence. But by mid-1960, having a dozen or so poems in the step-down line, he is convinced that the line will work just as well for an Englishman as for an American, and that the secret lies in reading the foot as a breath unit, as Olson had said ten years earlier in his "Projective Verse" essay. The real matrix for Tomlinson shifts from Williams to the Wordsworthian meditative line, and the proof Tomlinson needs is in reading Wordsworth's blank verse lines as already containing the triple cadences of the three-ply variable foot. For Tomlinson, therefore, the aim must be to marry the iamb to the variable foot. In other words, as he hears them, the staggered tercets resolve themselves back into the traditional iambic pentameter; they are ultimately variations on the blank verse line. For this reason Tomlinson uses the three-ply line in his translations from Machado (1960), since, for him, the standard iambic measure can and does play nicely "across and into the movement of the variable foot." And there is the crux: whether or not Williams's staggered tercets are essentially blank verse lines filed under another name.

Recall for a moment how for many years Williams himself inveighed against the old, inherited English forms, those forms for which he used the term "sonnet" as his metonymical signature. But, he warned, there were other, more pernicious influences, such as the all-pervasive blank verse line (the trouble was that when you used it, as Stevens's practice had shown, you felt compelled to say something important) and within that line the tyranny which the iambic measure imposed.[13] So, for example, in the forties Williams pointed repeatedly to the young Auden, Tomlinson's precursor by twenty years, as the figure of the Englishman who had come to the New World in search of a new line. In his lecture "The Poem as a Field of Action" (1948), Williams insisted that Auden had come to America because England could no longer supply him with the poetic means he needed were he to continue to develop as a poet.[14] And though Williams was kinder to Tomlinson, praising his 1958 volume, *Seeing Is Believing*, for its division of the "line according to a new measure learned, perhaps, from a new world," [15] there were no examples of the staggered tercet in that volume.

Anyone who has read even cursorily Tomlinson's eight books of poetry knows that there is indeed in his lines a propriety of cadence that belongs very much to the older English tradition: to Pope, Johnson, and especially Wordsworth, a measure that remains constant whatever the American influences on his poetry. Along the way, Tomlinson has listened to Pound, for example, especially the Pound of the Chinese cantos and the Confucian translations. He has listened to the syllabics and delicate cut-glass chimings of Marianne Moore; has listened, too, to the meditative patterns in Stevens. And he has listened, of course, to Williams. But Williams becomes strangely muted, a pensive Wordsworthian, finally, if we hear only Tomlinson's proprieties of cadence and not a voice twisting its slow way to its fitful conclusions, discovering flashes of resolution in the very process of the poem's unfolding.

Thus, Tomlinson's "Picture of J. T. in a Prospect of Stone" is much more sure of itself, much firmer than a poem like "Asphodel." Its very title, recalling Andrew Marvell's "The Picture of little T. C. in a Prospect of Flowers," points to the poem's real allegiances, and its ceremony of address, its playful balancings between lightness and seriousness—so much like the image of light playing off stone that is a favorite of Tomlinson's—suggest the Yeats of a poem like "A Prayer for My Daughter" more than Williams. The mode here in Tomlinson is dialogic, the poet asking and assuredly answering his own questions in a version of genial catechesis, as he muses over the kind of gift he would wish for his little daughter. What the eye sees, of course, is the shape of the staggered tercets, but what strikes the ear are the older verse forms deeply imbedded in the new, more flexible lines:

> to prove
> its quality the better and
> thus learn
> to love
> what (to begin with)
> she might spurn.[16]

The lines will not stay in this unstable solution (though the *prove-love* rhyme keeps the line slightly askew) but must rearrange themselves into heroic couplets such as Marvell might have given us:

> to prove
> its quality the better and thus learn
> to love what (to begin with) she might spurn.

Again, examine the final eight lines of the poem, with their syntactical and metrical regularity—

> —And so she shall
> but let her play
> her innocence away
> emerging
> as she does
> between
> her doom (unknown),
> her unmown green (PL, 18)

—and another pattern of loose octosyllabic couplets may be revealed:

> And so she shall but let her play
> her innocence away
> emerging as she does between
> her doom (unknown), her unmown green.

The eight lines contain three rhyme sets—*play-away*; *between-green*; *unknown-unmown*—giving to the lines the effect of a slight double focus. In addition, the sense of an ending is contained within the limits of that final, balanced sentence, with its nice analogue between his daughter's intimation of mortality and the long lovely years still ahead of her, as the poet captures her in this frozen moment stepping lightly across

> a sheep-stile
>   that divides
>   village graves
> and village green . . . (PL, 17)

There is in this pastoral a good deal of wry humor, the play of the intellect across an idea that we associate with an older, vanished world order: a world of ceremony, remnants of which Yeats found in Renaissance Italy and even in eighteenth-century Dublin, and traces of which Tomlinson, in his turn, finds now in Yeats, as he himself confronts a world that is destroying its architectural forms and aging monuments to the past at an alarming rate. But Tomlinson's short-lived experimentation with the Williams triad may, in the long run, have helped him to loosen his own rhythms and to return to a blank verse mode now notable for its delicate suspension, its phrasal modification, its hesitating stresses. Paradoxically, then, it may well be Tomlinson's contact with American free verse that has helped him to "hear" the voices of his own English fathers—Marvell and Pope and Wordsworth—more clearly.

Yet if Tomlinson's appropriation of the staggered tercet has been only partially successful, he has succeeded in taking over and making his own the short, clipped line which we also associate with Williams and the Objectivist poets Zukofsky and Oppen.[17] Tomlinson has in fact managed to appropriate the short, jagged line, with its tonal hesitations and its play of phrasal unit against linear segmentation, and to have made it as much his own as a poet like Robert Creeley in another way has made that pattern register *his* linguistic preoccupations. I mean specifically the kind of lines using either isostanzaic patterns or irregular paragraphs which we find in Williams as early as *Al Que Quiere!* and as late as *Pictures from Brueghel,* and which we find Tomlinson using with assured mastery in a volume like *American Scenes.* Consider, for example, the phrasal modulations, the line control, the finely tuned sense of the comic in the exquisitely told anecdotes of "Mr. Brodsky" and "Chief Standing Water." That mode obviously fits comfortably on Tomlinson, for he has continued to wear it, shaping it to his own specific needs. He employs this form masterfully in one of the most harrowing poems I have come across in a long while, the poem "Underground," which is too long to quote effectively here, since its sinuous continuities do not easily admit of dismemberment, even for scrutiny's sake. Ostensibly, this is a poem about one of those nameless characters one is bound to come up against if one rides the subway, tube, metro, or underground long enough. In this case we find ourselves staring at a tall woman, face toward the wall, as she sings and dances to herself, indifferent to the crowd of spectators which has assembled to watch her, the poet among them. Even when she finally gets on the train, she continues to stand, face toward the door, singing snatches of improvised blues amidst choked incoherencies. The observer, drawn by this figure, moves toward a comprehension that he is witnessing here a radical metonymic signature for the human condition and perhaps even more specifically for the orphic poet—that curious anomaly—and strains to get a glimpse of her face, of that which will identify and individualize her. But he cannot, can do nothing more than watch her beat time on the closed door panes of the subway car, where "the metal frame / masking the rest of her," / helps reduce her to a voice raised in distracted song, a flexed mouth "fulminating its song / into the tunnel."

But the most characteristic signature in Tomlinson is the exquisite modulation and clarity of observed detail he achieves when he works the blank verse line, adding as he does so to the manifold possibilities of that line as it continues to swerve in its downward trajectory from Wordsworth, Hardy, Auden, and Wallace Stevens. Consider, for example, the sensitive registration of phrasing in two pieces like "The Witnesses" and "Hill Walk," the latter of which ends with these shimmering, tremulous lines evoking a delicate memory of Provençal landscapes and ruined (Albigensian?) fortifications in early spring:

182 POST-WORLD WAR II POETS

> We contemplated no assault, no easy victory:
> Fragility seemed sufficiency that day
>   Where we sat by the abyss, and saw each hill
> Crowned with its habitations and its crumbled stronghold
>   In the scents of inconstant April, in its cold.

Or consider the sharp brilliance of a poem like "Swimming Chenango Lake," which manages to move beyond the limits of meditation into something like a ritualistic participation with the nonhuman other, the primal element, a "naked" reality. I do not see how any but a very few of those present at the convocation exercises at Colgate in May 1968, where Tomlinson first read his poem, could have grasped the poem's ontological precisions, regardless of how many times they themselves may have swum Chenango Lake. For this is a profound meditation on the limits of human knowledge which, in its ritualistic unfolding, directs us in almost Ignatian fashion (cf., for example, Roland Barthes's reading of the *Spiritual Exercises* in *Sade/Fourier/Loyola*) from description to meditation to participation to realization.

Tomlinson's two footnotes to this poem suggest his abiding interest in the significance and centrality of ceremony as a way of encountering and of controlling our immersions into reality itself. His first note quotes Lévi-Strauss's *The Savage Mind*, from the passage on the Hako, a Pawnee tripartite ceremony and invocation for the crossing of a stream (call these first, the moment of entrance, second, the movement into, and third, immersion), activities that correspond to Tomlinson's tripartite poetic ritual of meditation on the waterscapes of the lake as the swimmer prepares to enter the water (it is morning, autumn, winter is not far off), entrance (a froglike scissor stroke across the water's surface, skin to skin), and his own loss of self-identity as he immerses himself totally in that interior cold.

But, his second footnote reinforcing what the poem participates in, there are necessary limits to any such entrance. Evoking a Hopi ritual of passage from youth into manhood, Tomlinson quietly insists on the limitations of all metaphor ("the spirits [finally] remove their masks and the child sees that those he had taken for gods are only metaphors for gods: they are his uncles and kinsmen"). Now, as the poem approaches its own terminus, Tomlinson produces the illusion of having transcended the necessary limits of language itself. For a moment we can feel that almost nameless element, that interior, inhuman cold, which is both merciless and which "yet shows a kind of mercy," sustaining the observer become participant. The ceremony of the poem, then, enacts a baptism of *un*-naming, where self is thrown back on a preonomastic self, where the counters giving us the name "Chenango" in a language as irrevocably lost as those people who so named it begin to be construed now in another way. For it is the body itself, as it scissors through the water, de-creating the patterns observed in its untouched surfaces and immersed now in this alien element, this other-not-oneself, which must frame in an a-linguistic series of gestures a meaning all across this "all but penetrable surface."

In the poem's final lines, we, like the observer, having emerged from that element, are made freshly aware that there is a pattern of correspondences or at least of geometrical equivalents touching self and other. Perhaps it is a chiming between man and what we used to call nature, for Tomlinson has always rejected the notion of the autonomous imagination, opting for perception as a variation on a theme rather than as a pure fantasia. In any event, what he makes us realize is that all images are accidents (in an Aristotelian sense) and that reality does not move, necessarily, toward the human observer for its validation. The truth seems to be, instead, that reality is constantly going elsewhere, "incessantly shaping" itself according to its own necessities. All *we* may do is to learn how to participate—humbly and quietly—in that reality. The consolation is that, as we embrace it, it embraces us in its turn. For Tomlinson, then, the poem is, as he says, a rite, an initiatory ceremony, which is capable of bringing us into a closer relationship with our world. One of the most profound ironies in this profound poem, then, is the self-reflexive realization that even the metaphor of water as reality is only an approximation, since *no* metaphor can embrace that which we can only *call* reality.

It is here, then, in this kind of quiet, intensive meditative framework, in a tradition beginning with Wordsworth and running through the English tradition to our own time, that Tomlinson's poetic voice seems most comfortably at home with itself. Like Odysseus and Apollonius of Tyana—other travelers to distant and wild places—Tomlinson too has come to understand in some deeply rooted sense that it must be the long look homeward that finally points the real way in.

1977

Robert Creeley

"One of the few books I've ever had that was stolen," Creeley remembered in a lecture he gave in Berlin in January 1967, "—not by me, as it happened, but by a girl I persuaded to steal it for me—was William Carlos Williams' *The Wedge*. It proved fire of a very real order." That book, the book Williams had had so much difficulty publishing because of the war, had finally been brought out by Harry Duncan's Cummington Press in the fall of '44 in a small edition. When "I got hold of it," Creeley said, "its content was a revelation to me." [1] Thus Creeley, at forty, recalling Creeley at eighteen. For five years, between early '45 and early '50, when he finally screwed up the courage to write Williams directly (under the cover of doing business, i.e., beginning a little magazine), Creeley studied Williams's lyrics deeply and long, taking to heart Williams's dictum in his "Author's Introduction" at the head of *The Wedge* that

> When a man makes a poem, makes it, mind you, he takes words
> as he finds them interrelated about him and composes them—with-

out distortion which would mar their exact significances—into an intense expression of his perceptions and ardors that they may constitute a revelation in the speech that he uses. It isn't what he says that counts as a work of art, it's what he makes. . . .[2]

So, while he took accelerated courses at Harvard (taking time out to serve with the American Field Service as an ambulance driver in 1945, living in the feverish jungles of Burma and India, taking drugs daily just to keep himself from vomiting up his own bile in the intense heat) he kept the example of Pound and Williams before him as he could. And then, returning to Boston in the winter of '45, he enrolled once again at Harvard on the G.I. Bill, trying to finish up his degree, taking literature courses from F. O. Matthiessen (anti-Pound) and Harry Levin (pro-Eliot) in the Great Tradition.[3]

Slowly, though, the Harvard B.A. churned to a halt. First, there was Creeley's young family now, and a required math course which refused to go away. Besides, his final semester was turning into an abysmal anticlimax (two failures and an incomplete). And taking the steamer from Provincetown (where he was then living) to Boston—with the ship's bar open the two hours to and two hours fro—was not helping. Furthermore, whatever time he had left over he spent listening assiduously to jazz, while he tried writing short stories and lyrics in a mode that combined Williams with the syncopations of jazz. He found *Paterson*, like Pound's *Cantos*, intimidating for his own writing then, unlike *The Wedge* and Williams's lyrics of the later forties, which he followed closely in the little magazines. (There was, too, the important lyric example of Hart Crane—paradoxically—strengthened by Creeley's friendship with Slater Brown, Crane's close friend, who was down and out on his luck when Creeley came to know him in the mid-forties.)

If, however, *Paterson* was beyond Creeley at twenty-two, he could—and did—benefit from Williams's jagged couplets and tercets, quatrains and verse paragraphs. He charted Williams's line breaks and word breaks, his qualifiers and pronomial indeterminacies, his shifts from a rising to a falling measure and back again. And he studied as well Williams's prose statements—his "Introduction" to *The Wedge,* his *Letter to an Australian Editor,* and his attack on Eliot in "With Forced Fingers Rude"—in the intense cone-shaped light of the world of the little magazines, magazines like *Imagi* and *Tiger's Eye, Golden Goose,* and *Four Pages.* These, together with Pound's critical dicta as outlined in *Make It*

New, Pavannes and Divisions, ABC of Reading, and *Guide to Kulchur*,
formed his nascent poetics. A fragmentary sort of contact as yet, granted,
but enough to sustain Creeley in the batlike cultural isolation in which
he found himself. And enough to sustain his belief that there was a
viable alternative to the Eliotic and academic tradition which dominated
the literary scene in the half-decade following World War II.

"I think that in 1945," Creeley recalled sixteen years later,

> men of my particular generation felt almost an immediate impa-
> tience with what was then to be regarded as a solution. Many of
> us had been involved in this huge global nightmare, and we came
> back to our specific personal lives . . . feeling a great confusion. . . .
> So we had that reason to move upon something—upon a clarity that
> could confront these dilemmas more adequately than the generali-
> ties we had been given.

And then a "very specific example" of that clarity: "We also had . . .
Williams, who, in 1945, I don't think was even regarded as a minor
poet. It's curious to remember that." [4]

Still, Creeley managed to publish a dozen or so lyrics between '45
and '49 with that "specific example," decent lyrics for a beginner who
had yet to define himself as the hip Puritan he would "become." Those
first poems in the Harvard *Wake* and *Accent*—his initial forums—were
tight constructs, with the feel of jazz about them in their syncopated
rhythms and Williams-like line breaks. They used rhyme, most of them,
but these were internal rhymes or end rhymes which alternately refused
to call attention to themselves or brazen themselves out. They are the
lyrics that open *The Charm*, lyrics like "Poem for D. H. Lawrence" and
"Poem for Beginners," "The Late Comer" and "Gangster."

But the Provincetown lifestyle and the antagonist's relationship he
found himself in with regard to Harvard were having their toll. It was
time for Creeley to take his family and move, this time to an old farm
up near Franconia Notch in New Hampshire, at a place called Rock Pool
Farm in North Lisbon. The place would need work, but it had woods
and it had space. Here Creeley could raise his family and poultry and
prize pigeons, play jazz, think, think . . . and write. And then, in early
1950, the possibility of starting a little magazine (as yet nameless) with
another young writer named Jacob Leed, and the chance, too, to finally
make literary contact with Pound and Williams.[5]

The point of actual contact between Creeley (age twenty-three) and Williams (age sixty-six) begins, then, with a long, deferential, yet intensive missive posted from Littleton, New Hampshire, February 11, 1950, to Rutherford.[6] It is the initial groping to engage the master, and there is talk of starting an undefined literary magazine, and a request for the older man to contribute something. It is a beginning, hesitant as a New England spring thaw, but a beginning. And then, the formalities and the "business" of the letter done, the admission of sonship: "To be frank, I've put myself to school with your work, can think of very few others who've written verse comparable to your own" (YU).

"Dear Creely" (thus, in Williams's response twelve days later), "I completely agree with you as to your plans." Talk, then, of the current state of little magazines, of *Imagi* and *Poetry New York* and the now-defunct *Tiger's Eye*, talk of "the coast mags and the New Mexico mags and the Midwest mags," talk of the "chronic constipation" of Williams's old enemy, the *Partisan Review*. But there was nothing, "not a line of verse" (WU), to offer besides *Paterson* 4 (which was consuming Williams with its own formal insistencies and which he couldn't anyway let go). Nothing, then, to offer before summer at the least.

His letter answered, Creeley lost no time in offering his own counter-response. On February 27, he sent off a carefully composed five-page letter to Williams, hitting at the kinds of academic literary canons that Harvard, like so many other universities, had established after the war, singling out (with disgust) one well-known professor's grouping of Proust, Mann, and Joyce with Eliot's *The Waste Land*. But the avant-garde edge—as manifested in the little magazines—had also lost its sharpness by mid-century. Finally, he asked Williams—as he would shortly ask Pound—to describe his own "program" for writing, since what was especially needed was a gathering of forces, a direction, both a theoretical justification for the new poetry (yet to be written) and a way of creating a new vortex, a new center. (Amazingly, within a year Creeley, Charles Olson, Cid Corman, Denise Levertov, and Williams would be exchanging letters and ideas with one another, shaping a poetic, a distinctive new mode.)

"My own (moral) program can be briefly stated," Williams wrote on March 3 (the letter was published the following year as a kind of manifesto in the first issue of Cid Corman's *Origin*). "To write badly is an offense to the state since the government can never be more than the government of the words. . . . Bad art is . . . that which does not serve in the continual service of cleansing the language of all fixations upon dead, stinking dead, usages of the past" (wu). It was a version of what Williams would say two weeks later in his acceptance speech on receiving the National Book Award for *Paterson* 3, and, as such, necessarily broad in its moral insistencies. But, broad as it was, it was something Creeley could nevertheless use: a poetic that focused on a language rinsed as much as possible of its literary associations, an anti-Symbolist stance, the words sharp, distinctive, denotative, their energies supplied by their specific context and space. Not, not the accretions of time, but a style clean and bare and angular . . . as a Unitarian steeple. It was one Puritan's advice to another.

April 7: Could he, Creeley asks Williams, get a copy of Williams's NBA speech which he'd picked up over the radio? And could he reprint Williams's comments on T. S. Eliot and the uses of Milton—in *Four Pages*—in his own little magazine? As a way of focusing the new attack on the kinds of literary traditionalism still rampant in the academies? Yes, Williams answered, "if you find it has not gone stale." True, not many had seen it, hidden as it was in that obscure place, but the key men—those who mattered, finally—*had* seen it, and that fact might take away "a good bit of its punch" (wu).

But there is a new tone in Williams's voice here: a growing admiration for Creeley's (the name got, finally, right) critical intelligence, as now another figure moved to fight the good fight in the fragile yet enduring form of the little magazines. And it is "we," now, who need to get the new information out to "them," if only enough of the "stuff" can be assembled to make a difference. As for the National Book Award speech Creeley had asked for: Williams was sending that along (if he could find it), delighted that it had actually "travelled further than from my lips to the mike." Together, Williams and this young man might "dent them yet." Either that or face "our own destruction" (wu). The old war against turgidity, entrenchment, and sodden writing was underway again. Williams, as usual, was not one to take half-measures.

Sometime in mid-April, Williams wrote Charles Olson that there was a young editor up in the New Hampshire woods looking for good new work, for on April 21 Olson shot off two letters from Washington, D.C., one for Williams and the other for Creeley. Olson had already sent Creeley some lines via his friend Vincent Ferrini of Gloucester—"a lovely liquid thing"—which Creeley had apparently rejected with the judgment—in Olson's retelling of the gist of the matter to Creeley—

that Olson was nothing but "a boll / weevil . . . just lookin' for a lang . . . and i says . . . a man / god damn well has to come up with his own lang., syntax and song both. . . ." Olson finished this first letter to Creeley by telling him to watch out for an essay of his which would soon be appearing in *Poetry New York* on "PROjective Verse / vs. the NON-projective." [7] It was an essay that would—at length—give both Creeley and Williams (who was so floored by Olson's formulations that he placed a sizable chunk of the piece smack in the middle of his own *Autobiography*) a taste of what the new program for poetry would become.

And to Williams the same day (April 21), a letter that included these sentiments:

> I had to tell him [Creeley] he was off his trolley (had to remind him, there is a man's language, sure, and a man better damn well come to it, syntax and song both, but, that there is a language fit for each poem under hand as well. . . . i've dubbed it in the PRO VERSE, 'composition by field.' " (YU)

Thus, through Williams's instigation, with other energies gathering in early 1950: the beginnings of one of the most prolific and seminal literary correspondences in the field of contemporary American poetry. "Thanks for the push with Olson," Creeley wrote Williams at once. "I had seen some of his work, but nothing like what I have on hand" (YU). And, on May 29, Olson sent Williams a post card with these sentiments: "Thanks for, creeley"—*homo ludens* unable to resist the chance for throwing a few puns— "he / 's sure got ideas / And a nose, a nose! / and sense, he know / 's / where the business / is" (YU).[8]

Letters between Creeley and Williams about the proposed first issue of Creeley's magazine continued to shuttle back and forth up through the end of June, with Williams soon acting as an editor in shaping the magazine's contents. So, for example, he suggested Creeley's adding several letters he'd received from Srinivas Rayoprol, a young Hindu student studying in the states, as well as several poems by Donald Paquette, something of Byron Vazakas's, some prose by Paul Goodman, a long poem of Olson's, and the two prose pieces by Williams. But by July, the whole scheme had finally fallen through for lack of money. Years later, Creeley could admit that the magazine idea had been half a cover anyway, a way of getting up his courage to write to such immensities as Williams and Pound: "I would have been shy of writing them just to say, 'I think you're a great man,' or something. You know, I wanted to have business that gave me reason" (CP, 141). The initial "purpose," then, had failed. But something better—contacts with Williams and Olson which would last till those men were gone—had begun. They were contacts that were to produce a much more significant sense of "program."

For, whereas Pound's response to Creeley was to send long reading lists and injunctions, either directly or through Dallam Simpson, to study this or that text (it was Pound's way of treating just about everybody, including Williams himself, as *Paterson* 3 remembers in its own comic fashion), Williams's response was more practical, specific, to the point, something Creeley could *use*. "I remember," Creeley recalled in 1967, seventeen years after the event, "one time I wrote [Williams] a very stern letter—some description about something I was going to do, or this was the way things were blah-blah. And he returned me the sheets of the letter and he had marked on the margin of particular sections, 'Fine. Your style is tightening' " (CP, 141).

"I notice a definite tightening of your own style as shown by your letters," is how Williams actually worded it, returning five pages of Creeley's letter with four sections lined in ballpoint down the left-hand side. "The yeast's working in one case, so it's working" (WU). *That* kind of attention—not to ideas but to the way the words jostled or hit the page aslant—*that* could go a long way in the education of any intelligent young writer. It had a more practical use, even, than digesting Del Mar's *The History of Money* or following Simpson's injunctions to "review Plutarch's *Moralia* for the Simonides 'polis andra didaskei.' " [9] The trouble with reading lists like Pound's or his Harvard professors' was not that reading wasn't a primary and indispensable consideration for the artist, but that they tended to steamroll the neophyte, flattening him out and blocking the actual writing interminably, since there was always one more book to know. The important thing, finally, was to capture "the simplest idea coming like the most fresh, beautiful, sweet thing I cd ever get a grip on, because, dammit, it's mine." [10] For a writer writing meant, first and foremost, the *act* of writing.

September 1950: another momentary flurry of activity, with Creeley asking Olson for a recommendation with the Guggenheim people to write fiction for a year and wondering if Olson thought Williams might —as a kindness—also write for him. Go ahead, Olson told him (Creeley did), and Olson followed up with his own letter, generous and bearlike.

Williams, seeing now some of Creeley's early short stories (subsequently gathered in *The Gold Diggers*), praised them highly, both to their author and to the Guggenheim Foundation Committee (though it did, as Williams had warned him, little good). By the end of the year, then, despite these failures, Creeley had gained two friends—one who had already shaped and one who would subsequently shape his practice as a writer of prose *and* of poetry—two figures who were to crop up everywhere in Creeley's conversation, interviews, and essays, in part determining the very lay of his syllables on page after page for the next quarter of a century.

December 16: "The keystone, this most admirable piece of thinking about the poem that I have recently, perhaps ever, encountered" (UC). Thus Williams from Rutherford to Olson in Washington, D.C., fresh from reading Olson's "Projective Verse" essay in *Poetry New York*. He wanted a big piece of it for his own *Autobiography*, which he was deep into at that moment, for Olson's formulations had articulated Williams's own sense of direction and purpose, "affirming" his own conceptions about the nature of the poem. Olson, whose own fortunes at that juncture were low, was understandably giddy with the prospect of becoming the capstone to Williams's own *biographia literaria*. So, on the eve of his departure for Yucatan—where he was going to live more cheaply in order to be able to write—Olson dashed a letter off to Williams giving him whatever permission and encouragement he could.

Creeley, too, had read Olson's essay and admired it. In fact, many of the ideas in Olson's formulation had been worked out in the give-and-take of letters which had shuttled back and forth between himself and Creeley for the past eight months. "It is," Williams wrote Creeley in late December, "it is as if the whole area lifted. It's the sort of thing we are after and must have . . . a good useful thing for us to try out in practice" (WU). Never again was Olson to stand quite this high in Williams's estimation. Olson would shift in Williams's letters and interviews over the next decade in a game of shuttlecock with that other aberrant son, Allen Ginsberg, with now the one son rising as the other set: "Howl" up and "The Kingfishers" down; the *Maximus* poems up (some of them), and Ginsberg's Whitmanian lyrics down. Creeley, on the other hand, grew more tentatively in Williams's estimation, though it was in the long run a stronger and stronger acceptance of the man's ability—and the realization of that ability—to make a subtle music sometimes surpassing even his own.

In early '51 Creeley wrote Williams about shifting some of Williams's prose from his aborted literary magazine to Cid Corman's new *Origin* and Ranier Gerhardt's avant-garde German magazine, *Fragmente.* Swamped with the sheer weight of the *Autobiography,* and just weeks away from his stroke, Williams shot back a note giving whatever permissions were necessary. When Williams next heard from Creeley it was summer and Creeley was living in Aix-en-Provence, France. Creeley was reading Williams's early work, especially *In the American Grain,* and the just-published *Paterson* 4. The whole epic, Creeley told him, was "an organism, a continual growing in the head of whoever can listen" (YU). That was on the first of August.

Coincidentally—for it would have been several days before Williams received this letter—Williams wrote on August 2 to Cid Corman praising the second issue of *Origin.* As the first issue had featured Olson, so Corman had given Creeley forty pages of the second issue for his fiction, criticism, letters, and poems. Williams's response to this issue of *Origin* was, in fact, his attempt to evaluate the node of brilliant but sporadic energy emanating from this new literary magazine. For while he felt an "exhilaration and a sense of freedom" in reading through the issue, he was still "not impressed by all of it." No doubt about it: Olson and Creeley were both intelligent men, searching for something important but as yet undefined. And Olson's ideas—as the older man—had already proven invaluable to him (he was thinking, of course, of the "Projective Verse" essay). But he still wished Olson had taken his ideas and pulled them "together in firmer terms." It was a criticism he would reiterate several times in the years to come.

But of Robert Creeley he was even less sure. He liked Creeley's prose style, especially the attention to detail, but the young man was still very much "on dangerous ground":

> He's very unformed. This makes him susceptible to influences. I'm curious to know what France will do to him. . . . But if he comes back here unchanged, what good will it have done him to go abroad? I like him, I like him very much, he has an honest, enquiring mind; he puts down what he sees and seems listening internally to his own thinking.

But what would come of it all he didn't know. Like a father watching over an as-yet-unproven son, Williams would watch to see what developed. Creeley just might yet "turn out to be an important man." [10]

What Williams told Creeley was essentially the same thing, that he had already shown that he could write fine prose. And later, when Creeley was having second thoughts about the wisdom of having moved to France, it was Williams who told him to buck up and hold out. Wasn't Creeley, after all, acting as an "ambassador" of the new work? "From your own word you are seeing and talking with many discerning people in France, Italy and Germany who will be valuable to you as time piles itself up" (wu).

The richest correspondence, the one that outran any others of Creeley's for sheer quantity of energy and fruitful interaction, was not between Creeley and Williams, however, but between Creeley and Olson. Simply stated, the gap in age and expectations between Creeley and Williams was just too great to bridge. Creeley, for example, might continue to inform the older poet of what he was doing from time to time, and of course Williams could do the same. They could send each other their new books as they came off the press, and Creeley reviewed four of Williams's books between 1952 and 1962: the *Autobiography, The Desert Music,* the *Selected Essays,* and *Pictures from Brueghel.* Moreover, there is a pattern in Williams's later correspondences that repeats itself over and over with new writers: an initial and intense encounter until the writer establishes a footing, and then a kind of periodic wellwishing while Williams goes on to other writers. (This pattern, of course, is played by both partners, and the neophyte learns almost instinctively to follow the master—at a distance.) It was played with Creeley, Olson, Ginsberg, Corman (to a lesser degree), and others.

After all, Williams's most deeply felt influence on Creeley was not the correspondence. It lay, rather, in the fact of Williams's poems, poems that had etched themselves deeply into Creeley's mind years before. The *critical* correspondence for Creeley (in both senses of that term) was then the one with Olson, which ran to something like 750 letters on each side, of which a small sample was published by Creeley as the *Mayan Letters.* Creeley himself has recalled how intense the writing could become, especially with Olson, who, when he had something to say on a subject, would attack his typewriter, hurling long missives of six or eight pages at his correspondents as often as four or five times a week, sometimes for week after week. More than once Olson's typewriter simply gave way under that kind of barrage.

For Williams, however, the correspondence with Creeley meant writing at long intervals—a letter, two, three, a year, mixed with long periods when he was simply unable to write to anyone. In early April 1952, for example, Williams wrote Creeley about accepting the Chair of Poetry at the Library of Congress, his duties beginning in mid-September. He was getting old, he said, could feel the weight now of his sixty-nine years, and so wanted "to do ALL I can for you" and for the other writers in the front ranks of the avant garde. He had been reading the first issue of Ranier Gerhardt's *Fragmente,* the little magazine with which both Creeley and Olson were very much involved. He was pleased with it, seeing it as a sign of a new form that was beginning (as ever with Williams) to realize itself. It was as if *Fragmente* itself were the actual "REshaping of a world that is taking place," fragments, that is, not of the old, but of the new order (WU). But when Creeley wrote that November to Williams, asking if he had anything for *Fragmente,* it was Floss instead who answered: in mid-August, just weeks before he was to have begun his duties in Washington, Williams had suffered a severe stroke. There was nothing, then, to send, beyond Bill's best wishes.

It was not until the following fall that Williams could answer Creeley directly once again. On October 8, 1953, he sat down to begin a letter to Creeley, who was living now in Mallorca. Williams was trying to work off the nervousness he felt as he prepared to meet the public for the first time since his stroke fourteen months before. That very evening he was to appear on the CBS television talk show "Author Meets Critic," and the typewriter was interceding as a catharsis of sorts. It was a newsy letter, bringing Creeley up to date on the effect the stroke had had on him, followed by the "red stink" which had cost him—ultimately (and unfairly)—his Chair as Poetry Consultant to the Library of Congress. But he'd also been able to write "ten or twelve poems along a new line stressing the importance of measure" (WU). In December he wrote again to thank Creeley for sending along Larry Eigner's *From the Sustaining Air,* which Creeley had published through the Divers Press in Mallorca the previous July. He liked Eigner's poems, especially for their "complete relaxation," a quality Williams had come in old age especially to appreciate.

In the late spring of '54, Creeley sent along a copy of his own short stories called *The Gold Diggers,* which his Divers Press had published in March. Williams had these read to him and genuinely admired them. Their "very lack of development," he told Creeley, "only emphasized for me the more the vividness of the essential detail which is the very point to be remembered." The vividness of the essential detail. Creeley was growing, and so was Olson: "I'm at present trying to write a piece for Jonathan Williams on Olson's Maximus poem [1-10] which I have just read. It's by far his best work." The local theme—Gloucester— and the formal intelligence behind Olson's poem had impressed Williams. The writing here, he could already see, was "a tremendous improvement over much that has been written about the American scene in the past" (WU).

But what most interested Williams was Creeley's typescript of a review of Williams's *The Desert Music* volume, a review that was to appear in the summer issue of *Black Mountain Review* (which Creeley was then editing from Mallorca). This review, called "A Character for Love," stressed Williams's clarity and uncommon honesty in treating the theme of love. That Creeley should have stressed *this* theme owed much to the presence in this new volume of poems (written in that new measure Williams had mentioned the fall before) such as "For Eleanor and Bill Monahan," "Asphodel," "To Daphne and Virginia," and "The Yellow Flower." Creeley, watching the disintegration of his own first marriage and fascinated by the tentativeness, delicacy, and anguish of the fact of loving, was himself intimately involved with the very same theme in his own poems—those which would finally coalesce into *For Love: Poems 1950–1960*—and in *The Island*, his single novel, which examines the gradual dissolution of his first marriage.

"Let men do what they will, generally—there will be no statement beyond this," Creeley concluded, his eye on a passage from Williams's then-unfinished "Asphodel." "It is fantastic, to me, that Williams at such a time as now confronts him should be so incredibly clear" (QG, 116). But Williams had a disclaimer to make. Actually, he had "never come down as hard on that [theme] as I would like to or, better put, as I have dared to." And yet, by carefully selecting and juxtaposing key passages, Creeley had been able to "penetrate" to Williams's very "vitals" (WU).

Out of his own need, then, Creeley had struck the resonating chord. It would still be several more years before he could fully use in his own poems what he'd found in Williams by '54, and the poems themselves would for the most part be addressed to another woman—his second wife, Bobbie. But the lessons of the dancing master had been fully assimilated by the time Creeley came to write "The Rose" and "For Love" in the late fifties. We hear the altered rhythms as well as the syntactic strategies of Williams's late love lyrics in, for example, the closing lines of the title poem of *For Love:*

> Let me stumble into
> not the confession but
> the obsession I begin with
> now. For you.
>
> also (also)
> some time beyond place, or
> place beyond time, no
> mind left to
>
> say anything at all,
> that fact gone, now.
> Into the company of love
> it all returns.

And compare Creeley's lines to those lines in Williams's "Asphodel," which Creeley so admired:

> You understand
>   I had to meet you
>   after the event
> and have still to meet you. . . .
> I risked what I had to do,
>   therefore to prove
>   that we love each other
> while my very bones sweated
>   that I could not cry out to you
>   in the act.

The voices are distinctive and yet complementary. By 1960 Creeley had become, like his master before him, in Mallarmé's complex and elevated sense of the word, a subtle *syntaxier.*

November 1954: Creeley writes to express his dissatisfaction with Williams's just-published *Selected Essays*, especially with the omission of two pieces that had profoundly affected Creeley's own sense of development: "With Forced Fingers Rude" and the 1946 "Letter to an Australian Editor," both of which had attacked the Pound-Eliot literary canons. Williams explained that the *Selected Essays* were only half as long as he had hoped they would be, and that there were, in fact, enough essays lying around to double the size of the book. But Creeley, who was reviewing the volume for the *Black Mountain Review,* unsatisfied with this answer, wrote again in December to say he had shown the "Letter to an Australian Editor" to Robert Graves (there in Mallorca), who had liked its theme of the androgynetic mode. These pieces needed to be published, he stressed, and he was willing to bring them out himself if Williams consented. But Williams told him to let the matter rest where it was, at least for the time being.

In Creeley's December letter, however, there is a new preoccupation, a new sense of urgency in his voice. For the first time, there is an expanded discussion of poetic measure, a discussion central also to his review of the *Selected Essays.* Williams's "Statement for Cid Corman," which had appeared in the Spring '54 issue of *Origin* and which had closed the *Selected Essays,* was evidently behind the terms of Creeley's discussion. But Olson's letters to Creeley and Creeley's to Olson at this time were also concerned with the same questions of measure. It is, in fact, an issue that gathers into its center a host of figures in the mid-fifties: Ginsberg, Duncan, Olson, Creeley, Corman, Levertov, Lowell, Williams.

"I can see," Williams answered Creeley in mid-December, "that my concern with 'measure' gets under your skin yet it is . . . the neglect of any measure in modern verse which disturbs me" (WU). In his review, Creeley had quoted the entire text of Campion's lyric, "Kinde are her answeres" as an example of the *escape* from the necessity for a traditional measure. Campion, Creeley felt, had given his attention—like Williams—not to a measure, but rather "to the words and the rhythms which they carried in them, to be related then as they occurred." Campion's lyric could no more be "scanned" than a lyric of Williams's like "The World Narrowed to a Point." (And that latter is a visual and aural model of the very kind of thing Creeley was attempting then to achieve for himself.) The Renaissance poet's process, Creeley insisted with self-reflexive intensity, was "literally the same as that by which Williams himself writes, *or any man who can effect such things with words*" (emphasis mine). If, for example, one compared Campion's lines,

> Kinde are her answeres
> But her performance keepes no day;
> Breaks time, as dancers
> From their own Musicke when they stray,

with Williams's lines,

> The eye awakes
> perfumes are defined
> inflections
> ride the quick ear,

one would hear similarities apparent to the unstopped ear (QG, 104–11).

But Williams once again demurred. Contrary to Creeley's argument that there was a sameness between himself and Campion in terms of the strategic deployment of a variable measure which could be changed according to need, Williams read Campion's lyric instead as "one of the most subtly *measured* of all examples that I could choose from." No, Williams insisted, no doubt the fifties had its share of "instinctive, mad poets but the intelligence escapes them." Chaos or randomness or blind instinct were dead ends, uninteresting, finally. What was needed now was a sense of "the relative or variable foot," a disciplined measure which could at the same time retain all the freedom of the Greek choric dance, a measure consonant with "all the freedom that the intelligence justifies." He knew that he was opening a Pandora's box with this kind of talk of prosodic freedom: "I shrink to take responsibility for what the unskillful students . . . will do with this [new] line," he added, "but I don't for the life of me see how they can escape attempting it" (WU). And Williams was right; for all its tentativeness, new measures were to spring up over the next few years—in Lowell's *Life Studies* phase, Ginsberg's "Howl," Olson's later *Maximus* poems, and in Creeley's lyrics themselves.

But Creeley was confused by Williams's refusal to acknowledge any similarity with Campion, or even of a prosodic kinship between modern poetry and Elizabethan experiments with the lyric. Yet, for all his natural deference, Creeley could be as tenacious as Corman or Levertov when it came to questions of craft. Under that pressure, then, Williams finally backed off. "When it comes to your failure to be convinced by my recent strictures on the poetic line," he wrote on February 3, 1955, to Creeley (who was then at Black Mountain), "forget the whole thing. I agree with much that you say as far as I can follow it. Campion hasn't much to teach us concerning modern verse." And besides, "what if I may say so, do i finally [know] about Campion?" (WU). So much, then, for the nonce on the Campion issue.

But there was something more—and what Williams said to Creeley he said in one form or another to his other "disciples" of those years: "We are not even *near* a common enough agreement in the terms we are attempting to use to make us intelligible to each other. . . . I often feel that we are talking of the same thing but do not recognize it as such because we simply do not recognize it as such." It would take months of a daily give-and-take to "wear down the excrescences in the arguments that hold us off." In the meantime: better for each one to work "along his own line" and hope finally "a light will dawn" (WU). The issue did not come up again for five more years, while Williams and Creeley did work, each "along his own line," listening, finally, each to his own voice.

The letters still moved between the two men after 1955, though most of Williams's are missing, casualties, perhaps, of Creeley's uprootedness and domestic turmoil during these years. During 1955, Creeley is at Black Mountain with Olson as the college splinters, tragicomically, toward its final demise. It is also the year that Creeley and Williams meet for the first time (there would be three more visits). In mid-1956, Creeley is in San Francisco for a short time just as the San Francisco renaissance is about to experience its golden hour with Ginsberg's mad version of the beatitudes, "Howl," uttered prophetically before a large crowd in this proto-happening. "Creely [sic] is out here," so Ginsberg tells Williams in May of this year, "& will publish me and Kerouac & Bill Burroughs in London . . . and various other extremely interesting zen buddhists around here, all good poets, whom you met and influenced around Reed years ago, 1950? There is a kind of revival you would dig taking place. . . . Creely arrived and picked up at once also. . . ." [12]

By August, Creeley is at Ranchos de Taos, New Mexico, writing Williams his own version of the Frisco experience, of his having met Ginsberg, Phil Whalen, and Gary Snyder. He also mentions the possibility of printing Williams's introduction to Ginsberg's volume of early poems, *Empty Mirrors*. And, finally, he tells him that his ex-wife and kids are living in Connecticut, and that he is living alone.

New Year's Day 1957: an extremely moving letter from Albuquerque, New Mexico. He is teaching now, six classes a day to boys ranging

in age from ten to fourteen. He has just returned from a holiday visit
with Denise Levertov and Mitch Goodman down in Mexico. He is
still alone. And then a fifteen-month hiatus until April 1959, when he
writes from Alameda, New Mexico, to say that he is married again
and has two new daughters, the second—Katherine Williams—named
for Williams himself. His next letter, written Christmas Eve, is post-
marked Guatemala, where he has gone with his family to teach.

And then, in 1960: a series of letters once more taking up the question of measure. In January he talks of measure in Ginsberg, whose
poems—like "Howl"—"are a series of experiments with the formal
organization of the long line," something he personally can connect
with. About Olson and Williams he has this to say: "But god knows we
are blessed, any of us, younger, by having someone like Olson 'out
there.' . . . He clears a lot, just as you do—the example is unforgettable,
and forgives no embarrassment on any count whatsoever" (YU).

It is in response to this letter that Williams begins again talking of
measure, this time stressing the local idiom and the variable foot as the
very basis of the new measure. But, having seen some of Creeley's most
recent poems—those that make up the last section of *For Love*, including "The Rose"—Williams is ready in his letter of January 18, to sum
up Creeley's own achievement to date: "I don't know why I go on in
this way because of all the people writing about you need it the least.
You have the subtlest feeling for the measure that I encounter anywhere except in the verses of Ezra Pound" (WU). And even Williams
was willing to admit he couldn't equal Pound at his subtlest. "At your
best," he told Creeley—though this, he added, was "rarely"—"you perhaps surpass me with a passage that leaves me flat on my back but there
is never much of that. As you yourself say it is mostly unconscious when
something of that sort appears on the page" (WU). And so, after ten
years: a tribute, a qualified tribute, from the master (at seventy-six) to
the disciple (at thirty-three). Creeley had learned his lessons well—even
(from Williams's point of view) perhaps too well.

In August, Williams sends Creeley a mimeograph copy of his "American Idiom" paper, asking for comments. In September, Creeley comments, talks of new work by Gael Turnbull which he has seen, praises
Burroughs's *Naked Lunch,* and asks Williams again for permission to
reprint some of his work.

Fourteen months later, in November 1961: a letter from Creeley in
Albuquerque, with a cryptic reference to the death of his little girl, a

reference expanded only in June '62, explaining how she'd been caught in an earthslide when an arroyo gave way. It is a letter filled with pathos and sensitivity. And then, in the summer and early fall of '62, with Williams's health rapidly failing: three short letters from Creeley, praising Williams's final book of poems, *Pictures from Brueghel*, which Creeley is reviewing for the *Nation*. Now it is Creeley's chance for summations, as he makes this judgment on Williams's last phase. It is an evaluation that is both precise and to the point:

> I cannot make that judgment which would argue among the poems that this or that one shows the greater mastery. I think there must come a time, granted that one has worked as Williams to define the nature of this art, when it all coheres, and each poem, or instance, takes its place in that life which it works to value, to measure, to be the fact of. (QG, 120)

Williams's end, after so many strokes, came quietly, even anticlimactically, in March 1963. In a very real sense, his readers—and even more especially his sons and daughters—became, in both senses of that word, him. And none more so, perhaps, than the Creeley of *For Love* (1962) and *Words* (1967). Long before then, however, Williams's presence—his standards and admonitions—had become ubiquitous touchstones in Creeley's letters, interviews, essays, and—more subtly—in the craft of his fiction and his poems.

And though it is another story, it is worth noting that Creeley began soon after Williams's death to break with the former short lyric mode that had become Creeley's characteristic signature. Thus, Creeley's first attempt in the early sixties at a sustained fictional mode, *The Island*, in order to extend the range of his prose, and the prose improvisations, for example, of *A Day Book* and *Presences*, which in some ways recall Williams's improvisations of the twenties. And, too, the strong sense of continuity among the shorter lyrics in *Pieces*, that they are pieces (as with Williams's *Spring and All*) of a larger whole, that they signal an attempt by Creeley to incorporate disparate poems into a lyric continuum.

That is the story, of course, of a poet's attempt to unmake or deconstruct a too familiar sense of oneself. But *this* story, however, has concerned itself with the fragments of an early making: with the shaping of a poet and the variations possible in gridding one voice to another in the way of a tradition, while at the same time assuring that one is discovering a mode of speaking that will be distinctly one's own. The reality of that literary and human relationship is, of course, far more complex and vivid than a handful of residual documents can hope to show. Still, in the track of that complex interaction of poet with poet, certain luminous fragments do surface. And it has been the business of this piece to chart those fragments until a sense of order (tenuous at best, particularly when played against the tentative, exciting new music these two men were actually hearing somewhere out there, in the air, the thin air) might be allowed to reveal itself here.

1978

John Montague

John Montague published *A Slow Dance* and *The Great Cloak* three years apart, though their subjects—old laments and modern loves and their different musics—cover the same five-year period in his life. But for the accidents of economics and publishing schedules, these two sequences might have been printed together in 1975. *A Slow Dance* is by far the stronger of the two books and I cannot read it without thinking of the old, pre-nineteenth-century Irish tunes that belong to a primitive world with its convoluted melodic line, dirgelike and unearthly. Only Seamus Heaney among Irish writers today can compare with Montague when it comes to evoking this old Irish music with its vigor, its subtle webbing, its rainsoaked landscape of gray rock and burren, hedgerow and hawthorn and bog. And if *A Slow Dance* is not Montague's most ambitious book—that honor belonging to his earlier sequence on the Irish troubles, *The Rough Field* (1971)—then it is still his strongest and most satisfying to date, touching a world aligned to Ireland's distant past: somber, unrelenting, pagan, aristocratic, like fine fretwork in stone tracery.

It is Yeats who stands behind this music, though Montague has managed to come close to the unadorned, stubborn ground of Ireland's being without Yeats's Romantic overlay and without recourse to his vatic posturing and Romantic rhetoric. At its best, Montague's language is more attuned than Yeats's to the rare phosphorescence of Ireland's ancient past. There is in Montague a clearing of the field, a greater knowledge of the past understood in its own uncompromising terms, with less guesswork, less anxiety over generating all-encompassing Irish myths. What we hear are the old instruments resurrected: the shrill and beat of tin whistle, fiddle, harp, *bodhrán* and bones, as in the jagged rhythm of

> Darkness, cave
> drip, earth womb
>
> we move slowly
> back to our origins
>
> the naked salute
> to the sun disc
>
> the obeisance
> to the antlered tree
>
> the lonely dance
> on the grass. . . .

Or here, in the poet's tribute to the modern Irish composer, Ó Riada:

> two natives warming themselves
> at the revived fire
> in a ceilinged room
> worthy of Carolan—
>
> clatter of harpsichord
> the music of leaping
> like a long candle flame
> to light ancestral faces
>
> pride of music
> pride of race.

Yeats claimed to be among the last Romantics, yet forty years later we have still not escaped his valedictory note. Nor is this any less true for Montague. The difference, however, between his Romanticism and Yeats's is that he has cut his Romantic stance closer to the bone, making it more of a tribal affair, grafting his own line onto Yeats's late wintry branch: that stark, disconsolate, percussive line we find in the last plays and poems.[1]

Besides the melodic line there is in Montague the realist's lens, images heightened and isolated by the jagged contours of the lines themselves:

> His vestments
> stiff with the dried blood
> of the victim, old Tallcrook advances
>
> singing & swaying
> his staff, which shrivels & curls:
> a serpent ascending a cross.

Or consider this portrait of an old French colonel, retreating into the prison of the self, silent, sliding toward his own extinction:

> I heard the floorboards creak
> as, cloudhuge in his nightgown,
> he prowled the house, halting
> only when, gnawed by the worm
> of consciousness, disappointment
> at disappointment, he stood
> on the porch to inhale
> the hay and thistle scented
> air of a Normandy harvest;
> piss copiously in salutation
> towards a shining moon.

A Slow Dance reveals a great deal about how Montague takes hold of a subject and finds a style to work it with. He claims a field and marks it with his own scratches the way animals stake out territorial prerogatives. He wrestles forms—a wide variety of them, both closed and open—and makes them his own, even if it means twisting their necks into submission. He has used the sequence to ride over a sixty-four-page format (a limit defined as much by the printer as anyone). Of the four

sequences he published in the 1970s, only *The Rough Field* spilled over
to a crowded eighty-eight pages.

And these *are* true sequences. *A Slow Dance*, for example, begins with
a seven-poem section celebrating the old blood-hungry gods of Ireland.
The section salutes the old dolmens and stone circles that dot the Irish
and English countryside, dating back to a time before Ireland's memories of England turned so violently bitter. It is no surprise, then, that
in this ancient Ireland the venerable litany to the Blessed Mother should
give way to a litany for the Hillmother, the female earthsource, renewer,
delighter, beginning and end:

> Moist fern
> > unfurl for us
> Springy moss
> > uphold us
> Branch of pleasure
> > lean on us . . .
> Hidden cleft
> > speak to us.

A contrapuntal melody, the male of it facing the female, the slow,
stately dance cleansing and healing, putting one in touch with one's
humble beginnings in the earth and transforming the dancer into the
greatrooted blossomer. "Totally absent," a prose piece runs, "you shuffle
up and down, the purse of your loins striking against your thighs, sperm
and urine oozing down your lower body like a gum."

The poem's last section closes like a diptych. Lining up with the opening sequence, this powerful, elemental lament is for Ó Riada, the Irish
composer who worked so successfully in the old Irish musical tradition
and who died in 1971. It is an antiphon calling across to the slow dance
at the beginning of the volume, Ó Riada's impersonal, tormented music
merging with Montague's sad lines until we too hear that keening

> Beyond the flourish
> of personality, peacock
> pride of music or language:
> a constant, piercing torment!

There are moments of earned privilege in Montague's dirge when he
summons the whole weight of the presences of Ireland's tradition to

welcome their dead brother into the ancient blackness that for Montague is older than Homer, or Carolan:

> The slant of rain on void eye sockets,
> The shrill of snipe over mountains
> Where a few stragglers nest in bracken—
> After Kinsale, after Limerick, after Aughrim,
> After another defeat, to be redeemed
> By the curlew sorrow of an aisling.

For the most part, Montague maintains an icy control over his subjects; syntax chafes against line break and the chiseled images pluck pizzicato against eye and ear. But sometimes, ever the Irish republican, he slips over into sentimentality, especially when he tries to deal with human love. For if Ireland has its proud, aloof blind bards strumming the golden hairs of ancient harps, their visions blazing into the dark skull as words begin to tumble into the thin air, she also has her tradition of beerhall and pub, where patriotic ballads recall the old tragedies and stir us in spite of ourselves. No less a figure than James Joyce was wary of this all-devouring, sentimental popular music, with its come-hithers and "Wild Colonial Boys." Only by turning the tradition on its head and keeping a safe distance from those sirens was he able to escape that sentimentality which sometimes catches up Montague.

Looked at from the angle of cultural retrieval, however, Montague and the other Irish poets have been more fortunate than their American cousins. For if the English conquerors cut out the Irish tongue in the eighteenth century by proscribing Gaelic, the present-day Irish have grown a new one in order that they might once again sing the grave songs of their ancestors. Refined over millennia rather than decades, the old melodies have escaped the tyrannies of the musical bar and the English lyric tradition. And while it is true that few Irish would willingly surrender their facility with English to return to a language for which there are perhaps 20,000 native speakers (there are more speakers of Gaelic, for example, in western Massachusetts than there are in all of Ireland), still, what the Irish have done with their new tongue is extraordinary.

An old tongue and the old gods—half-effaced, mouldering, melting back into the steaming earth from which they once came—are elemental forces which Montague knows remain very much with us, as in the ritual bloodletting of Irishman against Irishman:

> we exchange sad notes
> about the violence plaguing these parts;
> last week, a gun battle outside Aughnacloy,
>
> machine gun fire splintering the wet thorns,
> two men beaten up near dark Altamuskin,
> an attempt to blow up Omagh Courthouse.

In the Iron Triangle, young British tank crews, eyes red with fatigue and fear, patrol gutted streets where anyone may harbor a bomb, not a homemade amateur sort, but a sophisticated model made by experts who have had ten years of practice in which to perfect their craft. So the killing trickles on in the north—in Tyrone and along the Falls Road or outside Belfast—at the average of one death each day. Under the shadow of the old gods the poet's countrymen continue to do what they have been doing for centuries, as his free translation from the eleventh-century Irish tells us. Still the Irish cry out and multilate their bodies, and "from this worship of dolour" they named one blood-stained field the "Plain of Adoration."

In Montague's world the passage of time is an allusion, for the old terrors still dominate his landscapes. So in one poem he recalls a night spent in a Belfast high-rise hotel, where "jungleclad troops" ransacked the Falls area, running down the "huddled streets" in search of terrorists, until the "cave of night" bloomed "with fresh explosions." Ireland's landscape of nightmares is like Bosch's fevered vision, where a "woman breasted butterfly / copulates with a dying bat" and a "pomegranate bursts slowly / between her ladyship's legs," her eggs "fertilizing the abyss."

A man racked with nameless guilt and a stiff pride, so his poems tell us, Montague is at home, finally, with bog and farmyard, tides and rivers, seagull and wren and curlew, with phallic tumuli and stone outcroppings, death and the scent of death, the release afforded by strong whiskey and copulation . . . all bought at the cost of the knowledge of his own mortality. He has not escaped his Jansenist background, though we know from these poems he has tried. Out of his struggle for some sort of order and his willingness to surrender himself to some kind of primordial fate, he has created a slow dance, a somber music, set to a few dark chords to which he clings as to a birthright.

When he turns in *The Great Cloak* to sing of modern love, as though he had won through to it, what we hear is a frailer, more fragmented music. Here the sequence follows the chronology of personal history in a triad Montague calls "Search," "Separation," and "Anchor," the sections that divide the text into thirds. These poems, he tells us in his quarter-page plot,

> should not only be read separately. A married man seeks comfort elsewhere, as his marriage breaks down. But he discovers that libertinism does not relieve his solitude. So the first section of the book ends with a slight affair which turns serious, the second with the despairing voices of a disintegrating marriage, the third with a new and growing relationship to which he pledges himself.

Approaching the subject of modern love, Montague has tried to use the strategy of detachment. It is thus Stendhal whom he seats across the entrance to the "Search" section of the poem, in order to reinforce the particular tone he is after: urbane, slightly amused, even somewhat disgusted and enervated by the rutting that goes on in (semi-) secret places. This man is hard on himself, harder than perhaps he need be. How studiously he avoids the personal, self-implicating eye in this first section. Both partners—or is there more than one woman enmeshed in Montague's curiously impersonal language and syntax?—remain unrealized shadow figures, tracks, where the bit actors—porters and provincial chambermaids and even flowers—seem to take up a more substantial space:

> *I shall miss you*
> creaks the mirror
> into which the scene
> shortly disappears:
> the vast bedroom
> a hall of air, the
> tracks of our bodies
> fading there, while
> giggling maids push
> a trolley of fresh
> linen down the corridor.

Flat, distant, even self-parodic, like "The Chess Game," in Eliot's *Waste Land* or the dreamlike world of *Last Year at Marienbad*, Montague's language struggles to cope with a world of tenuous love between a man and a woman. One thinks back to poems Montague has written about male camaraderie in which he remembers old friends from boyhood, all-night drinking sessions, a father finally applauding the poems of a son he does not quite understand. But in "Search," man and woman are wisps, ghosts: a hand resting on a table, a clenched fist, long fingernails stroking the skin like a butterfly caressing pollen, hands clasped defensively on small breasts, a closed hand trembling inside a more powerful one like some frightened animal seeking shelter.

It is a pattern of liaisons which has been repeated a thousand times, where

> Slant afternoon light
>
> on the bed, the unlatched
> window, scattered sheets
> are part of a pattern
> hastening towards memory.

This pattern hastening toward memory defines the whole first part of *The Great Cloak*, culminating in the terrible realization that the poet has after all been "searching through" the woman's body

> for something missing
>   in your separate self
> while profound night
>   like a black swan
> goes pluming past.

And so, for all its sense of a confession, "Search" remains very much a private affair, to be dealt with in the refined tones of a dozen cosmopolitan writers from Chaucer to Proust: a French set piece, almost, in spite of its Belfast setting.

But if terror and pain are kept in a minor key in the opening section of the poem, anger and suffering make themselves felt everywhere in the poem's center, as the poet's marriage to his first wife falls violently apart. We hear the pain growing, from the plangent cry of the screech owl in the June night air to the flat unhooded words of accusation flailing out against accusation, coupled with the knowledge that, certain things said and done, there can be no way out except separation. "We shall never be," the refrain insists, "what we were, again."

The problem for Montague here is to be fair to his first partner, despite his anger and hurt. One way for the "gentle man" to do that is to "assume / the proffered blame." But no use. Even in his recounting the old angers force their way to the surface: "It takes / two to make or break / a marriage. / *Unhood the falcon.*" Montague has tried to let his wife speak for herself in such poems as "She Walks Alone," and "She Daydreams, By the Blue Pool." "She Dreams," the strongest of the interior monologues spoken by the wife, points to one of the reasons —presumably—for the dissolution of this relationship. "I came to a place," his wife dreams,

> to where the eggs lay in the grass,
> I watched them for a long time, warming them
> With my swollen eyes. One after another
> The chipped and scraggy heads appeared;
> The embryos of our unborn children.
>
> They turn towards me, croaking "Mother!"
> I gather them up into my apron
> But the shape of the house has fallen
> And you are asleep by the water's edge:
> A wind and wave picked skeleton.

Childlessness is personal tragedy too deep even for the poet's words, and the bone sticks in the singer's throat:

> Grief, an unashamed,
> unconstrained, teeth-baring
> lament, one creature
> in a fury of loss
>
> bearing witness to
> the passage of another. . . .
>
> ("Lament")

This passage would seem to key the inner music of the whole middle section, before it subsides into the final lyric afterthought, a final visit to the old home on Herbert Street when these two were first married. To sing of old happiness is to recollect the old times: Georgian Dublin architecture, Nurse Mullen with their old black tomcat, the pony and donkey across the way. We feel Montague's lacerated wounds as he once again evokes that lost gossamer playland world, and we understand his failing attempts to keep faith with his wife's injunction not to betray whatever truth it was that belonged to them both.

The final section, "Anchor," like a kind of extended *Midsummer Night's Dream*, focuses on the dream of the girl who moved through the opening sequence and to whom the poet returns once more. Montague fleshes her out now, as she emerges out of the shadows to become first some mythic corngoddess and finally a woman named Evelyn. Days of wine and roses: a world of sweet-smelling hay and "warm Constable" scenes, where deer by night are disturbed by headlights until they are forced to move "stiff-legged, in short, jagged / bursts" at the couple's approach. As lyric gives way to lyric, we come to know this other woman more intimately, learning her little secrets and then her big ones: the shared intimacies and sudden, unexpected grace notes, the lullaby sung a little off key as the woman's wounds are touched. Thus Ceres gives way to another human being. And the new love leads—as with the old —to new quarrels. It is the pattern of fallen human nature reenacted once again. A man and a woman, like a team of horses, race together in the same direction, "close," yet "separate"; bitter quarreling is followed by sweet reconciliation, where thigh melts "into thigh, / mouth into mouth, breast / turning against ribcage." Love's old sweet song again, but with this difference, that in the book's last few pages, this new wife swells out with the promise of new life, caught up in the pattern of mother and child.

So "Protest" enacts the ritual of birth, with the poet present to comfort his wife in her need (Montague concentrates on her trembling hands, symbol of her vulnerability and need for comfort), "while our daughter was hauled / and forced into this breathing world," "born, as we die, reluctantly." Una, his firstborn, will inform everything he writes from now on with her presence: "love's invisible ink, / heart's watermark."

In the book's last two poems, Montague manages to see his two wives embedded in the seashore landscape of his new home. In the first of these, "The Point," he recalls the sound of the foghorn mourning like a cow who has lost her calf, a sound that brings home to us Montague's obsession with his first wife's barrenness. Once, the poem remembers, he had assisted at the futile attempt to save a calf whose neck had been broken during the violent transit into life. Now the memory of the cow's disconsolate crying after its lost calf echoes the disembodied cry of the foghorn off the coast of Cork; echoes too the cry of his first wife, and— finally—Montague's own deep cry, even as he insists—unconvincingly because the pain on both sides seems too great to be this easily accounted for—that the sound of the foghorn is nothing more than "a friendly signal in distress." As the poem ends and he bids a final good-bye to his first wife, he chooses to see the fog lifting to reveal their past in the same way that he now sees the opposite shore reveal itself, "Bright in detail as a painting, / Alone, but equal to the morning" of their shared life together.

The last poem is in turn addressed to Evelyn, and it too takes place along the Cork seashore by their new home. But now Montague's central metaphor is not the foghorn but the lighthouse. His new marriage, he says, must be—as all marriages are—a sailing out into unchartered waters, though the comfort of a sheltering home lies behind their excursions outward. Father, mother, child mark a new beginning, ambiguous as the image of the shore's edge itself, where the edge between domestic harbor and the vast sweeps of the Atlantic keep shifting, though for the moment they are quiet.

I am uneasy with *The Great Cloak*, though probably no more so than Montague himself was. He has moved beyond the momentary stasis of that poem's quiet edge, and that newborn child is now nearly seven. For even beneath those delicious embraces in the summer hay reminiscent of Constable's world, I can feel in the lines themselves a hornet swarm, a muscular tension, the deep angers and unresolved conflicts that also constitute one of Montague's strengths as a poet. What he managed to do in *The Great Cloak* was to wrestle his demons into some sort of formal pattern: a snarl of lusts, of anger, pathos, pain. But this sequence is—I think—only an interlude, an interruption, from that harsher, darker music one hears in *A Slow Dance*. It is that music that will probably draw him back to itself:

> Start a slow
> dance, lifting
> a foot, planting
> a heel to celebrate
>
> greenness, rain
> spatter on skin,
> the humid pull
> of the earth.

Transmute that music how he will, it will insist on rising to the surface again. It is Montague's own double-edged gift.

1979

John Berryman

Dante, Blake, Pascal, Baudelaire, Hopkins, Eliot: these, and Emily Dickinson and—at moments—Roethke . . . and Berryman. Figures in our post-Augustinian pantheon, and in the west, who have touched with their words the mudflats of the human condition and have reported back to us the sense of having been in their turn touched by the fiery or chilling finger of God. Consider this cluster of works in the short space occupying Berryman's own post-*Dream Songs* world: *Love & Fame* (1970), *Delusions, Etc.* (1972), *Recovery* (1973), and *Henry's Fate* (1977). When Berryman leapt from the bridge which crosses the Mississippi River at the University of Minnesota seven years ago, swerving slantwise toward the frozen river, only the first of these volumes had been born. But we, coming after, and picking up the fragments as best we can, can piece together from the scattered limbs of Osiris a pattern—a terrifying pattern—which includes in its grid an oasis of spiritual recovery before that battered self suffered its further disintegrations.

Much has already been made of Berryman's alcoholism. This is of course inevitable, since Berryman himself made so much of it, whether in the *Dream Songs* themselves or in *Love & Fame* or in his unfinished novel, *Recovery*, that thinly disguised fiction about a schizoid figure named Alan Severance (a name that one witty alcoholic character translates this way: " 'Alan' is harmony, right? Celtic, I believe. Your last name is wide open. Tearer-apart of people, disrupter.") Berryman was an admitted alcoholic, but it is his struggle against his condition that seems to me to mark the anxiety of the hell-trapped condition of modern man as much as any condition. It is this self-conscious, self-emptying struggle that in fact informs the movement of Berryman's best book, *Love & Fame,* to inform, indeed, nearly all the late poetry. My quarrel —such as it is—is with those critics who would try to explain away these poems as evasive techniques, lexical mannerisms, language distorted, lost control of, either by the delusions attendant upon alcoholism or by the recovery from that disease. Whatever truth there may have been in Berryman's belief that alcohol was necessary to spur the spirit on, to keep the muse in motion (a belief shared by other writers such as Hart Crane, Malcolm Lowry, F. Scott Fitzgerald, Eugene O'Neill, Hemingway, Faulkner), this much seems true: in struggling to arrive at the roots of his own spiritual malaise, in wrestling with those terrifying demons ensnared in the pickerel grass of the subconscious, Berryman has managed to speak with extraordinary force about the human condition in which we all—willy-nilly—share. To the point here is the longest of the five quotations that preface the *Delusions* volume: "And indeed if Eugene Irtenev was mentally deranged everyone is in the same case; the most mentally deranged people are certainly those who see in others indications of insanity they do not notice in themselves." And Eliot points the finger at every reader of *The Waste Land*, echoing his own dark encounter with Baudelaire: "You! hypocrite lecteur!—mon semblable—mon frere!" Exactly.

Reading *Recovery*, we are imaginatively transposed to the alcoholic's ward, where we can watch with apparent impunity the complex, devious moves and countermoves people will make to explain or defend their own self-delusions. What we soon realize, however, is that we have really been given an opportunity not so much to view *them*—as though we were London wags of two centuries ago taking a leisurely Sunday afternoon stroll through Bethlehem (Bedlam) hospital, who, having paid our entrance fee, are invited now to employ our riding crops to poke at or strike the more repulsive or unrecalcitrant idiots under our gaze—as to view ourselves, to see that, though sober, many of our actions and impulses, once scrutinized at their murky wellsprings, are anything *but* sane. The drunk reeling against the wall or vomiting over your rug or passing out in some sleazy tenement hall is simply more in the foreground of attention than most of us allow ourselves to be. For I have it on sufficient evidence—as even Jimmy Carter would admit—that our own thoughts and impulses and strong desires are as irrational and as Dionysian as the alcoholic's in his insistent frenzy. But then good psychoanalysts, writers, and confessors have known all that for some time.

Berryman had an enormous ego, as his poetry and criticism alone will show. He could be—and was—rude, insulting, dismissive, haughty, bullying, and his doppelgangers in *Recovery* admit to all these . . . and more. But there is in the poetry, in among the verbal evasions and aggressions, a vulnerability, an ability on Berryman's part to laugh at all his ego-flaunting peacock struts. And it is to this eye of self-assessment, this relatively calm eye at the middle of this Lear-like moving storm that dominated Berryman's life, that I would like now to turn my attention. And so to the fourth section, the marvelous close, of *Love & Fame.*

A word about the form of these "Eleven Addresses to the Lord." Here, as throughout the entire book, Berryman's characteristic formal signature is the quatrain, a form he also used almost entirely in his follow-up volume, *Delusions, Etc.* and that makes its presence felt in *Henry's Fate.* The form as Berryman uses it is amazingly—almost giddily—supple, the lines flexible, proselike, able to contract or expand at need. They can implode in on themselves, condensing to the "inimitable contriver" of the second line of the first address, or explode outwards, expanding into the theological qualifications of a line (from the same poem) like "and I believe as fixedly in the Resurrection-appearances to Peter & Paul," followed by the clipped parataxis of, "as I believe I sit in this blue chair." The addresses themselves range in length from the first (and longest), which is twenty-eight lines, to the seventh which is only eight. The average length (and six fall into this category) is sixteen lines—a paradigm of four fours. What makes cousins of all eleven is that each is, in fact, a direct address to the Lord: a prayer of thanksgiving, praise, confession, or petition. It is form, then, form imposing structure, discipline, tradition, order.

But what is most remarkable about these poems is the *mode* of address, the lexical encounter with the Other, which draws on and releases a magnificent spectrum of linguistic strategies. And unlike many of the language games Berryman uses in *The Dream Songs* in order to conceal or evade or dance about, here in this group of poems there is at heart a serious attempt to encounter, to join frightened self with that Other Self. Berryman's linguistic range is extraordinary; it can swing all the way from the use of special languages—the parlance, for example, of the radio astronomer or the biblical exegete or of the encounter session—to the lingo of blackface, showboat, babytalk. He is as well a brilliant manipulator of syntactic distortion, capable of wrenching the idiom until it yields its virtue, a manipulation that calls to mind, for me, the straining Hopkins of the terrible sonnets. Consider, for a moment, what Berryman can do with the language of astrophysics, exegesis, and encounter—mixed in with the traditional mode of the Old Testament hymn, as in the opening quatrain of "Lauds," which initiates the "Opus Dei" sequence of *Delusions, Etc.*:

> Let us rejoice on our cots, for His nocturnal miracles
> antique outside the Local Group & within it
> & within our hearts in it, and for quotidian miracles
> parsecs-off yielding to the Hale reflector.

Nothing in the Psalms will quite prepare us for that (though Auden—an early favorite of Berryman's—might come to mind in another key, as in his sonnet, "Petition"). At the other end of the lexical spectrum, Berryman is capable of doing a reputable imitation of the rhythms of jazz, the New Orleans strut, and blackface, all locked into the shattered frame of *Lycidas*, as in the eighteenth *Dream Song*, called "A Strut for Roethke," itself a pastoral elegy, lamenting the loss for all humankind and all nature of the brother singer:

> Westward, hit a low note, for a roarer lost
> across the Sound but north from Bremerton,
> hit a way down note.
> And never cadenza again of flowers, or cost.
> Him who could really do that cleared his throat
> & staggered on.

But in the "Eleven Addresses," Berryman shies away from both poles, choosing something closer to a middle register. A middle register, that is, for post-*Homage to Mistress Bradstreet* Berryman. For the ensemble of voices that we identify with the speaker of that poem and with the

Dream Songs, whom we know familiarly as Henry and Mr. Bones, here becomes Berryman, even to the extent of infiltrating that other persona of Berryman's, Alan Severance. "A poet's first personal pronoun is nearly always ambiguous": thus Berryman himself, speaking of the problem of the self-defined and idiosyncratic "I" that informs Whitman's *Song of Myself*. Here is Whitman's own solution to the poetic I —"the trunk and centre whence the answer was to radiate . . . must be an identical soul and body, a personality—which personality, after many considerings and ponderings I deliberately settled should be myself— indeed could not be any other." Quoting this very passage, Berryman comments that Whitman's voice is a voice "for himself and others; for others *as himself*—this is the intention clearly (an underlying exhibitionism and narcissism we take for granted)." And Berryman's gloss on the nature of the valve in Whitman's line, "Only the lull I like, the hum of your valvèd voice," is to the point here. It is a safety valve Whitman is speaking of, Berryman says, suggesting for him the sense of outlet of the poet as

> a mere channel, but with its own ferocious difficulties, [which] fills with experience [until] a valve opens; he speaks them. I am obliged to remark that I prefer this theory of poetry to those that have ruled the critical quarterlies since I was an undergraduate [at Columbia in the thirties]. . . . It is as humble as, and identical with, Keats's view of the poet as having no existence, but being "forever in, for, and filling" other things.

It is this sense of the "I"—as a constricted channel (constricted by all those things that make this "I" its idiosyncratic, specifically defined self) pouring out those things that have filled up the reservoir of the soul— it is *that* sense of "I" that Berryman employs consistently throughout his mature poetry. When he sings, therefore, it is with the range of voices we have come to identify with Henry. That voice has become as unmistakably Berryman's as Whitman's voice in *Song of Myself* has become Whitman's. Despite Berryman's disclaimer at the beginning of *His Toy, His Dream, His Rest* that *The Dream Songs* are "essentially about an imaginary character (not the poet, not me) named Henry, a white American in early middle age sometimes in blackface, who has suffered an irreversible loss and talks about himself sometimes in the first person, sometimes in the third, sometimes even in the second . . . ," it is this complex, painfully self-conscious voice that Berryman found himself using whenever he would let that valve fly open. (A look at Berryman's pre-*Bradstreet* poems should convince any lingering doubters.) The poetic "I" which we find in most English and American long poems of an autobiographical cast since *The Prelude* is not, of course, the voice the poet would ordinarily use in asking the waitress for a second cup of coffee or in lecturing on the New Testament to a group of undergraduates, and it would be shot down at once in a heavy group encounter session. But it does become, with time and practice, the "acquired" voice of the poet in the act of making a poem.

Given this framework, then, we can speak of the muted, humble, even serenely accepting voice of the "I" of the "Eleven Addresses," which I take to be as close to the poet as any voice can be said to be the poet's own, fairly synonymous at least with that five percent or so of the total mind he, like any person, uses when he feels he must articulate his feelings, even if it means releasing such impulses in the form of a poem or a prayer. And one of Berryman's most marked successes in these poems is the way he manages to play a specific, idiosyncratic, seriocomic voice against the traditional, rather rigid framework of praise and petition associated with the shaping of a prayer. What this mix produces is a compound of sentiments that are relatively straight-forward, honest in their doubts, quibbles, qualifications, even (yes) weirdly eloquent in their striving to avoid what we might normally consider eloquence.

Consider the strategy of the opening address as in some sense representative of all eleven. Each of this poem's seven quatrains is not only end-stopped; it is a semantically self-contained unit. (The only possible exception here—the only place where there is a slight running-over of sense—is at the juncture between the fifth and sixth stanzas, where the normal period terminus gives way to the more fluid comma.) The opening quatrain is an exercise in onomastics, a calling on the Lord, who is identified in turn as "Master of beauty," as "craftsman of the snowflake," as "inimitable contriver," and—more expansively—as "endower of Earth so gorgeous & different from the boring Moon." Such a convocation of epithets is close in spirit to the beginning of Hopkins's "Wreck of the Deutschland" (and it is Hopkins who will be indirectly summoned at the close of the tenth address to give his gloss on the real nature of fame). Here, then, are the opening lines to Hopkins's great ode, where God's own inscape is instressed in these terms:

> Thou mastering me
> God! giver of breath and bread;
> World's strand, sway of the sea;
> Lord of living and dead.

But even closer to Berryman's sentiments are these lines from Hopkins's sonnet in honor of St. Alphonsus Rodriguez (1888), where God is defined as the one who

> hews mountain and continent,
> Earth, all, out; who, with trickling increment,
> Veins violets and tall trees makes more and more.

Having evoked, then, the Arch Creator with such gorgeous phrases (three of which, incidentally, are self-reflexive and could apply on a smaller scale to the poet as maker himself), Berryman thanks that Creator "for such as it is my gift." That qualifier is of course all important, for that gift has been anything *but* an unmixed blessing.

The second quatrain by contrast is childlike, the good boy reporting his progress to his father. The poet has spent the better part of two days making up "a morning prayer to you / containing with precision everything that most matters." An interesting framing device, this, as the poet stands back in the midst of *this* prayer to comment in passing on that other prayer, an example of microcosmic contrivance, which has little, finally, in common with the acts of the "inimitable contriver" he is addressing.

The third quatrain is built around a parataxis, a Hebraic doubling, each completed sentence taking over half the quatrain's alloted space: "You have come . . . You have allowed . . ." These lines form the second thank offering to an apparently loving God for having rescued him not once but "again & again," even while he has apparently "allowed" the poet's brilliant friends (Delmore Schwartz, Randall Jarrell) to destroy themselves. The first thank offering indirectly comments on fame as the second comments on the love of the book's title. But both offerings are hesitant and qualified, and those qualifiers begin now to overrun the surface of the poem. If Berryman has been saved, if he still finds himself in his mid-fifties functioning, he has also been "severely damaged." But what is worth noticing here is the tone, which is one neither of hysteria nor even of resentment; instead, it teeters on a tightrope somewhere between comedy and pathos or, better, humility.

"Made a decision to turn our will and our lives over to the care of

God *as we understood Him,"* the third of Alcoholics Anonymous's "Twelve Steps" reads (the italics are mine). It is with the nature of the relationship between the poet and the immense Lord which he has been bold enough to address that Berryman's fourth quatrain is preoccupied. With all respect for his Addressee, Berryman finds himself suddenly in the awkward position of addressing the frankly unknowable, conscious that love for what is unknown is, finally, impossible: God is "Unknowable, as I am unknown to my guinea pigs." The only emotions he can feel confident exist in him as he addresses his Lord, then, are, first, *gratitude* for benefits received and duly acknowledged, and then *awe* before this rescuer. It is these two emotions, in fact, that dominate the first address; it will take several more addresses before Berryman can admit that what he feels most deeply is in fact love.

If the fourth quatrain compares Berryman's doubts about God's personal involvement with something as apparently trivial as people (Berryman by his own admission never had any problems positing a Deistic watchmaker off somewhere in the empyrean), the fifth and sixth quatrains take up the all-important issue for Berryman of a related question: the possibility of continued life after death. Neither science nor philosophy would seem to support such a notion, the poet readily admits, but, steeped in the tradition of New Testament exegesis, he is also ready to "believe as fixedly in the Resurrection-appearances to Peter & to Paul / as I believe I sit in this blue chair." (Which is fair enough, unless one questions whether one is indeed sitting in a blue chair. And just what constitutes the act of sitting? And what is blue? And what a chair?) This act of apparent affirmation must set up dissonances in any reader, for Berryman follows this conditional clause with another qualifier, namely, that these appearances "may have been a special case / to establish their initiatory faith." If the first stanza opened with a crescendo of qualified assertions, the sixth stanza has shifted us to the niggling brackets of the detached theologian, counting probabilities. With that, however, the last quatrain begins to round again on the poem's initiatory stance.

"Whatever your end may be," Berryman petitions, "accept my amazement," thus underscoring at once both his confessed *awe* before the Lord and wedging in at the same time the ambivalent resonances of that word, "end." Which end? God's End? He who has traditionally been thought of as eternal, both alpha *and* omega? Or end as purpose? But God's end in and for himself, or for Berryman? The embarrassment and

self-consciousness that the poet feels in addressing the radically unknowable even carries over into the seriocomic petition of his beseeching the Lord that he may remain vigilant to his promptings, in language
that echoes the psalmist's watchman waiting for the dawn but that at
the same time lugs into the poem's foreground the postcard image of a
British guard at Whitehall, standing "until death forever at attention."

So, even as the poet prays for constant vigilance, part of him sees that
what he is asking for is, at least for himself, at best improbable. After
making his request, a request that a fellow alcoholic, incidentally, would
tell Berryman in Group was a high-falutin' unrealistic Contract, Berryman ends his poem by half-asking, half-cajoling the Lord into giving
him assistance again, as he has so many times in the past. With this
much quieter petition, the poem rounds on the same epithet with which
it began, with one final qualifier—this one an onomastic tribute to the
Lord who somehow sees more deeply into Berryman than even Berryman's qualifiers will admit—as now he addresses the Lord as "Master
of insight & beauty."

Having attended to alpha, our exegesis would be incomplete, asym-
metrical, ateleological, without some consideration of omega. The
eleventh address is one of the shortest and certainly one of the most
poignant of Berryman's addresses, as though, approaching the volume's
terminus in silence (the inescapable condition of all books), the poet
were forced by the gradual stripping away of his linguistic strategies to
say what is in his mangled heart, and to utter it as devoid of verbal
coy or decoy as possible. The last poem recapitulates the conclusion of
the first, but with an important difference, for it is about Berryman's
willingness, after all, to stand at some kind of attention—or at least to
remain, as best he can, attentive.

There are three quatrains here, the first two centering on two early
Christian martyrs, examples culled from Berryman's long reading in
the Loeb edition of the Church fathers. (Has he not already informed
us in "The Search" that he began "the historical study of the Gospel /
indebted above all to Guignebert / & Goguel & McNeile / & Bultmann
even & later Archbishop Carrington"?) The first example is of the
young Germanicus, who, cowboy-fashion, "leapt upon the wild lion in
Smyrna" to the crowd's wild applause, "wishing to pass quickly from
a lawless life" (Berryman's own deepest wish—and placed in a classic
situation: dying before an admiring crowd in the public amphitheatre).
The second example is of the octogenarian Polycarp, faced with the

"choice" of death by burning unless he renounced his Lord, asking now with a certain inestimable grace how he could be expected to renounce the One who had done him no harm in all those years. Placing his own condition against these two paradigms of witness by martyrdom, Berryman petitions in wrenched syntax the same Lord whom they served that he too may be permitted to offer his own comic, inadequate (yes, qualified), but nonetheless authentic witness:

> Make too me acceptable at the end of time
> in my degree, which then Thou wilt award.
> Cancer, senility, mania,
> I pray I may be ready with my witness.

Composition of place, two exempla, an embarrassed petition barely wrenched from the poet, but uttered nonetheless. Ironically, the poem itself *is* Berryman's own best witness.

Finally, something should be said about this sequence as conclusion, as an honest deflation of the speaker's ego, commenting on the progress of the poet's fortunes with love and fame. Throughout this volume of poems, Berryman's twin themes have been the speaker's preoccupation with those two conditions. This double theme is present from the opening poem, "Her & It," to the close of the book. "Her," incidentally, is a lost love, a girl he was once in love with—and for that matter may *still* be in love with—who probably "now has seven lousy children," and "It" is a questionable fame: "my publishers / very friendly in New York & London / forward me elephant cheques." In fact, *Love & Fame* is a study in the transformation of those two all-encompassing, all-engrossing abstractions. Consider one pole of these intertwined, twinning terms in the closing stanzas of "Drunks," a reminiscence from the poet's undergraduate days, when he was at a New Year's Eve party at his mentor's home—"crawling with celebrities"—where his friend H

> . . . got stuck in an upstairs bedroom
> with the blonde young new wife of a famous critic
> a wheel at one of the book clubs
>
> who turned out to have nothing on under her gown
> sprawled out half-drunk across her hostess's bed
> moaning 'Put it in! Put it in!'
> H was terrified.
> I passed out & was put in that same bed.

So much for the erotics of the New York publishing world, for one measure of love and fame. For Berryman's own sense of the proper perspective in dealing with these themes, however, we will have to place that wild scene against the tenth of the addresses, the poem that I take to be the key, if you will, to reading the title in its most corrective light, devoid of delusion. It is here that Berryman confesses, finally— and despite his earlier qualifiers—that he has indeed fallen "back in love with you, Father,"and asks that his Lord may "Come on me again" (and the sexual pun is surely inescapable) "as twice you came to Azarias & Misael." Love.

And as for fame:

> Oil all my turbulence as at Thy dictation
> I sweat out my wayward works.
> Father Hopkins said the only true literary critic is Christ.
> Let me lie down exhausted, content with that.

It is Berryman's prayer that he may come to see that Christ's judgment on the artist's work may be accepted as sufficient. "Fame," Hopkins had written to his friend Canon Dixon in 1878, "whether won or lost is a thing which lies in the award of a random, reckless, incompetent, and unjust judge, the public, the multitude. The only just judge, the only just literary critic, is Christ, who prizes, is proud of, and admires, more than any man, more than the receiver himself can, the gifts of his own making." If Hopkins—whose magnificent corpus of poems remained in manuscript for thirty years after his death—found the standard he articulated here absolute, precise, exact, and exacting, Berryman must have found it—finally—impossible to follow in more than wish:

> Will I ever write properly, with passion & exactness,
> of the damned strange demeanors of my flagrant heart?
> & be by anyone anywhere undertaken?

That passage seems to capture as well as anything Berryman's anxieties about his craft and his name. If he cannot really follow Hopkins's heroic standards, though, at least he sees them as a distant possibility, a way of getting out from under the debilitating effect of fame as the critics and reviewers only can dispense it.

With the "Opus Dei" sequence—which opens Berryman's next (posthumous) volume, *Delusions, Etc.* and thus seems to comment ironically on the "Eleven Addresses"—the voice is much more qualified and uncertain, noticeably more hesitant and even schizoid. (Which, for example, is the real delusion: to accept the sorry self as one finds it, with all its manias, incessant hungers, egogratifications, and so on, or to try to radically alter that self by capitulating to an onomastic peg-board Other that may not, in fact, after all even exist?) Still, the "Eleven Addresses to the Lord" did constitute a kind of oasis for the at-wit's-end Berryman, did provide a space where the poet could address his God, could, in the very lay of his syllables, find some relief from the feverish heat of the poor self grating against itself. For having achieved this with such consummate verbal skill at a cost to the self that only the poet could have measured, for this—among other things— Berryman deserves our affection and—though it is too late to matter much to him, now—our praise.

1980

Robert Pack

Leonard Baskin might do his portrait, using the Clifford photograph on the paperback cover of Pack's *Waking to My Name*.[1] The shadows darkened, the weathered lines of the poet's face at fifty etched in, the rock set of the jaw, the slight downturn of the lips, the eyes peering out from behind the bone fortress with that quizzical mixture of irony and vulnerability. You come away from reading this volume of 250 pages that cover Pack's life as a poet—twenty-five years of it—with the sense that a man has dressed over some deep wound with an extraordinary array of bandages. At times he can make even his early masters—Keats and Stevens and Hardy and especially Robinson and Frost—seem light and gay, for he refuses to look away from the fact of death in the same way that Baskin's drawings refuse any consolations before the same fact. Pack's own death (waiting for him somewhere down the line), his father's death, his children's eventual deaths, the death of everything he treasures now even as he understands that someday he will have to let it all go. "On what premise might an art be based that would free it from a dependence on violence as its primary source of energy and thus lead the artist from the maker's happiness back again into life?" Pack asks. In returning to something believable, some supreme fiction, he suggests in his 1975 essay, "Art and Unhappiness," "the artist might become a model for us all, adding a tranquil perspective out of his ordering power" so that he might free his "voice from dependence on irony or cynicism."

Pack means what he says, and he has tried to establish a poetics based on creating a Wordsworthian tranquility for our time which he demands and needs. When Pack reads modern fiction and nonfiction and poetry (and as director of the Bread Loaf School of Writing he is inundated with it), I can imagine his ironic smile as he reads of violence and more violence, of murder, suicide, rape, incest, fellatio, sodomy, and the thousand strange faces violence can be made to wear. His answer to these faces is the counterproposition of limitation and its promise: the Vermont countryside (though he is an ex-New Yorker in the way Frost was an ex-Californian), a wife of twenty years, three children, a mother, a sister, and a father who in a sense "deserted" him by dying when Pack was sixteen. Out of this recognizable world Pack has chosen to build his classical, anti-Romantic world, snatching what domestic pleasures he can against the lengthening shadows of death and oblivion. Like Candide, like Stevens's Crispin, Pack wants to cultivate his small garden in relative stability and peace. Ironically, critics and some of his fellow poets have taken him at his word. But what they have not gauged sufficiently—and what Pack himself has underplayed—is a potential for anger and violence in himself which he has had to learn to control. Wordsworth is indisputably somewhere in the background as Pack's progenitor, but Pack's world is a lot darker than that Romantic's ever was, as relentlessly dark, perhaps, as Frost's was.

Pack's real father is Keats rather than Wordsworth, in spite of what Pack has said to the contrary. I mean the Keats of the late odes, fronting the fact of death, the Keats we hear in the odes to melancholy and the nightingale and the urn, the poet hopelessly trying to make time stand still, trying to warm himself by the fire of the imagination (and even succeeding for a few brief moments), a man trying to wrestle with his own death (in spite of whatever he can find to say to the contrary) and trying to console himself—and others—as he inevitably goes on losing that battle. And therein lies Pack's terrible strength, which makes him harder to read sometimes than Hardy. (I once heard Pack recite Frost's "Out, Out . . . ," about the death of a boy whose hand is ripped off by a mill saw. I was gasping by the time Pack had finished, stunned for days after by Pack's evocation of that small death. I had heard Frost's poem before, had even taught it, but for the first time I deeply felt that boy's irretrievable loss at the marrow.)

Anger. Consider for example the poem that begins Pack's new selected, a recent poem called "After Returning from Camden Harbor." The speaker is recalling a sullen trip back home to Middlebury with his wife after a few days at the shore. He is angry with her for whatever reason (since in a marriage of any duration anything can be enough to start an argument). He has turned defensive and sullen and inward, wanting to speak, needing to speak, but afraid that speech would be speech seeking the wrong thing. Worse, it has rained at the seashore, turning this vacation ground into a landscape exactly duplicating Pack's own troubled mind, so that inner and outer weather have once again conspired. Sadly, the speaker realizes the futility of his own anger, does not want to stay angry since anger is itself wasteful, poisoning more of the limited time he knows he has left with his wife. He tries therefore substituting one image—the roiling sea "with sailing boats / rearing like horses against the flat slap / of foaming waves"—with another domesticated image: "a plain, translucent pitcher, quiet with milk, on a yellow tablecloth / brightened by morning sun." This in turn becomes a "green pitcher of milk" and the image is meant to replace the impinging reality of a green chaotic sea. The realization of love, like the realization of the poem, Pack insists, is a matter of choice and thus a matter of words, of giving order to the chaotic turmoil of chance swirling within and without. The garden *must* replace the wild, insane sea both around and—even worse—within us. For this measure of order, limited as it is, is really all we have.

The poem's happy surprise of form is concealed until the close when we realize that, in all this furious disorder, Pack has managed to provide us with an intricate sestina. Pack's poems are filled with such difficult forms used deftly, masterfully, and I find myself admiring his use of them almost in spite of myself. Perhaps it is the heritage of Whitman and Pound and Williams, but I distrust such forms in American verse, and from their actual practice I would guess most American poets writing today (with a few notable exceptions) feel the same way. But Pack uses the sonnet, the rondo, the villanelle, the ballad, the sestina, the blank verse dramatic monologue—with urgent rightness. As here, where he has his wife break the sullen silence of the trip back to Vermont by communicating the neutral information that a computer, "given six random words / and the idea each sentence must include them, / all repeating in the final line— / composed a poem that furiously made sense." Those six words—three nouns and three descriptive modifiers—Pack, true to the furious logic of his sestina, repeats together as the last line of his poem: *"idea water asleep furiously green words."* We go back to the opening of the poem and find that, sure enough, all six words have already been introduced in the first four lines of the poem and then repeated over and over in the poem's succeeding lines. This is not mere cleverness but the demonstration of a civilized and passionate wit, choosing to order those six random words, uttered by his wife/muse, into a poem celebrating his love, in spite of his very real anger, for the very real woman sitting there beside him. Like Robert Hass's "Meditation at Langunitas" with its final repetition of the single word, "blackberry," a word that has come by poem's end to carry so much meaning, Pack's poem dares even more in terms not of nostalgia for an early love but rather of celebration of something so much more difficult to do convincingly: to choose to praise married love in the midst of anger itself. Not idealized love, then, but a love, frayed, tired, committed to the long haul, a love that means trying to compose a sense of domestic order—of *choosing* to do just that—when every fiber and nerve end in us feels like throwing the whole relationship with its crushing human limitations over the side and beginning again with the chimera men sometimes call, to their own chagrin—and the woman's—the Perfect Woman.

Marriage and poetry go hand in hand in Pack's poetics. Out of the chaos of anger and confusion and the illusion of infinite choices before us, we choose this word and that woman, composing day by day an order so that we may realize the good we can possess rather than plunging after what Pack sees as the short-term pleasure and long-term vacuity of essentially anonymous sexual liaisons. Pack may well be a proponent of the Paterian aesthetic; he may be in some senses a latter-day Marius the Epicurean attuned to the various registers of the pleasure scale (as a poem like "The Last Will and Testament of Art Evergreen," with its rich sensual catalogues, will attest to), but out of that aesthetic he has created a fierce moral construct which informs—*in-forms*—the very core of the man's poetics. For Pack, the decision to create a circumscribed happiness out of the dark void of Genesis, in other words the choice to create the poem, is at heart a moral choice reflecting on our very humanness. *I choose, therefore I am what I am.* Call it the Cartesian fable of Popeye.

One reason Pack has not received more critical attention is that, though he cannot have escaped being a Romantic, he has tried very hard to write a classical poetry in a Romantic age. It is as though he knew that this age is the age of Lucifer the over-reacher, spawning another generation of sons and daughters swerving from their poetic fathers. We live with another generation of poets whose strongest voices appear to deny the limits of language, intent on the distinctive sounds each can make. We still want distinctive, individuating voices; we want to sound ourselves as John Cage, breaking all the traditional values of music, is able to sound himself. We still want, as Hopkins knew in his own heart, to taste ourselves no matter what the cost. And this denial of our place in the chain of humanity, the necessary realization that we are children of very human progenitors and not of the gods, leads us, in Pack's view, to the dangerous illusion that we are immortal, that we are gods as the serpent in the garden promised us we would be if only we rejected the father.

But Pack places himself boldly against such illusions. He is painfully aware that we are limited by ourselves. Having lost his own father early, Pack knows—chillingly—that this makes him next in generation to go into the silence. Like his masters, Keats and Hardy, Frost and Stevens and Yeats, he has been made aware of his own limitations. Bloom has already brilliantly observed that the knowledge of limitation is itself a temptation to be overcome; too great a preoccupation with limitation, with the shadow of death, renders us powerless. Pack has wrestled with the shadow of this covering angel in that his formal patterns of image and syntax have rendered some of his earlier poems static and unrealized, their energy straining for release but caught by the cold serpent's medusa gaze. Hopkins—another of Pack's favorites—ran the same risks and for some of the same reasons: that he was placing himself squarely against over-reachers whom he admired while he struggled to set up an anti-thetical poetic. For Hopkins it was Shelley and Byron and Keats and especially young Swinburne just as for Pack it would seem to be Berryman and Lowell, Plath and Sexton, and—more recently—Ashbery and Merrill, as much as he might seem to admire these poets for their own demonic energy.

I don't think any less anger or fear informs Pack's poetry than theirs; he can see as well as anyone the verbal pyrotechnics of an Ashbery, a

Merrill, even a Tate. But he has opted —this repressed Romantic—for another kind of poetry somewhat out of favor now in the United States: a poetry of statement, of formal complexity aligned to an older tradition, a poetry of moral purpose which insists on returning the reader to the world as we live it, better able to live in that world ambiguous because we have come to better terms with it. Readers naturally feel uncomfortable when someone has designs on them. But every poet has designs on the reader. What helps Pack particularly is the distance of formal design, the distance of wit, the distance of irony. And yet, ironically, it is against this same mask of irony that Pack has tried to distance himself so that we may believe what he says. Repeatedly he has divested his protective masks to reveal himself in all his human limitations. It is a paradox that the anger Pack would transform reveals itself in his poetry as a demonic energy, an energy, thankfully, which even prose statements and poetic maxims or witty and convoluted word games cannot quiet or tame.

This is why a poem like "The Kiss," dedicated to the youngest of his three children, Kevin, evokes such strong emotions in us. It is early April in Vermont in this poem. It is still cold and the ground frozen, but there is the promise of another planting season in the air. Pack is at home with this Vermont countryside; he has made it as much a part of his poetry as Frost and Robinson once made New Hampshire and Maine a part of theirs. It is a rugged pastoral we are offered, Pack presiding here as Pan, his "boot-grooves packed with mud" until they have become "cold cleft toes." Like a latter day Franciscan, he helps apple trees through yet another harsh New England winter. There are fresh turds on the ground near the trees where starving deer have come to strip the bark for food and Pack takes in "the faint waft of skunk" carried by the wind: visual and olfactory images he cherishes because they sharpen the edge of his pleasure while reminding him of the human limits of our pleasure. As in other poems, he sees the "female curves" of distant hills and gives his mind to sexual fantasies until he realizes the cost to spirit of such illusions and remembers "what thoughts I must / hold back to let my careful body thrive / as bone by bone it was designed to do."

He is the presiding genius of this scene, tending the apple trees "as if to dress / a child for school" and he must husband his energies wisely. Suddenly he is visited by his youngest son, trying to launch a huge bat kite in the April wind until it takes a nose dive and crashes into one of Pack's apple trees. Then, like Vito Corleone in *The Godfather*, Pack takes, not a serrated orange peel, but some of the protective aluminum foil from the apple tree he has been tending, makes two enormous fangs, and goes running after his son across the field until, his heart banging in his chest from the unaccustomed activity, he catches his boy and wrestles him to the ground. The boy is both delighted and terrified by that passionate force and the father, no longer Pan now but a very demon, is overcome with longing for his youngest. Here is his own flesh, his own blood, he sees, and he sinks his mock vampire fangs into his son's warm neck to suck "deeper / than I have known." Raw violence, transformed by a father's need to possess what he knows must quickly move away from him if the son is to flourish in his own time. The boy cannot understand his father's longing, will not understand until he himself has earned his own fatherhood, but many of us who are parents will know at once what Pack intends. "In our struggle to survive with purpose," Pack tells us, "what we need is an art in which the indigenous happiness of art, its order-giving power, is wedded to an idea of goodness—a goodness that is attainable in daily life. When this idea of goodness is passionately held, the theme and spectacle of evil may be treated without exploitation, for the deprivation or loss of good feelings (as in friendship or love) will be powerfully felt, and the power of the longing for their restoration will replace the increasing need for shocking stimulation that the imagery of violence generates." This desire to evoke and restore good feelings is what Wordsworth calls the "tranquilizing power," and it possesses the "wondrous influence of power gently used."

Pack's ostensible strategy in "The Kiss" would seem to follow his prose formula here completely. Yet the poem does not finally behave in a Wordsworthian fashion for me. One reason, I think, is that Wordsworth's pantheism with its benign nature has been replaced in Pack with a psychological ambivalence we associate with Freud and Otto Rank. Rather than end with an image of tranquility and of power gently used, Pack closes this fine poem with the powerful and poignant image of a father trying to sustain his own too mortal life by usurping his son's. He is in fact fed by the boy's warmth, an image the more poignant because Pack has once again become aware that his own world is so quickly gone. But in the poem he has not yet given over, not yet made the sacrifice he understands he must someday make of letting go so that his son may flourish. Instead, he desperately clings to what he loves, knowing, even as he composes his poem at his typewriter, that the scene he is reenacting is already in the past. And it is that saving ambivalence, that dissonance in Pack's formal constructs, that saves him. In short, his poems are greater than his own prose criticism tells us the poem can and cannot be and go beyond the limits Pack has told us the poem should not be able to go.

To read through *Waking to My Name* from beginning to end is to come to an understanding of the ways in which, over the past quarter century, Pack has matured as a poet and as a man. This volume gives a representative selection—containing about two-thirds of the poems that have appeared in seven previous volumes beginning in 1955. In Pack's case this presentation has been crucial because it shows how the darker side of this poet is defined in gradual stages, thus revealing by stark contrast the special light Pack has also earned for himself. I have read Pack's poetry regularly since the publication of *Home from the Cemetery* in 1969 and long ago came to admire his toughness, his paradoxical tenderness, his irony, his composed, sardonic, witty surfaces, his unusual civility (in the sense in which, say, Richard Wilbur and Charles Tomlinson would understand that term). Reading Pack I see one possible successor to Frost and Stevens in terms of tone, colloquial strategy, formal imperative. It is time now for a reassessment of the man, something Pack has not yet adequately been given, though his poems certainly deserve it. For the man is hardly written out, and his latest work, which I have read in manuscript—a volume consisting of a series of complex, interwoven dramatic monologues spoken by what I can only call a representative human family placed in Vermont —shows that Pack at fifty is still working, and still waking into his own name.

What we hear in him is a voice that has been struggling over the years, despite the polished surfaces, to come into its own, beginning in 1955—the year Wallace Stevens died—with a competent collection written when Pack was still only in his early twenties: *The Irony of Joy*. It is a derivative voice we hear in this book (for how except in a handful has it ever been otherwise?). But already Pack's signature is upon these poems. His is a strong voice, the poems tough, poignant, declamatory, hard-edged in their structure. Like so much poetry written in the academic mode in America at that moment of our literary history, Pack's is a poetry aligned to figures like Nemerov, Wilbur, Jarrell, and Bishop. Here is poetry with a moral grain which depends on the fathers, on the traditional structures and recognizable voices passed down by them. The close of "To the Family of a Friend on His Death" catches the tone of this first book, a first effort so much better in spite of its limitations than the first efforts of many young poets:

A man
Is not the sum of fortune of his gifts;
You want his life. Somewhere some still break
Familiar bread in happiness,
Draw in the sweetness of abundant breath.
What good is it to know your early joy
Depended on his death?

But Pack was not satisfied with a poetry of detachment and irony masking a real sensitivity and so—in spite of the academic vogue for irony in the 1950s—Pack's next volumes show a development in a formal mastery wedded to a colloquial line, together with a new calculus of emotional responses. The Pack who wrote *A Stranger's Privilege* (1959) and *Guarded by Women* (1963) shows the impact of Freud and of Yeats, the Yeats we recall in Roethke's Yeatsian poems. This is Pack in his late twenties and early thirties, a poet very much involved in his craft and already capable of writing some very good poems. There are poems of social protest here, poems of an apocalyptic baroque verging on Bosch, Freudian and grim fairy tales, poems that rewrite the biblical myths of Genesis (in fact the whole Pentateuch), to give voice to Pack's own need for beginnings. Among my own favorites here are "Neanderthal," "Adam on His Way Home," "The Shooting," and especially "South Beach," this last for its combination of strong rhetoric and the colloquial in a poem that realizes a setting in the way early Wilbur or Snodgrass or the Lowell of *Life Studies* did:

Two children splash along this beach
As if this summer's day will have no end.
I lie back on my towel, cover my face
With the *New York Times,* and think things through
As the ocean rasps upon the shore
By the breaker where our dog was killed.
In the blown sand and the water's spray,
I tell myself that all is vanity,
Even accepting vanity is vain;

> I do five extra push-ups, take a dip,
> Relieved at last by the absence of hope,
> And feel then, tightening on my lips,
> The white, determined smile of the drowned.

Whether we accept our fate or refuse it is of little consequence to fate itself. No poem can alter our fate by even a hair; it can only release us, release our muscular tensions by giving us a moment of pleasure and a glimpse into the truth of our human condition. And for Pack that is quite enough. One of the things therefore I take pleasure in is the way Pack has co-opted and subdued Yeats's late tragic gaiety in his own lines: "I tell myself that all is vanity, / Even accepting vanity is vain."

With *Home from the Cemetery* (1969)—his fourth book of poems —Pack arrives at his maturity. This is still for me his strongest single volume, as important for his development as *Spring and All* was for Williams's development, both books published too in their makers' fortieth year. There is not a throwaway poem in the entire book and some of Pack's best lyrics—sardonic, mordant, bitter, wry—are here. This volume contains the beautifully touching poem to the poet's infant son, the baby's arrival in the midst of the father's own angers and frustrations. "Welcoming Poem for the Birth of My Son" closes with the baby's coming at Christmastime, just the worst time of all for the poet. And yet, finally, perhaps the best time of all:

> He comes, crowned in his ears and fuzz,
> In a dazzle of fingers and toes, making
> Miracles with his glad eyes;
> He walks in the sun-struck kingdom of penguins
> Enraptured on their eggs, crying GOOD WILL
> To that angered city where my love hides.

There are also several very good social fables here, registering Pack's anger and dismay at what was happening to America in the late sixties, poems like "The Unificationizer" and "Burning the Laboratory" and— one of my favorites—"Love," which I understand more only as I grow older. Another is "The Stone," which may owe something to Ted Hughes's gothic animism or to Roethke's infantile animism but which makes particular sense when one considers the Vermont landscapes and the old stone walls which line the country roads with their dark shadows. And—too—when one understands the nature of Pack's own hunger for life and motion. The volume contains two major poems. The first is "Home from the Cemetery," a haunting Roethkean pastoral meditation which recounts the poet as a young man moving among the final landscapes surrounding his father's death in 1945, an attempt made twenty-five years after the event to come to terms with that wounding loss. The other poem is Pack's most ambitious—though not his most successful: "The Last Will and Testament of Art Evergreen."

"Last Will," seventeen-pages long, is a testament in thirty parts; it has been justly praised by figures as different as Anne Sexton and Lawrence Raab. A complex effort, it deserves a careful and extensive reading impossible here. Essentially, however, the poem is a dialogue between an old man who is near death named Art Evergreen (the name of course suggesting the poet's own sense of how we survive our own extinction) and a younger man named Jack who records Art's wishes and in so doing, it turns out, may well be Art's real son. One of Pack's preoccupations here as elsewhere is with the sense of continuity, the older poet handing on to the son (or daughter) what has already been handed on to him. It is a broadly, weirdly comic poem in which Art, over the course of a day (any day, since our lives are a succession of days anyway ending in the final and shortest day), gives away his body—his eyes, ears, nose, mouth, the rest of it at the same time teaching his amanuensis, Jack, how to use the very senses life gives us to enjoy. "I leave my eyes to you, Jill, both nearsighted," he quips, trying to teach his wife—one of four who all happen to be named Jill—to

> Wonder back through them to sunlight whipping
>   white on tacking sailboats;
> Or sledding over the dip of a hill,
> See the unfurling smoke of children's voices.
>   Past rainbow conch shells,
> See salt-shiny toes of sandpiper girls
>   swinging hands;
> Yellow trefoil fields; masquerading skunks;
>   the clown-glee of raccoons
> Parading through their moony paradise
>   of garbage pails. . . .

In turn young Jack Jackson (Jack son of Jack) tries to comfort the old man, who is soon to lose a world of things finely seen, by telling him that really he shall not miss such things since the "advantage of being dead / is that one sees nothing," that his eyes then will float like stars in the vast interstellar darkness, "boneless body / Spiralling away" and that moon craters will form where once his ears were so that self "will never enter them again / To hear sand slushing" as it did when once he walked the shores. Cold comfort that; yet, if we are to enjoy the light, Pack warns us as others have earlier, we must first become aware of our own deaths. And so Art Evergreen comes finally to lash out at what he considers the idea of God himself, that false father in Pack's world. Or, better, the ideas of God we have inherited over centuries: Egyptian, Greek, and Roman deities, various beast gods, even Jahweh with his "fire-fanning wings with feathers overlaid / hue upon brightening hue / Into a rainbow spanning the covenant, seascape, / breath-filled void." Thus does Art dismiss the second-rate imagination of Genesis to replace it with his own world. And though Pack admires Hopkins, he parts with him on the comfort of the resurrection, for in his world there is no resurrection beyond a comic re-creation (out of Stevens) where Art might leap up "naked hi ho / out of bed, prancing erect / On your pet hog, your cape streaming, singing / *The Star-Spangled Banner,*" where he may finally embrace the Perfect Woman, who—it turns out— would still be another woman named Jill. For Pack it will never happen, though we may hope for a kind of immortality in the millions of sons and daughters Art can affect by his evergreen words, including these words of his major comic pronouncement, a *last* will and a last testament meant to replace the Old and New Testaments themselves. "How long can I go on writing this," the poem ends, "keeping you alive?" And for once the voices of Art and his son and heir Jack and the Maker of this poem and of this world—a god-figure named Pack—collapse into one. By looking at the worst life has to offer we can hope for renewal, for some happiness in our own time. This comic/moral mode recalls at times the exacerbated voice of Stevens at forty-two, composing his own early last will and testament: "The Comedian as the Letter C."

Nothing But Light (1972) is a consolidation of what Pack had achieved in *Home from the Cemetery.* It is a satisfying volume with poems like "The Pack Rat" (the artist as comic collector of things, the artist as lover, as father, as husbandman), the moving and evocative "My Daughter," the terrible poem, "The Children," about casualties among children all over the world, as in that still green memory of Vietnamese children running down a road, their clothes, skin and hair on fire from an American napalm shell exploded on top of them. And there is the inexorable pressure of "The Plea of the Wound." Two poems in this book stand out powerfully above all the others: "Prayer to My Father While Putting My Son to Bed" and "Now Full of Silences." Harold Bloom has described them as "unique consolations in the abysses of family romance, firm achievements of a deliberately 'reasonable romancer' who has individualized his own distinguished middle way." Both are exquisitely moving, quiet and tender, almost Virgilian in their resonances. Listen to the opening of the first:

> Father of my voice, old humbled ghost,
>   ragged with earned earth,
> Teach me to praise those joys your last sleep
>   still wakes in me.
> What can I hold to? What can I tell this boy
>   who at moonrise
> Picked a vase of asters, purple and white,
>   now holding back from sleep
> Another trusting moment, listening
>   to my voice,
> To what it says?

Pack will not be hurried in his meditations, in the earned fruits of what he has disciplined himself, cell by cell and word by word, to say. And for one who would question the metaphysical efficacy of prayer, he does a good job of understanding the silent places of the heart and the heart's affections. Here we are, he says in "Now Full of Silences," "keeping watch over the stony fields / we are learning to forego" as the poor, dumb innocent animals in Noah's menagerie climb up the planks of the ark to "leave for the last spaces / full of silences / Which our words fill emptying themselves, / watering the final pity / We once taught the gods when we walked / among them." We no longer walk as gods now but rather with the animals, sharing their common fate as we all go into that same silence uttering even as we do the talismanic words the gods themselves once spoke to us. Perhaps, Pack hopes, we too go up the ramp in pairs like the animals, confirmed in our deaths as,

> hand in hand, as we have always done,
>   we walk into the past.

Pack's poetry lacks the insistent egobeak of so many American poets, crying out with their thin wares: *hear me, hear me*. His civility has cost him, probably, much critical attention. Nevertheless these poems rest secure in their achieved craft and human wisdom. In that sense Pack is truly one of the sons of Wallace Stevens.

Keeping Watch (1976) consolidates Pack's achievement. There is, for example, "Pruning Fruit Trees," with its two voices intersecting in a harrowing dithyrambic counterpoint, the voice of the stoic fronting death and the voice of elegy. There is the cosmic joy of "A Spin around the House," as the father, in a spontaneous and happy mood, begins to dance and whirl around the kitchen after dinner until his children, caught up in his dervish mood, lift "their blue glasses / over the spinning table / as their laughter splurges through the galaxy." There is the Stevensian sequence, "Maxims in Limbo," recalling "Like Decorations in a Nigger Cemetery," though Pack's 101 maxims and axioms are both more blooded and more accessible than Stevens's, if less challenging. There is, too, the poem, "Feeding the Birds," which captures the essential Franciscan spirit of the late Williams of "For Daphne and Virginia" and "The Mental Hospital Garden."

Finally, there are two poems that need special mention. The first is "Jeremiah," a love poem responding subtly to Williams's "Asphodel" and employing Williams's step-down triads, first moving to the right and then reversing themselves and moving to the left. The second is "The Ring," that touching prothalamium, a lyric of continuities employing the circular strategies of the greater English ode. Pack is a master of layering and manipulating time to reveal what is so essential to his poetic vision: the circular patterns through which we all move, repeating in our lives the gestures of our parents, which will in time be repeated by our own children. For whatever individuality we may achieve must be seen in conjunction with the way we repeat and repeat and repeat. Pack suggests this in his rhetorical patterns, his syntactic echoings, dependency on refrain, repetition of sound patterns, end rhymes, assonance, the repetition of entire lines, the repetition of key images. As here in the figure of the ring, which is first of all the wedding ring passed down from parent to poet, and which will someday be passed on to the poet's daughter. But the ring is also the arc of the apple branch reflected (and completed) in the pond, the circle of the moon and time, the halo of the necessary angel who guards the household, the arc of epithalamium completed in the death of the parent who gives himself or herself so that the child in turn may live out his or her days fully and the pattern we call life may continue. Perhaps, Pack suggests, his own father saw his daughter's eyes reflected in his own wife before he died, as now he sees in his mind's eye his own daughter's eyes, the arc of anticipation thus completed (in time) in the arc of memory:

> I hand the groom the ring
> and step back in the house
> an angel guards, beside the moonlit window
> where my mother paused,
> when her husband died, and turned the ring half-circle
> where the lord and lady
> cannot see. And there, reversed, again
> she waits in apple light,
> as slow wind shifts the laden petals
> in her hair, the pond,
> under the tree, for him to wed her now,
> as I do thee.

I have already spoken about some of the new poems in *Waking to My Name*, but a number of others besides "Camden Harbor" and the title poem need mentioning. I single out "The Twin," "Learning to Forget," "The Stained Glass Window," and particularly the finely modulated "Looking at a Mountain-Range While Listening to a Mozart Piano Concerto." This last reveals something of Pack's long attention to classical music, to Bach and Mozart especially and their genius for repetition and variation which Pack has sought for in his own poems, which, he has said, have at their core a "musical soul." Musical repetition, he tells us, means returning "to the crucial scenes of one's past, or the compulsion to face apprehensions and fears that have not been (and may never be) resolved." So in his poems where repeating phrases and images recall those scenes that bring us happiness, though they can also "be the dramatic necessity of returning to memories or ideas that still cause distress or even dread." The act of returning brings with it the concomitant hope of mastering emotions that threaten us, showing us at least how we may learn to endure them. Poetry, then, as Stevens would have agreed, "by affirming design, can celebrate the mind's power to confront its own despair" since that despair is grounded in what we are and in what we as a species have done to ourselves. "Brightly the piano asserts its melody," Pack's Mozart poem has it, and it is a melody we can hear in the poem's finely achieved blank verse lines:

> the orchestra gathers its colors to reply,
> true to the law that everything responds,
> nothing is left unanswered, that variation
> extends the self—as if one's life were made
> essential in a piano's theme, departing
> then returning one to what one is.
> And now again it is the piano's turn,
> and now the separate instruments, again
> as one, move onward to their chosen end
> beyond which nothing else will be desired.

Thus, in a meditation on the nature of Mozart's art, Pack reveals his own penchant for a Paterian aestheticism Stevens himself understood: the amassing harmony of one's life under the shadow of the urn, life understood in its essential and repeating patterns so that even our own deaths can come to be accepted as part of that unalterable pattern. In accepting such limitations Pack has found sufficient light by which to make his way and make his *ars poetica.* His poems proclaim that he has come to accept the human and necessarily limited aspects of the love he can give—and receive—from wife and friends and children. It is not the frenetic anonymity and shadow fruit which he believes Romantic love holds out for us to eat. In a sense Pack has become his own maker, his own final father, an aging Adam in a postlapsarian world, waiting for the flood to engulf him as he knows it must at last, but choosing in the meantime to walk with a very real Eve (or Jill) who shares his mortality and his warmth with him. It is a vision that must suffice, and will. We could do worse than listen to what Pack's poems have to teach us.

Intimacy has become Pack's consuming theme in middle age, a consoling intimacy which I rarely find in American poems, either because the wisdom and the difficult ability to record that wisdom is lacking, or because most contemporary poets seem capable of dealing adequately only with what Hopkins once called the dull dough of selfyeast. There is danger in Pack's working with these quiet themes, of course; the danger that the poem will become trite, unconvincing, bourgeoise in the

Marxist sense. Characteristically, Pack avoids the frenzied, the Dionysiac, the ecstatic, for something quieter and more solidly in the middle ranges. Because he has, many have read his stoic control as a comfortable prosiness. Yet Pack is anything but a comfortable poet. He knows darkness intimately, and has opted, like Williams before him, for the light. And he can sing, exquisitely. As in his new poems appearing in the little magazines and quarterlies. They are dramatic monologues which belong to the tradition (too long left in disuse) Frost made available to us more than half a century ago. With the dramatic monologue Pack extends his own voice to include father and mother, sister and brother, son and daughter: in short the whole human family tree. *Faces in a Single Tree,* containing Pack's most recent work, is (at present) composed of some thirty long poems which together provide us with a world in the sense in which Hardy and Faulkner and Anderson earlier composed worlds out of Wessex and Yoknapatawpha and Winesburg. Pack has naturally chosen Vermont and its people, and though that world is sketched in rather than painted in great detail, he has managed to make these poems resonate with a complex of feelings that, while they sometimes evoke Frost's presences and sometimes Browning's grotesques, are very much a part of Pack's circumscribed but distinctive experience. Together these monologues comprise an extended poem on the theme of intimacy. Some of the new pieces are sardonic, some scarifying, others poignant; many of them reverberate long and hard in the imagination. One comes away from these poems feeling one has heard these voices before, seen these words revealed somewhere else. For they are the same preoccupations we have found in Pack's earlier lyrics. But, as Pack's variations on intimacy are played out now in these dramatic monologues, we become aware of new currents of feeling, new patterns, new realizations.

I am impressed by the control and convincing quality of many of Pack's new poems, but a few I find stunning. These newest poems do not lend themselves to excerpting. They are too interwoven, depend too much on subtle repetition and variation. The language is familiar, colloquial, quiet, prosaic, unhurried. "Inheritance," for example, is a Wordsworthian poem in the tradition of "Michael." A father is talking to his son about the young man's future, trying to explain why he must disappoint him by not letting the son get into heavy debt at the beginning of his business career. It would not, he tells his son, be fair to be indebted to the father. No, the young man should not be mortgaging his future to pay off his past but should rather think about what he owes to the son he himself will someday have. We pay the father back by passing on ourselves to our own children and someday, the father tells his son, some

> cool October afternoon, when he
> is splitting wood with you, and you
> are resting on a stump beside the sumac
> blazing in the last warmth of the sun,
> he'll take his T-shirt off, and as the axe
> descends, you'll watch his shoulder muscles flex
> and then release beneath his flawless skin.
> A waterfall, you'll flow out of yourself. . . .

Even as he speaks, this father has been splitting wood with his own son. The talk goes on, things are said and left unsaid. At the poem's close the speaker remarks that another long, cold winter is coming on. Which reminds him then of something *his* father once told *him,* that earth is first our home and finally our grave. He remembers it was a day like this and he was raking leaves when his father told him that:

> I stood
> before him, naked to the waist, sweating,
> thinking of your mother, trying to decide
> what I would say when I proposed to her.

What has been so poignantly left unsaid is the realization—long after the fact—that the speaker's father had in his time seen the inevitable separation of his son from the nest and—in that sudden realization—had willed to empty himself of himself. Call it a celebration of the fact of familial pattern repeating itself, as here, tactfully, tacitly, the father tells his son how much he loves him and that he too is ready to empty himself for him, giving him now his real inheritance: the covenant of a future at one with the past from which it stems.

Pack began publishing in the same year Allen Ginsberg, three years his senior, read "Howl" to a crowd in San Francisco. He has survived to see the Confessionals rise and tragically set in their own short red sun. He has bided his time, trying to find a way through the same world that Plath and Sexton and Jarrell and Lowell and Berryman each tried

244 POST-WORLD WAR II POETS

to find a way. The results of that search, having shaped themselves over a quarter of a century, have now been gathered in *Waking to My Name*. One feels the fact of mortality everywhere in these poems, the sense of loss, the calculus of costs, the seriousness of all that life in the pause between birth and death has to offer us. Nature giveth and taketh away. And even as phoebe and chickadee clash in the radiant summer fields around him, even as he knows that his own name—poet —is pulsing now at fifty, Pack also knows that his own heartbeat is there to remind him "that most of the full of my life is behind me." Pack is more than a veteran craftsman. He is a poet of the penates, the old, despised but still-vital household gods whom we ignore at our own peril. He is a health-giving presence, this leech-gatherer. Read him.

1982

Thomas Merton

The Literary Essays of Thomas Merton (New York: New Directions, 1981)—a 600-page book—contains nearly all Father Merton's literary remains, that is, those fugitive critical pieces—introductions, reviews, essays, even his Master's thesis on William Blake—that he wrote between the late 1930s and his death in 1968. There are fifty-three pieces here, ranging from the very short to the monograph-length essay, all arranged by Merton's secretary at Gethsemani, Brother Patrick Hart. Gethsemani, you will recall, is the Cistercian Abbey in Kentucky where Merton spent the second half of his relatively young life, that is, the twenty-seven years from 1941 until his death at fifty-three. Brother Hart has divided Merton's specifically literary remains into four parts followed by three appendixes, though in Merton's case literature and religion keep passing through each other, refusing to remain within their own generic bounds, so that literary *aperçus* spangle brilliantly with theology, Zen, and mysticism in a way that Merton made his own. Part 1 consists of seventeen essays written during the last decade of Merton's life, when Merton turned his attention to a wide range of figures which included Blake (an early preoccupation reconsidered thirty years after), James Joyce, Pasternak (with whom Merton corresponded in the late 1950s), Faulkner, Edwin Muir, Julien Green, Louis Zukofsky, Simone Weil, Roland Barthes, J. F. Powers, Flannery O'Connor, William Styron, Rolf Hochhuth (author of *The Deputy*), and the black novelist William Melvin Kelley.

Merton's late preoccupation with Albert Camus makes up the second part of the book: seven essays written on this clear-eyed antagonist of Christianity, seven essays written over a two-year period, forming a monograph in themselves. It is evident from these pieces that Merton had meditated long and consistently on the implications of Camus's novels, journals, and interviews and that he found it important to be able to establish a strong counterargument to Camus's commentary on the state of modern society to show where Camus's thinking was logically taking him. For Merton, Camus is not an absurdist and certainly not a nihilist. He was in fact a humanist in the classic mold who had already constructed a vision of hell and another of the via purgativa and seemed bent on creating a vision of a world reclaimed by a clear-eyed love when he was killed in an automobile accident. Whatever, Merton found it important to face off against this worthy antagonist, this dark brother whose strictures against the religious mind in our time were as compelling as St. Thomas Acquinas found the inquisitive and doubting mind of his Jewish and Moslem counterparts in the thirteenth century.

Part 3—barely twenty pages long—collects Merton's short introductions (done mostly for the New Directions annuals in the 1960s) to the Spanish, Portuguese, and Latin American poets he was translating then. These include Ruben Dario, Pessoa, Vallejo, Cardenal, and Andrade. Part 4—"Related Literary Essays"—consists of six essays written between 1953 and 1968 on such topics as the "Theology of Creativity," "Poetry and Contemplation," and "Why Alienation is For Everybody," and they are much more dynamic than their rather heavy titles might suggest. This is followed by three appendixes: Merton's Columbia Master's thesis on "Nature and Art in William Blake," fourteen essays and reviews that Merton wrote between 1938 and 1940, prior to his entering the monastery at Gethsemani; and two tape transcriptions of Merton's talks on Faulkner's novels. The thesis on Blake reveals a man still in his early twenties already capable of handling literary and philosophical ideas competently and with something of that clarity that would become a mark of Merton's thinking. Its particular beauty is its ability to demystify Blake's art and to place it in both its historical and its ideological context. (The thesis, incidentally, can be read as a veiled autobiography, for the strains of Christian and Eastern thought that Merton unraveled in Blake were the same that helped shape his own thinking for the next three decades.) The essays and reviews (1938–40) were written mostly for the *New York Herald Tribune* and the *New York Times* on such figures as Aldous Huxley, Vladimir Nabokov, John Crowe Ransom, John Cowper Powys, E. M. W. Tillyard, and C. S. Lewis. Of all of these, it is the encounter with Huxley's vision of contemporary society that most fully engaged Merton. The Faulkner pieces, where you can almost *hear* Merton in the classroom, were talks given to a group of the younger monks on Sunday afternoons, when Merton would wind his way up from the Hermitage—that rugged cinder-block structure where he was allowed more of the solitude he so craved—to talk about the religious and monastic life, using "secular" figures like Faulkner as often as not as examples of contemplative and sapiential literature.

One approaches Merton's *Literary Essays* as one might approach a volume of St. Thomas's *Summa,* for we know at once that we are in the midst of serious literature, a literature asking the big questions. And the very way Merton puts together a paragraph or an essay demands an act of attention such as is demanded of us when we read Camus or Roland Barthes or an exegetical passage of the Johannine gospel by Raymond Brown. I do not mean to suggest that there is a turgidity or lugubriousness in Merton any more than there is in the other writers. Rather, what I want to suggest is that we are in the presence of a mind that has thought long and carefully about what it wants to say. Moreover, Merton was a natural teacher—Master of Novices at Gethsemani but also a Zen Master for all practical purposes (vide his extraordinary *Asian Journal* and *Zen and the Birds of Appetite*)—and so he keeps circling back on a point, listening carefully to whatever objections might be raised against his line of rigorous thought and attempting honestly and without rhetorical camouflage to answer the objections that might be brought against his position.

This is why the essays on Camus are still so important for us, for Merton heard in Camus the true voice of the questioning atheist (or, perhaps more correctly, the agnostic), a voice that had made the conscious choice to alienate itself from a radically absurd society, a voice that consistently and at great personal cost refused to join the pack, whether the pack be the consolidated voice of the Catholic Church (that being for

Camus the most visible face of Christianity) or the voice of the French Marxists, with whom Sartre for example had joined forces. The engagement with Camus is all the more important because one senses how deeply Merton was drawn to him, and one has only to remember Merton's own spiritual journey as described in *Seven Storey Mountain* to realize that he saw in Camus's position one that he, except for his conversion experience, might well have arrived at.

But Merton continued to grow and to change in the most alarmingly unorthodox ways throughout his life, to the dismay of all who wanted to claim him for their own. And those who years ago read Merton's autobiography will be surprised at the changes Merton continued to undergo throughout the 1950s and 1960s. To read his biography (a good one, for example, by Monica Furlong) is to witness some of the changes that parallel or even anticipate the most radical metamorphoses that have come out of Vatican II. Merton himself came to look somewhat askance at what he recognized as his own earlier posturings, even as he came to understand along his pulse what being a monk really meant. A year before his death, for example, he wrote of Faulkner's Ike McCaslin (*Go Down, Moses*) that in spite of McCaslin's initiation and vision in the wilderness, he still remained "a failed saint and only half a monk." But then he added that, after spending twenty-five years in a monastery, he had come to see that it was "extraordinarily difficult for *anyone* to be more than that, and most of us are not even that far along." He would not have excluded himself.

Those changes in the self are caught here in the very stylistic habits of the young reviewer and graduate student with the self-assured, aloof, and cocky stance of the Catholic convert who had read Jacques Maritain and the Catholic apologists of the 1930s, writers every bit as earnest as their Communist apologist counterparts. Consider the tone and all-inclusive sweep of the following, written when Merton was twenty-three: "In any context of social control, the word Love has so often been used by charlatans, evangelists, and movie producers that it is less convincing than the better advertised patent medicines." Or this: "Biology and economics in their most elementary forms have been hashed up into various theories of the sovereign state to fill our uncritical need for some kind of philosophy." And then compare these words (which actually say less than we think they do) to the following, written when Merton was forty-five (and then only with the proviso that we take them as a tentative formulation) :

How shall we prepare ourselves to consider the theology of creativity? The secular caricature is a futile and demonic attempt to squeeze divine powers out of man. Since there is no genuine creativity apart from God, the man who attempts to be a "creator outside of God and independent of him is forced to fall back on magic. The sin of the wizard is not so much that he usurps and exercises a real preternatural power, but that his postures travesty the divine by degrading man's freedom in absurd and servile manipulations of reality.... Wizardry...obscure[s] the light, dim[s] man's vision, and reduce[s] him to a state of infatuated self-absorption.... This bending back upon himself, this fixation upon the exterior self was, for St. Augustine, one of the principle elements in the fall of Adam.... Creativity becomes possible insofar as man can forget his limitations and his selfhood and lose himself in abandonment to the immense creative power of a love too great to be seen or comprehended.

This is an insight absolutely central to an understanding of the poetics of Gerard Manley Hopkins as well and is diametrically opposed to the Gnostic formulations of a critic like Harold Bloom. It is, moreover, an insight into the nature of creativity which would not have been possible to Hopkins without the self-imposed silence of his seven years of Jesuit training or to Merton in our time without the rigorous discipline of his early Trappist training. Merton's is a very strong mind, tough yet also patient, willing to listen to all objections or cavils or attempted rebuttals, and where a logic by its very structure refuses to be answered, he will say so and pass on. His is a mind made strong with years of contemplation, long hours of solitude, the discipline of rising morning after morning at 2:00 A.M. to begin another day, a mind that fell in love with the rhythms and cycles of nature and the regular hours spent in prayer (especially the poetry of David's Psalms), a mind "hip"—in the jargon of the sixties—to questions of nuclear disarmament, racial unrest, women's rights, the emerging Third World nations, alienation, and the problems with the hundreds of panaceas (from free sex to anti-intellectualism) offered in his time to solve these dilemmas.

There is of course a certain unavoidable repetitiveness in these essays. They were, after all, written for specific occasions, whether as reviews or for periodicals like the *Sewanee Review, Thought, Jubilee,* the *Critic,* or lesser known outlets like *Katallagete* and *Motive.* And when Merton was preoccupied with a subject—as he was with Pasternak and later with Faulkner and Camus—many of the same ideas (refleshed each time) reappear in different essays. (Remember that it was T. S. Eliot himself who reminded us that this repetitiousness in a writer signaled certain key ideas or obsessions, *leitmotifs* if you will.)

Merton remains—in a word he provided for others—a truly sapiential writer. One of the wonderful things that he learned in his wide and deep reading was that figures like T. S. Eliot, Melville, William Carlos Williams, D. H. Lawrence, and Faulkner provided us as readers with "a privileged area for wisdom in the modern world," more so, often, than did the reading of modern philosophy and theology. Such wisdom writers, he maintained, sought "to apprehend man's value and destiny in his global and even ultimate significance." Such writing was "not an initiation into a world of abstractions and ideals" but rather awakened in us a "communion with the concrete." Moreover, it had the capacity "to bridge the cognitive gap between our minds and the realm of the transcendent and the unknown, so that without 'understanding' what lies beyond the limit of human vision, we nevertheless enter into an intuitive affinity with it, or seem to experience some such affinity." The finesse of that last comment, Merton's characteristic habit of acknowledging those who might not understand the experience of *sapientia* and so might want to call into question the experience itself: it is that which helps explain Merton's wide appeal.

And yet, for me, the central experience of reading Merton is not to be found here in his literary essays, anymore than I find the essential Hopkins in his journals and sermons, helpful as they are in providing a fuller picture of the man. Toward the end of his own relatively short life that other Thomas—the Dominican from Aquino—had an experience—sapiential, mystical—which made him say of the scientific compendium that was his extraordinary *Summa* that it was all so much straw to him now. Coincidentally, a week before he died by means of accidental electrocution (touching a faultily wired fan in his room in Bangkok), Merton recorded an experience whose strong yet comforting light had the effect of transforming his *Asian Journal* and—by extension—everything that he had written in his literary essays. Merton had come to Ceylon as part of his spiritual journey to witness the giant Buddhas at the monastic complex of Polonnaruwa and what he experienced as he walked alone among the Buddhas he found difficult to express in words. The Ceylonese Catholic vicar general with whom he had traveled refused to walk with him, not wanting to come into too close proximity with these "pagan" statues. So Merton removed his sandals and walked over the wet sand and grass toward the standing and reclining Buddhas towering peacefully over him. What he records of this experience verges on something like very great poetry:

> Then the silence of the extraordinary faces. The great smiles. Huge and yet subtle. Filled with every possibility, questioning nothing, knowing everything, rejecting nothing, the peace not of emotional resignation but of Madhyamika, of sunyata, that has seen through every question without trying to discredit anyone or anything—*without refutation*—without establishing some other argument. . . . I was knocked over with a rush of relief and thankfulness at the *obvious* clarity of the figures. . . . I was suddenly, almost forcibly, jerked clean out of the habitual, half-tied vision of things, and an inner clearness, clarity, as if exploding from the rocks themselves, became evident and obvious. . . . I mean, I know and have seen what I was obscurely looking for.

The difference between this passage and the passages from Merton's *Literary Essays* is the difference between the opening passages of T. S. Eliot's *Burnt Norton* and the closing passages of his *Little Gidding:* the movement from an honest questioning, a sincere attempt as Christian apologist to "establish some other argument" or at least demonstrate the viability of one's own line of reasoning, and an achieved—if you will—grammar of assent, a clarity bordering on *hilaritas* and seeming to emanate from the dancing rocks themselves. That is where Merton at fifty-three ended his own search. What *The Literary Essays* gives us is another part of the record of a rare and beautiful mind which remained honest and vulnerably open to the search and which still believed that one could *in time* come to touch something of the truth.

1982

Notes

The Poem as a Field Action: Paterson

1 *Milton II*, collected in *On Poetry and Poets* (New York: Noonday Press, 1961), pp. 165–83.

2 "With Forced Fingers Rude," *Four Pages*, Galveston, Texas, no. 2 (Feb. 1948): 1–4.

3 *The Selected Letters of William Carlos Williams*, ed. John C. Thirlwall (New York: McDowell, Obolensky, 1957), p. 227. Hereafter cited as SL.

4 "Against the Weather: A Study of the Artist," collected in *Selected Essays of William Carlos Williams* (New York: New Directions, 1954), p. 197. This collection hereafter cited as SE. When Charles Olson read this essay, he wrote Williams half-jokingly that he had stolen heavily from it. (Unpublished letter, dated December 5 [1939], in the William Carlos Willams collection of manuscripts in the American Collection at Yale.) Olson's "Projective Verse" essay, published in 1950, would appear to bear that statement out, in the sense that Williams acted as the central influence in shaping many of Olson's ideas and emphases.

5 SE, 205–6.

6 The working papers for "The Poem as a Field of Action" are now in the Poetry Collection at the State University of New York at Buffalo. Hereafter

cited in notes as BU. These consist of an early draft in the "Red University Notebook" and seven drafts (most of a few pages in length and written first in pencil at odd moments snatched and then corrected in ink) and the last a seventy-one page sheaf, with many corrections in pencil, ink, and red and blue crayon, marked up in the same fashion and with the same tools as the *Paterson* manuscripts.

7   Reviewing Zukofsky's *Notes on ANEW* for the Winter 1947–48 issue of *New Quarterly of Poetry,* for example, Williams praised his friend's poems as "fertile, prolific in possibilities" for a revolution in the poetic line that might well be a direction for the future (p. 11). Zukofsky's major breakthrough, Williams believed, was his "new understanding of the line structure," a metrical pattern *discovered* in the language of his own day" (p. 12). Here were lines that could "expand physically before the pressure and the speed of thought." In that lay "the new. And the release. And the happiness" (p. 14). The poem Williams particularly drew attention to as containing in its fullness the new line Zukofsky had worked out is his very fine "No. 42," reprinted in his *All: The Collected Short Poems, 1923–1964* (New York: W. W. Norton, 1971), pp. 109–11.

8   The inability to change enough had seriously affected Eliot's own poetry, Williams strongly felt. In fact, he could hardly think of Eliot without thinking of a potentially fluid line moving into marmoreal rigidity, stasis. So, for example, when he finally did get to meet "the Eliot" in mid-November 1948, when Eliot gave a reading at the Library of Congress in Washington, Williams sent his friend Robert McAlmon a picture postcard of the Statuary Hall in the Capitol with the comment that, though he personally liked Eliot, "now that I have met him, the party last night [following the reading] closely resembled the reverse of this card." (From the collection of Norman Holmes Pearson.)

9   Auden's immediate popularity among American audiences from the late thirties on not only angered Williams; it seemed to threaten the very direction he was hoping American poetry would take. In his unfinished collaborative novel, *Man Orchid* (written in late 1945 and early 1946 and published posthumously), Williams recalls a poetry reading that he shared with Alfred Kreymborg, Malcolm Cowley, and Auden himself—three old-timers and this young Englishman in his early thirties—held in the Great Hall in Cooper Union in April 1940. Even five and a half years later he can still not forgive his American audience for their uncritical acceptance of all things English:

> Remember at Cooper when the young Englishman read his verse to that supposedly tough bunch. I was there. Remember? There were a couple of American poets, not too hot but hitting along the line I'm telling [an authentic American line.] Well, this young English poet with his smooth Oxford accent got up and smiled at those lunks and said, I hope you'll pardon my accent, I can't help it! And they almost drowned in their own slobber they were so tickled to grant him any small favor that lay to their eager hands. Their faltering hands! And he read them

his verses, and very good sweet verses they were and—they raised the roof with their gracious huzzas. It was magnificent to hear and to see. See *A Williams Garland: Petals from the Falls, 1945–1950*, ed. Paul Mariani, *Massachusetts Review* 14, no. 1 (1973): 85. Hereafter cited as MR.

10 See Williams's review of *The Man with the Blue Guitar and Other Poems* in *New Republic*, Nov. 17, 1937, p. 50.

11 *The Necessary Angel: Essays on Reality and the Imagination* (New York: Vintage Books, 1965), p. 77.

12 Letter of December 19, 1946, to José Rodriguez Feo in *Letters of Wallace Stevens*, ed. Holly Stevens (New York: Alfred A. Knopf, 1966), p. 544.

13 "An Approach to the Poem," in *English Institute Essays, 1947* (New York: AMS Press, 1965), p. 68.

14 Ibid.

15 Ibid., p. 69.

16 Williams's attitude toward Hopkins continued to shift. At one point he calls him "a great early innovator" and at another point his effects are "constipated." But one of the neatest observations Williams made on Hopkins was in pointing to the man's sharp, "brutal" chin in his notes to "The Poem as a Field of Action" as a sign of Hopkins's control over his forms as a counterbalance to their "dream" content. He might dream on in his poems of his logocentric world, but it was in his hard, brilliant ability as a craftsman that he caught the sensuous reality, the very pulse of his "abrúpt sélf."

17 After his teaching session at the University of Utah in July 1947, Williams and his wife went to visit Mesa Verde with their old friend Robert McAlmon and stayed at the local hotel in Cortez. Out of that visit came Williams's "The Testament of Perpetual Change" (*The Collected Later Poems*, rev. ed. [New York: New Directions, 1963], p. 103) with its interlinear grid (in italics) taken from the opening lines of Bridges's *Testament of Beauty*. Williams's and Bridges's lines, laid thus side by side, chime remarkably in their cadences (though the tone, lexis, and content of each writer clearly inhabit quite different worlds). A study of Williams's poem would show, I think, in what ways Williams's own practice is a "testament" of perpetual change.

18 See "The Later Pound," an essay Williams wrote on January 13, 1950, and published in MR, 124.

19 See "A Study of Ezra Pound's Present Position," an essay Williams wrote between January 21 and 23, and published in MR, 118.

20 By 1950, after he had read the *Pisan Cantos*, Wiliams saw that Pound *had* developed, not in those quotable "purple passages" that kept dragging Pound back into the past, but in the "common text," where the "heavy work" of any long sequence was done, and done beautifully. Remove Pound from his library and evidence of his ear for the native cadence could still shine through with extraordinary sensitivity.

21 This is the same argument he had with Stevens and Eliot, different as they

were in other respects. In an unguarded moment, Williams put the crucial difference this way:

> Pound has given up his earlier attempts and gone over to "ideas." As he has said, "You gotta have something to say, Bull. If you ain't got something to say, you can't write." . . . But suppose both have something to say . . . , as there are at least several important things to say. Both being equal in that and both being poets, then the next step is the implementation itself that will determine their value *as poets.* It is even conceivable to me that, though one may have something important to say and the other next to nothing to say, the second may still, judging him by his resources as a poet, be the more "virtuous" person. At least the possibility seems there.

This is a crucial statement of Williams's distinction between the poet as a person of ideas and the poet as a person of action, creating the poem itself as a field of action. In his lecture delivered at Briarcliff Junior College on November 29, 1945, Williams stressed the distinction between prose, where the writer put one's thoughts on paper and the poet, whose poem was "evidence of that within the man or about him by which *he* is thought." The idea, and that way of phrasing it Williams had taken from the opening of Rimbaud's *A Season in Hell.* Williams's "Memory Script," entitled "Verse as Evidence of Thought," is in BU.

22 In a letter to Parker Tyler (February 9, 1946), Williams recalled being asked if he could give "any evidence of the 'new way of measuring' in anything . . . I myself had written at any time. It was a fair question but one I shall have to postpone answering indefinitely." And then he conjured up the image of the Mendelejeffian table of periodic weights:

> Years before an element was discovered, the element helium, for instance, its presence had been predicted by a blank in the table of atomic weights.
>
> It may be that I am no genius in the use of the new measure I find inevitable; it may be that as a poet I have not had the genius to do the things I set up as essential if our verse is to blossom. I know, however, the innovation I predict must come to be. Someone, some infant now, will have to find the way we miss. Meanwhile I shall go on talking. (SL, 243)

23 MR, 120.

24 Working papers for "The Poem as a Field of Action," p. 53. Hereafter cited as PFA.

25 Ibid., p. 54.

26 In his working papers (PFA), Williams refers to the example of his friends, Charles Scheeler, the painter, and his Russian wife, Musya, the dancer. He relates this story at length at a critical juncture in his *Autobiography,* just after quoting from Charles Olson's "Projective Verse" essay (1950). Thus, the Scheelers serve as a concrete example of the field theory of poetry. What Scheeler had done was to settle down in a small stone cottage, one of the few structures remaining on what had formerly been a Hudson River colonial

estate with its own sixty-room mansion and outlying buildings. By reorganizing that field (the estate, which had had its own formal center) around his new center, Scheeler had "married" himself to a "present-day necessity," less grand than the past, but containing the "seed" of a new intelligence, a new structure, created out of the elements of the past, and had filled it with *local* artifacts (Shaker furniture). It had been taken, by this transference of new values, into a new context, into a fitting place for Scheeler's Russian wife, his muse, to dance.

27 In early 1947, Williams wrote that it was the handling of the caesura, the break (or breaks) *within* the line, that held out the "greatest hope I have discovered so far for a study of the modern line" (MR, 122). The expanded use of the caesura might well prove to be what quantity was to Greek poetry.

28 SL, 163.

29 Ibid., 214, 216.

30 Abbott/Williams correspondence at BU.

31 SL, 230, 232.

32 Ibid., 234–35, 236–37.

33 Williams, who knew Freud's *The Interpretation of Dreams*, was in full agreement with Freud that the content of the poem was indeed "a dream, a daydream of wish fulfillment." It was "always phantasy—what is wished for, realized in the 'dream' of the poem—but . . . the structure confronts something else." What the structure confronts, of course, is reality itself. ("The Poem as a Field of Action" in SE, 281.)

34 Cf. Williams's comment on the figure of the emergency squads of the omnipresent authorities—the critics, the universities—who, once they detect a trickle of new energy escaping from the dams they have built, "rush out . . . to plug the leak, the leak! in their fixed order, in their power over the water." And also, in the same essay review, the image of the old poetic line as a "grill . . . before a prison window" and the new line as "the grill gone" ("A New Line is a New Measure," *New Quarterly of Poetry*, 2, no. 2 (1947–48): 10.

35 "Letter to an Australian Editor," *Briarcliff Quarterly* 3, no. 2 (1946): 207.

36 That Williams needed a line like the staggered or step-down three-ply line after his crippling strokes, needed their more meditative resources, can in part be demonstrated by listening to his reading on the Caedmon LP, *William Carlos Williams Reading His Own Poems,* of poems like "To Daphne and Virginia" and "The Host" in the new measure, where the pace seems correct, next by listening to his reading of "The Yachts" that same day—June 6, 1954—and then by listening to his reading of the latter poem recorded nine years earlier (in May 1946) and issued in *An Album of Modern Poetry: An Anthology Read by the Poets,* edited by Oscar Williams. Listening consecutively to William's's two recordings of "The Yachts," one realizes that at sixty-two he was reading the poem nearly twice as fast as he was at seventy-one.

37 SL, 251–52.

The Eighth Day of Creation: Rethinking Paterson

1   Yale Collection of William Carlos Williams. Permission to quote from the Williams materials, both published and unpublished, is hereby gratefully acknowledged to the Williams Estate.

2   The figure of Cress (Cressida) appears as the female correspondent in *Paterson 1* and *Paterson 2*. Her letters are in fact part of a larger number of letters Marcia Nardi began writing to Williams in April 1942. During the winter of 1942, incidentally, Williams reread Chaucer with renewed interest; he was especially taken with Chaucer's psychological rendering of Cressida.

3   From *Spring and All* (1923), collected in *Imaginations,* ed. Webster Schott (New York: New Directions, 1970), p. 116. Copyright 1970 by Florence H. Williams. Hereafter referred to as SA.

4   SA, 89.

5   In *The Necessary Angel: Essays on Reality and the Imagination* (New York: Vintage Books, 1965), p. 160.

6   In "Against the Weather," collected in *Selected Essays of William Carlos Williams* (New York: Random House, 1954), pp. 196–218. Copyright 1954 by William Carlos Williams. Hereafter cited as AW.

7   AW, 107, 205.

8   *The Autobiography of William Carlos Williams* (New York: Random House, 1951), p. 347. Copyright 1948, 1949, 1951 by William Carlos Williams.

9   Among Williams's unpublished papers at Yale. Hereafter referred to as Calas.

10 Letter from Allen Ginsberg to William Carlos Williams of June 6, 1950, part of which Williams included as one more scrap in the grid of his collage, *Paterson 4*, pp.194–95 of the current (seventh) paperback printing.

11 Xerox copy of unpublished letter from Williams to Louis Ginsberg, February 1952, in Yale Collection.

12 *Selected Letters of William Carlos Williams,* ed. John D. Thirlwall (New York: McDowell, Obolensky, 1957), pp. 312–13. Copyright 1957 by William Carlos Williams.

13 *Paterson 5*, pp. 236–37.

14 *Paterson 1*, pp. 6–8.

15 *William Carlos Williams: The American Background* (Cambridge: Cambridge University Press, 1971), p. 152. Mike Weaver includes a black-and-white plate of *Fata Morgana* in his study.

16 William Carlos Williams, *Paterson,* Book 2. Copyright 1948 by William Carlos Williams. Reprinted by permission of New Directions Publishing Corporation.

17 *Pictures from Brueghel and Other Poems* (New York: New Directions, 1962), p. 3. Copyright 1954, 1955, 1959 by William Carlos Williams.

18 Yale Collection.

The Hard Core of Beauty

1 "Effie Deans," in *A Recognizable Image: William Carlos Williams on Art and Artists,* ed. Bram Dijkstra (New York: New Directions, 1978), pp. 128–29.

2 The original of this letter is in the William Carlos Williams Collection at the University of Texas at Austin. Printed with permission.

The New Aestheticism: A Reading of "Andromeda"

1 *The Letters of Gerard Manley Hopkins to Robert Bridges,* ed. Claude Colleer Abbott (London: Oxford University Press, 1955), pp. 87 and 128. Hereafter cited as *Letters to Bridges.*

2 *The Poems of Gerard Manley Hopkins,* 4th ed. (London: Oxford University Press, 1967), p. 277. Hereafter cited as *Poems.*

3 From Wain, *Essays on Literature and Ideas* (London, 1963), pp. 113–31. First published as a Chatterton Lecture, 1959, in the *Proceedings of the British Academy.* Reprinted in part in *Hopkins: A Collection of Critical Essays, Twentieth Century Views Series,* ed. Geoffrey H. Hartman (Englewood Cliffs, N. J.: Prentice-Hall, 1966, pp. 57–70.

4 For example, Mrs. E. E. Duncan-Jones (Elsie Phare) has shown that two early poems (July 1864) of Hopkins, which he signed "Mrs. Hopley," refer to the *Times* account of Mrs. Fanny Hopley who was suing her husband for divorce. The husband, a schoolmaster, had just completed a four-year prison term on charges of having beaten Reginald Cancellor, one of the pupils, to death. When we recall how much Hopkins disliked his own headmaster, Dyne, we can see why he would follow the *Times* account and write two satirical pieces from Mrs. Hopley's point of view (whom, by the way, Hopkins seems not wholly to have exonerated). The wrecks of both the *Deutschland* and the *Eurydice,* on which he based two of his poems, were reported in the *Times* as well as in the *London Illustrated News.* And when he composed his late "The shepherd's brow" in April 1889, he had in mind the Eiffel Tower, then nearing completion for the Paris Exhibition and which he could have read about in the newspapers on the same day he wrote the poem. While it was being hailed in the papers as the world's tallest man-made structure, Hopkins may have viewed it in his final illness as merely another of man's vanities, another Tower of Babel. He even composed a comic triolet, a form that the English Parnassians took so seriously, on the London *Times* itself. So this most isolated of all Victorian poets breathed in and assimilated not only the natural beauty around him, but the public world of the dailies as well. Compare also his concern about the British defeat at Majuba, the Irish Question, Parnell, Gladstone, Disraeli, unionism, and many other contemporary issues.

5 Evidence in the poems of just such a tendency, especially to sing of masculine strength and boyish beauty almost exclusively, and certainly sublimated in Hopkins, can be found, for example, in "The Handsome Heart," "The Bugler's First Communion," "Felix Randal," "Brothers," "To What Serves Mortal Beauty?" "The Soldier," "Harry Ploughman," "Epithalamion." Hopkins's fascination with virile beauty and his heroic determination to check this "dangerous" impulse helps, I think, to account for some of the nervous, erotic energy one experiences in reading his poetry.

6 "The Virgin and the Dragon," *Yale Review* 37 (September 1947): 33–46. I am indebted to Norman H. Mackenzie for this suggestion.

7 In a letter to Ignatius Ryder, S.J., written in July 1868, Hopkins, about to enter the Jesuit seminary, writes: That reminds me to say that the subject [of his proposed article for a review] wd. be Wm. Morris' last poem and the medieval school of poets. To make matters worse *The Earthly Paradise,* the poem in question, I cannot get. So far as I have got I am dull and abstruse.... Still I shd. like to sing my dying swan-song" (*Further Letters of Gerard Manley Hopkins,* ed. Claude Colleer Abbott [London: Oxford University Press, 1956], pp. 53–54. Hereafter cited as *Further Letters*). Ten years later, writing to Dixon, he praises "Morris' stories in the *Paradise,* so far as I have read them" (*The Correspondence of Gerard Manley Hopkins and Richard Watson Dixon,* ed. Claude Colleer Abbott [London: Oxford University Press, 1935], p. 3. Hereafter cited as *Correspondence*).

8 In a letter to Dixon in June 1886 (*Correspondence,* pp. 133–34), Hopkins writes at some length on Burne-Jones's paintings, admiring their genius, spirituality, and invention, but expressing dissatisfaction with their technical flaws. Morris had always intended Burne-Jones to illustrate "The Doom of Acrisius" for The Kelmscott Press, but neither lived to see the task through. The unfinished Perseus series was, however, collected with "The Doom of Acrisius" in 1902 in a limited edition by the publishing house of Robert Howard Russell.

9 I am indebted to James Ellis (*The Bab Ballads*) for this information.

10 See *A Century of Whitman Criticism,* ed. Edwin Haviland Miller (Bloomington: Indiana University Press, 1969), p. 40 and passim. See also Harold Blodgett's *Walt Whitman in England* (Ithaca, N.Y.: Cornell University Press, 1934).

11 *Letters to Bridges,* pp. 154–55 and passim. Hopkins admits pointedly here to his attraction and repulsion for Whitman.

12 The bulk of Saintsbury's review is reprinted in *Letters to Bridges* as "Note P," pp. 311–16.

13 Letter of April 3, 1877, in *Letters to Bridges,* p. 39 .

14 See especially Hopkins's letter to Baillie of March 1864: "There's no place like home.... You can only see *The Times* and *Saturday* [*Review*] and nothing else" (*Further Letters,* p. 207).

15 Did Swinburne's stanza,

> The earth-god Freedom, the lonely
>> Face lightening, the footprint unshod,
> Not as one man crucified only
>> Nor scourged with but one life's rod;
> The soul that is substance of nations,
>> Reincarnate with fresh generations;
>> The great god Man, which is God,

with its praise of freedom in appellatives traditionally reserved for Christ, serve as an echo when Hopkins composed "God's Grandeur" (February 1877)? Besides the terminal rhymes of "[un]shod," "rod," and "God," there is the "lightening" (shining), "generations," as well as the incarnational and regenerative themes of both poems. If so, he would again be borrowing from Swinburne's technique while radically transforming his content.

16   To complicate matters, Swinburne also called for a "noble and chaste" art "in the wider masculine sense." See his "Notes on Poems and Reviews" (1866), a reply to the critics of his *Poems and Ballads* of the same year.

17   *The Journals and Papers of Gerard Manley Hopkins*, ed. Humphry House (London: Oxford University Press, 1959), p. 166.

18   *The Swinburne Letters*, ed. Cecil Y. Lang (New Haven: Yale University Press, 1960), 2: 253.

19   David Anthony Downes, *Victorian Portraits: Hopkins and Pater* (New York: Bookman Associates, Inc., 1965), p. 48 and passim. It may be significant that on the back of a note from Pater to Hopkins saying he would come to dinner on May 20 of this year, Hopkins wrote some lines on the difference between the amoral good and the moral right, including these:

> What makes the man and what
> The man within that makes:
> Ask whom he serves or not
> Serves and what side he takes.

20   *The New Republic* (London, 1877), Book 5, chap. 1, pp. 356–59. Italics mine.

21   The image of the soul, pictured as a woman awaiting her deliverer on a rock or foundering ship while the sea rages around her, is an image Hopkins employed in "The Wreck of the Deutschland" (stanza 29, ll. 7–8), and close parallels occur also in "That Nature is a Heraclitean Fire" and in the fragment, "On the Portrait of Two Beautiful Young People," where Christ is again the beacon in the storm. There may also be a pun on the verb "alight" in "Andromeda."

22   Hopkins was here echoing one of two sources: either "the utterly utter" Bunthorne, a lightly veiled figure of Wilde in Gilbert and Sullivan's *Patience* (1881), or a contemporary *Punch* cartoon by George du Maurier. Although du Maurier frequently singled out Wilde for his barbs, this particular cartoon lampooned the entire Aesthetic Movement as "too utterly utter." In thus echoing *Patience* or *Punch*, Hopkins's own bias seems apparent. See

also Hopkins's letter to Bridges of June 28, 1881, where Wilde's name seems to be intentionally misspelled as "Wild" (*Letters to Bridges*, p. 134).

23   *The Renaissance* (New York: Meridian Books, 1961), p. 108.

The Cry at the Heart of "The Wreck"

1   *Further Letters of Gerard Manley Hopkins*, 2d ed., ed. Claude Colleer Abbott (London: Oxford University Press, 1956), p. 135.

2   *The Sermons and Devotional Writings of Gerard Manley Hopkins*, ed. Christopher Christopher Devlin, S.J. (London: Oxford University Press, 1959), p. 197.

3   I should like to modify here what I wrote in my *Commentary* concerning the mode in which Hopkins means us to understand how it was that the nun "fetched" Christ. Except for a few very minor points, I would still stand by my reading of "The Wreck" presented there. But I no longer maintain— nor have I for several years—that Hopkins meant his readers to believe that Christ had literally walked the waters of the Thames that December night and that the nun's cry was in fact attesting to that kind of miracle. At the time I wrote that chapter, I had recently read Elisabeth Schneider's *The Dragon in the Gate* and had been impressed by her arguments supporting such a reading. Now, six years later, I believe that when Hopkins spoke of "real fetching, presentment, or 'adduction,'" of a real presence as opposed to "mere vision," that such fetching does not have to take the form of a ghostly presence; the presence Hopkins is speaking of is, rather, one felt so certainly in the very center of the heart that the heart responds with its own counterstress, its own utterance. Hopkins clearly believed in miracles and signs, and made no secret of it, but, as James Finn Cotter has said in his impressive study, *Inscape: The Christology and Poetry of Gerard Manley Hopkins*, Hopkins "would hardly invent one where eyewitness reports gave no grounds for its occurrence." The real center of Hopkins's ode is much more firmly rooted in the Christian experience than Schneider's reading suggests.

4   *The Letters of Gerard Manley Hopkins to Robert Bridges*, ed. Claude Colleer Abbott (London: Oxford University Press, 1955), p. 60.

5   *The Journals and Papers of Gerard Manley Hopkins*, ed. Humphry House (London: Oxford University Press, 1959), p. 146.

6   There is, both in this poem and elsewhere in Hopkins's poetry, a kind of daring play with Christ's/God's name, especially when the poet is under extreme emotional stress. So, for example, I believe that Hopkins was well aware that many readers, reading the nun's words, "O Christ, Christ, come quickly," might be tempted to read them as an empty expletive, Christ's name evoked the way most of us do when the hammer finds the thumb instead of the nail, for example. Under extreme stress, we might evoke that name as a sign to which the whole self is foredrawn, or we might use it as an empty cipher. So, it is "for Christ's sake" or "for God's sake" or "O Christ, Christ," and we "lash," then, 'with the best or worst / Word last."

A Poetics of Unselfconsciousness

1 From Hopkins's commentary on "The Second Week" of the Long Retreat, in *The Sermons and Devotional Writings of Gerard Manley Hopkins* (London: Oxford University Press, 1959), pp. 179–80. Hereafter cited as s.
2 From Hopkins's commentary on "Creation and Redemption" during the Long Retreat (November 8, 1881), S, pp. 200–201.
3 Harold Bloom, *The Anxiety of Influence* (New York: Oxford University Press, 1973), pp. 20–21.

The Sound of Oneself Breathing

1 In Father Boyle's "Time and Grace in Hopkins' Imagination," presented at the 1976 MLA seminar on Hopkins.
2 In conversation with James Finn Cotter. See also Cotter's seminal *Inscape: The Christology and Poetry of Gerard Manley Hopkins* (Pittsburgh: University of Pittsburgh Press, 1972), passim.
3 *Further Letters of Gerard Manley Hopkins,* ed. Claude Colleer Abbott (London: Oxford University Press, 1956), p. 433.
4 Letter of June 13, 1878, in *The Correspondence of Gerard Manley Hopkins and Richard Watson Dixon,* ed. Claude Colleer Abbott (London: Oxford University Press, 1935), p. 6.
5 Ibid.
6 Cf. Hopkins's letters to Bridges of March 20 and April 29, 1889 in *The Letters of Gerard Manley Hopkins to Robert Bridges,* ed. Claude Colleer Abbott (London: Oxford University Press, 1955), pp. 301–6.

Charles Tomlinson

1 Russell Davies, *Review,* nos. 29-30 (Spring-Summer 1972): 49.
2 Calvin Bedient, *Eight Contemporary Poets* (London: Oxford University Press, 1974), p. 1.
3 See Alvarez's anthology, *The New Poetry* (Harmondsworth, England: Penguin Books, 1962), which leads off with four Americans: Lowell, Berryman, Sexton, and Plath, all but the first of whom were suicides. See, too, his introduction to the volume, defending his selections.
4 "The Art of Poetry," *The Necklace* (1955; rpt. London: Oxford University Press, 1966), p. 14.
5 See Donald Davie's argument for this connection in his *Ezra Pound: Poet as Sculptor* (New York: Oxford University Press, 1964), pp. 112–114.
6 Among those who have used the staggered tercets successfully, I might mention Robert Pack and John Malcolm Brinnin.
7 "Abstruse Considerations," *Poetry* 104, no. 4 (1964): 243. See also Robert Duncan's rejoinder in "A Critical Difference of View," *Stony Brook,* nos. 3-4 (Fall 1969): 360–63).

8 Or perhaps blank verse was the basic staple to which he would, by testing and circuitous perambulation, return, which may come to the same thing.

9 *Journey to Love* (New York: Random House, 1955), p. 30. Parenthetical page references in the text, preceded by JL, are to this edition.

10 *Spectrum* 1, no. 3 (1957): 59.

11 Ibid.

12 Tomlinson's letters to Williams are now among the Williams papers in the American Collection at Yale.

13 See, for example, Williams's open letter to Kay Boyle, meant for inclusion in *Contact* (1932), but not printed until *The Selected Letters of William Carlos Williams*, ed. John Thirlwall (New York: McDowell, Obolensky 1957), pp. 129–36; Williams's review of Wallace Stevens's *The Man with the Blue Guitar and Other Poems, New Republic,* November 17, 1937, p. 50; and *A Garland for William Carlos Williams,* ed. Paul Mariani, in *Massachusetts Review* 14, no. 1 (1973), passim. Hopkins, too, felt the same metrical claustrophobia seventy years earlier, seeing it as analogous to the tyranny imposed on melody by the four-beat bar.

14 "The Poem as a Field of Action," in *The Selected Essays of William Carlos Williams,* ed. William Carlos Williams (New York: Random House, 1954), pp. 287–88.

15 "Seeing Is Believing," *Spectrum* 2, no. 3 (1958): 189.

16 *A Peopled Landscape* (London: Oxford University Press, 1963), p. 18. Further parenthetical references in the text, preceded by PL will be to this edition.

17 The following material, cut from the essay as it was originally published, is here restored for the balance it provides toward any initial assessment of Tomlinson's poetry.

Robert Creeley

1 Robert Creeley, *A Quick Graph: Collected Notes and Essays,* ed. Donald Allen (San Francisco: Four Seasons Foundation, 1970), p. 64. Further textual citations will be to QG.

2 Reprinted in the *Selected Essays of William Carlos Williams* (New York: New Directions, 1969), p. 257. Quoted also by Creeley in QG, 64–65. All previously unpublished materials by William Carlos Williams, copyright 1984 by the Estate of William Carlos Williams. Published by permission of New Directions Publishing Corporation.

3 See Creeley's interview with John Sinclair and Robin Eichele in *Contexts of Poetry: Interviews 1961–1971,* ed. Donald Allen (Bolinas: Four Seasons Foundation, 1973), pp. 46–52. Further textual citations will be to CP.

4 See Creeley's interview with David Ossman in ibid., pp. 9–10.

5 See Jacob Leed's lively reconstruction of this period (from February to August 1950), when he and Creeley tried to put together their little magazine, in "Robert Creeley and *The Lititz Review:* A Recollection with Letters," *Journal of Modern Literature* 5, no. 2 (1976): 243–59. Creeley dubbed his

prospective magazine the *Lititz Review* after the small town in Pennsylvania near the farmhouse where Leed had set up his rickety, unworkable press, bought for a grand total of ten dollars. When Leed's right wrist was broken in a car accident in May, Creeley drove down to try to help him set type in a last-ditch effort to save the magazine, but the press was too far gone. After a day working over the machine, both knew it was useless. It was left to Creeley to notify his contributors—Williams among them—that there would not, after all, be any number of the *Lititz Review*.

6 Creeley's letters to Williams are among the Williams papers in the American Collection at Yale University (hereafter cited as YU); Williams's letters to Creeley are in the Rare Books & Special Collections at Washington University (hereafter cited as WU).

7 Olson's letters to Creeley and Creeley's to Olson are in the Special Collection at the University of Connecticut, Storrs (hereafter cited as UC), as are Williams's letters to Olson. Olson's letters to Williams are in the American Collection at Yale University. Olson's first letter to Creeley of April 21, 1950, was published in *Maps No. 4* (1971): 8.

8 See also Creeley's interview (1967) with Lewis MacAdams in CP, 142: "But the first person, curiously, to give us access to Olson was Vincent Ferrini. He heard from Cid Corman that I was trying to get material for a magazine, and so Cid had asked Vincent to send some stuff, and then Vincent undertook to send some of Olson's. And my first reaction was that I wrote back saying, "You're looking for a language." And, boy, did he ever come back on me!"

9 Robert Creeley's "A Note followed by a Selection of Letters from Ezra Pound," *Agenda:* "Special Issue in Honour of Ezra Pound's Eightieth Birthday," 4, no. 2 (1965): 11–21.

10 This letter of Creeley's was returned, and is therefore in the University of Washington collection. Internal evidence would date it May or June 1950.

11 Quotations in these two paragraphs are from Williams's letter to Cid Corman of August 2, 1951, in the Williams collection of the Humanities Research Center at the University of Texas, Austin (hereafter cited as UT).

12 Letter of May 24, 1956, from Allen Ginsberg to Williams. Part of this letter (though not the section quoted here) found its way into the text of *Paterson* 5. Williams's letters to Ginsberg are in the Special Collection at Columbia University, with copies at Yale.

John Montague

1 One other poet comes to mind when I read *A Slow Dance,* the H.D. of the *Trilogy* and *Helen in Egypt.* Montague is as much the druid priest as H.D. is the ancient priestess.

Robert Pack

1 *Waking to My Name: New and Selected Poems* (Baltimore: The Johns Hopkins University Press, 1980).

Acknowledgments

Grateful acknowledgment is made to the following publishers and journals for permission to reprint copyrighted material.

New England Review/Bread Loaf Quarterly for "Reassembling the Dust: Notes on the Art of the Biographer," *NER/BLQ* 5, no. 3 (1983).

The Iowa Review for "The Poem as a Field of Action: Guerilla Tactics in *Paterson*," *The Iowa Review* 7, no. 4 (1976).

Twentieth Century Literature for "The Eighth Day of Creation: William Carlos Williams' Late Poems," *Twentieth Century Literature* 21, no. 3 (1975).

Sagetrieb for "The Hard Core of Beauty," *Sagetrieb* 3, no. 1 (1984).

The Poetry Society of America Bulletin for "Williams on Stevens: Storming the Edifice," *The Poetry Society of America Bulletin* 70 (Winter 1980).

Victorian Poetry for "Hopkins' 'Andromeda' and the New Aestheticism," *Victorian Poetry* 11, no. 1 (1973).

Loyola University Press for " 'O Christ, Christ, Come Quickly!' Lexical Plentitude and Primal Cry at the Heart of *The Wreck*," in *Readings of the Wreck: Essays in Commemoration of the Centenary of G.M. Hopkins' The Wreck of the Deutschland,* ed. Peter Milward, S.J., and Raymond Schoder, S.J. (Chicago: Loyola University Press, 1976).

Renascence for "Hopkins: Toward a Poetics of Unselfconsciousness," *Renascence* 29, no. 1 (Fall 1976).

The Hopkins Quarterly for "The Sound of Oneself Breathing: The Burden of Theological Metaphor in Hopkins," *The Hopkins Quarterly* 4, no. 1 (1977).

Parnassus for "Vespers: Robert Penn Warren at Seventy," *Parnassus* 4, no. 1 (1975) and for "Fretwork in Stone Tracery (John Montague)," *Parnassus* 8, no. 1 (1979).

Contemporary Literature for "Tomlinson's Use of the Williams Triad," *Contemporary Literature* 18, no. 3 (1977).

Boundary 2 for " 'Fire of a Very Real Order': Creeley and Williams," *Boundary 2* 6, no. 3 and 7, no 1 (Spring/Fall 1978).

The Best Cellar Press for " 'Lost Souls in Ill-Attended Wards': Berryman's 'Eleven Addresses to the Lord,' " in *A Book of Re-readings in Recent American Poetry* (Lincoln, Neb.: The Best Cellar Press, 1979).

The Massachusetts Review for "Fresh Flowers for the Urn: Reassessing Robert Pack," *The Massachusetts Review* 23, no. 4 (1982).

American Book Review for "The Literary Essays of Thomas Merton," *American Book Review* 5, no. 1 (1982).

William Eric Williams, Paul Herman Williams, and New Directions for permission to reprint published and unpublished materials of William Carlos Williams.

Library of Congress Cataloging in Publication Data
Mariani, Paul L.
A usable past.
Includes bibliographical references.
1. American poetry—20th century—History and criticism—Addresses, essays,
lectures. 2. Williams, William Carlos, 1883–1963—Criticism and interpretation
—Addresses, essays, lectures. 3. Hopkins, Gerard Manley, 1844–1889—Criti-
cism and interpretation—Addresses, essays, lectures. 4. English poetry—20th
century—History and criticism—Addresses, essays, lectures.
I. Title.
PS323.5.M37 1984   811'.52'09   84–2613
ISBN 0–87023–445–5